LOVE'S DAZ...

"I'll teach you how
he faced Laura in t
while the thunderstorm raged outside. "I
suspect you would make a very good
student."

"You don't need to teach me to be wicked,"
Laura lied. "I already am."

She kept her eyes open as Cash's arms slid
around her. She didn't even have to think
about what was happening. Cash made it so
very easy that she knew only the thundering
sensation of his kiss combining with the fury
of the storm—until she felt his hand inside
the newly unbuttoned flaps of her coat, and
shock raced through her like lightning.

"Do I go too fast, Laura?" he whispered as
she stiffened and then shivered when Cash's
hand moved to the fastenings of her shirt.
But his kiss merely traced her cheek, leaving
her the freedom to say yes or no . . . before
his hand found what he sought and his warm
flesh touched hers. . . .

"A splendid read. I thoroughly enjoyed it."
—Constance Day O'Flannery

SHELTER FROM THE STORM

by

Patricia Rice

AN ONYX BOOK

ONYX
Published by the Penguin Group
Penguin Books USA Inc., 375 Hudson Street,
New York, New York 10014, U.S.A.
Penguin Books Ltd, 27 Wrights Lane,
London W8 5TZ, England
Penguin Books Australia Ltd, Ringwood,
Victoria, Australia
Penguin Books Canada Ltd, 10 Alcorn Avenue,
Toronto, Ontario, Canada M4V 3B2
Penguin Books (N.Z.) Ltd, 182–190 Wairau Road,
Auckland 10, New Zealand

Penguin Books Ltd, Registered Offices:
Harmondsworth, Middlesex, England

First published by Onyx, an imprint of New American Library,
a division of Penguin Books USA Inc.

First Printing, March, 1993
10 9 8 7 6 5 4 3 2 1

For the Rices—for your love, your support, and for being there—this one's for you.

Prologue

Cairo, Illinois
May 1865

Tear spots stained and blurred the ink of the elegant script of the letter in Laura's hand as she read it once more. She had received few of these missives through the years of war and turmoil, and they always carried bad news. The first one had come at the end of that first year of war, telling of Aunt Ann dying of some mysterious ailment that had left her too weak to eat. Then there had been Uncle Matt a few years later. He couldn't actually be called a casualty of war; he had been too old to march with the army, but the war had killed him just the same. When the Union gave his last few male slaves a "pass" to join the army, he'd had an apoplexy from which he never fully recovered. Perhaps it was better that he hadn't lived to see the army grant passes to their families earlier this month. Laura had wondered how Stoner Creek Farm had been run since then, and reading this letter gave her some clue.

With Lee having surrendered and Lincoln dead, the war was nearly done, and Ward was still alive. Handsome, gallant Ward Breckinridge, pride of the Kentucky Rifles, shot and imprisoned, and now home, only to die—if Sallie's letter were to be believed. Laura shook her head as she reread the words. Sallie had never tended to be hysterical, but this letter came close to it. Ward had seemed the ideal husband for her: competent, self-assured, wealthy even without Sallie's rich lands, and patient. Ever patient. Sallie had always been a terrible flirt, but Ward had outlasted all her other beaux. The night he had walked into the ballroom wearing his blue-and-gold uniform had brought Sallie to her senses. It was the best thing she had done in her life, marrying Ward, and

7

they had had but a few weeks out of all these years together.

Laura wiped her eyes with a plain-edged handkerchief from her skirt pocket. It seemed as if the Kincaid luck and charm had finally dwindled to an end with the name. Stoner Creek was all that was left, and from Sallie's letter, that might not be for much longer.

Laura set the stiff pages on the small oak dresser at her side and rose to stand at the dormer window of her attic room. The heat was already climbing, and it was still early in the morning. She'd thought about that letter all night, and she'd finally made her decision, but it had been the hardest decision of her life.

The muddy unpaved streets below couldn't compare with the rippling emerald green of the pastures at home. The crude wooden storefronts here were no replacement for the sun-burnished patina of old bricks and white-painted porticoes of Stoner Creek. Even the people lacked elegance. She was tired of sewing drab linsey-woolseys and calicoes, and she ached to see the lavish silks and satins of home.

But still it had been a battle to decide to send that telegram saying she was coming home. It was an admission of failure, a throwing away of nearly four years of her life. She would have to go back to the same penniless dependent role she had fled before, only this time it would be worse after having this taste of freedom.

Laura glanced down at her stiff widow's weeds, then strode determinedly to her writing desk. The telegram would go out before she opened the shop this morning. She had saved enough money to pay the fare. She would return with her head held high and clothed in the respectability of black. No one would have to know her shame. No one.

If only she could remember she was a woman grown, and not the love-starved child of long ago.

It has been alleged, and not without some color of plausibility, that Kentuckians are belligerent by nature. We do not deny it. The crest of the state shows two gentlemen in swallow-fork coats, holding each other firmly by the right hand. The intent of the picture is plain. So long as they hold hands, neither can reach for his hardware.

—Irvin Cobb
Paducah, Kentucky

1

Stoner Creek, Kentucky
August 1850

Sitting stiffly in her crisp new petticoats and crinoline with dimity eyelet pantaloons peeking out beneath, six-year-old Laura Kincaid didn't dare mop the perspiration forming on her brow. Her father would have declared all this lace and horsehair utterly ridiculous for an afternoon ride, but her father was dead, and Sallie had insisted this was what ladies wore.

Laura glanced circumspectly at her nine-year-old cousin's willowy back. Sallie had a lovely Arabian mare with ribbons braiding her mane that matched the multifarious ribbons of Sallie's delicate batiste gown. In pastel blue with all the ribbons fluttering in the faint breeze, she looked as cool as a pitcher of water from the spring. Her blond naturally curly ringlets bounced beneath her matching bonnet, never falling flat and limp as Laura's hair did now. She stuffed a lank strand of brown back into her bonnet and straightened her parasol with annoyance. Parading to town dressed like a peacock didn't have the same appeal as it had earlier in the coolness of the tree-shaded porch, and she squirmed irritably in her hot new clothes.

Sallie's mare wandered to a halt, and Laura glanced up from her sulk to find the cause. They had passed from the tree-lined lane of the farm into the rutted road leading into town. On either side of the gravel-and-dirt path spread fields of towering tobacco. Laura hadn't quite determined the extent of her uncle's lands yet, but the peeling whitewash on this fence did not resemble the newly laid stone fences of Stoner Creek Farm. She assumed these must belong to a neighbor, and she looked with curiosity to the half-naked occupant of the tobacco bed.

From the dark eyes filled with suspicion that he turned toward them, Laura judged him to be a few years older than Sallie, although they appeared to be much the same height. Still, the boy's shoulders had begun to fill out, and when he lifted the hoe to his bare shoulder, muscles rippled along his arms. His hair was black and unkempt, curling about his neck where sweat dampened it. Baked by the summer sun, his skin was darker than any white man's she had ever known. Traveling as she had with her father, Laura had seen many sights and all sorts of people. This one fitted no category that she could name, white or black, and she stared at him openly.

He didn't even notice her. His eyes never left Sallie, even though his suspicious gaze had turned insolent at her cousin's question concerning his mother. He made some reply as his gaze fully absorbed all the fancy frills and furbelows adorning Sallie's white-and-golden beauty. It was with reluctance that he turned to give Laura a cursory look upon Sallie's polite, if condescending, introduction.

Still in awe of her cousin's plenitude of charm, wealth, and beauty, six-year-old Laura felt she had little to offer in comparison, and she understood when the boy's attention swiftly returned to the older girl. But she could not resist the opportunity to satisfy her curiosity, and when it seemed apparent Sallie would move on without further explanation, she spoke up.

"Pleased to meet you, Cash Wickliffe," Laura murmured politely as she had been taught, before she launched into her real interest. "Why do you not have slaves to work this plot? I thought tobacco was slave work."

Sallie halted her mare to give her younger cousin a contemptuous look. "Come on, Laura. If you can't keep a civil tongue in your head, I'll not take you with me again."

She began to trot away without even saying farewell to the boy, who stared after her with the oddest expression in his piercing eyes. When Laura didn't immediately follow, he turned his gaze to look upon her fully for the first time.

"I come cheaper than slave labor," he offered without a hint of scorn as his gaze swept over her flowered bonnet and layers of flounces and petticoats practically standing upright from her position in the sidesaddle. "You must be the orphan cousin Sallie's folks took in."

The statement was made with the same lack of rancor as Laura's question. Both were singularly rude, but neither one appeared to object to blunt honesty.

"My pa died in a steamboat race," she said bravely, although his death was still recent enough to bring tears to her eyes.

He quickly changed the subject to the enormous black dog patiently sitting at the side of the road beside her pony. "He yours?"

Laura brightened. "That's Franz. My pa gave him to me for my birthday last year."

"He's bigger than you. What kind is he?"

"Laura Melissa Kincaid, you come on right now, y'hear! Or I'll tell Pa on you." Sallie had turned her mare and brought it cantering back to retrieve her wayward charge.

With a slight wave of her hand Laura nudged her pony into catching up with her demanding cousin's. The Newfoundland ambled along behind.

"You don't go conversing with white trash like that, Laura Kincaid! Didn't your folks teach you anything?" Sallie grabbed the pony's bridle to ensure Laura's captivity.

"They said to always speak when spoken to," Laura replied defensively. "I was just trying to be polite."

"You don't have to be polite to the likes of that. He's no different from Henry or Jemima, and you don't carry on conversations with them."

Since in her loneliness Laura had carried on quite a few conversations with these house servants, she didn't argue the point, but sought enlightenment. "Why? He seemed nice enough to me."

Sallie rolled her expressive blue eyes. "How did you get to be such a baby? Can't you tell he's not like us? His mama's a quadroon from New Orleans. And his pa is a no-good drunken scoundrel, Pa says. They tenant-farm that piece of land and Cash works for wages for Mr. Watterson. He don't even own the clothes on his back."

Since Cash hadn't worn any clothes on his back, Laura worked at this new knowledge a little while. She knew about New Orleans. She'd just been there this past winter and had been impressed with the beauty of the delicate scrollwork and flowers and airy balconies. The ladies had all been beautiful, too, and she had spent many a hopeful hour admiring the selection, wondering if her father would choose any of them to replace her mother. They had smelled much as she remembered her mother, and spoke in the same soft, purring accents. But she knew nothing of quadroons and didn't understand why a lady from New Orleans would be someone to speak of with scorn.

She frowned and puzzled over these comments as Sallie kicked her mare into a canter again. It did little good to question Sallie. She always knew everything and was impatient about imparting any of it to anyone else. Her answers were always more puzzling than the questions. Laura would wait and ask Aunt Ann. Her answers were not always satisfactory, but they were always quiet and polite. There was no danger of disturbing Aunt Ann's peace of mind with persistent questioning. "Maybe" was a decisive answer for her.

Later, in the coolness of the evening, Aunt Ann looked up from her perpetual embroidery with something close to surprise at her niece's question. "Cash? Why in heaven's name was Sallie talking to Cash? I vow, that child will flirt with anything in breeches. You just stay away from him, Laura. He's not our kind."

"But Sallie said his mama is sick. Shouldn't we visit her?" Laura clung tenaciously to her subject. She didn't much care one way or another about insolent boys who worked in tobacco patches, but the promise of a lady from New Orleans kept her captivated. Her aunt's soft Southern accents were pleasant, but they did not remind her of her mother's lovely French one.

"Visit the Wickliffes? Certainly not, Laura. They're not our tenants. Go on and play now, child."

Defeated, Laura wandered off to the kitchen, where she played with Franz and listened to the odd drawls of the slaves as they cleaned up after the evening meal. Franz wasn't supposed to be in here, but as long as he didn't get boisterous, Jemima didn't complain. Laura didn't belong in here any more than Franz did, but she didn't belong anywhere else either. With no one to talk to but the dog, loneliness overwhelmed her as it had every night since she had been brought here.

No one came looking for her until bedtime. By then her new pantalets and crinolines were dusty and disheveled and her brown ringlets had fallen flat and limp about her face. Sallie took one look at her and made a face.

"You'll not be any beauty, I'll be bound. Wait until Pa sees you." She caught Laura's arm and jerked her in the direction of the study.

Uncle Matthew little resembled his suave younger brother, Laura's father. He was the same height, but years of comfortable living had given him a portliness that did not lend itself well to quickness of movement. He preferred to sit back in his chair, smoke his cigars, and give orders, making the world come to him rather than going out to see it for himself. He raised his bushy eyebrows slightly at the sight of his niece in sadly rumpled clothing, and he looked to his lovely daughter for explanation.

"She was in the kitchen playing with the dog," Sallie answered scornfully, without need for the question to be voiced. Long ago she had learned both her parents would promise her anything, but if she actually expected to get it, it was her father who would provide.

From behind his slightly graying side whiskers Matthew Kincaid smiled indulgently. "Well, there are worse crimes, I suppose. Why don't you scamper upstairs, Laura, and let Amy clean you up and put you to bed?"

Weary now, Laura eyed his ample lap with longing. Papa used to always pick her up and hold her and tell her of his day's adventures before carrying her off to bed. She desperately needed that familiar reassurance now.

"Isn't my papa ever coming back?" she whispered tearfully.

"I'm your papa now, child. You go get some sleep and you'll feel better in the morning. Maybe you can sit with Sallie in the schoolroom and start to learn your ABC's."

She already knew her ABC's, but she could tell by the tone of her uncle's voice that she had been dismissed. Dispiritedly she trailed off to the upper reaches of the house, leaving Sallie with her father.

"She's not very grateful." Sallie flounced down upon the settee, spreading her new crinoline admiringly over the plush velvet upholstery.

"She's a baby yet. I'm looking to you to take good

care of her. She's never had a home before. That brother
of mine was always a rover. It's only a miracle that he
didn't take the child on that last trip." Matthew sipped
at his whiskey and contemplated the pastoral landscape
on the wall, depicting two small boys and a lady in white
in one corner, with hills of rich land and Stoner Creek
filling the rest of the canvas. "You be nice to her,
y'hear?"

Hearing a story behind his warnings, Sallie encouraged
him eagerly. "How come I don't remember Uncle
Mark?"

Matthew sighed and tapped his cigar against the glass
tray. It never seemed strange that he spoke to his daughter as most men would a wife. Sallie was always there;
Ann was not. Not in the mental sense, anyway.

"Your uncle married a woman beneath his station,
some French singer he met in New York on one of his
travels. My father forbade him to bring her home, so
he didn't. He never came home again, even after your
grandfather died. Proud and stubborn, the fool. At least
he had the sense to name me the child's guardian in his
will. There's no telling where she would have ended up if
he hadn't left those papers with their landlady." Silently
Matthew contemplated the memory of the garish blond
who had brought Laura to the farm last spring. Landlady,
indeed. Mark had headed straight downhill after his
wife's death. It had taken a healthy sum to pay off the
woman and get rid of her. He suspected there were dozens of other debts out there somewhere, but he felt no
qualms at ignoring them. Mark had led a gambler's life,
and those who gave credit to gamblers deserved their
fate.

"What happened to her mama?" Sallie prompted him
again when it was obvious her father's thoughts had
trailed off.

"She died a couple of years ago. Now, hadn't you better be off to bed too?" Matthew lifted his eyebrows again
in a manner not meant to be disobeyed.

"Yes, sir." Sallie hopped up but couldn't refrain from
asking one more question. "Does she have to stay with
us always? She's an awful baby."

Matthew frowned and rose to his full towering height.
"From now on, she's your little sister, and you'll take

care of her just the same. She's a Kincaid. Don't ever forget it."

Sallie gave a reassuring smile, dropped a curtsy, and walked off with all the stateliness of a nine-year-old princess. A Kincaid, indeed. She wouldn't be at all surprised if Laura's mother wasn't a quadroon just like Cash's. Imagine anyone marrying so foreign a creature as a dirty, dark Frenchwoman when Kentucky was known for the beauty and quality of its belles.

She fully intended to be the most beautiful and sought-after of them all, one of these days. After all, Stoner Creek Farm would one day be hers, and there wasn't a man in the world who wouldn't do anything to have Stoner Creek Farm. She had only to choose among them. It would take a long and intensive study to make her choice, and she didn't mean to wait until the last minute to do it.

At almost the same time that Sallie was sedately preparing for slumber, twelve-year-old Cash Wickliffe trailed up the path to the tar-paper shack he called home. Night had fallen, but the day's heat still left the stench of bubbling tar. The pigsty of the shack next door added to the heavy odors of this barren patch of Watterson land. The stench was worse in this humidity, when no wind stirred the air, and Cash hurried to the door, fear pounding through his veins as always when he entered his home.

It wasn't fear of his father. He had reached an age when he could stand up to anything his father could mete out, despite the fact that he was bone weary after fourteen hours of labor. The fear that followed him in the door was a fear of death, and his eyes quickly searched the gloom to find the room's one bed.

He smiled in relief as a gentle voice called from the pillow. She had not bothered to light the candle. There was little need for it under the circumstances. She could scarcely lift her head any longer to do the fine sewing that had put food on the table for the first years of his life. Cash crossed the dirt floor to kneel down and give his mother a hug.

"Pa gone to town again tonight?" he asked in resignation, reaching for the medicine that should have been administered hours ago.

"He's a bitter man, Cash. You have to understand that. He gave it all up when he married me. He couldn't know how things would turn out. You just remember he's your father, and show him the proper respect."

Her gentle admonitions did not strike the same chords of guilt and shame that they used to. Ever since he had learned that his hard-earned wages went to buy his father's whiskey and pay his gambling debts, Cash had not been able to look at his father in the same way. "Things" had never turned out well for him because he drank and gambled, not because his lovely wife was a "woman of color." Cash wished there were some way to make his mother see that, but she would never hear a word spoken against the proud Southern gentleman who had broken all the rules to marry her. He would have to be grateful. He had a name, he supposed, for all the good it did him.

He kissed his mother good night and sat down to his birthday dinner of cold beans and stale cornbread. To ease the hatred burning inside him, Cash conjured up the pastel vision of Sallie Kincaid stopping to speak with him today. Someday he was going to be richer than the Kincaids, have a bigger house than Stoner Creek, and marry a woman like Sallie. Maybe he would even marry Sallie. She was pretty enough to make people forget who he was, and the whole town of Stoner Creek would have to look up to him with respect.

Then let his father try to steal his wages.

2

Laura came out of the dry-goods store with a small bundle of needles and thread in her hand. Now that she was nine, Aunt Ann had promised her her very own sewing box if she could complete hemming Sallie's new gown. Hemming was boring, but the sewing box would have nice new scissors and measuring tape and chalk, and with the scraps she had saved from the dress, she could make an elegant gown for her doll. She already knew what the gown would look like, and her fingers itched to get started.

Franz patiently rose to his huge feet as she stepped out to the brick walk. The main street of Stoner Creek had recently been paved with McAdam's new surface, reducing the level of mud and dust considerably. But the presence of a constant stream of horses and carriages on Court Day had contributed more than the normal share of refuse on the street. Laura turned up her nose in distaste at the odor.

She glanced around for some sign of Henry in the confusion of men and horses. Aunt Ann would probably have fainted had she known her niece had gone to town on Court Day, but Henry wouldn't tell and no one else would miss her. If she were to finish that hem, she had to have thread. And Henry's errand to pick up a repaired bridle had seemed fortuitous. What difficulty could she get into in just a few minutes?

Men from throughout the county came to town on Court Day. Small farmers in jeans and hickory striped shirts mixed with the wealthy landowners in linen coats and silk waistcoats discussing the upcoming election and Cassius Clay's latest outrage. All along the main street vendors set up stands touting patent medicines and other nostrums. A tooth doctor had set up his booth on one

corner, and a pair of minstrels strummed banjos on another for the coins thrown in their hats. In front of the
courthouse there was a lively argument going on over the
price of a horse, and similar transactions would occur
throughout the day. By evening, whiskey and tempers
would have erupted into enough brawls to fill the tiny
jail, but the day was young yet. Laura tapped her small
booted foot to the lively tune of the minstrels and waited
for Henry to return. She found Court Day rather
exciting.

Despite the earliness of the hour, loud voices and
shouts from a crowd down toward the tavern attracted
her attention. With more curiosity than wisdom, Laura
wandered in that direction. She didn't know what men
liked to fight about, but Uncle Matt was always full of
tales of the latest feuds. Politics seemed to be the most
popular argument, and even Uncle Matt got stirred when
some of the neighbors came over and started arguing
elections and such. There seemed to be a mighty to-do
every time the issue of slavery was brought up. Since the
Great Compromiser, Henry Clay, had died two years
ago, the arguments had grown more vociferous, and
Henry's distant cousin Cassius seemed to be the instiga-
tor of most of the turmoil. She didn't understand much
more than that. She knew Uncle Matt's Henry and Jemima were slaves, but they were far better off than some
of the white folks in town. That was what Uncle Matt
said, and she had seen the truth of that with her own
eyes.

As she drew closer to the brawl, Laura saw that the
crowd seemed to be surrounding a man on a horse who
was shouting incoherently and wielding a whip. She recognized Mr. Watterson from the farm next to Uncle
Matt's, and her nose turned up in more distaste than she
had displayed at the odor emanating from the street.

Watterson was a fat, florid-faced man of uncertain
temper, at best. Henry and Jemima stayed out of his way
when he came to visit because his way with slaves was
not gentle, even when they were not his own. Rumor
had it that he'd had to sell off all his house servants to
cover massive debts, and the few field hands seemed to
be dwindling rapidly. Since he'd had to advertise run-
aways numerous times in the last few years, the cause of

the dwindling number remained vague. Most of his work was done by hired help, and if possible, he treated them worse than his slaves, since they were worth nothing to him.

Shouts of encouragement mixed with voices of protest as the whip descended again, and Laura felt a sickness in the pit of her stomach as she approached. No animal should be treated so cruelly. How could those men stand idly by and behave as if this were another cockfight? At least the cocks were equally armed. A man with a whip against a defenseless animal was no such thing. She was only nine and small for her age, but she would tell the nasty man to stop it. Even Watterson couldn't lift a hand to a Kincaid.

The crowd shifted as she approached, and Laura gave a gasp of horror at the sight finally revealed. No animal stood beneath the thunderous lashes of that whip, but a boy coated in blood. Her fingernails dug into her palms as the whip sliced through the air once again, laying open another stripe on the boy's broad shoulder. The boy had tried to grab the whip as it whistled past him, but the blow knocked him to the ground. Before he could rise, the whip struck again, tearing open what remained of the shirt across his back.

"Damned disobedient young pup! Who do you think you are, swearin' out a complaint against me? I'll teach you who's boss here. Your pa owed me a heap of money before he died, and you're going to pay back every cent if you have to work till you drop!" The exclamations were accompanied by the slash of the whip, crippling the skinny boy, who still tried desperately to regain his feet.

"Someone orter stop him before he kills the boy," one bystander protested laconically, spitting a wad of tobacco juice toward the street.

"He's just white trash, and not all white at that. Watterson's got the right on it. He ain't got no call to be filin' a complaint against a man who gives him room and board."

So sick to her stomach that she felt fury steaming out her ears, Laura contemplated kicking the ignorant yokel who spoke, but her soft leather boots wouldn't have much effect. Fists clenched in pain as the whip struck again, shuddering as if she had been the one struck,

Laura knew what she had to do to stop this horror, but she closed her eyes and prayed first, hoping Papa would hear her. When he had given her Franz, her father had taught her all the commands that Franz knew, but there was one she had been forbidden to use except in dire danger. She had never used it and did not know how it would work, but she felt her father would understand if she tried it now.

Taking a deep breath, she opened her eyes and cried, "Kill, Franz, kill!" and pointed in the direction of horse and rider.

Laura didn't know how the dog would differentiate among the many, but she prayed her father or the good Lord above was watching over her. Someone had to put an end to this travesty.

Franz dashed loyally in the direction indicated. Before any could stop him, the huge black animal hurled forward and fastened his massive jaw around Watterson's thigh.

The man's high-pitched scream scarcely reached Laura's ears as she dodged into the crowd to grab the boy lying sprawled in the street. The men around her were more intent on the spectacle of Watterson fighting the devil-dog than on his hapless victim. Laura tugged the boy's arm and he lifted a blood-streaked face to gaze at her dazedly. The dark eyes cleared quickly at the sight of the young girl still in her brown winter velvet pulling at his arm.

"Come on, we got to get out of here," she commanded, tugging again as if her small frame could lift him from the street.

Rage and fear overcoming the torment of his body, Cash found his feet and dodged through the crowd at the heels of his avenging angel. Several men shouted warning of his escape, but Watterson was beyond caring. Fighting the unyielding jaws of the dog, he reached for the pistol he always carried in his jacket pocket on Court Day.

Laura's back jerked at the sound of the shot, but she did not turn or falter in her footsteps. She had a destination in mind, and she did not swerve from it. In the face of such courage, Cash could do no less than follow, although instincts acquired in years of ill treatment screamed a protest. He needed to steal a horse and ride out of town before Watterson came looking for him. Instead, he raced after the tiny figure darting down a side alley.

Heedless of the dirt and trash littering the carriage alley behind some of the town's larger residences, Laura lifted her skirts to aid in running and glanced over her shoulder to be certain Cash still followed. He was limping badly and blood poured from a cut over his forehead, but he was right behind her, his long legs keeping pace at a distance.

She opened a back gate leading into a small garden behind a converted carriage house, once the grand residence of a polished barouche. The driver's quarters and eventually the entire building had been converted into a cottage and office for the town's only physician. The elderly and once wealthy owner of this magnificence had gladly accepted Dr. Broadbent's offer to purchase the empty carriage house. It now had a respectable entrance to the street, but Laura preferred this rear entrance under the circumstances.

She was panting as she pounded on the office door, and as Cash caught up with her she unceremoniously threw open the door and entered before any could answer her knock.

The odors of alcohol and formaldehyde mixed with the scents of lemon and some other sweet-smelling concoction as Laura lunged into the stifling room the doctor had partitioned off for his laboratory. The man bent over a microscope looked up with an expression of dismay and disapproval until he registered Laura's tear-streaked face. When the blood-caked boy stumbled through the door, he immediately set aside the machine and assumed a brisk air of professional efficiency.

"Laura, run into the house and have Kate bring us some hot water. You, boy, come with me."

Relieved that someone of competence had taken control of the matter, Laura ran to do as told. Dr. Broadbent was young, and many of the older people refused to consult with him, but Uncle Matthew knew his family and had brought him out to the farm on any number of occasions to treat various injuries and sicknesses among the household and servants. Laura liked the serious young doctor, who always took time to laugh and talk

with her, and she had taken to visiting with his sad-eyed
wife whenever she had the opportunity. Sallie had informed her that Mrs. Broadbent had consumption and
was sad because she couldn't have children, but Laura
understood little of that. She just knew Kate was one of
the kindest people she knew.

Between them they managed to carry the heavy pitcher
of water to the office, where Dr. Broadbent had taken
Cash. Stripped to his trousers, Cash sat bravely on the
cot, flinching only when the doctor applied soap and antiseptic to his wounds. As Kate unwound bandages and
found ointments as ordered, Laura settled quietly in a
corner out of the way, trying desperately not to think of
Franz.

"I'll have the devil who did this," the doctor gritted
out between clenched teeth as he applied needle and
thread to the skin gaping over Cash's eye. "He should
have been strung up long ago. The man's inhuman."

"If they didn't string him up for killing Caleb, they
sure won't do anything over the likes of me." Mentioning
the slave over whom he had filed the complaint, Cash
glanced to the corner where Laura sat apparently forgotten in the bustle. "That was a mighty big dog. You
reckon it might have got away?"

Laura's eyes lit with sudden hope. "Do you think he
might? I better go see."

Before she could leap to her feet, Kate caught her
shoulder and held her down and Dr. Broadbent frowned
sternly at the pair. "Neither of you is to go out in that
street again today. Laura, is your uncle here? I'll send
someone for him."

Laura shook her head. "Just Henry. He's at the
harnessmaker's."

Only a look passed between husband and wife before
Kate hurried off to send someone after the black servant.
Laura appeared ready to cry again as she glanced toward
the door.

"Couldn't I just go look, Doctor? Franz may just be
hurt, and he'll be looking for me."

"I'll go. Watterson will be healing himself at the sa-
loon. I'll find him." Cash started to rise from the cot.

"I'll take a switch to you myself if you try any such
damned fool thing." The doctor shoved him back down.

"Laura didn't sacrifice her dog just so you could go back out there and get yourself killed. I don't even want to know how that child got mixed up in this thing. I'll have a word or two for Matthew Kincaid before this is over, but right now the two of you will sit right where you are. Henry will look for the dog."

Cash's jaw set stubbornly, but whether in defiance or against the pain, it wasn't easy to tell. He suffered in silence while the physician started on the long stripes across his shoulders.

In the interest of politeness, Laura offered, "I heard your mama died, Cash. I'm sorry. She was a nice lady."

Cash grimaced as the antiseptic went over another cut. "That Mrs. Kincaid's idea to send the fruit? It was mighty kind of her."

This was a polite euphemism to cover up what they both knew Laura shouldn't have done. Laura had been the one to visit the tar-paper shack on numerous occasions, not Mrs. Kincaid, and the thought of sending fruit would never have occurred to the vague woman inhabiting the upper rooms of Stoner Creek. Laura kept up the polite facade in front of the doctor. "It's the least that we could do." Lapsing into childish honesty, she added, "I don't know why people always send food. I don't remember being very hungry after Papa died."

Dr. Broadbent snorted and looked over his spectacles at the small girl wrapped in silks and velvets in the corner. "Food feeds the vultures who show up after any death. It saves the mourners from needing to provide for them."

"Jonathan!" Kate entered in time to hear her husband's cynical comment. "They're just children. You mustn't speak so."

A gleam came to the doctor's eye as he looked to his young wife and back to the two "children." Laura's hazel eyes still blinked suspiciously with tears, but there was a maturity behind them that her elder cousin had yet to display. And the furious dark eyes of the fifteen-year-old under his hands had probably never known a child's joy. But he wouldn't spoil his wife's innocence unnecessarily.

"My apologies, madam," he answered with a hint of irony.

"The boy has gone to fetch Henry, and I've fixed up

the bed in the back room. You will want to watch him for fever, won't you?"

Cash jerked beneath the doctor's hand, attempting to slide away. "I'm obliged to you, but I got no money to pay, and I'd better be getting along before Watterson comes looking for me. I don't want to cause no trouble for nobody."

Broadbent's long, slender fingers dug into the boy's shoulder and held him without effort. "Watterson won't come near here if he values his life. I've threatened to file charges against him before. This time I'll do it, and he knows it. You'll stay, and when you're better, you'll help around the place to work off the debt. I heard you're good with horses, and I've been thinking of replacing that old mare of mine."

It was like handing a peppermint stick to a baby. Cash sat down and looked warily at his benefactor. His lean dark face had never learned to smile, and suspicion was its most common emotion. When the doctor ignored his reaction and continued to work on the multitude of welts, the boy glanced to Laura's corner. The sight of her huddled form surreptitiously wiping away a tear relaxed the tautness in his shoulders to a degree. A new look of shrewd intelligence appeared on his grimy face.

"I already filed charges. I'm supposed to be over to the courthouse today. He killed Caleb and he damn near killed me before this. I don't let no man get away with that, begging your pardon, ma'am, sir." He dodged an apologetic glance to the doctor's pale-faced wife.

"No jury from around here is going to find against a landowner like Watterson when a boy like you is pressing the charges. You'll only cause yourself more grief. Count whatever your father owed him as paid and leave it at that, for now. When you've got your full growth and made something of yourself, then you come back and right the wrongs. Learn patience, boy."

Cash's mouth set in a grim line, but he seemed to be absorbing this advice and filing it away for future reference. Laura listened in amazement as he dropped the subject of his enemy and broached another.

"I'm real good with horses and I'm a hard worker. These cuts won't slow me down. I can start work today, if you want. Maybe after I show you how much I can do, you could give me a small wage. I don't mean to be beholden to nobody."

"Your mother told me she'd taught you to read and write and do figures. That's the hardest work you'll do until these gashes are healed. You'll earn your keep, don't worry, and you'll get fair wages when you're ready to earn them."

The buggy and a terrified Henry arrived in the back, and Laura ran to the old black servant's arms as he exclaimed and held them out to her. The tears that she had been holding back streamed down her face now that she had the comfort of solid arms around her. Henry glanced up to the questioning eyes watching this performance and shook his had sorrowfully.

"C'mon, Miz Laura, we take you back now. We let Marster Matt take keer of things."

Laura looked up in horror. If Uncle Matt knew Henry had taken her to town on Court Day, he would have a proper fit. She shook her head until her loosened bonnet fell. "Oh, no, you mustn't say a word. We'll say Franz followed the carriage. He's dead, isn't he?"

Henry nodded slowly, his eyes brimming at the sight of her brave tears. "I'm feared so, Miz Laura. It was real quick-like. He didn't suffer none."

From his seat on the cot, Cash spoke up. "I can't bring back your dog, Miss Kincaid, but someday I'll make it up to you, I promise."

In the security of the trusted servant's arms, Laura turned to watch the boy's face, and nodded politely. Despite all the warnings she had been given three years ago, she had found the row shack that once housed Cash's bedridden mother and drunken father. His mother had been a lovely, gentle woman who had done mending until the last days of her life, to help keep bread on the table. She accepted payment only in food so his alcoholic father couldn't spend it at the tavern. This was the woman the world condemned because one of her grandparents was black. It looked to Laura like Cash's aristocratic father was the one to be scorned, but her opinion didn't count. Cassius Wickliffe had no means to talk of repaying anyone, but Laura believed him. Strangely comforted, she held up her hand in farewell as Henry carried her out to the carriage.

3

Choked by the steel corset required by Sallie's hand-me-down London smoke-gray riding habit, twelve-year-old Laura Kincaid glared at her image in the oval mirror. Sallie had looked dashing and elegant when she had worn this habit. The scarf on the high top hat had floated gracefully about her shoulders and her blond curls had danced beguilingly from beneath it. In contrast, on Laura the scarf hung limply halfway down her back, the skirt's long train made her trip, and the hat balanced precariously on the sedate chignon which was the only answer to her obstinately straight hair. She should have stayed with her own old velvet habit instead of accepting Sallie's offer of hers.

But she would be thirteen this summer, and it was time she began looking like a lady. Sallie had looked like a lady at nine. Laura despaired of ever obtaining that status. When Sallie had been thirteen, she already had a bosom and a tiny waist and knew how to flaunt them. At sixteen she was drawing beaux as flowers draw bees. Laura glanced down at her flat chest and straight figure and gave up in disgust to wander to the window to watch the scene below.

Sallie sat gracefully upon her bay mare, laughing and chattering as half a dozen young men on expensive horse-flesh milled around her, doting on her every word. Ward Breckinridge was by far the most handsome, in Laura's opinion, but Johnny Clay had a certain dashing charm, and Todd Payne was known to be rich as Croesus. Even Dr. Broadbent came over to make a gallant bow, but his wife had only just passed away and he did not linger long.

If Dr. Broadbent were here, then Cash could not be far behind. At eighteen he had grown well over a foot taller than when the doctor had first taken him in. He was still more lean and wiry than these well-fed country gentlemen, but Laura had seen him lift injured colts in his arms and carry stacks of firewood that Sallie's beaux would never have dared dream of lifting. Even though Dr. Broadbent had undertaken the formidable task of making a gentleman out of him, Cash wasn't accepted into Sallie's wealthy, aristocratic circle. He remained an oddly mysterious figure on the outskirts of society, his dark saturnine face often seen at large affairs but never engaged in the idle flirtation that was the main reason for most gatherings.

Laura picked up her long skirts and petticoats and started for the stairs. She was too young to be a part of the gay party below, but she would ride with the other women and children gathering in the hall and parlor. It was much too early in the season to have a barbecue, but the Breckinridges welcomed any excuse for a party. The announcement of their eldest son's engagement and the early warm weather were sufficient reason to invite the countryside for a weekend of barbecue, dancing, and visiting.

Maybe she could slip by Uncle Matthew and go outside to find Cash. He would want to know how the puppy he had brought her last fall was doing. Franz the Second, as she had dubbed him, wasn't a puppy any longer, but a gentler, friendlier companion couldn't be found. Cash had trained him to sit and heel and fetch and even to growl warningly if anyone approached suddenly, but although neither of them had spoken of it, the new Franz had not been trained to attack.

Laura's small figure in the absurd hat and too-long skirts was scarcely noticed as she wandered across the lawn of fresh spring grass in search of Cash. She was a child and beneath the notice of Sallie's lofty companions. She had never cultivated the interest of the other children laughing and screaming and racing through the abelias and mock oranges. And since Aunt Ann and Uncle Matthew were the only adults responsible for her and they were seldom around, Laura had complete freedom to wander where she wished.

She found Cash in the stableyard, where she had suspected he would be. His frock coat was flung over a fence rail, and in shirt sleeves and silk waistcoat he stood among the horses examining the hoof of the massive stallion he had trained for Dr. Broadbent. The horse was so strong-willed that the doctor seldom rode him and never harnessed him to the buggy. He had bought a gray gelding for general use. The stallion was simply an elegant showpiece.

"I'll have one of the stableboys look at him if he's picked up a stone," Laura called as she ungracefully clambered up the fence, trailing her long skirts.

Cash lowered the hoof, gave the horse a solid pat, and strode across the paddock to join her. Even the tight trousers and Wellingtons and cravat couldn't make Cash look like a gentleman. His dark locks had a habit of tumbling where they would, and frequently touched his shirt collar in defiance of local custom. He was too lean, too dark, and too harsh to look upon to be mistaken for one of the laughing, charming, polished young gentlemen on the front lawn. But he was the only one of his age who managed to spare the time to speak with a lonely child.

"That's quite a fancy get-up, Miss Laura. You going somewheres?" Cash smacked his large hand flat against her top hat, straightening its precarious balance while jamming it tighter on her head.

Laura stuck her tongue out at him. "Uncle Matt said I could ride with the others to the Breckinridges'. We're almost ready to go. Are you coming?"

A dark gleam escaped his hooded eyes, and Laura almost detected a trace of smile on his thin lips. "I'm coming. If you've got a few extra coins you're willing to gamble, I know a surefire wager you can place them on this evening."

Excitement lit Laura's small face at this hint of a secret she wasn't supposed to know. The men gambled all the time on horse races and cockfights and other sports which ladies weren't supposed to know about. They always did, of course, but they never took part in them. Cash was actually telling her about what the men would be indulging in tonight. Sallie would die to know about this.

"Is there going to be a race?" she inquired eagerly.

"Now, I'm not supposed to tell you these things. You gotta keep quiet. But I have Doc's permission to race

Jupiter over there, and unless an act of God interferes, he's going to win big. I could turn your coins into a lot of dollars you wouldn't have to account for to anybody."

Cash watched with amusement as Laura's small face grew solemn at the enormity of his proposition. He could almost see the wheels turning inside that head of hers. She looked no more than a little trained monkey perching there, but he knew better than any that she had more courage than many men he knew. He owed her more than a favor. He owed her the prospect of a whole new life. He rather fancied she would enjoy being in on his moment of glory.

Laura considered his proposition carefully. She had two gold dollar coins that Uncle Matt had given her for her birthday last July. She had hoarded them carefully all these months, uncertain what would be the best use to put them to. If she gambled them, she might lose them entirely, but she didn't think Cash would gamble his own hard-earned wages on anything that wasn't a certainty.

"Will you place the wager for me?" she asked anxiously. She would never know how to go about doing it herself.

"If you'll trust me with it. Or you can give it to Doc. He'll be there too."

With a sudden defiant grin Laura started down the fence. "I'll just be a minute. You wait right here, y'hear?"

Cash almost had to laugh as she raced off toward the house. She had sounded just like her beautiful cousin ordering one of her beaux around. His dark gaze drifted to the group of young people gathered on the lawn. Sallie's golden hair sparkled with all the glory of the sun, and he felt the black need cracking through the volcano of his insides. All his life he'd been aware of what he'd been denied because of the accident of his birth. Someday he would have it all. His gaze fastened in determination on the elegant portico and sun-washed brick of the graceful mansion. Someday they would have to recognize the son of a New Orleans quadroon, whether they liked it or not.

Laura slipped through the shadows of the shrubbery in the late-evening light. The April air had turned cool, and

she pulled the shawl tighter around her shoulders. Thank
heaven she'd had the sense to pack the pretty brown
wool gown Uncle Matt had given her for Christmas. Sallie's summer batiste had sent her scurrying into the
warmth of the Breckinridge parlor hours ago. She could
sit and gossip with the ladies if she liked. Laura had
better things to do.

Dew was already dampening the long grass when she
reached the pasture where the men were gathered. Beyond the trees there was still sufficient sunlight to see
the horses and their owners milling about. Several of the
horses would have black jockeys, and these stood to one
side from the frock-coated and top-hatted gentlemen.
The spectators wandered through the pack of horses,
talking knowledgeably of the horses' antecedents and
lines, confirming wagers already made or drumming up
new ones.

Laura found Dr. Broadbent's stallion standing beneath
a tree, idly munching grass, unattended. She frowned at
this dereliction of duty. If Cash meant to race this horse,
shouldn't he be tending to him and stirring up interest in
wagers?

Keeping to the shadows of the stately elms along the
fencerow, Laura wandered closer to the loudest group of
men. She recognized Ward Breckinridge's tall frame and
then began to place others of Sallie's beaux among the
group. They were passing a flask and enjoying themselves more than the occasion warranted. They had probably been tippling all day.

She cast her glance around again and found Cash idly
leaning against the fence, chewing on a piece of grass.
She glared at that piece of grass suspiciously. Cash never
chewed on grass like some ignorant farm boy. She
jumped when one of the young men discovered him at
the same time she did.

"Hey, Wickliffe, you got any wagers on this run?"
Todd Payne nudged one of his companions and grinned
as Cash turned in his direction, his dark eyes wary as he
perused the group.

"I wouldn't wager on any of those nags out there if
you paid me." His reply was enough to boil the blood
of any horse-proud Kentuckian even if it weren't coming

from a tenant farmer. Backs stiffened everywhere within hearing.

"You're too cowardly to take a chance, you mean," a voice called out.

"Nope. I'd bet on Jupiter if he were running." Cash dropped his grass stalk and nodded toward the bored stallion.

Laughter filtered through the crowd. It was well known that Jupiter's genealogy was uncertain and scarcely of the finest. That was why the doc had been able to afford him. And there wasn't a soul present who didn't know that doc couldn't handle the miserable animal that his lackluster ward had trained. The horse had never been raced, and for good reason.

"How much you willing to wager?" one wag inquired.

Laura watched as Cash shrugged nonchalantly. How could he be so calm?

"He's too good a horse to risk in that miserable pack. I haven't got enough to make it worthwhile."

Todd Payne hooted. "What kind of odds are you looking for? Even at five to one you'd be getting more than the lazy beast deserves."

Five to one! Laura's eyes glowed as she calculated the winnings her two dollars would make. She would own a fortune. She could buy Franz his own bed and buy herself some of that lovely taffeta that Aunt Ann said she was too young to wear. She would sew it into a gown more gorgeous than anything Sallie owned. She waited for Cash to snap up the bait.

Cash simply shoved his hands in his pockets and continued to gaze with a sneer at the horses beginning to line up at the end of the field. "Still ain't worth it. I've only got twenty bucks to my name, and Jupiter's worth more than ten times that amount. You rich folks just go on about your business."

"Ten times! That wretched animal couldn't even breathe the dust of Ivanhoe out there. I'll bet you two hundred to your twenty that your animal can't even place." To Todd Payne, this sum was scarcely a gambling amount. He already had wagers larger than that with the others listening to them now.

Insolently Cash looked the wealthy college boy up and down. "How much you give me to win?"

"Five hundred!" Fury and liquor overcame common sense, but there was no backing out once a wager was made. Excitement trembled through the growing crowd, and more wagers were hurriedly exchanged as Cash pulled off his coat and headed for the horse.

Laura stood in the shadows and listened with incredulity. Five hundred dollars! That had to be more money than there was in the world. She was good at arithmetic, but it took a few minutes to calculate how much of that her two dollars would earn. Just as the number fifty came to mind, she saw Doc Broadbent meander over and exchange words with several of the older men. He gestured toward Cash and the stallion, and more money hastily came into view. My word, but even Doc was taking wagers on the outcome!

Laura could scarcely keep her excitement to herself as Cash mounted the huge stallion and trotted in the direction of the waiting field. Fifty dollars! She could buy a whole new wardrobe for fifty dollars. She could buy a horse for that much. Two horses. The possibilities seemed endless. Now she understood why men got so excited about gambling. This was why her father had carried her up and down the rivers for endless miles while he played at cards. With that kind of easy money to be had, who wouldn't?

Those thoughts swiftly sobered as Laura's faint recollections of seedy hotel rooms and sleeping on cotton bales returned. What was so eagerly won could be even more speedily lost. Should Cash's arrogance not pay off, the two dollars she had saved for nearly a year would be gone. She would still have a roof over her head and food on the table, and so would Cash, but it would be a painful setback. She prayed Dr. Broadbent wasn't wagering too high. Worse yet, she hoped Uncle Matthew wasn't here. He would certainly take up the wrong end of those odds. Although Stoner Creek was one of the largest farms in the Bluegrass, it wasn't cash-wealthy enough to cover too many of those kinds of bets. The vague thought of losing everything on such a silly pastime filtered uneasily through her mind.

She could scarcely bear to watch as the horses took off, but she could not turn away either. Holding her breath and peeking out from beneath lowered lashes,

Laura gripped the lower rails of the fence and watched
as Cash's big stallion stayed in easy stride with the pack.
From her position behind the fence, the trees interfered
with her view of the far end of the field, and without
thinking, she scrambled over to get a better look. Jupiter
was pulling ahead, and she jumped up and down in excitement, clenching her fists and praying as the men
around her screamed and hollered and cursed vividly.
She scarcely heard them. Jupiter was ahead! Straining
his mighty legs, he pulled farther and farther afield, his
rider never laying a whip to him. Laura screamed in victory as he crossed the line well ahead of the thoroughbreds behind him.

The furious curses this win produced jarred Laura back
to her surroundings. Todd Payne's face was positively
livid with drunken anger and his fists clenched as Cash
swung his scarcely heated mount around to trot back.
The Breckinridge boys were counting out their money
and murmuring fainthearted platitudes about debts of
honor, but Laura heard others scoff that Cash was no
gentleman and there was more trickery than honor to his
victory. Their anger astonished and worried her.

Before she could run to Cash with a warning, Doc
caught her by the shoulder and gently pushed her back
toward the fence. "Get out of here, Laura. This is no
place for a lady."

"But Cash—"

"I know." Grimly Jonathan Broadbent lifted Laura to
the top rung, his face a study in stern lines and planes
when it came even with hers. "Cash can take care of
himself. Go on."

With one last despairing look over her shoulder at the
drunken young men going out to meet the victor, Laura
ran back to the house.

The next morning there were hushed murmurs in the
far corners of every room but they instantly quieted at
the approach of young ears. The men were scarcely to
be seen anywhere until noon, when the house party
began to break up early.

Laura peeked surreptitiously at the black eyes and
bandaged noses beneath top hats as the young men rode

off, but she held her tongue. They didn't even know she existed. The ones she wanted to see were Doc and Cash.

But Uncle Matthew ordered his party home before she'd had a chance to find either one of them. Instead of gallantly riding in a cloud of dust surrounded by beaux as she had when she arrived, Sallie was forced to ride with Laura in the carriage, unaccompanied by any of the gentlemen. Laura knew that meant someone was in disgrace, but she didn't think it was Sallie. Her cousin chattered all the way home of the heads she had turned, without giving a sign that anything was wrong.

Since Laura didn't think Uncle Matt knew of her escapade, she figured it had to be Sallie's beaux who had behaved badly. She wished she knew what had happened after she left. From the blood and bruises, she assumed there had been a brawl, but that was scarcely unusual. It was rumored Todd and Ward had already drawn pistols in a duel over Sallie. Hot tempers flared frequently in these parts. But that usually wasn't sufficient to put them in disgrace. She worried about Cash.

So when Doc Broadbent appeared down the lane later that evening, Laura ran to the front porch to meet him before the rest of the family could usurp him. She would never catch his attention while Uncle Matt and Sallie were around.

His cheek sported a vivid bruise, and he suddenly looked very young as he spied Laura and tousled her hair. He couldn't be much more than twenty-eight, but the weight of his responsibilities always made him seem much older. Laura gave him a tentative smile as he sat on the porch rail and reached in his coat pocket. Nothing could be seriously wrong if Doc was smiling.

"Cash tells me this packet belongs to you. I'm not going to inquire the wheres and hows of it, but I suggest you not let your good folks hear of it. They might not be quite so understanding." He removed a small pouch from his pocket and passed it to Laura.

It weighed heavy and jingled and crackled, and she stared at it in awe. Even Uncle Matt couldn't have that much money. She lifted her small solemn face to meet Doc's gaze. "Where's Cash?"

The smile disappeared from his face and he shook his head sadly. "He's gone, Laura. He bought that ornery animal from me last night and left with his winnings. He was right to go. This isn't any place for him. He's better off on his own now."

Laura heard the pain and sorrow in the doctor's voice that his words didn't reveal. After Kate's death, Cash had been all the family he had. Now he was truly alone. She touched his hand gently.

"He'll be back, won't he?" She said it with as much promise as question, both seeking and giving reassurance.

The doctor shook his head. "Not if he's smart, he won't. He's headed out West, where men are judged by what they do, not who they are. This place won't ever let him forget that he's not one of them."

Alarm briefly crossed Laura's face. "But I'm not one of them either. Will I have to go out West?"

A gentle smile touched his lips as he patted her hand and stood up. "You've got a wealthy uncle to look after you, child. Be glad of it. He'll make you a Kincaid or shoot any man who denies it. Now, smile and think of what you're going to do with all that money."

4

As she remembered those words, Laura's smile was as grim as the doctor's had been the night of the race. That pouch of money Cash had won for her had taken her out of Stoner Creek as certainly as his winnings had taken Cash. Not knowing where or how to spend such an enormous sum, she had saved it until that fateful summer when she had turned seventeen.

Laura glanced over the railing to the Ohio River slowly drifting by. She could see Louisville coming up in the distance. Almost halfway home. She tried not to remember those last painful days when she had fled the safety and security of Stoner Creek for the humiliation of Cairo, Illinois, but the journey from Cairo to home was

a long and tedious one, and she had nothing better to
do than think.

At the river landing in Louisville, Laura accepted the
offer of a carriage ride from a matronly woman returning
home and found herself in the train station with time to
spare. The soaring heights of the L&N depot made no
impression on her as she fought off memories of that last
trip through here as a terrified, determined seventeen-
year-old. Four years had brought maturity but little else.
The whole country had gone to war and torn itself asunder while she sat in a tiny country town and sewed garments for other people. Her only strong memory of those
years was humiliation, and she had plenty of that to
spare.

Taking her seat on the train, Laura straightened her
widow's veil and politely tried to adjust her position on
the worn cushions without disturbing the other passengers around her. The unshaven soldier on the seat opposite jarred painful memories, and she tried not to look
at him, not to remember a time when boys had donned
those uniforms proudly and bravely. She was not yet
twenty-one and still she felt like a decrepit old woman.
All that hope had disappeared years ago. All she had
left now were memories.

She closed her eyes and tried to sleep as the others
were doing, but the constant rumbling and belching and
jerking of the train kept her just on the edge of sleep
where memories and dreams intermix. She didn't have
the money or even the pride to wear the multitudinous
petticoats she had worn that long-ago summer. Her traveling gown clung almost indecently to her knees now as
she tried to arrange her legs more comfortably. She
didn't care. It was cooler this way, and no one looked
twice at a small nondescript widow of uncertain means.
There were widows to be had aplenty anymore. Men
were the scarcity.

Laura's thoughts jerked back to the summer of '61,
when she had worn so many petticoats to her birthday
ball that she could scarcely sit down. Sallie had insisted
that the hooped crinoline she wanted to wear would not
be sufficiently graceful for the elegant silk she had been
allowed to don for her seventeenth birthday. As always,
Laura followed Sallie's fashion sense, but in the heat of

that July evening she began to rebel against her cousin's strictures.

It was Laura's ball, but Sallie still received all of the attention. The guests would arrive and smile politely at Laura and say things like "So you're seventeen now. My, haven't you become the lovely young lady," before taking Sallie's elbow and going off for an animated chat over the latest gossip. Always cast in Sallie's shadow, Laura had never learned the trick of prattling about nothing. Sallie did it too well for Laura to even compete.

Watching her cousin lead off the dancing with Todd Payne while she had to be satisfied with Uncle Matt's dutiful guidance, Laura vowed she would find a suitor all her own, one who wouldn't even know Sallie was alive. She smiled dreamily as she imagined her handsome prince walking through that door, his eyes only for her. He would come up to her immediately and sweep her onto the dance floor and not release her until the end of the evening. By that time everyone in attendance would realize how lovely and graceful and charming she was, and they would all regret that they hadn't taken notice before.

The fact that she was scarcely five-feet-two and had only thick lengths of pale brown hair to commend her had little to do with Laura's fantasy. Her eyes had darker, longer lashes than Sallie's, but who would look close enough at her plain face when he had Sallie's laughing golden loveliness to admire? But Laura was certain her prince would look beyond her simplicity to the worthiness beneath. Certainly all men wouldn't be led astray by a pretty face.

When Ward Breckinridge and several of his companions entered the room wearing the blue and gold of the Seventh Calvary, Laura's fantasy took a sudden dive. They looked so dashing and handsome in their tightly tailored coats, their dress shoes polished to a high luster, their sabers gleaming in the candlelight, that every eye in the room swerved in their direction. Taller than the others, Ward in particular stood out with his captain's bars and epaulets flaunting his captain's rank. Stunned by his new status, Sallie drifted away from the other young men in plain civilian garb and attached herself to Ward's elegant arm for the rest of the evening.

While Sallie admired Ward's uniform, Laura wondered at the blue color of it. The Breckinridges had more slaves than almost anyone else in Kentucky. Had they really fooled themselves into thinking that if Kentucky remained neutral and their son openly supported the Union that they would be allowed to keep those slaves when the war ended? It seemed a popular misconception, along with the belief that the war could last only a few months. Laura had overheard enough male conversations to believe Dr. Broadbent was closest to the truth. The Confederacy wouldn't give up their slaves and way of life until every last one of them was dead, and until the slavery issue was resolved one way or another, there would never be peace.

Still, she couldn't help but be drawn to the glory of the Union cause they supported, and they did look exceedingly dashing compared to the more neutrally dressed young dandies around them. With Sallie firmly attached to Ward's arm, the others were left to play the field, and for a change Laura found herself in favor as the other young men came up to her to ask for the requisite birthday dance.

One of the soldiers was new to her, and his darkly cynical face caught her fancy. He was not so tall or broad-shouldered as the others, but there was something about his dark eyes and bored attitude that held her attention. When she realized he was returning her look with interest, she blushed fiercely and smiled up at her current partner.

Not minutes later Ward was introducing her to Marshall Brown of Cincinnati. He bowed gallantly over her hand, gave her that special smile she knew was reserved for her alone, and led her onto the dance floor.

After that, the evening was the closest thing to heaven that Laura had ever experienced. They talked of everything and nothing while they danced. He took her into protective custody around the crowded refreshment table, securing her cups of punch while hovering charmingly at her elbow. They danced some more, and when the ballroom reached stifling proportions, they slipped through the open French doors to walk in the gardens.

Marshall Brown might be a Northerner, but he was the most enchanting man Laura had ever met. He never once glanced at Sallie, he had little interest in the rowdy drinking of the other young bachelors, and he squired Laura about as if she were precious porcelain. So much attention all at once went straight to her head, making her giddier than strong wine. She even allowed him a brief kiss, reveling in the masculine strength of the arm around her and the faint musky taste of his mouth on hers.

The scent of faded roses and potted gardenias forever marked that night in her memory. After everyone had retired for the evening, Laura slipped down to the garden to retrieve the petals to press between her Bible pages. Finally she had found her prince.

Marshall returned the next day and the next. Laura learned his unit wasn't the same as Ward's, but neither unit was fully formed or prepared to move out. There was time yet in these last days of summer for moonlight and roses. She grabbed at her one chance for heaven with eagerness and gratitude.

By the end of those two glorious weeks Sallie was formally engaged to Ward, an occasion which produced an endless round of parties. Every night Laura went to bed praying Marshall would speak for her by the next night. His attendance on her at every festivity was remarked, and rumors were already flying. Surely he would speak before he had to march off to war. He had as much as promised already.

Remembering the night he had won her the scarlet ribbons in the Breckinridges' rifle shoot, Laura smiled confidently to herself. He had held her in his arms that night, touched her in places she knew were sinful, but he had told her he wanted her, that she was the prettiest girl in the county, and that someday soon she would be his. She knew what that meant, and each day she waited eagerly for Uncle Matt to say Marshall had spoken to him.

The night that she flew down the stairs in her best rose taffeta with the daring low neckline and Uncle Matt stood at the bottom of the stairs instead of Marshall wasn't the worst night of her life, but it rated second, surely. Laura glanced around in bewilderment. Marshall had sent her a spray of pink roses to go with her gown, and she was eager to show him the results. Sallie had laced a small posy into the ringlets crimped above one ear, and the others were inserted in the wide sash at her waist. The heady perfume of the roses alleviated the need for artificial scents.

Uncle Matt took Laura's arm and led her toward the waiting carriage. Gruffly he tried to explain away her bewilderment. "Your beau has thought it best to join his unit in Louisville. You will meet someone who will be much better for you one of these days."

Alarmed rather than comforted, Laura halted and stared up into Uncle Matt's sympathetic eyes. "Why would he leave without telling me? What happened?"

Matthew shrugged his heavy shoulders, and taking her elbow, forced her into motion again. "I had a talk with Ward about the man's family. He's not our kind, Laura. You can do better. You've been looking very well these last weeks, and don't think it hasn't been noticed. You'll be flocked with suitors tonight."

Not our kind. The words cut like a knife through places still tender from similar wounds. Her father had been forbidden his home because he chose to marry a Frenchwoman. Cash had had to run away because his mother was a Creole. And now they had forced Marshall to leave for some equally trivial reason. His family probably didn't date back to Virginia. His antecedents weren't listed in Lexington's Blue Book. He didn't have a dozen aunts and uncles and cousins and second cousins scattered about the Bluegrass like daisies in a field. He wasn't one of us.

Well, neither was she. Laura's eyes flashed fire as she entered the ballroom that night. She danced with every man there and pried information from each one of them. By the time she left that night, she knew the name of Marshall's unit, where they were currently stationed, where they would be going, and had a vague idea of how to get there. That was all she needed. That, and the pouch of gold stored in her dresser underneath her chemises and pantalets.

She could carry only a carpetbag of clothing, but she felt confident that Marshall would take care of whatever necessities she had to leave behind. She was prepared to face the fact that he would be gone for months of war. She could wait as long as she knew he would be coming

back to her. She didn't need Stoner Creek and its aristocratic inhabitants. She needed love.

She was sorry to disappoint Uncle Matt and Aunt Ann,
but they still had Sallie. They would be better rid of a
plain and increasingly rebellious dependent. Like her father, she would run off to be with the one she loved.
Laura had only a vague recollection of her parents, but
she believed they had been happy.

She changed trains an enormous number of times. She
sat in railroad stations and hired buggies to get from one
depot to another before she could even get to Louisville.
She had never traveled so far since her father had died,
but she couldn't turn back now. Once she had left the
protection of family, she was a lost woman. She had no
choice but to keep on going when her arm ached from
carrying her bag and her eyes felt gritty from soot and
lack of sleep. The trains were crowded with soldiers, but
she had the sense to take a seat by the most formidable
matrons she could find.

When she reached Louisville, she discovered Marshall's unit had already moved out, and resignedly Laura
found her way to the steamboat platforms. At least boat
travel was a little more elegant than the small-gauge train
lines she had been forced to use. She had only to stay in
the safety of the ladies' cabin. The tedium grated on her
already frayed nerves, but she concentrated on the happy
reunion to come.

The night she arrived in Cairo, Laura definitely rated
as the worst night of her life. It seared her memory with
a wound so deep she would never escape the scars of it.

Cairo was little more than a mosquito-infested mud
hole. Landing on the rickety wharf, her bag at least a
hundred pounds heavier than when she started, she
stared at the ghastly little town with tears in her eyes.
She was hungry, but nowhere looked safe to eat. She
was parched with thirst, but she didn't dare enter one of
the taverns littering the street parallel to the river. Her
fashionable gray traveling gown had wilted to bedraggled
inelegance, and her modest bonnet had lost its feathers
along with its starch in the humid river heat. The worst
of it all was, she didn't have any idea where she was
going.

Stoner Creek had only one small respectable hotel and

a rooming house. She had never dreamed Cairo would
be any different. She had thought she could make a few
inquiries and then she would be in Marshall's arms again.
That was only one of her many mistakes.

She gazed down the long street in the deepening twilight and decided she had no alternative but to find a
bed to sleep in and look for Marshall in the morning.
Out of all the sprawling taverns and bordellos and storefronts, she could see one tall facade with a respectable
porch and imitation balcony that might possibly be a
hotel. She turned her weary feet in that direction.

The streets were filled with soldiers and horses. Obviously Marshall's unit hadn't left yet. But from the looks
of their celebrations, this might be their last night on the
town. She had to avoid several overeager young drunks
as she wended her way through town.

When she reached the hotel lobby the clerk regarded
her warily, and Laura had to remember her position. A
single woman traveling alone and looking for a man not
her husband would definitely be an object of suspicion.
With a brief flare of her usual humor, she introduced
herself.

"I am Mrs. Marshall Brown. I don't suppose my husband has chosen this respectable establishment for his
abode, has he?"

The clerk still continued to watch her warily, but when
he reached for a room key, Laura's heart leapt with excitement, and she scarcely noticed his look. She couldn't
believe it. Luck had finally found her! After all these
days of misery, she had come home.

A porter came to claim her bag, and joy carried her
tired legs up the stairs. She didn't even stop to consider
the enormity and audaciousness of this step. In her mind,
they were already married. The formalities could be met
on the morrow. Tonight she would be with Marshall
again. She couldn't wait to see his face when she entered
the room.

To her disappointment, he wasn't there when the porter unlocked the door for her. She should have expected
that, but it deflated her joy to some degree. Giving the
porter a coin that brought a flashing smile, she closed
the door in an eager swirl of skirts surveyed the room
that would be her wedding chamber.

It certainly lacked elegance. The cuspidor by the door smelled as if it hadn't been emptied or cleaned since it had been placed there. She couldn't tell what color the curtains over the one small window or the coverlet on the bed were meant to be. They had faded to a neutral hue somewhere between dull gray and beige. The narrow floorboards had no cover, the cheap pine dresser had no adornment of any kind, and the washstand held only a cracked bowl and pitcher.

Well, it wasn't moving or belching smoke and soot. Laura took off her hat and set it on the dresser and contemplated her next step. Marshall couldn't be blamed for the town's lack of accommodations. She had only herself to blame for following him to these seedy quarters. She could have wired him from Louisville if she had known, but she had wanted to surprise him. It served her right if she surprised herself.

Laura was so tired, all she could think of was washing and slipping into a clean nightgown and climbing between the covers, but even in her innocence she knew the enormity of climbing into a man's bed. She didn't know what happened there, but only fallen women and wives were allowed that privilege. That seemed an odd combination, and she wrinkled up her nose at the connotations it wrought, but she couldn't stand around looking dismayed all night.

She took off her dusty jacket and washed her face in the tepid water. She unpacked her toiletries, let down her hair and brushed it out and plaited it. The hour grew later and the candle burned lower. The humid air in the room didn't diminish even when she opened the window. An army of mosquitoes persuaded her to close it a little later.

Restless, Laura pulled out her fragile lawn nightgown. It was a child's gown, but she didn't know that. Her only thought was that it had only a small cap sleeve and required no corset or petticoat. It would feel divine just to have that one piece of lawn against her skin instead of all of these trappings she had lugged around for days. Perhaps Marshall wasn't coming back tonight. Presumably the army had a camp nearby. He must have had to stay in it this night. Surely it would be all right to go ahead and wash and go to bed.

It was only a matter of minutes to put thought into action. The heavy traveling gown came off with only a little persuasion. Laura untied her petticoats and neatly folded them beneath her gown. There was no room in her carpetbag for them and she didn't have the nerve to open the dresser where Marshall kept his clothes. She was growing increasingly nervous by the minute, but she had thrown caution to the winds and had to abide by her choice.

Remembering Marshall's quiet charm, she forced herself to relax. He would do everything that was proper in the morning. Surely he had to come back and pay the hotel clerk sometime. He would be thrilled to see her, but not if she were dirty and exhausted. She had to get some sleep.

She removed her stays and buried them under the petticoats. Wearing only stockings and chemise, she washed as thoroughly as she was able. Then, hesitantly listening for telltale footsteps in the hall outside, she pulled off the long-sleeved chemise and quickly squirmed into her nightgown. Then she sat on the edge of the bed to remove her shoes and stockings.

The candle had nearly guttered out by the time she was done, and, relieved, Laura blew it out. The stifling heat seemed a little less miserable now that she was clean and the cool lawn gown was all that covered her. Her breasts tingled as the soft cloth brushed against them, and she felt odd as she swung her legs between the sheets of Marshall's bed. A lump formed in her stomach, and tensely she lay listening to the strange sounds in the hotel around her.

She was almost asleep when she heard the staggering footsteps outside her door. A long-forgotten memory briefly flashed through her consciousness, the sound of her father's footsteps as he returned to their cabin on the boat. She always knew when he had had a bad night and had been drinking by the sound of his footsteps outside the door.

As she fought for full consciousness, Laura realized it couldn't be her father, but the key turning in the lock came before she remembered where she was. Eyes so heavy she could scarcely open them, she could only gaze in dismay as a candle lit the darkness and Marshall appeared in the doorway.

This wasn't the dashing, debonair Marshall she remembered in tailored uniform and smelling of bay rum. This Marshall hadn't shaved in days, his shirttails hung partially out of his buckskins, and he seemed to have lost coat and cravat. He also stank of cigar smoke and cheap whiskey, returning even more unpleasant memories. Laura pulled the sheet up to her chin and stared at him uncertainly.

Marshall returned the stare, his incredulous gaze taking in the sight of a neatly plaited braid over a childish nightgown, bare ivory arms, and a woman's curves hidden beneath a thin sheet. He staggered, found a chair, and collapsed into it.

"Laura?" His befuddled brain managed to summon the name, and he stopped while he was ahead. Let her do the talking while he gathered his scattered wits.

"Marshall, I am sorry. I didn't think you would be returning until tomorrow. I had to come. Don't you see? You should have come to me before you left. I could have told you that it didn't matter." Nervously Laura sat up in bed and poured out bits and pieces of phrases she had been practicing for days. They didn't seem to go together as smoothly as she had planned, but she didn't know how to remedy that right now.

His head began to clear as he remembered the humiliating encounter with this girl's uncle that had sent him packing from the pleasant social whirl of Stoner Creek. She was as much responsible for that humiliation as her uncle, wearing all those silks and satins as if she were a wealthy young lady deserving of his attention. And look where it had landed him. His incredulity turned to a sneer.

"What doesn't matter? That you have no money? That you're as penniless as I am? Did you come here with some romantic notion that you could live on love alone? Or did you have the sense to empty your uncle's safe before you left?"

Laura watched in horror as Marshall grabbed her reticule from the dresser and emptied out the few remaining coins in there. She had sewn her extra cash into the lining of her carpetbag, but her tongue stuck to the roof of her mouth and she could say nothing. He was drunk, very drunk. He didn't know what he was saying.

Marshall pocketed the few coins in disgust, then sat down again to remove his boots. He continued to stare at the pale, dark-lashed face of the small female in his bed. She wasn't exactly what he would call voluptuous, but beggars couldn't be choosers. He threw his boots to the floor and watched in amusement as her eyes grew wide with horror.

"As long as you came all this way, I won't deny you the pleasure of my company, my dear. I've had a rotten night, and I could use a little comfort. If your uncle hadn't thrown me out I could be in the warm arms of that little maid at the Breckinridges' tonight. I always thought I could make a good Southerner. I can drink whiskey with the best of them, gamble as unwisely on the horses, and appreciate the sweet taste of dark meat come day's end. Don't you think that qualifies me, sweetheart?"

Shocked into paralysis, Laura could only watch as he removed his trousers, leaving only his long shirt and his stockings to cover his nakedness. She stared at his hairy knees in growing horror and did not dare raise her eyes as his words battered her with their subtle cruelty. He had never been interested in her. He only wanted the kind of life he had thought she would bring. It had all just been a pleasant and amusing episode for him. It had never concerned him that her affections might be engaged in the process.

As he approached the bed, Laura regained her senses and fled from the other side, tearing the sheet away with her to wrap around herself. Marshall staggered at the suddenness of her flight, then caught himself on the edge of the bed. Drunker than he thought, he lowered himself to the mattress where she had just been and gazed at her outraged innocence in self-indulgent amusement.

"You might as well get some pleasure out of this debacle, Miss Kincaid. I'll not marry you, but I'll teach you what it takes to be a whore. Your uncle isn't going to welcome you back with open arms, and you'll have to live somehow. Come here and I'll show you that it's quite a pleasant way to live. You won't even have to wear those hated crinolines and petticoats again."

Laura looked sick as he threw her whispered confidences of nights before back in her face. She had thought she was being daring and sophisticated by confiding such things under his encouragement. Instead, she was only providing him with some titillating tidbits to bandy about. How could she have been so blind about his interest in her?

As Marshall sprawled out in the bed and watched her cowering in the corner, Laura realized her mistake. He was interested in her, but not for the reasons she had so romantically imagined. He had seen her as a ticket to wealth at first. Now he saw her as an object of temporary pleasures. His interest was in himself; all she had seen was its reflection. She shuddered and sat down in the chair he had just abandoned.

Marshall shrugged and closed his eyes. "When you get tired of sitting there, come on over. I'll not be going anywhere soon."

His soft snores filled the air shortly after. Laura sat and watched the candle he had lit until it guttered out. Except for Marshall's snores and the pounding of her heart, the night was silent. Rigidly she clung to the protection of the sheet and stared into the darkness. She closed her mind to his words, refused to think of the future. All she could do was cling to the present and pray that the horror would end.

When she woke, she was curled on the hard wooden floor, and Marshall was gone. She stared at the empty bed in disbelief and wondered if it had just been a nightmare. The empty reticule on the floor belied that thought.

The man at the desk below shattered any other illusions she might possess. Addressing her as "Mrs. Brown," he politely informed her the troops had moved out early this morning and that her husband had said she would take care of the hotel bill. The expression on his face and the sheriff leaning over the far end of the counter warned of the futility of argument.

5

As the rolling hills of bluegrass slipped by the train window, Laura began to relax and even managed a pleasant smile for the soldier in the opposite seat. Almost home. Home, to shaded lawns and green pastures and frolicking yearlings. To Henry and Jemima and Doc Broadbent. To the cool porch and spacious rooms of Stoner Creek Farm. She might be arriving as a dependent once again, but at least the quality of life would be a significant improvement over these last few years.

Marshall's hotel bill had eliminated her small hoard of cash. She couldn't have returned home then if she had wanted to, even if pride would have allowed her to admit her foolishness. At the headstrong age of seventeen she could never have admitted her error. Even now she was content to hide it, even after all these years of scraping to get by, knowing how wrong she had been to follow her heart and not her head.

She had nearly starved those first few weeks while she washed dishes and scrubbed floors in return for a place to sleep. It had been humiliating to an extreme, devastating to the few remnants of her pride. But once she explained her husband was in the army, people began to look on her more kindly. Eventually she had found work sewing the overflow from one of the dress shops in town. After a while she knew enough people to start taking in mending and sewing on her own. The town was poor and her earnings were meager, but she had managed, until eventually she could even hoard a penny or two, always with the distant dream of Stoner Creek in mind.

After a year or two of this life, everyone in Cairo knew her, and several of the women she went to church with began to question her about Marshall's whereabouts. Laura had lied about letters when questioned, and after

Marshall's unit was involved in a particularly bloody battle, she didn't mention the letters anymore. She simply donned black shortly after, and all questions had ended. Little did the good ladies know that she merely prayed the wretch was dead.

The widow's weeds had worked wonders in Cairo, and Laura felt confident they would do the same in Stoner Creek. She had written Sallie that she and Marshall were married. Who was there to protest she was not? To this day she had no idea if Marshall had survived the war, but he would certainly never return to Stoner Creek looking for her if he had. It was a perfectly safe little lie that lent her respectability. Sallie wouldn't be interested in anything else, and the lie hurt no one.

The *Bluegrass Special* rattled into the Stoner Creek depot, and Laura rubbed at the dirty glass in hopes of seeing familiar faces. The war had sporadically struck at this wealthy area of Kentucky, but only Morgan's raiders had done any amount of damage, she knew. They had pillaged the countryside, driven the Union Army in circles with the antics of their telegraph operator and his false messages, and destroyed the property of Union supporters wherever they could. But they had left the town of Stoner Creek relatively intact. The depot looked only a little older than when she had left.

The only traveling gown Laura owned was the same one she had left in. She had grown an inch or more since then, and her bosom was a little fuller. It had taken long hours of work to lower the hem, tighten and add ruching to the unfashionably full sleeves, and let out the bodice seams, but Laura was quite proud of her handiwork. Black braid hid the seam and hem lines and added the touch of mourning necessary for her widowed state. She stepped off the train in almost the same elegance as she had once entered it.

On the platform Laura searched for someone to help her carry the carpetbag holding all her worldly possessions. She had very little money left after paying for meals and fares, and she had no idea of the cost of paying someone to take her out to the farm. She had hoped Henry would be here to meet her, but as she looked at the strange faces hurrying by, she realized she had only been conjuring up fantasies of the past, not the reality of the present.

Things had changed, but she had just been too caught up in her memories to notice it. As she carried her bag out into the street, Laura could see that the number of black faces around her had diminished considerably. Usually the drivers of the buggies and farm carts were black, and the servants tripping along behind their mistresses carrying packages were black. None of these familiar sights greeted her now. She had been imagining a place that no longer existed.

Although Kentuckians claimed the Emancipation Act had had no effect on them, since they were not among the proscribed secessionist states, the military had declared martial law and issued passes to any black person seeking one, Laura had read in the papers. Obviously the slaves had taken their freedom and left. She couldn't blame them, she supposed. There was little enough here to make a living for a white man unless he owned land. With no education and no training, what could a black man do? Outsiders were never welcome. Freed slaves would be anathema to a community like this. She wondered where house servants like Henry and Jemima might go.

It became obvious that no one had come for her, whatever the case might be. She had wired Sallie of her arrival, but she had no idea of the conditions at the farm. Perhaps they had no servants at all, and with Ward ill . . . Laura refused to think further than that. Too much had been lost in these years. She wouldn't create more losses in her mind.

Doc Broadbent would know how things stood. Perhaps he'd know somebody who could give her a ride. She lifted her heavy bag and started down the street.

People stared as she went by. Several gentlemen lifted their hats to her, but intent on her purpose, Laura paid them little heed. Isolated on the farm, she had learned little of the townspeople other than that they always remarked upon strangers. If they recognized her through her short veil, they didn't give evidence of it, so she assumed they thought her a new arrival. Even so, it felt odd to have men lifting their hats to her. When she was here last, she had always been trailing Sallie, and it was always Sallie who attracted notice.

Going in by the back gate, Laura caught Doc Broadbent just hitching his horse to his buggy. She halted hesitantly, not wishing to interfere if it were an emergency. Nearing thirty-five, he was still a young man, but he moved with an old man's slowness. His lined face looked tired and stern, and she wondered if he had ever remarried. Certainly there ought to be a plenitude of women available from whom to choose. He wasn't rich, but he was comfortable. And if his angular face wasn't exactly handsome, it possessed an intelligence and kindness to make up the lack. Laura rather thought the late president's face looked much like that, although the doctor's wasn't as harsh-boned as the daguerreotypes she had seen of Mr. Lincoln.

Just as she determined to step forward, he looked up. She could see him hesitate as she walked toward him, and then his mouth began to turn upward in a weary smile of welcome.

"Laura! Laura Kincaid, as I live and breathe! You came back!" His glance then encompassed the black bonnet and bands of mourning, and his smile faded. "Sallie told me you lost your husband in the war. I'm sorry, child."

Laura shook back the encompassing bonnet and let the sun shine on her hair in a gesture of relief and freedom. "It's been a long time, Doc. There's nothing to be sorry for. How's Ward? I told Sallie I'd be back to help, but there wasn't anyone at the station."

He immediately finished fastening the bridle and offered a hand to lift her up. "Come on, I was going that way. You'll be a sight for sore eyes out there, I reckon." He climbed up in the seat beside her and clucked the mare into a walk. "Ward's about as well as can be expected. A healthy young man like that has a hard time adjusting to the life of an invalid."

An invalid. Laura could not imagine that gallant young man as an invalid. Or Sallie dealing well with one. She grimaced slightly to herself at the thought. "Tell me what's been happening since I've been gone. Sallie's a terrible correspondent. I only hear when someone dies

or takes ill. And have you heard from Cash? It's the
funniest thing, but I've been remembering him lately."

Jonathan Broadbent chuckled and flicked his whip as
the carriage rolled into the street and headed for the
country. "Sallie's a caution, I don't deny. It's been hard
for her, with both her parents dying like that, and now
this business with Ward coming home injured. It'll do
her good to have a level head around. Whatever anyone
might say, you're the Kincaid with the best head on her
shoulders. Even Cash noticed it when he wasn't too busy
looking out for himself. I had a letter from him just the
other day. He doesn't say much, just that he's doing fine.
He made it out to California when he left here, you
know. It seems he has a bit of land and some horses,
but he's not one to puff himself up, so I can't rightly tell
how he is except by reading between the lines."

They gossiped companionably on the way out to the
farm, Doc not noticing that Laura evaded personal
questions by turning them all back to him. Lonely for
someone who would listen instead of telling him their
problems, Doc unconsciously fell under the spell of a
woman who said little but listened well. By the time they
reached the stone fences of the farm, he felt as if they
were closer friends than they had ever been before, and
Laura began to feel as if she had come home at last.

When they drove between the stone posts of the farm,
Laura scanned the tree-lined lane eagerly for the first
sight of the house. The warm bricks appeared through
the thick foliage of elms and pin oaks. She caught a
glimpse of a dark shutter and a window, then a corner
of the columned porch.

They lurched around the bend and the whole house
veered into view. Laura sat back in satisfaction as she
observed the immense security of those familiar walls.
The ivy had climbed farther up the side chimney than
Uncle Matthew had ever allowed, but she liked the effect. The paint on the shutters had faded some, and the
paint was beginning to peel around the columns. As she
looked closer, she could see the vast expanse of emerald
lawn had not been cut in a long time, the mock oranges
and abelias hadn't been trimmed, and honeysuckle was
taking over the rose garden. Sallie had never been much

interested in gardening, so the disorder didn't dismay Laura entirely.

The shock came when the carriage rattled around the drive and she could see the burned ruins of the once-glorious stables. She had expected neglect. Things had not been going well when she left, and the war would have drained away the labor and finances eventually, but there had been no battles in this area. Even Morgan had left them alone. What could have happened to the stables?

Jonathan caught the surprise and alarm in her look, and a measure of concern filled his eyes as he shook his head. "The aftereffects of war, Miss Laura. All the thousands of men who once fought for our country and against it are now trying to make their way back home or discovering they have no homes. They've been fighting for four long years, many since they were boys. Fighting is the only life they know."

That didn't explain the stables, and Laura watched him expectantly, waiting for him to continue.

He slowly wound his whip as he spoke. "There's no excuse for what they do, of course. They can't go on fighting forever, but around here it looks like they're going to try. There's one group that calls themselves the Raiders, and they'll use any excuse to lynch a black man or steal from a Union supporter. They've been helping the slave owners hide their slaves and keeping them penned up so the soldiers can't find them. Then there's the Regulators, who've decided the law can't protect peaceful citizens, so they set out to make their own law and order."

Jonathan shifted uncomfortably on the cushioned seat of the ancient barouche as he sought words to continue. "If you'll pardon my language, Miss Laura, it's just another excuse for rape and pillaging, one group getting even with the other. I shouldn't be saying these things to a lady, but you have a right to know what to expect. The Raiders came out here one night looking for trouble. Ward held them off with a rifle and one servant, but he couldn't save the stables. They stole the last of the horses and burned the stables to the ground."

Laura sat silently, gazing at the blackened brick walls that were all that remained of Uncle Matthew's pride and joy. She had read the tiny articles in the Louisville *Courier* occasionally mentioning a "murderous raid" or "abominable acts of marauders," but she had never associated those articles with Stoner Creek. The war was over. Why keep fighting it?

Jonathan climbed down from the carriage and came around to offer her a hand. She accepted it gratefully, needing his reassuring squeeze as she glanced up the steps to the house. What had she returned to? And why?

No servant hastened to open the gracious double doors. No stable lad rushed to take the doctor's horse and feed it a handful of grain and wipe it down. No laughing faces appeared in the windows, and no one came running around from behind the house. There was no sign of welcome at all. Even Sallie's golden head didn't appear to adorn the bank of once-sparkling front windows. And Uncle Matt's booming voice would never resound again through the hallway, commanding everyone to present himself. It was a strange homecoming, and Laura ascended the porch stairs slowly.

They knocked, and a dog barked vehemently from somewhere inside. Eventually a slight maid in worn calico and dirty apron opened the door, accompanied by a large animal that could only be Franz the Second. The maid nodded at the doctor in recognition, stared rudely at Laura, who had given a cry of joy and bent over the dog, then hurried off somewhere down the wide uncarpeted hall.

Gently Dr. Broadbent pried Laura from the animal and led her after the maid. "This way. No point in making Ward come to us."

Still holding the dog's collar as they traversed the hall, Laura puzzled over the conflicting information she had received so far concerning Ward's health. From Sallie's letters she had assumed him to be on his deathbed. Doc had called him an invalid, yet he had been able to hold off a gang of cowardly marauders. That didn't sound like any invalid she knew.

They entered what had once been Uncle Matt's study just as the maid hurried out. She bobbed a curtsy and scampered in the direction of the kitchen.

The draperies were pulled and the room was in semi-darkness as they entered, but Laura could discern the form of a large man seated in a chair as Franz went to join him. Ward's voice was the same warm, friendly drawl she remembered as he reached to pull back the heavy curtains.

"Doc! What brings you out this way today? I can see you've brought me some lovely company." His eyes turned inquiringly to the woman in the gray traveling gown and black bonnet at the doctor's side. His eyes widened as she shook off the concealing hat and pulled it away from her face. "Little Laura! For goodness' sake! I don't believe it. Look at you. Why, last I remember, you were a gangly-legged filly just making your debut. I'd make a bow if I could, but you'll have to accept my hand instead."

Ward took her mittened hand in both of his and squeezed it warmly, giving Laura the reassurance and welcome she needed. It took a moment longer before she realized he wasn't sitting in the desk chair, but in some contraption with wheels. When he came around the desk to greet her more politely, she could see the outlines of his legs beneath the blanket, but they didn't move as he rolled into the room's center.

"Have a seat, both of you. Lottie's gone for some lemonade. Sallie should be here any minute. My mother and sister-in-law came to fetch her for some tea party."

Laura settled her skirts on the old velvet settee and tried to recover her tongue. Between the neatly trimmed bands of his sideburns, Ward's face was thinner than she remembered, and the gold of his hair had faded somehow. He no longer sported the tanned healthiness of a man who preferred the outdoors, but his eyes were still warm and vaguely amused as he waited for her to speak. She had never been much for words around him, and he must have realized she had not changed.

"You don't know how good it is to see you looking so well, Ward." She managed to finally formulate a complete sentence. "After Sallie's letter, I imagined the worst."

A shadow crossed his face as Ward glanced down at his useless legs, but when he looked up again, he was smiling. "Well, to Sallie, my inability to dance probably is the worst. I daresay I'd feel the same if our positions were reversed. So, tell me, little Laura, where have you been hiding out all these years? I never thought that rogue Marshall had it in him to settle down. I'm glad I was wrong. You look prettier and happier than I ever remember seeing you."

They were still exchanging news when the front door opened and the patter of light feet and the rustle of silk and crinolines hurried down the hall. Sallie flew through the doorway in a burst of sunshine, carefully coiled ringlets dancing golden in the light as she threw aside her fashionably feathered hat with its gauzy streamers and stretched out her arms in exuberant welcome.

"Laura! You've come at last. How dreadful of you to leave me like that! I cried myself to sleep for weeks. You've come to stay, I hope. Why, I don't know how we've done without you."

She grasped Laura's hand charmingly, turned her plea to the doctor for support, and completely ignored the man sitting patiently in the chair behind her. Her pretty face was as animated as ever as she kissed the doctor's cheek and pulled Laura down beside her on the settee, and Laura had to sigh with exasperation as she realized one thing hadn't changed—Sallie's self-centeredness.

Disengaging her hand, she glanced from her cousin to Ward. "I don't want to be a burden to anyone. I'll do my share to help around here if I stay. But, Sallie, I think this is something you need to ask Ward. He may not want another useless female around. I've been taking care of myself for four years now; I can continue to do so. I don't want to live on anyone's charity."

Sallie opened her mouth to speak, but Ward interrupted before a sound could come out. "Laura, this is your home. You don't need my permission to stay. Just be aware that we're likely to work you half to death if you do. Neither of us has ever been known for unselfishness."

Sallie gasped with indignation, the doctor coughed and turned his head away, and Laura gave Ward a relieved smile. One of them had matured over these years, at least. She held out her hand in agreement.

"Done. I'll live in the lap of luxury and work like a slave. It seems a fair exchange to me."

Laura hadn't underestimated the situation with that brave declaration. Stoner Creek had never relied heavily on slave labor, but there were certain tasks that the local population considered the province of blacks alone and therefore beneath their dignity. Combined with the loss of healthy workers due to the war, the manpower needed to run a large farm was severely limited. Only planters wealthy enough to pay the highest wages could afford to continue operating on the same scale as before the war.

And Stoner Creek was far from being wealthy. Laura didn't mean to pry, but when Sallie came home from town with her arms loaded with packages and Ward's expression took on that look of pain Laura had learned to recognize in her first few weeks back, she knew all wasn't well.

Since her return, Laura had taken over the tasks of helping in the kitchen and overseeing the weekly laundry, for which workers were imported from town for that day only. She had not dared ask Ward if they might have more help to trim the gardens or clean the house. What labor was available went into the fields, and she didn't question the wisdom of this decision. Their livelihood came from what could be grown in the rich acreage beyond the lawns. If there were money available for house servants, Ward surely would have provided them.

So Sallie's extravagance on the frills and furbelows so dear to her heart could be the only reason for the pained frown between Ward's eyes as he watched her rush upstairs with her new acquisitions. The first few times this happened, Laura politely turned her back and walked away, but the day she had to hoe the kitchen garden herself because the maid, Lottie, declared she wasn't getting paid enough to do it, Laura stalked into the study after Ward.

She found him poring over the farm ledgers, his ink-stained fingers and the stacks of scribbled papers across the desktop giving evidence that he had spent the better part of the morning in this occupation. She took a seat beside the desk and waited patiently for him to look up.

He looked so tired and unwell that Laura's heart went out to him, and daringly she covered his hand with her own, bringing his restless scribbling to a halt. "How bad is it, Ward? I can see that half the crops haven't been planted, and without the foals to sell in the fall, we'll be hurting, but surely we've cut enough expenses to get by?" She knew all about cutting expenses from hard experience. It didn't seem odd to discuss such a subject with a man who could scarcely have considered the possibility of limited cash in the past.

A thin smile appeared on Ward's lips at her worried expression. "Don't you fret about it, Laura. I can't walk or ride a horse, but I can still manage a few things. You go on up to bed now."

Those were the kind of words she had been hearing all her life, and a sudden fury swept through Laura. She had just worn her hands to the bone to keep from hiring another expensive servant. Did he really think she was totally incompetent? She was no longer a child, and it was on her tongue to tell him so, but the way Ward passed his hand across his brow in weariness made her bite back the angry words. His pride was at stake as much as hers. It seemed a shame they couldn't work together to solve the problem, but the barrier between them was greater than she had remembered.

Laura rose stiffly but did not go without a few parting remarks. She felt she deserved that much. "Uncle Matt refused to sell our slaves even though he said they cost too much. He wore out too many fields planting tobacco. This place was losing money before I left. Whatever shape it's in now is not your fault, Ward, but it looks like it's up to you to make changes. I'll help in any way I can, but you have to tell me what to do."

As she moved toward the door, she heard Ward speak her name, and she turned to look at him questioningly.

In the light of the oil lamp his thin face looked shadowed, and her stomach jumped nervously at the ghostly image she saw there. Dr. Broadbent said he was healthy. She didn't dare think otherwise.

"Laura, if you would . . ." He seemed embarrassed, and hesitated before continuing. When she waited patiently, he was forced to go on. "See if you can talk to Sallie. I could have hired three good laborers with the money she spent today. I know I owe her a lot for not being able to give her the kind of life she expected, and it's hard for me to deny her anything, but she has to see that things have changed. No one has the money to go out and buy as they did before."

"The whole world could turn upside down tomorrow,

Ward, but Sallie wouldn't change. I'll speak with her, but you'd best write letters to all her favorite shops here and in Lexington and in Louisville and everywhere else, telling them not to extend any more credit. We might not change Sallie, but we can change the world around her a little bit. It is a very small world she lives in, you know."

Ward's smile was bitter as he nodded his head in agreement. "I know. I'll take your words into consideration. Thank you, Laura."

He wouldn't do it, she knew as she climbed the stairs to her bedroom. Sallie slept in her lonely glory in the master suite upstairs while Ward hauled himself into the cot in the study each night. Never would it occur to Sallie to rearrange the rooms so she could sleep downstairs and take care of her husband's needs. And never would it occur to Ward to suggest it. He would protect Sallie and her way of life until his dying day. Laura wondered what Sallie had ever done to deserve such devotion.

Her talk with Sallie the next day was as unsuccessful as she had expected. Her cousin looked up with surprise when Laura broached the subject, then smiled and waved her hand to dismiss it. "Don't be silly, Laura. Why, I only spent a few dollars yesterday. Surely a few dollars won't bankrupt us. Ward wouldn't want me to go to his nephew's christening in old clothes, would he? Of course not. By the way, I've invited his family and the rest of the guests over here afterward. I think it's time we began socializing again. Papa always said he sold more horses at a party than he ever did at market."

Laura stared at her aghast, but Sallie seemed perfectly oblivious of the cannonball she had just exploded. They didn't even have enough hired help to scythe the grass. And what horses did she think they would sell?

Biting her tongue to hold back harsh phrases, Laura calmly agreed. "Very well. The christening is Saturday, isn't it? We'll have to have wine and champagne, fruit for the centerpiece, more ice than we have left in the icehouse. Someone will need to slaughter and dress a hog . . . I don't believe we have any more hogs, do we?" She began ticking their material needs off on her hands. "I'll tell you what, Sallie. I'll go into town and see about supplies. You find a cook who knows how to make some-

thing besides fried chicken and greens, a half-dozen
maids to set this place to rights, another half-dozen gar-
deners so our guests won't have to wade through the
lawns, and by Saturday we'll be ready. We'll just have
to serve the food and drink ourselves, though. I don't
think we'll have time to train house servants."

Sallie glared at her, picked up an ostrich-feather fan
on her dresser, and switched it back and forth. "Well, I
declare, Laura, you needn't get so snippety about it. I'm
just trying to help, after all. Just because I can't cook
and clean doesn't mean I can't be useful. I'm good at
parties. Ward knows that. He ought to be grateful that
I'm trying. Why doesn't he buy some yearlings, if that's
what bothers him? That's what Papa would have done."

It was always pointless to talk reason to Sallie. Everything was always someone else's fault, someone else's
responsibility. Laura had learned the only way to deal
with it was to drop the subject. When she observed the
house was not magically cleaned and the lawns were still
not tended, Sallie would find some way of blaming someone and call off the party. That kept the aggravation
level to a minimum.

It was one particularly humid day at the end of June
when Ward painfully rolled his chair to the porch to join
Laura as she broke beans from the meager garden. Steve,
Ward's older brother, had just left, and after being
cooped up in the stuffy study with him all day, Ward
looked worn and melted. His shirt collar had lost its
starch, and irritably he pulled at his cravat to loosen it.
Always formally correct, he wore his coat and waistcoat
still, but at Laura's questioning lift of her eyebrow, he
began to struggle out of the top coat.

"Help me out of the blamed thing, Laura. You'll excuse me this once?"

"I not only excuse you, I sympathize. I want to know
the fashion arbiter who dictates women must wear long
sleeves except in evening. I'll wager she's a Yankee."

Ward grunted his thanks as she helped him off with the
coat. "Well, it's evening. Where are your short sleeves?"

The pale brown silk she wore was one she had owned
before the war. It had a high neck and pleated bodice,
and a high waistline that was exceedingly out-of-style,

but it made a sensible day dress. Laura lifted the limp skirt wryly.

" 'Tis evening, but not an evening gown. When you have to clean and press your own clothes, you become more cautious of changing frequently."

Ward frowned, but Laura's lack of fashion wasn't what was on his mind. With her thick hair modestly caught back in a net, Laura would almost appear matronly, but he had grown to know her better these last few weeks. Her dainty face and expressive eyes hid nothing, but he seldom saw anger there. He had learned to appreciate her quiet beauty as opposed to Sallie's more flamboyant good looks. He gave a ragged sigh and wiped his brow with a handkerchief, waiting for Laura to return to her seat. She carried the scent of some faint cologne with her, and he realized it had been a long time since he had been gifted with the fragrance of a woman's cologne in his nostrils.

"My brother wants to buy some of that bottomland adjoining his farm. It's good for horses, and we haven't got any anymore. I'm thinking of selling."

Ward didn't ask for her advice, but it was in his voice. The land had become his when Matthew died. Kentucky law was based on English common law, and a married woman couldn't hold property. Her husband was even entitled to her wages. It didn't seem fair, but in this case it was justified, Laura knew. If the land had to be sold, Ward would get a much better price for it than Sallie.

Laura shuddered when she thought of what it would have been like had she married Marshall, or if Sallie had married someone like Marshall. He could have sold the whole farm and disappeared with the proceeds when he grew tired of temporary amusements. In that, he and Sallie were much alike. How she could have been so blind and ignorant kept Laura perpetually confused when she thought about those days. She wasn't at all certain that her judgment was sound if she could fall for the likes of Marshall Brown.

"I hate to sell that stretch," Laura answered thoughtfully with a small frown. "It's prime land. Couldn't we sell something else and buy a few horses?"

Ward looked dubious. "Maybe. Do you think Sallie will object to selling anything off?"

Laura gave him a wry look as she pushed the rocker with the tip of her toe. "She doesn't have much choice, does she?"

Ward turned his chair so he could watch her gently rocking, her fingers snapping and sorting even in this fading light. He had never desired a quiet, unassuming woman before, particularly one who occasionally displayed more intelligence than he, but at this moment his needs were such that she seemed the perfect solution. In the twilight her skin glowed as if illuminated by moonbeams, and she was as feminine and dainty as any woman he could ever remember. Even Sallie seemed almost boisterously large in comparison. He smiled and reached out to touch her hand, halting her constant motion.

"Laura, you're too young to waste away your life out here. Why did you come back?"

She glanced up in surprise at Ward's sympathetic tone. He had always been a handsome man. His golden hair and chiseled face held women spellbound when he turned his charm their way. The chiseled features were slightly lined now, but she still wouldn't mind tracing her fingers over the dent in his chin, just below that mobile and rather seductive mouth. She smiled at his sudden concern for her.

"I was too young to waste away my life out there. Why do you ask?"

Ward frowned at her facetious answer, but it was a thoughtful frown, and his fingers wrapped around hers as he weighed his words. "You've been a married woman, Laura. I won't offend your maidenly modesty if I speak of a man's needs?"

Laura's free fingers clenched indecisively in her lap. She was glad the half-light hid her embarrassment. "I doubt that I ever possessed much maidenly modesty, Ward. I've never been like Sallie, you know."

"I know," he said softly. "That is why I felt free to speak to you. Sallie does not see me as a man anymore, but I am. Only my legs are useless, not the rest of me. It's been a long time since I've had a woman. Your coming here reminds me of that every day." He hesitated, searching for proper words for an improper request. "I thought, perhaps, if you should ever feel those same needs . . ." Ward drew away his hand and made a gesture of disgust. "Oh, hell, Laura, I'm not any good at wooing without horses and dancing and romantic strolls through the gardens. Forget I ever said anything."

Laura hid her flush of embarrassment by clasping her hands in her lap and staring at them. She had a very good idea of what he was talking about, but yet she didn't. She felt vague needs and desires when the air filled with spring and restlessness was everywhere. She felt the same when she stripped naked in the privacy of her room and daringly slept that way in the summer heat. But she had never associated these strange stirrings with Ward, and she could not now, although, much to her chagrin, she tried.

"You think you've shocked me, but I assure you it is a pleasant shock. I am an exceedingly wicked woman, Ward, more so than you'll ever know," Laura murmured quietly as he gazed morosely over the overgrown lawn. "I'll take your offer as a compliment, even though I cannot accept it. I know Sallie very well. She's all the family I have. I hold her at fault for her treatment of you, but I cannot in all conscience rectify her mistakes."

"Even if you wanted?" he asked with wry humor, the darkness between them forgiving all.

Laura dared turn her face to him again. "Were it not for Sallie, I would say yes in a minute. It would probably be wrong for both of us, because we are nothing alike, but you're still an attractive man, and you are right, I am a lonely woman. In which case it might be much safer for both of us if you found someone less hampered by Sallie than I am."

Ward looked startled, then grinned. "Any suggestions?"

Demurely Laura returned to her beans. "Whatever happened to that accommodating maid your parents kept?"

6

Jettie Mae began work the next week. A slight-boned, handsome coffee-colored woman of about Sallie's age, she had already had two children of distinctly lighter color than herself. Whoever their fathers were, they had paid well to keep their secret, and she had no need to leave the county as so many of the other slaves did. From the flash of her eyes when she greeted Ward, she was not averse to adding to her income.

Laura watched in amazement their reunion as old friends, but discreetly left before Ward offered the position of his full-time "nurse." He really did need someone to help him with the excruciating difficulty of just the daily routines of dressing and taking care of himself. For a long time Dr. Broadbent had seen that he had a male assistant for these chores. Lately Ward had assumed them himself, but Laura judged that Sallie's extravagances had led him to decide he could afford a few of his own. Jettie Mae looked to be quite competent about helping him achieve those desires.

In truth, the newcomer to the household turned out to be an eager worker. She bossed the kitchen maid into producing decent meals for "Mr. Ward," and in consequence they all ate better. The downstairs study and parlor that Ward had adopted as his own became scrupulously clean. She changed and washed all his linens and had no objection to doing others as long as she was paid for it. Sallie regarded her as a laundry maid and scarcely saw her relationship to Ward. Jettie simply rolled her eyes and her hips and minced away in imitation of Sallie's corseted walk when the lady of the house turned her back.

Laura found herself grinning at instead of reprimanding the bold nurse. Jettie's presence had made an immediate change in Ward, and she could find no fault in anyone who returned his laughter and relaxed the lines on his face. The house seemed less solemn and dismal now, and the growing number of chores looked less hopeless.

So it was with considerable surprise that Laura greeted Jettie's frantic arrival late one night with her two youngsters in tow. Her dark eyes showed gleams of white as Laura cautiously opened the front door and she shoved in. No servant had entered through the front doors before, but that wasn't Laura's concern now. The fear in Jettie's bold face caused her insides to shrivel.

"Where's Mr. Ward? Them Raiders are comin' ag'in. They done been to my place, but I heerd about it and got out fast. They be here next."

Ward called out from the study, and they could hear the squeak of the wooden wheels against the floor. "Laura? Who is it? What's wrong?"

The two women exchanged glances, and Laura held out her arms for the smaller child. "I'll take the children upstairs. They'll be safe there. You tell him."

Jettie gave her a measuring look, then an approving nod before handing over her youngsters. Laura hurried them upstairs without another word. Securing them on cots in the old nursery, she gave them some old toys off the shelf to keep them quiet, then ran back down the stairs. Sallie had gone to Lexington with the Breckinridges for the wedding of a distant cousin of both families. She wasn't expected back until late the next day, a circumstance that had made it easy for Laura to decline the offer to accompany her. Someone had to stay with Ward and mind the house. Laura wasn't certain whether she was sorry or grateful she had been the one to stay behind, but she had too much else on her mind to worry over it.

Ward was already loading his rifle and giving Jettie instructions on how to use the pistol she held in her hand when Laura came back down. At her entrance, Ward looked up in relief. "Good. Go see if that worthless Lottie is around. She can make enough noise in the kitchen to make them think it's occupied. We're going to get a horse after this. One of these days I'm going to have the sheriff out here to see what we have to put up with, but there's no way of notifying him tonight."

"What about the field hands? Some of them have been using the cabins out back. I can go get them." Laura lifted the other pistol on the desk. She had never handled one, but the basic principle seemed simple.

"They're likely to be the ones showing up tonight with hoods on. They're riled because I hired Jake Conner instead of a white man, and they're using Jettie as an excuse to come out here."

Laura must have looked puzzled, for Jettie grinned and explained further. "They say Jake and me done replaced white men. You think I'se replacing any white man?"

Ward gave her a look of irritation, but Jettie only grinned further and lifted the pistol to sight along the barrel as he had showed her.

"Well, Jettie, we could always send you outside to explain, but I'm not certain Mrs. Breckinridge would appreciate it." Laura tried to look along the barrel of her pistol as Jettie was doing, but it made her look cross-eyed. "Hadn't you better show us how to load these things, Ward?"

"Laura, you don't need to be down here at all. You just wake Lottie and get back upstairs." Impatiently Ward rolled the chair to the window and scanned the drive again.

"Like hell, I will," Laura muttered under her breath, picking up her skirts with one hand and clenching the pistol with the other. She caught Jettie's laughing glance and knew she had been heard, but Ward was intent on other things. She swept out without deigning to give him the reply he deserved.

She dragged Lottie from her bed and set her to watching the west side of the house while Laura kept an eye on the east, by the old stables. The Raiders couldn't come through the north without climbing over the roofs of the slave quarters and the old kitchens. Their more likely route would be the front drive guarded by Ward, but Laura didn't wish to risk any surprises.

She heard the pounding of hooves before she could see them. Lottie stole back to whisper they were all on the front lawn with torches, but she was too scared to watch. Laura handed her the pistol and warned her to fire it if anyone tried to come around to the side. Then she ran down the hall to see these monsters of inhumanity for herself.

There were only ten or twelve of them, and they were busily pounding a rough timber cross into the long grass. Some of them wore black hoods, others covered their heads with what looked to be pillowcases with eyeholes cut out. Chances were good she would recognize most of their faces had it not been for the disguises, and Laura longed to go out there and jerk the silly costumes from their heads. The guns, rifles, and torches in their hands prevented any such action. She held her breath as they waved the flaring tar-pitch branches. It hadn't rained much in weeks, and the grass was as dry as tinder out there.

The marauders cursed as they worked to stand the cross up straight, and in the torchlight the scene had an eerie quality to it. Several men stayed on their horses, keeping rein on the riderless mounts, while another man nailed what looked to be parchment to the trunk of an old oak. She'd seen these signs screaming "nigger lover" before, but she had always closed her eyes to them. What on earth could they hope to accomplish with this insane display?

Laura's palms perspired nervously as she watched the torch flames dancing against the backdrop of trees. The house was brick and too large to stampede through as they had those of some of the smaller farmers who had refused to join in their battle against the forces of change. The farm's biggest outbuilding had already been burned; they had stolen the more easily accessible valuables in the last raid. All that remained was the house and its contents. The Raiders had never struck at one of the big houses. Did they think Stoner Creek to be the weakest defended? She wished for a cannon to show them differently.

As the hooded intruders began to dump bundles of dry sticks beneath the cross, Laura grasped their intentions. White fury shot through her, but there wasn't time to curse and rail and call them the blackguards they were. She raced back to Lottie and the kitchen.

"Fill all the buckets and pans you can with water and carry them up front. Hurry, or your skin won't be worth a plugged nickel."

She needed the stable blankets, but they had been lost with the last fire. Swiftly Laura ran up the back stairs to the blanket closet and grabbed an armful of the heaviest woolen ones. She ran down and dumped them on the kitchen floor, where Lottie hurriedly pumped at a pail of water. She wished for two pumps, or three, but it was too late for wishes. Hauling the first pail of water, she hurried to the front of the house, where Ward and Jettie watched helplessly as the torches were laid to the tinder.

"Jettie Mae, go soak those blankets I left in the kitchen. Ward, I'm going out there. Shoot the first man who raises a gun."

Without waiting for Ward's refusal or outraged admonitions, Laura carried her pail to the front door. Stoner Creek was all the home she had. She wouldn't let a band of idiots burn it down around her.

The men outside looked startled when the door opened. They relaxed their cautious stances somewhat when only a slight female appeared in the entrance.

They stood so close that Laura could smell the sweat of fear and lathered horses, but her eyes were only for the flames rapidly licking at the tinder and the lawn. Without looking at the men standing behind the fire, she dumped the first pail of water on the flames.

Surprise and anger could be heard as she marched back across the porch and met Jettie Mae carrying another bucket. She exchanged the empty one for the full one, turned around, and repeated her action. The flames began to splutter and smolder.

Ward's rifle crackled from the front window as one of the men started forward to stop her. That raised a yelp of pain and voices of consternation. Laura hurried back to the house again. There hadn't been time to fill another bucket, but Lottie appeared with the first soaked blanket. This wouldn't be as easy, but Laura straightened her back and ignored her clamoring heartbeat. It had to be done and there was no one else to do it.

A shot rang out over her head as she approached the flaming grass again. She jumped and nearly lost the blanket as a sliver of wood leapt from the column beside her. Ward's expensive Spencer rifle exploded a second time, presumably finding the culprit. There was a scream of pain and the curses multiplied as she swung the heavy wet blanket over the flames licking through the grass toward the house.

"We ain't toleratin' no more nigger lovers in this here town, y-hear!"

Laura ignored the angry voice and returned for the bucket Jettie handed to her. It would be like arguing with Sallie to try to answer such idiocy. She'd as soon speak to the devil.

"Give us the niggers and we'll leave you alone!" The voice continued obstinately as Laura submerged the fire beneath the cross with another bucket of water.

She didn't know whether they meant Jettie or Jake or both, but she didn't stop to inquire. Jake was probably still sleeping in the cabin out back. She wondered if Lottie had had the sense to go out and warn him.

The minutes seemed to drag like hours as she hauled heavy buckets and blankets with arms tense with terror. It would take only one lucky shot to put an end to her insane display, but she had counted on their being hesitant about shooting a woman, a white woman, at least. If they had been drunk, it might have been a different matter, but they weren't drunk enough to fire on a Kincaid.

Ward ended the standoff by firing at the horses. They reared in terror and jerked one of the men—or a young boy, judging by his size—holding the reins from his seat. His screams brought the others running to catch their valuable mounts. While they fought and cursed and brought the animals under control, Laura threw another blanket over the last of the flames, returned to the house, and shut the door. Shortly after, the sound of rapid hoofbeats carried into the distance as the disgruntled men left without their prey.

Laura slowly sank to the floor, shaking all over as she realized the battle had come to an end. She had done it, but she couldn't control the tears pouring down her face or the shivers racking her body. She wrapped her arms around herself and sobbed.

Jettie solemnly wrapped her in a dry blanket and helped her to her feet. Using every vile curse in his vocabulary, Ward jerked his chair into the hallway, only to watch helplessly as Jettie led Laura up the stairs. Still terrified, Lottie took one look at Ward's expression and ran back to the kitchen. The horror was over for now. Its repercussions would wait until morning.

Dr. Broadbent rode out immediately after church services the next day. Without any of the inhabitants of Stoner Creek coming to town to report the incident, rumor still managed to trickle to town. The sheriff had heard, but without a summons, he preferred to stay out of it. The doctor cursed him roundly and rode out alone.

He found Ward still in bed and Jettie Mae complaining vehemently as a wan Laura wielded a scythe to mow down what grass hadn't burned the night before. She wore an old cotton gown of pale yellow from which she had defiantly cut the sleeves. Round ivory arms flailed weakly at the offending grass, and he realized it was the aftereffects of shock more than strength that kept her going. Hurriedly the doctor swung off his horse and caught the scythe before she could swing it again.

"In the house, Laura. You'll do yourself an injury out here, and then where would we be?" He threw the scythe aside and forcibly dragged her by the arms toward the porch. The blackened scars on the bottom steps and the wide swathe of burned grass along the front testified to the closeness of the call.

"Lord a'mercy! It's 'bout time someone did that. I tried to stop her, but I done thought she'd mow me down! Jist wait here a bit, and I'll fetch somethin' cool to drink," Jettie exclaimed as they entered the house.

Doc seated Laura on the brocade cushions of the parlor sofa, picked up one of Sallie's fashion magazines, and waved it in a cool breeze toward Laura's heat-flushed face. "You ought to be in bed. You look like warmed-over death. I thought you were the one with a little sense around here."

Tired of fighting, Laura leaned against the sofa back and let the cool breeze dry her face. "There's no sense left in this world, Doctor. It's gone stark, raving mad. Perhaps I should go along with it."

There were times when he secretly believed this too, but this was a lady brought up to be protected from such harsh reality, and Jonathan's reply was that of a gentleman. "I think we've known each other long enough to drop the formalities, Laura. Why don't you just call me Jonathan?"

Laura wearily lifted one eyelid, and a wry smile played at the corners of her lips. "*Et tu*, Brutus?"

He looked momentarily confused, but Jettie hurried in with a tray of iced lemonade, and he was relieved of making any reply.

"Mr. Ward's awake and callin' for me. I'll tell him

you's here." She sashayed out with a mixture of motherly concern and delight.

Jonathan followed her departure with a skeptical gaze before politely seating himself on the chair beside the sofa and lifting a cool glass as if this were a formal occasion. "I take it she's the one that the ruckus was all about?"

Laura made an effort to sit up politely and straighten the strands of hair escaping her hasty chignon. "Ward needs a nurse," she replied defensively.

Jonathan regarded her heightened color with cynicism. "I daresay he does. That doesn't mean you need to suffer for his choice."

"No one should have to suffer for his choice," she retorted hotly before catching herself. She really was rather overwrought to speak out like that. She had learned long ago that quiet words and actions suited her place and accomplished more. The startled look on the doctor's face at her strong language proved the correctness of her beliefs. Fortunately, the sound of a carriage arriving gave her the opportunity to change the subject.

Sallie entered the house in a graceful breeze of petticoats and cologne and ribbons. Laura felt the shabbiness of her own hastily altered cotton in the presence of her cousin's cool elegance, but she was accustomed to the feeling. The carriage driver carried in Sallie's trunk, and she airily waved the old man to haul it upstairs while she floated into the parlor folding her parasol.

"Whatever in heaven's name has been going on while I was gone, Laura? Did you decide to barbecue the lawn?" She gave her gloved hand to the doctor as he rose with her entrance. "So happy to see you, Dr. Broadbent. Are you two having a cozy little chat? Am I intruding?"

Her light tone indicated the impossibility of any such occurrence, and her next words underlined it. Taking off her gloves, she gestured toward the tray of empty glasses. "Laura, why don't you fetch some lemonade for me? I'm fairly parched from that ride. I don't think I'll journey that far again. Why, I . . ."

Her monologue threatened to go on as Laura rose to take the empty glasses. Still standing, Jonathan caught her arm and motioned her back to the sofa, ignoring Sallie's voluble chatter. "Sit. You are not to lift a hand for the rest of the day. That's an order."

Sallie stared at him in wide-eyed incredulity but wisely made no protest as Laura returned to her seat under the doctor's orders. Rather than get the lemonade herself, she sat down and finished drawing off her gloves.

"It's much to hot to move about anyway. Dr. Broadbent, what brings you out here today? I hear the Paynes have bought the old hotel. Todd was always a good friend of ours. Do you think he'll succeed?" When the doctor made a noncommittal reply, Sallie turned restlessly to Laura. "I think I'll ask Jettie to pour me a bath. That journey has left me literally drained. I'll lie down and take a little nap before dinner. Or are we just having a cold collation again today? I swear, we never have any decent meals around here anymore. You really ought to look and see if we can't find a good cook. Then maybe we could have a small dinner, at least."

Laura hid her amusement at the doctor's expression when subjected to the full brunt of one of Sallie's excited monologues. She was an intelligent woman with too little to occupy her thoughts. There really wasn't a mean bone in Sallie's body. On the other hand, there wasn't a selfless thought in her head.

Before Sallie could depart, Jettie returned wheeling Ward in his awkward chair. His wife gave him an absent-minded look, smiled pleasantly, and excused herself. Ward grimaced, then turned his attention to his guest.

"What brings you out, Doc? Don't tell me Laura sent for you, because I won't believe it. She has some insane idea that she's invulnerable."

Jettie winked at Laura and whisked out the door, closing it gently behind her. Wishing she were taking Sallie's bath and nap, Laura rose to leave the two men to discuss the previous night's episode. She was too tired to hear the farce rehashed one more time.

"If you'll excuse me, gentlemen, I need to make myself presentable, then I will see about dinner. You will stay to have a bite to eat with us, won't you, Doctor?"

"Laura, if you get up one more time, I'm going to hog-tie you to the chair. Unless you tell me you're going upstairs to take a nap, I'm not letting you out of my sight." Jonathan rose threateningly before her, forcing her back toward the sofa.

Ward watched with suspicious eyes as Laura's brown

head bent with a slight blush and didn't raise to meet the doctor's eyes. Jonathan wasn't an excessively tall man, but he was taller than Laura's petite stature, and he appeared exceedingly protective as he caught her shoulders and steered her back to the chair. Physically, the two were well-suited, both of medium stature, pale brown hair, and slightly proportioned. Ward scarcely had time to absorb this startling fact when the doctor turned determined gray eyes in his direction.

"Ward, if Miss Laura doesn't object, I would like your permission to court her. I realize now isn't the appropriate time to begin my addresses, but I wanted you to know where things stand."

Laura's startled eyes lifted to Jonathan's slim frame as he confronted their host. Never had she considered his interest in her as anything but a fatherly one. Yet, seeing him now, his long serious face solemn, his slender hands relaxed and confident as he waited for some reply, she realized she had underestimated him. Jonathan Broadbent resembled her in more than stature. He was a quiet, resourceful man who got things done. Even if it had never occurred to her to look at him as a potential husband, she knew she would agree to be his wife.

Ward met her startled gaze, and a flicker of sadness appeared in his eyes even as a small smile curled his lips. "Well, Miss Laura, do you have any objection?"

Her knees quaked almost as badly as they had the night before. She had made a very large mistake in her one and only suitor. She had reason to doubt her judgment in matters of this consequence, and she had resigned herself to a life alone. To accept Jonathan's suit meant subjecting herself to the ordeal of coming out in society again. But if she would ever trust anyone again, it would be Jonathan Broadbent.

Vowing to start where she meant to leave off, Laura boldly returned to her feet and met Jonathan's look as squarely as her height would allow. "I am honored at your interest, sir, and I offer no objection, but you will forgive me for reminding you that I am not Sallie. I do not even know how to be Sallie. So please don't expect me to look or act like her, even if I am a Kincaid."

She swept off despite their protests. She couldn't wear her hair in elegant curls or balance fashionable hats upon her chignon. She wasn't tall enough to look graceful in long trains or formal gowns. She couldn't wave her fan and look interested at a party where the only topic was gossip. She couldn't do that and wouldn't try. She was old enough now to know better.

As her feet pattered down the hallway in the direction of the kitchen, Ward sent his worried guest a laughing look. "Sit down, Broadbent. If you're looking for a helpless female to protect, you're looking up the wrong tree, my friend. Do you want to hear how that dainty, demure little package held off a dozen ruffians single-handed?"

Jonathan turned a dubious gaze to the weary lines of his patient's handsome face. "No, I want to hear how you're going to get along without her."

7

August 1865

Cassius Marcus Wickliffe leaned his broad shoulders against the post of the captain's deck of the steamboat and drew thoughtfully on his cheroot as he gazed over the muddy brown waters in the boat's wake. They had just pulled away from Cairo and were headed up the Ohio, and he was seriously doubting his sanity in choosing this river instead of the broad expanse of the Mississippi just on the other side of the bank.

He could always get off at Paducah and turn back, he supposed. He didn't have to go on with this fool's journey. But he really had no reason to go back. Grimacing at this stark realization, he flung the cigar over the side, watched the wind carry it safely past the lower deck to the water, then raised his languid length to its full height and started for the stairs to the main salon.

A gambler who had judged him an easy mark at the beginning of the journey slapped him on the back as he entered the salon. "Cash, just the fellow I don't want to see. Go away and titillate the ladies, why don't you, while I find me an easier partner to complete this table."

Cash gazed down at the table, where two neatly attired gentlemen sat sipping bourbon and shuffling a deck of cards expectantly. Both wore the tailored linen coats, expensively embroidered waistcoats, and high top hats of wealthy men returning from a successful business trip. Old urges flared briefly, brightly, and with reckless disregard to the gambler's anxiety and his own new status, Cash pulled out a chair and sat down.

"Don't mind if I do, thank you, Jack. Gentlemen, how do you do? My name's Wickliffe, Cash Wickliffe. And yours?" He enjoyed throwing out his name and waiting for the signs of recognition or nonrecognition. In the West his name was met with discreet admiration and perhaps some wariness. The farther east he came, the less likely anyone was to recognize him. He had a feeling that was about to change, and not for the better, but these gentlemen apparently weren't from Kentucky. They nodded politely in nonrecognition.

The dapper gambler hid his dismay and resignedly settled in the remaining chair to make the introductions. After names were exchanged, the older man pulled out his gold pocket watch, noted the time, snapped it closed again, and as he tucked it away, gazed at the newcomer's lean dark face with speculation.

"You ain't from these parts, are you? What's your business, Wickliffe?"

The polished cards snapped briskly on the table in front of them. Cash idly scooped his up and fanned them as he spoke. "I'm from California, sir. Grand territory, where the streets are paved with gold if you kill enough prospectors for it, and the ladies are sweet as honey as long as you stick to the golden streets."

Jack gave Cash a nervous glance as he threw out his stake and discarded a card. "In other words, Mr. Wickliffe here made his money drifting across country and built himself a fancy ranch with the proceeds."

The younger man laughed and threw in his coins. "That sounds like a warning. Are you a professional gambler, Mr. Wickliffe? If so, I'll start counting my cards. I don't cotton to being cheated."

Cash unbuttoned his expensively tailored black frock coat, pulled a coin from his gold brocade waistcoat and flipped it to the table with lazy grace. His long brown fingers circled the cards without fanning them open again. "Every successful businessman is a gambler, sir. I don't claim to be anything else. One who counts his cards can usually play the odds; you should be safe."

"Why do I have the feeling you're glossing over the truth, Wickliffe?" The older man perched his hand of cards on his paunch to better peruse it. He missed the momentarily bleak expression in the stranger's dark eyes.

"Because who would listen to crude reality, sir? I have an appointment with a lovely lady at six, gentlemen. Shall we play?"

By the appointed time, the stack of coins in front of Cash considerably outweighed those before the other players, and they regarded his impending departure with relief.

"Give us a chance to earn it back later, Wickliffe?" the younger inquired politely.

A hint of a dark smile played for a brief moment upon the harsh face as Cash pocketed his winnings. "I don't expect to be free until morning, gentlemen. Perhaps some other time."

They watched as he strode off to greet an impatient lady tapping her slippered toe outside the salon. At Cash's approach, a beguiling smile spread across her lovely face, and she took his arm with a flirting look from beneath long lashes. The men watched the graceful sway of her hips all the way down the promenade deck.

"She his wife?" the older man inquired, clipping off the end of his cigar.

"Not likely," the gambler answered resignedly, scooping up the small sum Cash had allowed him to keep. "Why should a man like that marry when he can have all he wants without the strings attached?"

The other man grunted, drew deep on his cigar, and expelled the smoke in a single ring before replying. "For money and power, of course. Watch out for hungry men, they'll eat you alive."

The younger man pocketed his few remaining coins with a grimace. "Why didn't you give me that warning earlier?"

At dawn a few days later, Cash was out on deck watching the sun rise over the horizon that would all too soon include a view of his destination. The lady in his cabin wouldn't miss him until he was gone. She wasn't his reason for questioning his sanity in getting off at the next stop.

He didn't know why he had decided to return. The initial excuse had been a desire to improve his breeding stock with some high-quality thoroughbreds from Kentucky, but the arduous task of getting them back to California scarcely made the excuse creditable.

He was bored. That was part of the problem. In the eight years since he had left this place, he had traveled across country, learning to gamble from professionals, working on railroads when desperate, riding herd on cattle when he had contemplated the idea of settling in Texas. He hadn't found another place like Kentucky until he had reached the northern valleys of California, and there he had stayed and built his initial nest egg into a considerable sum. He wasn't wealthy by California standards, but he was comfortable. And bored.

White teeth flashed in a sardonic grin at himself. He'd never thought to see the day when having money would bore him. He still remembered all too clearly the tarpaper shack that leaked every time it rained and dripped icicles when it snowed. The scars of working as another mans' slave still marred his flesh as well as his mind. His hatred of the ignorant fools who had allowed his mother to die unheralded and despised had not diminished with time, but wealth couldn't bring her back to life or replace the love he had lost with her passing

Perhaps that was why he was returning. The only saving grace he had ever known was here in the lush bluegrass of Kentucky. He remembered the soft, cool voices of the women, their delicate perfumes, their elegant walks. He had been an outsider looking in, but he remembered them more distinctly than the dim image of his drunken father. He'd met with nothing like them in all his journeys. And it was time he began to look around.

He wondered how the inhabitants of Stoner Creek had survived the war. The wealthy would have bought their way out of conscription, but many were young and hot-headed enough to take to battle. The Breckinridge men had probably marched off in glory and to the sighs of the women. He knew Doc Broadbent had sense enough to stay out of the conflict. He would really enjoy seeing the old cynic again. His infrequent letters had the power to make him homesick more than thoughts of his mother, simply because they reminded him of a better time, a time of choices and possibilities.

Cash drew out his cheroot as the smoke of Louisville began to cloud the skyline. He had come this far; it wouldn't hurt to go a little farther. He was curious to know which of the aristocratic young men Sallie Kincaid had chosen. Doc had never seen fit to mention her in his infrequent letters. Perhaps there would be a whole new crop of young lovelies to choose from. 'Twas a pity he couldn't wait another ten years or so to marry. He could come back and court some daughter of Sallie's, give her proper fits. His sardonic grin didn't reach his eyes.

That was the challenge he really sought. Doc had mentioned the older Kincaids were dead and the farm was having trouble. The idea of owning Stoner Creek Farm someday had always been in the back of his mind. He would take it with or without Sallie, but a house like that needed a woman like Sallie to adorn it. Stoner Creek offered one more exciting challenge he had yet to conquer. It was time to accept the duel.

As he gave himself up to the idea of going home, Cash's memory caught on the image of a determined little urchin in top hat and too-long skirts. She would be married by now too. He wondered what kind of husband she would have chosen. Funny to think of that little monkey married and having children, but he'd rather like to see her again, just to see what kind of woman she had grown into.

*   *   *

The branches of the overhanging oak provided ample shade from the afternoon sun, and the August breeze blowing over the rippling creek created pleasant sensations as it played with Laura's skirts. A thunderstorm the previous day had swept away the humidity, and the air was fresh and clean for a change. Even the grass had regained some of its springtime color, and the fields and woods around the bridge seemed to shimmer in emerald greens.

Laura gazed at the tiny diamond in the box she held in her hand, and her heart beat nervously against her ribs. This should be a moment of joy, but she was more terrified than she had been as a six-year-old arriving at Stoner Creek. She gazed up to Jonathan's familiar angular face for reassurance, but found only further concern there.

"I know I must seem as old as your father to you, Laura, but it's not as if you were still a young debutante. You're a grown woman now, a widow who knows what life is like. I'll not press you to make a choice just yet, if you're not ready. I just want you to know what my intentions are."

In that moment Laura knew how easy it would be to love this man. Wonderingly she touched his taut cheek, and watched hope flare briefly in his eyes. He was a curious, sensitive man, too sensitive for this world, and he covered the flaw with a worldly cynicism that struck a chord in her. In some ways they were too much alike. Neither of them belonged to the gay society around them, but they were caught up in its whirl just the same. They were observers more than participants. She wasn't at all certain that was a healthy basis to establish a marriage on, but it was more than she had in common with any other man of her acquaintance.

If her soul cried out for something more, for life and love and a freedom for the energy and vitality that she kept so carefully hidden, Laura could not help but realize she had little chance of finding better than Jonathan offered. At times she still dismayed him. He was better than Ward at understanding that she had her own mind. He didn't expect her to be the useless trophy that Sallie was. Perhaps Jonathan would prefer it if she were more conformable to his opinions, and perhaps she would learn to bow to his wishes when they did not interfere too strongly with her own. She had learned not to expect marriage to be the hearts and flowers her romantic youth had envisioned. There would be compromises. She could only hope she had found a man willing to accept that the compromises worked both ways.

Laura slid her hand shyly back to her lap. She had kissed only one man in her life. She knew it was expected of her now, but she had no idea how to begin. "I don't think a woman could ask for a man better than you, Jonathan."

There was no hesitancy in her voice, only shyness, and Jonathan touched her chin to turn her face in his direction. "Does that mean yes? Or that you still wish to think about it?"

Laura loved the honesty of his gray eyes, the way hope lingered there with eagerness and perhaps a hint of amusement. All doubt fled, and she returned his honesty with courage. "I would have said yes that first day you asked Ward to court me, but I feared you would realize your mistake in time."

Jonathan grinned at the pert little face smiling up at him from the bulky old-fashioned bonnet. He swept the encompassing silk back from her face and touched his hand to the light brown of her hair. "I'm not old enough to make a fool of myself over a pretty face. I've known you for what you are since you were a little girl, Laura. You don't scare me any."

At the relieved laughter in her eyes and on her lips, Jonathan bent to take what he had been dying to sample these last weeks since he had declared himself. His mouth closed firmly over hers. He felt the slight ripple of shock course through her, and then he was oblivious of everything but the feel of a woman, a lady, in his arms for the first time in what felt like forever.

Laura felt the passion rise behind the gentleness of Jonathan's touch, and she knew a momentary fear. She was a fraud, and he would soon know it. What would he do then? Her fears froze her in his arms, but he didn't seem to think that at all odd. He gentled his kiss, brushed his lips across her forehead, and settled her more intimately against his shoulder. The leather hood of his old barouche hid them from the road, but anyone passing by would recognize the carriage. This was not the time or place for intimacy. Laura relaxed as all he did was slide the ring on her finger.

"Name a date, my love. After waiting all these years to make up my mind, I find I am suddenly impatient. I would have you in my house, under my roof, as soon as possible."

The thought was terrifying in its immensity. All she had ever known was Stoner Creek, with the exception of that horrible time in Cairo. Her memories of the days before Stoner Creek were too vague and hazy to count. Stoner Creek was her home, but he was asking her to leave and make another home with him, a home that another woman had once shared with him. She was being nonsensical. If she were truly the widow he thought, she would snatch at the opportunity he offered. Instead, she was terrified beyond all rational thought.

She could not let him know that. Jonathan was a proud man, and a sensitive one. She would never hurt him. She should be as eager as he, and she would not disappoint him. Carefully removing her bonnet so the breeze could ruffle through her hair, Laura turned to meet his gaze squarely. "I see no reason to linger. We neither of us require a large ceremony. Just whatever time it takes to notify friends and family and find a preacher."

He couldn't possibly hear the nervous pounding of her heart or read the lie in her eyes. Jonathan's narrow face lit with quiet joy, and he pressed one last kiss to her lips. "I knew you would make me happy," he whispered against her lips, and Laura buried her head against his shoulder to hide the tears as he held her in his arms.

8

Cash scraped his chair back from the drink-stained table and began to stash his winnings in his pockets. He didn't know why he had come here, of all places, on his return to his boyhood home. The stale stench of cigar smoke probably dated back to the years his father had haunted these environs. From the lines on their faces, he dared say the scantily clad women leaning over his shoulder had been there then too. They would all know his name, but none had asked it.

The gamblers at the table were much the worse for the night's excesses. It was near noon now, but the heavy thunderclouds outside gave the appearance of darkness through the filthy window of the bar. The flickering oil lamp made sallow masks of their weary faces, and Cash wondered in disgust if his own looked as dissipated as theirs. He felt no regret at pocketing their cash. He had not stolen it; they had given it away, fools that they were.

When he rose none too steadily to his feet, the one who had lost the most made a howl of protest. "You can't leave yet! A man don't leave when he's winning. Give us time to earn it back."

Cash had finally placed a name to the face and knew the man to be a well-to-do planter who had made him sit in the kitchen when he had accompanied Doc to the man's sickbed. The man had already placed the deed to part of his acres on the table, and it wouldn't be a moment's work to take it, but self-disgust prohibited any further excesses this day. Cash shoved his chair back under the table.

"Where I come from, a man would have to be a fool not to walk away when he's winning. It's been a pleasure, gentlemen, but it's time I took some sleep." For some odd reason he didn't care to analyze, he had carried his

Stetson to the table, and he put it on now. The low-crowned light felt looked oddly out-of-place among the top hats of the wealthy and the crumpled slouch hats of the tenant farmers, almost as out-of-place as Cash felt.

Before he could walk away, one of the farmers rose from the table and grabbed Cash by the shoulder, shoving him toward the wall. He was a big man with broad shoulders and a belly falling over his belt, with arms hardened by years of manual labor. As a hush fell over the room, it was obvious the man was accustomed to having his way, and they waited for the slender newcomer to bow to his wishes.

"We don't take to smart-ass strangers telling us how to play the game, mister. Now, sit back down there and take your medicine like a man. The game ain't done until we say it is."

It didn't take a second to size up the man and his strength and determine which ploy would work best. Size was the only advantage the farmer had, Cash decided, but he wasn't in the mood for a fracas. With a sigh, he removed his Stetson and set it down, then straightened his shoulders to ease back the man's hand. He dusted off his light linen coat, and at this seeming acquiescence, the man stepped back a little. When the tension had lightened to the degree desired, Cash balled up his fist and let swing with a right to the man's belly. He followed it with a double-fisted blow to the back of the man's neck as he bent over in pain. It was a dirty blow, but it worked. The man crumpled with a moan and a gagging sound that forewarned of the contents of his belly soon to be expelled.

Politely retrieving his hat, Cash nodded and stepped over his opponent's prostrate figure. A yell from behind him caused him to pause and raise an inquiring eyebrow.

"What's your name, mister?"

For the first time since he had walked into the tavern, Cash offered the semblance of a smile. "Cash Wickliffe, Sam. Tell Junior down there when he comes around that I still owe him one or two more of those, so he'd better not get too close next time."

He received some sardonic satisfaction from the unholy hell erupting behind him as he walked out, but as the thunder rolled overhead, Cash glanced at the clouds and felt the moment slip away. He had once dreamed of making that kind of scene, but the reality was more bitter than sweet. In those few hours at the table the had probably won more than his father had ever lost. It only served to prove how poor a man his father had been.

But he had gained some information that might provide an even better revenge. Giving the heavy clouds another thoughtful glance, Cash headed for the stable and the horse he had bought upon his first arrival. It wasn't much of a nag, but he needed some transportation, and the mare still had a lot of stamina left in her. He wasn't quite certain yet how to present himself to the planters who owned the horses he wished to acquire. But in the meantime he would take a look at that land he had reason to remember so well.

The only land he had ever considered acquiring here had been Stoner Creek Farm, but the temptation to possess Watterson's farm was considerable. Watterson had been a lousy farmer and a worse manager. He knew nothing of the land, and in consequence it had suffered from years of neglect. Cash didn't think it had improved any in his absence, but the opportunity to buy it for a song was tempting. The fact that Watterson was now dead and couldn't appreciate the irony of it dimmed the revenge slightly, but it wasn't an opportunity Cash could ignore.

As he rode out of town and along the creek that had given the town its name, Cash tried several scenarios in his mind. He could buy Watterson's farm and restore the house. The neighbors, out of curiosity, would have to come by. It was as natural as breathing to them to stop by and welcome a stranger. He could see the women now in their swaying skirts and fanciful bonnets, carrying homemade pies and baskets of aromatic bread. The picture tickled him endlessly, until he remembered he would have to give his name when he signed the papers. One whisper of his name would end their curiosity. He was no stranger to welcome, but a wolf to avoid. Son of a well-known Southern family but born of a quadroon, white trash, with no place he could call his own. Why in hell had he come back here to these people who knew him for what he was?

His mood shattered, Cash turned his mount off the

road and through the fallen gates to Watterson's farm.
He had the money now to make these people scrape and
bow if he wished, but he wasn't certain any longer that
that was what he wanted. It would be fitting revenge for
the way they had treated his mother, but he had sense
enough to know that revenge was a fool's dream, a fantasy from his childhood. If he bought this farm, it would
be because he could make something of it, and, perhaps,
of himself. He wanted to be recognized for himself, not
for who his parents were.

Which was like asking people to recognize him as a
penguin when it was obvious he was a grizzly bear. Thin
lips curling in a wry smile, Cash discarded fanciful notions and began to survey the remains of the abandoned
farm to discover its worth.

It didn't take long to determine that the house was
nearly uninhabitable, the fences destroyed, and the barns
in poor condition. No crop had been grown in this last
year, and the fields lay in tangled skeins of honeysuckle
and miniature forests of locust trees. The pastures that
should have fed horses had turned from lush bluegrass
to stinkweed and thistle. With a touch of drunken mas-
ochism, Cash rode out the tobacco lane that had once
housed his family and the other tenants in tar-paper
shacks. Little remained of the community but a cracked
and peeling lean-to. He stared at the crumbled bits of
rotting wood and debris that had once been his home—
now covered in Johnson grass and accented with an oak
sapling—and he took off his hat and let the growing wind
blow through his hair. He couldn't very well call this
coming home. There had never really been a home to
come home to.

Having paid his last respects to his childhood, Cash
turned his horse back toward town. Stopping to examine
one last barn that promised to be a little more substantial
than the others, Cash noted a slight figure riding across
the lower pasture in his direction. He didn't think the
rider had seen him yet, but he couldn't help lingering to
see who it might be. The horse came from the direction
of Stoner Creek Farm, and curiosity had the better of
him. He had been here only a few days, but he'd heard
some of the gossip. The Kincaids were down on their
luck, and the mighty Ward Breckinridge didn't have what

it took to turn it around. But Cash's fantasies of Sallie took a long time dying, so he waited, remembering the golden girl in ribbons and laces on her proud mare.

As he waited, Cash thought he recognized the horse as the old gelding Doc Broadbent had insisted on riding even when he had the brilliant stallion at his disposal. That thought made Cash grin slightly, and he waited even more eagerly for this touch with the past. He hadn't looked the Doc up yet, no more than he had the Kincaids. He had naturally gravitated to the lower levels of his past, but perhaps things were turning around.

Laura saw the lone figure beside the barn and debated the wisdom of approaching, but the gathering clouds and increasing wind warned of a storm about to break, and the horseman appeared vaguely familiar. Drawn by a curiosity she did not often display, she continued her progress toward the only nearby protection from the coming storm.

Once the stranger took off his foreign-looking hat, she knew him instantly. In the saddle, he sat taller than she remembered, and his shoulders were broader and less lean than they used to be in Doc's hand-me-down frock coats. She knew enough about tailoring to recognize the expensive cut of the linen he was wearing now, and the silver thread embroidering his black waistcoat cost a minor fortune in this postwar economy. Cash had done well, but the shadow of yesterday's beard on his jaw and the disheveled state of his overlong hair gave evidence that his character hadn't improved with his financial status. As Laura drew closer, she gave his weary eyes a dubious look, but she held out her hand in welcome.

"Jonathan didn't tell me you were back, Cash. Welcome home."

The use of the name "Jonathan" didn't warn him. Cash watched that unsmiling, pert face as if it were manna from heaven, and began slowly to grin as he took her neatly gloved hand in his and bent over it politely. "Miss Laura, it is a pleasure. I see you have grown into your hat." He gave the rakishly tilted piece of fluff on her hair an approving look. It wasn't new by any means, but it suited her more than that castoff of Sallie's had.

Cash had always looked at her as if she were real and not her cousin's shadow, and Laura responded to his attention as she always had, with perhaps a little more of a thrill than she remembered. She withdrew her hand from the protection of his with some reluctance and studied the rakish lines of his face as she spoke. Cash wasn't handsome in the same way as Ward, but there was a darkly attractive cynicism in the angle of his lips that held her gaze.

"I see your taste in horses has declined," she replied without a hint of her usual shyness with members of the opposite sex. Ward she had come to know as a brother and could speak to occasionally with honesty, although he continued to look at her askance when she did so. With Jonathan she had been too busy playing the part of courted lady to really touch on topics that required anything more than memorized lines from Sallie's past. But she and Cash shared secrets that left them open to each other. That hadn't changed, even if it had been over eight years since they had seen each other last.

Some of the weary lines disappeared from around Cash's eyes as his grin relaxed. "It was the first animal I could find that wouldn't bow in the legs when I got on it. There seems to be a sad dearth of good horseflesh hereabouts. How can that be?"

"The war," she replied simply. "They took everything that could run, walk, or crawl into battle. A few made it home, but not many. Won't you come back to the house? We're likely to get caught in the storm, but it's better than standing here waiting for it to happen."

Cash ignored the polite invitation as he studied the pure features of the woman beside him. He remembered Laura as a rag-tail twelve-year-old too gangly for her gowns and too small for her huge eyes. Now that she was grown, all her parts had come together to make a delicate package of perfection. Those huge green eyes were still there and still too large for her heart-shaped face, but they possessed an intelligence he hadn't realized he had missed. The worn but neatly tailored riding jacket emphasized the smallness of her waist and the roundness of her breasts, and a familiar longing built inside him. He fought the feeling as he quizzed her carefully.

"Doc makes a lousy correspondent, but I seem to remember him mentioning you running away to get married. Are you and your husband staying at the farm?"

Laura took a deep breath at the bluntness of his attack. She had forgotten Cash's directness, the one that so matched her own. She could wish now that he was more like the polite society in which she wandered. No one else had questioned her point-blank on her past. She didn't like to lie to Cash, but there was no way she could tell the truth. She smiled lightly and patted the gelding's head. "The war disposed of husbands as easily as horses. I'm home with Sallie and Ward now. And you? Have you come back married and prepared to settle down?"

That was what Cash wanted to hear right now. And he wanted to see the flirtatiousness in her eyes. Perhaps he was more drunk than sober, but Laura Kincaid looked just right for all his wants of the moment. He had had a fair sampling of war widows through the years. He owed Laura Kincaid more than his life, and he would never trifle with her, but the honesty between them never allowed for trifling. If they both wanted the same thing, there was no point in denying themselves. And Cash recognized the look in her eyes. He had seen enough women look at him in that way to know what it meant. He had only to make certain he wasn't misinterpreting it.

"Marrying isn't my style, and I'm still considering the settling-down part. What do you think the neighbors will say if I buy this place?"

Laura grinned wryly, and warmed by the approving male look in his eyes, responded with honesty. "They'll curse the war and no-account upstarts and down their bourbon in two gulps instead of three, but you don't really care what they say, do you?"

"Nope. Do you?"

"Not much. But being a dependent relative, I don't let that get about very often. You'll keep my secret, won't you?"

"I'll keep anything you want to offer. You don't mind my staring, do you? I can't believe little Laura has grown into such a stunning woman."

The praise startled her, but it shouldn't have. Cash was looking at her as if he wished to devour her, but at the same time, he played the part of flirtatious gentleman, just as Sallie and her beaux had done all those years ago. Laura had never played that game, even with Marshall, and she suddenly found it very exciting. Cash's words and the look in his deep-set eyes held seductive hints that made her heart pound a little faster.

"I thank you for admitting that I am a woman and not a little girl. People around here have some difficulty noticing. Perhaps it's my size. But then, I suppose I should expect such words from the town's bad boy. Have you grown into a bad man, Cash Wickliffe? What have you been doing with yourself?"

She was flirting with him. Cash had never expected to see the day, but he wouldn't lose the opportunity now. The scent of the chase was in his nostrils, sending his blood singing. She wasn't his usual type of woman, but right at this moment she was just what he needed. By tomorrow, perhaps the feeling would wear off, but for now little Laura Kincaid had succeeded in burying the hurt-filled memories he had just uncovered. For that reason alone he would want her. But there were a dozen other reasons staring him in the face, starting with that petal-soft Southern skin. Damn, but he wanted to touch her.

"I have grown into an exceedingly wicked man, madam. And it wouldn't be polite to tell a lady what I have been doing. But I'd be more than willing to show you." Cash raised one eyebrow and gave a leer that brought an infectious laugh to her lips.

"That's terrible! Do you practice faces like that in the mirror? Oh, I am glad you're back, Cash. It's been terribly tedious around here, and I haven't laughed like that in too long."

Cash didn't want to hear the tears behind her laughter. Laura had always been a solemn youngster, but when she laughed, it was as if the heavens opened and sunshine poured down. He wanted the sunshine right now, and he worked to gain it.

"Then I shall have to come and cut capers on your front lawn and balance pails of water over doors to douse your callers and set you to laughing so hard you'll fall into my arms from weakness. What makes you laugh, Miss Laura? I'll provide the show if you'll just tell me what you like."

He was smiling. She couldn't remember the boy Cash ever smiling. The sight sent warm shivers along Laura's flesh. She had never noticed the humorous curve to his

lips, nor how deep and pleasurable was the gaze from
his dark eyes. They were brown, she decided, with curious golden shadings somewhere in the depths. Their intensity now caused a ripple of excitement to begin
somewhere in the vicinity of her rapidly beating heart—
or lower. And a terrible thought occurred to her, one
that she couldn't hold back, and her body suddenly felt
too full for her clothes.

"I don't know what I like. It's been too long." She
was suddenly shy, but her words had a boldness that
she'd never intended. They startled her when they came
out, but Cash only smiled more and reached to touch
her face. He wore no gloves, and his fingers were rough
and callused against her cheek.

"That's a pity, Laura. You shame the stars when you
laugh."

She hadn't expected what came next either, but she
didn't resist when it happened. It seemed the natural
extension of these feelings swarming through her and of
the look in his eyes as he bent toward her. This was
Cash, and she trusted him. When his lips settled across
hers, she closed her eyes and sighed with satisfaction.

Besides Jonathan's, the only kisses she had ever known
were Marshall's and Laura couldn't remember them
being so pleasant as this. She tasted the whiskey flavor
of Cash's mouth, but the smooth tautness of his lips held
her captive. She didn't respond at once, and he moved
them carefully across her mouth, seeking, caressing gently, until she tentatively turned her chin more fully in his
direction, and her breath left her in a rush when his
tongue touched her just briefly. She reached for him
then, touching her gloved hand to his cheek, holding him
just a little closer so their mouths could meet more
firmly.

The excitement flowing from Cash's lips to hers stirred
the imps of Satan in Laura's soul. This was Cash, a man
she would trust with her life, but a man with reckless
adventure in his blood, a man who had admitted he never
meant to marry or settle down. She understood fully
what he did, even as she parted her lips at the pressure
from his. He thought her a widow ripe for seduction. He
meant nothing by these kisses. She had learned that
much from experience. Kisses didn't mean love. Kisses

didn't necessarily mean affection. Men scattered kisses and compliments where they would to obtain what they wanted. Even Sallie's husband, the wonderful gentleman Ward, used these little lies to hunt his prey. But even that knowledge didn't stop her.

The horses were growing restless. Thunder clapped almost directly overhead. They couldn't go on as they were. It was impossible to touch while clinging to a saddle and reins. Leaning forward in her sidesaddle was dangerous at the best of times; when she wasn't under control, it was foolhardy. Laura reluctantly moved back from the temptations Cash's tongue offered, but his hand strayed to her hair, staying her.

"We're going to get wet, *pequeña*. Do you have any objection to sharing a barn with me?"

She didn't understand the exotic Spanish, but the seductive timbre of his voice made his meaning as clear as if he had said "bed" instead of "barn." Laura stared at him in alarm, but the look on Cash's face was more tender than heated. No one had ever looked at her like that. She knew they needed the shelter of the barn. She knew she could stop him if she wanted. And she knew she didn't want to stop him.

She had a very good reason for nodding silently and accepting Cash's hand as he assisted her in dismounting. Huddled between the two horses, he stood more than a head taller than she, and she didn't dare look up to meet his eyes. A thick lock of coal-black hair fell across his dark brow as the wind picked up, and she had the urge to push it back. Lightning flashed in a brilliant arc above the pin oaks along the fence, and when Cash turned to lead the way into the barn, Laura offered no resistance. She was doing a terrible thing, but for a very good cause.

Jonathan expected her to be a widow. He thought her an experienced wife who had known the passions of a husband and would be satisfied to settle for the affections of an older man. He thought he was protecting her. He would never have offered had he known she was still an untried virgin. He would insist that she find a younger man, that she be properly courted as befitted her station. He would never have asked her to be his wife had he known the terrible truth. And he would surely discover the truth on their wedding night. She knew that much about what happened in the marriage bed.

It was odd that she had saved herself to bring her virtue to her husband's bed, only to discover herself betrothed to a man who would be horrified to know of it. She had not dared to explain to Jonathan for fear he would no longer wish to marry her, knowing he would never marry her if he knew the truth. At the same time, she hated deceiving him. She loved Jonathan. She loved his honesty, his carefully hidden sensitivity, his kindness. She didn't love him with the passion she had thought she had felt for Marshall, but with a maturer love that didn't require passion. She loved him and never wanted to hurt him.

But what he didn't know wouldn't hurt him. Laura glanced diffidently to the silhouette of Cash's angular face as they entered the mustiness of the old barn. Cash would never tell. She could explain to Cash later. She wouldn't hurt Cash with the truth. But she could hurt Jonathan. It was odd, knowing these things, but she knew them with an instinct that she couldn't deny, just as she had known what she had to do that day she set her dog on Cash's assailant. Some things were meant to be.

9

The first patter of rain against the unshingled roof startled Laura, and she hesitated. The heavy clouds concealed what little sun might have entered the cracks between the planked walls, but in the dusky light Laura could see enough to know Cash was turned toward her, and she could well imagine the question in his eyes.

Not daring to touch him, she loosed her horse's reins and lifted a hand to her hat, taking it off and brushing her hand through her hair to smooth it. The tension between them slacked slightly, and she felt more than saw Cash's appreciate grin.

"We're as likely to get wet in here as out there. Are you having second thoughts?"

"I can't think of anyone with whom I would rather share a barn." The words tripped off her tongue as if spurred by the devil. Laura wasn't at all certain that she knew herself at this moment. There was still time to cry a halt, but she didn't seem to have any intention of doing so.

Cash chuckled low in his throat and caught her hat, setting it carelessly on the horn of her saddle. He touched her cheek, then brushed a wisp of hair from her forehead. The touch was gentle, warm, and thoroughly exhilarating.

"We're two of a kind, I fear. You were always a little hoyden, no matter how hard you tried to conceal it. And I don't believe I ever worked very hard to hide my rather rebellious nature."

" 'Sullen' is more like it. You looked as if you'd bite the hand off anyone who approached you. I think there were times when you actually snarled. I loved it when you did that. It was something I always wanted to do."

Cash threw back his head and laughed. The sound was not so much joyous as accepting, acknowledging the truth of her words. Taking the reins from her, he led the horses to the side of the barn away from the wind and tied them to a post. He slammed closed the sagging door, but without a latch to hold it, it merely leaned inward, keeping out the worst of the storm.

He walked back toward her and held out his hand. "I'll teach you how to do it, if you like. I suspect you would make a very good student."

She could take his hand and smile and say something innocent, and they would spend the afternoon sitting on that moldering haystack reminiscing. Or she could walk into his arms and learn what it was like to be a woman. It didn't take a push from the devil to do the latter. She did it with eyes open, feeling Cash's arms slide around her as smoothly as if they did this every day.

"You don't need to teach me to be wicked, Cash. I already am."

"The gambler's daughter, come home to roost? Pardon

me if I find that hard to believe. You're every inch the lady, Laura, and always were. Although, admittedly, there aren't very many inches." Cash grinned down at her in the darkness just long enough to feel her ire rise before bending to do what they had come here for. He didn't know how far she would go, but he was more than willing to find out.

She kissed like a virgin, and if he thought about it, he'd venture to guess that she hadn't been married long before the war claimed her husband. But he didn't want to think about it. That would entail imagining a husband who didn't kiss her often, and from there the image would deteriorate rapidly. So he pulled her closer and proceeded to teach her what she should have known all along.

He was right. She was a good student. Too good. As her lips parted, inviting him with a sweetness that he hadn't known in a long time, if ever, Cash gave a violent shudder of relief and gathered her into his arms. He would never admit how much he needed this gentle touch, how the hairs on the back of his neck rose in anticipation as tender hands wrapped there and slid upward. Even through the thickness of her riding jacket, Cash could feel Laura's soft breasts crushed against him, and there was a heaviness in his loins that could be satisfied in only one way. He had never imagined a homecoming like this, but he was eager to pretend that someone welcomed him, someone as warm and soft and loving as this woman.

The seductive invasion of Cash's tongue took Laura by surprise, but when she learned to accept this intimacy, she responded to the sensation with delight. She didn't even have to think about what was happening. Cash made it so very easy that she knew only the thundering sensations of his kiss combining with the fury of the storm—until she felt his hand inside the newly unbuttoned flaps of her coat, and shock raced through her like lightning.

"Do I go too fast, Laura?" he whispered against her ear as she stiffened. "I can dally as long as you like, but I thought you would want it like this. Am I wrong?"

His breath murmured against her hair and his words seeped through to her from somewhere deep inside his chest. The hand caressing her through the thin linen of her shirt didn't halt, but increased its pressure, and the point of her breast rose in aching response to the need to be touched. Laura shivered as Cash's hand moved to the fastenings of her shirt, but his kiss merely traced her cheek, leaving her the freedom to say yes or no.

"Don't stop," she managed to push from her tongue, before his hand found what he sought and she arched in excitement as his warm flesh touched hers.

Never had she known what pleasure could be gained from so mundane a source as her body. For twenty-one years she had merely cursed her lack of height and grace and her smallness of form, and covered herself with the whims of fashion or fortune. A body was to feed and bathe and to carry her where she wished to go. But now Cash was teaching her a different use. Laura felt alive as she had never been before. She could feel the blood rushing through her veins, feel heat rising and moisture forming where she had never known it. And all because a man had touched her where she had never been touched before.

"Let's see if we can't make ourselves more comfortable." Cash stole another kiss and caressed her breast before glancing up to survey his surroundings. It seemed a shame to take her in a seedy barn, but he was too starved to wait for better circumstances. Besides, the thunder and rain overhead and the musty darkness below satisfied some urge inside him, and he suspected she felt the same. They were much too alike, even in their differences.

Cash quickly removed the saddles and blankets from their horses and arranged the thick wool on top of the remains of a haystack. Laura hesitated behind him, and he was aware that she had never done anything like this before. She was no bold wanton to toss and have done with. When he was satisfied with his arrangements, Cash stood and turned to offer her one last reprieve.

"You know what I am, Laura. I don't want to do anything that will lose you as my friend, but that's all I will ever be. I can't even promise to be here on the morrow." He waited for the denial to reach her face, waited for the recognition of the degradation any liaison with him would ensure, but all he could see was the luminous green pools of her eyes. Perhaps he was blind drunk, but he couldn't see anything but her fair hand reaching to touch his face, a hand divested of the glove she had worn earlier.

"I think that's why I'm here, Cash. But I don't want to think about it. Pretend I am a stranger. Pretend I am Sallie, if you must. But just this once, I need someone to hold me, to help me be strong."

Her words were like faint blows in the dark. Cash thought they bruised her more than they did him. He grasped her jacket lapels and began to pull the tight garment from her shoulders. "I don't know what kind of husband you had, Laura, but I don't think I would like him. You don't need to be Sallie. You're a beautiful woman on your own." Even as he said it, he envisioned the vibrant golden goddess that was her cousin in his arms, but he quickly thrust the image away. Laura was small and dark and quiet, all that her cousin was not, but no man could say she wasn't lovely. He carefully laid her jacket across the top of the blankets, then reached for the pins in her hair.

Laura let him remove the pins and tuck them safely away in his pocket. Her hair tumbled in an erratic cascade over her shoulders, and she was grateful for the darkness which concealed its unruliness. He touched her hair reverently, then parted it to find the nape of her neck and draw her forward.

"Don't believe me, then, Miss Pig-head. You'll see soon enough."

His words were nearly lost as their lips met, and Laura felt they were more for himself than for her, but they sent a thrill through her that she never would have felt had they been polite flattery. This was Cash, and she knew what she was doing. Her arms reached to encircle his neck.

A few minutes later she was no longer certain that she knew what she was doing. She was lying atop a bed of smelly hay with a man's heavy weight covering her, and her head was spinning with the heat of his kisses. She felt as if she were on fire and the blaze was rising faster than she could control. She felt only flaring gratitude and relief when Cash peeled back her shirt and unlaced her corset and chemise, and then the fire heightened as his hand touched her skin.

She writhed with the ecstasy of it. It was sheer madness, but she couldn't help herself. Cash's eager praises were like songs in her ear, and his hand melted her flesh into wanton waves of sensation. She wanted to touch him as he did her, but he was fully dressed, and she didn't know how to correct that situation. Her hands wandered through Cash's heavy hair, flattened against his chest as his kisses strayed daringly lower, and clung to his shoulders when his lips moved over the aching mounds of her breasts.

Had she known what it would be like, she would never have dared this, but knowing now, Laura could not stop. She cried out as Cash's tongue sent spiraling flames of pleasure from her breasts to somewhere in her center. She was becoming hazily aware of the heaviness where his hips pressed against hers, and the throbbing that began there was as frightening as it was exciting. But Cash didn't give her time to think about it, just as she had asked.

From that day forward she would never forget the heavy wet scent of the moisture-laden air as the hooks and buttons of her riding skirt came undone beneath Cash's skillful fingers. The heavy lengths of wool slid from her hips with the cumbersome folds of petticoat, and the cool drafts from the storm caressed her skin. As she realized he was uncovering her very plain and unadorned drawers, Laura knew a moment's panic and embarrassment, but Cash's attention seemed focused on her face and ears as he spread kisses like warm honey across her skin, and she gave herself up to this enchantment.

She managed to loosen his cravat and stroke the hard tendons of his neck through a barrage of thunder, and Cash's warm murmurs of encouragement led Laura to attempt the fastenings of his shirt. She no longer felt the chill and damp of the weather for the steam that seemed to be generating between them. She wanted to touch his skin, feel his chest against her breast, and know all of him at once.

But the tides of passion moved faster than Laura's inexperienced fingers. Just as she succeeded in uncovering a small fraction of the mysterious dark curls on his chest,

Cash's fingers dipped below her waist to the open seam of her drawers, and Laura cried out with the exquisite torment of this forbidden touch.

The sudden explosion of rain and hail against the barn roof warned that the time to turn back had ended. Cash's gentle kisses suddenly became urgent, demanding, and Laura raced to keep up with them. With her chemise hem hiked up above her waist and the bodice open to his questing fingers, she was nearly naked, but that no longer seemed enough. Heated lips suckled at her uncovered breasts and strong fingers took inconceivable liberties until the rush of pleasure became almost a panic for something she didn't know how to achieve. Laura caught her fingers in Cash's hair and pleaded wordlessly for reprieve, and his deep groan of desire and need struck new heights of urgency.

His mouth returned to plunder hers, and Laura sighed in relief at this familiar pleasure. She was aware of his hand between them, rearranging his own clothes, and she let him take over, knowing he would help her find the meaning of these pressures carousing crazily between them. She used her tongue as he did his, and was rewarded with another moan of pleasure and the crushing of Cash's body against her as he pulled her closer.

The sudden awareness of the hard shaft of heat between her thighs nearly shocked and terrified Laura from the pinnacle of desire where Cash had raised her. Never had she tried to imagine the differences between men and women, nor the means by which they came together in the marriage bed. To suddenly have that recognition thrust on her brought an insidious fear curling up from the inside and fluttering outward. This was what Jonathan would do to her when they were married.

There was scarcely time for the fear to take root. Long fingers once more touched her intimately, and this time Laura didn't back away, but rose unconsciously to meet the secret they offered. She didn't know where to turn or how to escape the fiery urges rendering her helpless. She felt a complete loss of self as Cash parted her legs wider and rose above her. Instinctively she knew what was coming, and in a last desperate attempt at self-preservation, she opened her eyes to plead for a halt, only to fall beneath the intensity of the dark look in Cash's eyes as he bent once more to capture her lips.

The pain when he entered her was brief, but sufficient to make her momentarily stiffen and gasp deeply of the storm-laden air. Cash tore his mouth away and cursed as he glared down at her pale face against the blankets, but the damage was done and not to be repaired. Shaking his head to clear it of questions or any thought at all, he moved more carefully until he was completely sheathed in the narrow entrance to her body.

He had to concentrate on her pleasure to rid himself of his dismay. She waited pliantly beneath him, eager for the rest of his lesson. Lesson! Damn, but he felt a cradle-robber. Yet he couldn't stop the powerful urges of his body as her hips moved tentatively beneath him. He should have taken all her clothes off, taught her the full sweetness of her body, but it was too late for that now. He had taken her like a stag in rut, thinking her in the same state of need as he. How was he to know she was as innocent as the day she was born?

Other than her lack of practiced tactics, he would not know it now. She responded to his touch with passion, took his thrusts with a growing eagerness that nearly destroyed his control. His dismay gave way to the challenge of teaching her what it meant to be a woman, and Cash applied all that he had learned the hard way over the years to this single lesson.

And she almost ended up teaching him anew what this joining between man and woman could be. It wasn't just the pleasure and relief of his body, but something deeper, more primeval and instinctive, just beyond the boundaries of conscious thought. Cash reached to grasp it, groping for it in the dark as Laura took him and welcomed him and did a dance of rapture beneath him as he joined her again and again. And then it was beyond his grasp as his body gave in to her beckoning and exploded with a rapture of his own, leaving nothing to thought but pounding waves of sensation in the electrified air around them.

They dozed briefly, completely satiated and drained of consciousness. The thunder drifted away, and the rain became a gentle patter on the wooden roof. The breeze brought a cleaner, sweeter scent as the heavy humidity dissipated and evening approached. Only the unmistakable rustlings somewhere in the hay beneath them gradually stirred them back to reality.

Cash woke first, carefully lifting his heavy weight from her slenderness and gazing into Laura's flushed and peaceful face with genuine curiosity. And then his expression hardened and he disentangled himself, waking her more fully.

Laura knew where she was. She had heard the rustlings and knew that a haystack was no place to be. But the heavy warmth of the man holding her had taken precedence, and the security of his arms had relaxed her usual caution. When he abruptly moved away, she woke with a jerk and quickly reached to cover her unforgivable nakedness in the cool, dusky air. She had no fear of the mice in the haystack, but she felt unexpectedly vulnerable beneath Cash's deliberate perusal.

"Why do I get the feeling that I've just been used?" he asked calmly, with only a hint of his usual sarcasm.

Laura stared at him blankly, then flushed, hastily pulling her chemise to rights and tying it with trembling fingers. Cash was still almost completely dressed, with only his open shirt and the dark shadow of curls beneath giving him a slight aura of unrespectability. She was the one who appeared wanton, and she hastened to correct that situation as she fumbled for a reply.

"I thought the feeling was mutual," she answered defensively.

"And so it would have been, had you been the experienced widow I expected." While she was otherwise occupied, Cash adjusted his trousers and fastened them. He couldn't help feeling a slight revulsion at himself for taking her like some whore he didn't have time to please. Why hadn't he just thrown her skirts up and had at it and been done? "I think you owe me some explanation. Why did you lie about being married?"

Laura heard the harshness in his voice then and knew its cause. They had always been open and honest with each other, and she had broken that bond. That was the price they had to pay for growing up, she supposed. They had never really been friends before. They didn't know each other well enough to be friends. They were scarcely more than casual acquaintances, after all. Which made what she had done even more reprehensible.

Laura sighed and turned her back on him as she struggled with her corset. Cash caught her shoulder and took the laces from her hands, swiftly pulling them taut. They tightened until she nearly gasped, before he relented and tied them off. The intimacy of the gesture left her even more unsure of herself. He now had a hold over her that no other man possessed. Why had she been so certain earlier that she could trust Cash not to take this any further?

She lifted her gaze shyly to meet his forbidding stare. An angry tic pulled at the muscle above his cheekbone, and she wondered irrelevantly if there might not be Indian blood in him. His dark face had the angular lines of the Cherokee, but this was scarcely the time or place to question him about his origins. That was something she should have considered before she took him to her bed, instead of seeing him as the hero of her childhood.

"You're right, I do owe you an explanation, but I'm not certain how to give it." Resignation laced her voice as she felt around in the dark for her skirt and petticoat. She was oddly grateful that he couldn't see the darn holes in the frail cotton. The petticoat had been pretty enough when Sallie first handed it down to her, but that had been nearly ten years before. It had seemed senseless to replace the old-fashioned petticoat when crinolines were all the style; she couldn't afford the expensive cages even if she had wanted one. She should be grateful she hadn't grown in stature, so that the material still covered her to the ankles.

The sated feeling of earlier had passed, and Cash felt rubbed raw and aching as he politely rose and turned away while she completed dressing. He wrapped his hand around a post and stared at the barn door while he listened to the rustle and whisper of her garments as she pulled them on. Even the smallest and most defenseless of the Kincaids had succeeded in puncturing his rather faulty armor. Grimly he clenched his teeth and tried not to remember how sweet and heady had been the pleasure of their joining. Any thoughts he might once have allowed to enter his head of taking a Kincaid mistress were definitely quenched. There were enough men out there ready to plant a knife in his back. He didn't need a woman to do the same.

"Doc said you ran away to get married. I take it that the marriage never came about." Unable to endure her continuing silence, Cash took the initiative.

He heard the bitterness in her laugh and jerked reflexively. He didn't want to know her troubles. He wanted to continue imagining her as the cosseted pet of wealthy society. She wasn't going to allow it, however. She answered, at last.

"He lost all interest when he learned I was only a dependent relative with no wealth of my own. He'd had visions of drinking bourbon all day while being waited on hand and foot by me and our slaves, then pleasuring himself all night—without me but with our imaginary slaves, I suspect. Even the maids were preferable to me, it seems. I suppose I am lucky that I am not as pretty as Sallie, or I wouldn't have had to do what I did today. I am quite certain he was capable of rape if I had been at all desirable."

The bitterness was quite unmistakable now, coupled with a cynicism Cash didn't think one so young should know. But then, he had known it at a much earlier age. Lifting his shoulders in a shrug of resignation, Cash turned around.

She was almost fully dressed and struggling with the hooks at the back of her skirt. He took a stride forward and spun her around. She was no bigger than a sack of meal, and she felt highly breakable and easily punished in his hands. Yet she accepted his touch without cringing, accepted it with all the trust and innocence of earlier. His rage dwindled, and he felt only a tiredness in his soul as he carefully placed each hook in its proper place.

"I don't know how long ago this happened or what you looked like then, but if you in any way resembled what you are now, the man had to be blind, pet. I'm not in the habit of troubling to seduce prune-faced old maids."

His reassurance was given as firmly and matter-of-factly as his hands on her hooks and fastenings. Cash wasn't one to offer mindless flattery, and Laura smiled slightly at the thought. "I thank you for the compliment, Mr. Wickliffe, and I will try to keep it in mind for future reference. Perhaps when I see you seducing other women, you would be so kind as to rate my appearance with theirs so I might better gauge my attractions."

Finishing his task, Cash caught her shoulders and shook her slightly before swinging her around to face him. Those mesmerizing eyes stared back up at him without a hint of emotion, and he grimaced. "I ought to slap you, Miss Laura, but that's not exactly what I feel like doing right now." She flinched at the sarcasm in the "Miss Laura," but he felt like hurting someone else besides himself right now. When she fully realized what he wanted to do, her eyes widened and she backed away a step.

The temptation to pull her back was great. He had just possessed her body, touched her as no man ever had, and he had the need to reassure himself of that fact by repeating it. Even fully garbed in yards of that damned material, she was wholly desirable, but he'd had enough torture for this day. Cash released her.

Laura's shoulders sagged slightly at the removal of his strong hands, but then she straightened her spine as she had been taught and faced him squarely. "I didn't mean to trick you, Cash. I knew you thought me something I wasn't, but things just happened so fast. . . . I'll not do it again, I promise. I just thought . . . Well, men do it all the time, and it wouldn't hurt just this once, for a good cause."

Cash's laugh was sharp and bitter. "For a good cause? That's a new one, sweetheart. Since when is an itch like ours a good cause?"

Laura tightened her lips and glared at him for this rudeness. "To you it was just an itch, perhaps, although that's certainly a crude way to put it. But to me it was freedom. What are the chances that Doc Broadbent would marry me if he thought I wasn't a widow?"

He'd been shot once, and the shock was much the same, jolting through him with a force that knocked him backward. Cash glared at the little asp who had gone for his jugular, then marshaled his considerable resources, and placing his hands on his hips, fought back. "One in a million, brat. The Doc prefers whores. Now, tell me what the hell you're taking about."

It didn't take long and it didn't taste sweet, but when

she was done, Cash held her in his arms and let her
weep, then gently kissed her good-bye. It was the very
least he could do for his fair rescuer, for the Doc was a
far better man than he would ever be.

10

Laura washed the evidence of her sins from her body
when she returned to the house, but she couldn't cleanse
her mind or soul. In the dim light of the lantern that
night, she removed all her clothes and stared down at
herself with some wonder, touching the aching points of
her breasts roused by the damp night air, feeling them
respond to her touch as they had to Cash. Daringly she
let her hand wander farther south to splay across her
abdomen, and a dazed look replaced the wonder as she
tried to imagine how they had fitted together to create
that miraculous harmony. She didn't allow her hand to
stray any lower. It seemed somehow a sacrilege to touch
that place where they had joined. She was glad she had
not seen the male instrument he had used to enter her.
It was better that she did not know the details.

But after she had drawn on her nightdress and climbed
between the sheets, she couldn't help but let her mind
wander to the night when she must share a bed with her
husband. At least now she wasn't ignorant of what would
happen there. She could come to Jonathan with all the
experience of a married woman. But somehow she could
not get the picture right in her head. It ought to be Jonathan's slender shoulders and light hair bending over her,
not the black hair and sharp features of the quadroon's
son.

It was easy to keep herself too busy to think about it
during the day. The daily household chores would keep
an army of women busy. Ward had learned to lean on
Laura when he needed eyes and ears outside the house,

and with the harvest only a short time away, she was riding out to the fields more often than ever. And then Jonathan was out more frequently now that she wore his ring, and they had to entertain more than they were accustomed to.

The day that Jonathan rode out in the company of Cash, Laura felt her insides lurch, but after making the first polite greetings, the men closeted themselves in the study. Laura closed her eyes and breathed a sigh of relief that she did not have to meet Cash's eyes in casual conversation. She was a woman and entitled to her own decisions. If she wanted to take a lover, she harmed no one but herself, and she was old enough to accept that fact. But she was somehow not quite ready to converse with a man with whom she had been physically intimate while in the company of her fiancé.

After they departed, she found Ward sitting at his desk, staring out over the fields that eventually led to the stone fence separating this farm from the Watterson place. He looked up at Laura's approach, and smiled faintly. "Somehow I always thought I would climb higher than the white-trash product of a union between a drunkard and a whore. Did Jonathan tell you that Cash is buying the Watterson property?"

Laura winced at this bluntness, but she replied with a modicum of calm, "Does that bother you?"

Ward sent her a sharp look. Sallie would have been outraged had she been here. She would have ranted and raved about the state of the world that it could allow such riffraff to pretend to society. Laura surely ought to show some displeasure at the fact. Perhaps she was innocent of the gossip, but he was beginning to realize that behind the innocence of those large eyes, Laura knew a lot more than she ought to. He frowned and tried to phrase the question delicately.

"I know Jonathan took Cash in as his ward some years ago, but that's not to pretend we don't know his origins. And from all I hear now, he hasn't fallen far from the tree. I admire and respect Jonathan, Laura, and I'm proud to know you'll be his wife, but I'm uneasy about the fact that we might have to entertain a man like Cash Wickliffe. Sallie isn't going to take it well."

Laura wanted to vent her fury in a screech of rage and

an inquiry as to whether Ward knew her own origins or
not. Her father was a gambler and a drunkard as much
as Cash's. Her mother was a French actress. But because
she was a Kincaid, she was acceptable and Cash was not?

But she had learned the folly of rash reactions long
ago. Men tended to ignore the opinions of women when
it suited their purpose, and they certainly never heeded
the opinions of women in a rage. She would get nowhere
by telling Ward just exactly what she thought of him and
his bigoted, hypocritical family. There were other ways
that were more successful, if not as satisfying.

"It's not Sallie's choice, Ward. Uncle Matt accepted
Cash here out of respect to Jonathan. You need only do
the same. You're the man of the house. Sallie will have
to respect your decision."

Those were words Ward wanted to hear, and he nodded with relief. Both knew she only mouthed platitudes.
Sallie would rant and rave if she wanted, and make life
a living hell for Ward if she could, but Laura was promising that she would blunt the sharp edge of her cousin's
wrath. They both had what they wanted without a word
of argument being offered.

Not that Laura truly wanted Cash underfoot every
time she turned around. The prospect of meeting him
over a dinner table was enough to make her insides
quake. But that fear had nothing to do with his origins
or his new property. It had more to do with the fact that
she didn't know how she was going to look Cash in the
eye while Jonathan sat by her side.

She didn't know why that hadn't occurred to her before. Perhaps she had thought Cash would never stay,
that he would return to whatever life he had led these
past years and leave her safely alone. But that fallacy
was easily exploded as the activity on the old Watterson
farm increased at a record pace, and all the town could
talk about was Cash Wickliffe and his fortune.

After listening to the speculation at the general store
that Cash meant to build a racetrack and open a gambling hell and whorehouse on the farm, Laura put down
the articles in her hand and turned around and walked
out with a sickness churning in her stomach. For the
hundredth time she wondered why she had ever returned
here, but when she nearly walked into Jonathan and he

caught her securely in his competent hands, she relaxed and breathed again.

Looking up into her fiancé's intelligent face and concerned expression, Laura allowed herself a small smile. "Sometimes it is just so good to know that there is one person in this town with a head on his shoulders. Why aren't there more of you around, Jonathan?"

The concern didn't instantly evaporate, but Jonathan relaxed his grip and politely set her fingers on his arm to lead her toward the carriage. "Can you imagine a world with nothing but old cynics sitting around carping about the state of the world? No, it's much better to have a variety, my love. We just have to learn to take the good with the bad."

"But why can there not be more of the good? Look at what those ignorant Raiders did to those poor families over at Tobaccotown. There was no excuse for that. The wages they make doing white people's laundry and hoeing fields wouldn't feed a single man in this town. What was the point in burning those shacks and trampling their gardens? Don't they think the world big enough for black and white?"

"There's nothing you can do about it, Laura, so there's no use in fretting. If it gives you any satisfaction, the Regulators strung up one of the men who did it, not that that will stop anyone." He assisted her into the two-seated carriage and climbed up beside her. "Now, there is something you can do for someone else if you would like. Old Bessie Whitehall is down ill and I need to stop by and take a look at her. She doesn't cotton much to me seeing her with her clothes off, and it's not easy to examine her through six layers of musty underpinnings. Could I impose on you to act as my nurse just this once? I promise I'll not ask it often."

There was a hesitancy in his question that made Laura examine Jonathan's expression more closely. Seldom did they have long or weighty conversations. They fenced around each other like two stray dogs in the road, both being careful to stay off anything that might be considered the other's territory. Laura thought she knew Jonathan as well as anyone could, but then, she had thought she had known Cash too. She was beginning to realize she was seeing only the surface and believing that to be the whole person. So she examined the question more closely, realizing that he was touching on subjects that had never before come between them. Just the mention of "underpinnings" in polite conversation was taboo, but if they were to be married, they would need to do more than discuss them. He was offering a glimpse of the intimacy that would have to develop between them if they were to have any relationship at all, and in so doing, he was offering a piece of himself.

That had to be hard for the solitary doctor to do. Reaching out to touch Jonathan's hand as she had never done before, Laura nodded. "It's not an imposition. I want to help you whenever I can."

A flicker of relief crossed Jonathan's face, and he squeezed her fingers before lifting the reins. "You may regret that offer someday, but I'll hold you to it now."

By now the whole town knew of their engagement, and people smiled in condescending approval as the carriage rolled through town. It was as if they all enjoyed a secret that the newly betrothed lovers did not, and Laura felt vaguely embarrassed by their knowing smirks. If Jonathan noticed them, he gave no sign of it, but pressed on toward his patient.

The thunderstorms of the previous weeks had not cleared the air as usual, but left it hot and humid for this late in the summer. Puddles of rainwater still sat in the fields and muddied the ruts of the roads. Rain barrels overflowed and sat in mossy mud that began to stink as the heat of the day climbed. The odor was more rancid than sweet as it had been with the earlier rain. There hadn't been a big storm in ten days or more, but still the moisture clung to the clay ground and pooled in green puddles where the sun didn't go. Laura swatted at a mosquito disturbed by the carriage's passing and pulled the wide muslin sleeves of her gown tighter at the wrist. She wished she had gone ahead and tried to update the gown by making cuffs from the rows of ruffles running the length of the sleeve, but she had never found the time. The loose sleeves were cooler, but they didn't prevent flies or mosquitoes from finding her arm.

At least she had on one of Sallie's crinolines and looked respectable as she entered the modest house of one of the matriarchs of the community. Signs of economy were everywhere: in the faded horsehair of the sofa that would have been replaced in better times, in the sight of only one servant in a uniform that had shiny spots from wear, and in the tarnish of the tea tray that no one had the time to polish. But the stuffy air of respectability still permeated the crowded rooms, and Laura felt almost an impostor as she entered the sickroom on Jonathan's arm to be introduced to the invalid.

But the old woman couldn't know Laura's rebellious nature or her sinful life just by looking at her, even though she watched Laura suspiciously through wire-rimmed glasses. Despite the fact that the patient was burning up with fever, all the windows in the tiny bedroom were closed and draped, and a coal fire was burning in the grate. Steam practically inundated the room as Jonathan tried to examine his recalcitrant patient.

By the time he and Laura between them had persuaded the old lady out of her robe and parts of her nightdress and the chemise she wore beneath it, perspiration was pouring down both their faces. Jonathan had already begun to frown before he began his examination, and after only the briefest of questions to the little maid hovering nearby, he hastily withdrew Laura from the room.

Slamming shut his bag and cursing under his breath, he gave the maid orders for caring for the fevered patient, then briskly took Laura's arm and walked her from the house. He was silent as he helped her into the carriage and set the horse at a furious pace toward the farm.

Laura didn't dare catch his arm, but clutched her reticule in her lap and carefully broke the silence. "I didn't finish the shopping, Jonathan. I need to go back to town."

Grimly he lashed the reins. "You won't be going back to town anytime soon. I want you and Sallie and Ward to stay away from town until I come for you. I should never have taken you with me. Damn, but you'd better stay away from Sallie and Ward for the next few days. If you feel any sign of fever, get word to me as quickly as you can. Hell and damnation, but I'm a fool. You'd think I was some lovesick adolescent with mush for brains. I'm sorry, Laura. Forgive my ranting."

He was talking to himself as much as to her, but his

words were sufficient to turn Laura's stomach into knots. Tightening her clasp on the beaded bag in her lap, she said stiffly, "It's yellow jack, isn't it? I didn't think this late in the season . . ."

"Neither did I." He turned and gave her a quick look. "What do you know of yellow jack?"

"I had it once, in Cairo. The summers there are horrendous. The river is practically at everyone's door and you can swim through the air in the summer. Everyone gets it. You'd better turn around and take me back to town. I don't know if I can give it to Ward, but there's no sense in taking chances. You'll need me before this is over with."

Jonathan slowed the horse and stared down at the pale face of the small woman at his side. She wore her hair drawn back in a knot at her nape, but the heat had loosed dainty wisps hither and yon, spoiling the severe effect she had attempted. In the billowy sleeves and graceful swathes of white muslin adorned with delicate sprays of roses that covered her slight frame, she appeared too fragile to withstand a breeze, but she was claiming to have survived a disease that killed over half of its victims. Meeting her eyes now, Jonathan saw the steel behind the soft hazel, and nodded in satisfaction. She was a fighter. He had known that. In his awkward attempt to play the gallant, he had just forgotten.

"I don't like it, but you're right. If you've had it once, you won't get it again, but it's likely to be a long fight, Laura. Are you sure you know what you're doing?"

"I told you, I've lived through it. It doesn't go away, the memory. I'd rather it would. I'd rather go hide out at the farm and pretend nothing is happening, but I can't. If Bessie has it, there will be others. We can only hope it won't be severe. It is late in the season, after all."

Jonathan stopped the carriage in a nearby drive. On an impulse he seldom gave in to, he wrapped an arm around Laura's slender shoulders and pulled her to him. He felt her surprise at the kiss, but he imagined there was a warmth for him there, and he indulged himself a little deeper. His first wife had been younger than Laura when they married, but her kisses had tasted much the same. The innocent sweetness after all these years of professionals made him feel masculine and invulnerable.

For a moment Jonathan almost forgot Laura was a widow and wise to the ways of the world. When he remembered, he pulled her more firmly into his arms. There had never been a time when this had seemed possible before, and there might not be time again in the next weeks. He would steal just these few minutes for himself.

The shock of Jonathan's demanding kiss and the strength of his hold as he pressed her to him kept Laura from thinking of anything else. His cheek was smoothshaven, and his lips were fuller and softer than the ones she remembered so clearly. When she reached to touch Jonathan's hair, it was cropped short and her fingers became entangled in nothing more satisfying than the stiff collar at his nape. But still, she did not find his touch repulsive, and when his hand cautiously brushed the side of her breast, she felt a jolt of anticipation.

The sound of horses coming down the road brought the interlude to a hasty end. Two men Laura remembered from her uncle's dinner table rode up with knowing grins on their faces, greeting the doctor with joviality and hiding their smiles as they made polite bows to her. When they rode on, she hid her flush behind her hands as Jonathan turned the carriage around.

He gave her a quick glance from the corner of his eye as he urged the horse toward town. "I seem to be spending the day apologizing, Laura. But this time I'm not really certain I'm sorry. They know we're betrothed and that neither of us is exactly inexperienced. It's not quite the same as if you were still a debutante."

"I know. Just be patient with me. It's been a long time." Laura told herself she wasn't lying. It had been a long time since her presumed husband had kissed her. That was all he was talking about. But the difference in their ages and experience had never seemed to loom so wide as it did now. She cast him an uncertain look at the confidence and impatience in his voice. He expected her to be more certain of herself and of him. A widow would be. She would have to learn not to be embarrassed by what was after all a natural act between a man and his betrothed.

But Jonathan's thoughts had already traveled on to the disease threatening the town, and he gave her no further reason to question what had happened between them.

Laura tried to quell her doubts by turning the topic to the fever and what should be done in preparation for it, and she was satisfied that she and Jonathan were closer for having this time together.

They were greeted back in town by another urgent call to the bedside of a toddler. Jonathan left Laura there, applying cold compresses and ordering sheets soaked in cold spring water while he traveled on to the next call at the hotel. By the end of the day it was apparent that his worst fears were confirmed, and before the epidemic could take wing, they sent a message to the farm explaining the situation and asking for a change of clothes for Laura.

Not knowing how the fever spread, fearing to contaminate innocent people, Laura didn't dare stay with the few women acquaintances she had in town. Jonathan summoned Jettie's mother to come and stay as chaperon and cook for the sake of appearances, but both knew the servant was for show only. The fact that they were to be married eased the pressure, and with the epidemic uppermost in everyone's minds, there wasn't time for the normal gossip to have its way. They would suffer the consequences later, when there were less important matters to consider.

Not that there was time after those first few days for anything immoral, were they given to such activities. The black servant acted as message center, sending them both in different directions as the fever raged and swept through town. While Jonathan grabbed a few hours' sleep on the sofa, Laura would be with a weeping mother and her houseful of children. While Laura collapsed in exhaustion on the wide bed that would be hers when they married, Jonathan was riding into the countryside to tend row shacks of tenant farmers and their families laid low by the disease. If they saw each other at all, it was through bleary eyes as one or the other went out the door.

To Laura's surprise, Cash became the intermediary between town and country. He first arrived with the change of clothing she had requested. She stared at him in weary disbelief and incomprehension when she discovered his black-coated form hovering on the doorstep with her trunk in hand. "Cash?"

He took one look at the disheveled gown she had slept in, the dark circles beneath her eyes, and shoved his way into the house. "It's worse than the reports, isn't it? What in hell is Jonathan thinking about to let you stay here?" Cash threw the trunk he was carrying to the floor and turned to face her defensive position. She had never been very big or outrageously beautiful, but the sight of her pale face and weary posture tugged at something hitherto unknown inside of him, and he wanted to rage at a world that would treat her so.

"It's not Jonathan's choice, Cash," Laura responded quietly but firmly. His obvious anger made this confrontation easier. She couldn't have survived sympathy or concern, not while her whole body ached to be swept into the comfort of his embrace. "I've had the fever, and I know how to nurse it. I can help here, but I can only be a danger out at the farm. If you're going to come into town like this, you'd better not go back near Ward. There's no point in taking any chances."

Cash was on the verge of making another protest when a small boy ran up on the porch, his tear-streaked face speaking what his stuttered words could not. Laura reached for the small satchel of medicines Jonathan had left for her use. "If you want to make yourself useful, there's two dead at the Harrisons' and the coroner has been busy at the cemetery all night. Someone needs to remove the bodies before the infection spreads."

Grasping the boy's grimy hand, she hurried from the house, leaving Cash to run his hand through his hair and stare after her.

Thereafter, Laura found Cash manning a wagon carrying the dead to the trench dug in an open field outside of town, waiting in Jonathan's parlor with messages from Ward, and once, laying a brute of a fellow low in the road when he tried to steal the horse of a family trying to get out of town and away from the fever. Each time, Cash stopped to speak and inquire after her well-being and Jonathan's, but he never offered a hint of the intimacy between them.

Laura was grateful for the reprieve. She had no strength for the emotions that would swarm over her should Cash so much as express an overfamiliar concern. She needed his detachment in this time of overwhelming grief. Exhaustion wasn't her worst enemy; but the anguish every time she arrived too late to help or when help simply wasn't enough threatened to tear her in two. Her emotions were too close to the surface and too volatile to be played with under these conditions. She closed them off carefully and strained to keep up the physical demands pressed upon her.

A sudden downpour followed by a cold spell slowed the number of new cases of fever dramatically. Laura came home in the middle of the night to throw herself across Jonathan's wide bed, only to find him already there. Too exhausted to move another inch, she lay down beside him, fully dressed, and fell into a sound slumber.

When she woke, he was gone, but he had removed her boots and pulled the covers over her. The thought of Jonathan taking the time to do even that much brought a slight smile to Laura's face as she wearily rose to face the day ahead. It was possible this marriage could work. They just needed time to become accustomed to it.

That thought didn't last much longer than Cash's arrival upon the doorstep as she hastily drank the coffee handed to her by the silent servant. With almost a whole night's sleep behind her and no new cases waiting to start the day, Laura had a better grip on what was happening inside her. The sight of Cash's lean masculine frame outlined in the doorway sent a tremble through her middle that shouldn't be there, and she had to physically fight the urge to throw herself into his arms and weep. For the first time, she saw the compassion in Cash's eyes, the dark shadows beneath his skin, and knew he was as near to breaking as herself, although not necessarily for the same reasons. Seeing him like this, not as the coolly arrogant rebel who defied society, she knew she had wronged him in some terrible way, but it was too late to correct it now.

Stiffly she gestured him toward the parlor, but he merely shook his head.

"I just came from the farm. Ward's ill. Where's Jonathan?"

It didn't take more than those few words to shatter the future. Laura sent Cash on the way with directions to Jonathan and collapsed into the nearest chair. Ward with his damaged body and weakened strength couldn't possibly stand up to the fever that had cut a wide swath through young and old. Please, Lord, don't let it be the fever.

11

Ward Breckinridge was the last victim of the yellow fever that swept so briefly through Stoner Creek that September. As they laid him to rest in the family cemetery of the farm that gave the town its name, a crowd that cut across society's lines appeared to pay their respects, despite the steady gray drizzle permeating the day.

He had been a soldier in the war that had so devastated them all. He was the son of one of the wealthiest families in the county. He was the husband of one of the most beautiful women in a society known for its beautiful women. He had lived here all his life, had crossed the path of everyone in the area, and everyone came to acknowledge his passing. If they mourned the passing of more than the man in the coffin, no one had the words to express it.

Sallie wept dramatically behind her veil of black as the rain beat down around her. Ward's family stood cold and stiff at her side, huddling under umbrellas. Laura stood aloof, with only Jonathan squarely by her side. When the first clods of dirt fell hollowly against the wooden coffin and the crowd turned toward the house, the layers of society seemed to split apart around these two islands of grief as they paid their respects. The planters and their wives and families naturally gravitated toward Sallie and the Breckinridges. The servants and the townspeople and the merchants stopped to offer their condolences to Laura, as if Sallie were too far from their reach.

Only Cash managed to somehow bridge both. Coming to stand by Laura's side, he offered the protection of his umbrella and took her arm, firmly steering her toward the dwindling crowd around Sallie, leaving Jonathan to bring up her other side. Guarded on both flanks by respectability, Cash offered his hand in sorrow to Ward's family, saying the proper words to express his grief and theirs. If any of the Breckinridges were startled, they were too polite or overcome with emotion to show it, and the guests that remained were treated to the sight of Cash Wickliffe walking side by side with Sallie Kincaid Breckinridge as the family turned toward the house.

Masses of food had been imported to serve the overflowing crowd, but Laura didn't have the heart to touch it. She escaped to the study where Ward had slept and stayed all these long months, but it seemed somehow hollow, and she couldn't find the security of his presence there as she had hoped. The ledgers sitting on the desk were just pieces of paper, and the writing inside them bore no part of the gallant gentleman who had scribbled it. The silk hat hanging on the stand was just another object to collect dust and not the rakish chapeau that once sat like a crown upon a golden-haired king.

As she turned to leave, a rustle from the corner startled her, and Laura swung around to find Jettie Mae clinging to an abandoned frock coat, tears streaming down her cheeks. It didn't take any thought for the two women to come together in each other's arms, their grief shaking them with previously unshed tears as they found sympathetic shoulders.

Jettie's sobs didn't lessen, but increased as Laura gradually regained control and tried to console her. Laura knew very little about the saucy "nurse" who had been closer to Ward than anyone else these last months. From her actions the night of the Raiders, Laura knew her to be brave and loyal and not a little reckless. From what she had seen of the woman with her children, she knew her to be a good mother. But the fact that Jettie had obviously borne more than one child by men not her husband and had easily agreed to be Ward's mistress stood between them like a fence without a gate. They came from two different worlds, but the grief between them served as a bond of communication.

"Hush, Jettie, it doesn't do any good to cry. He's gone, and tears can't bring him back. He wouldn't want you to grieve like this, would he?" Laura tried to reassure herself with these phrases. She didn't know what Ward would have wanted. She had never tried to understand him, any more than she had anyone else. It was a failing she had, she knew. She had given him words to describe him and file him in her mind, words like "brave" and "gallant" and "handsome" when he had dated Sallie, "weak" and "hurt" but still "gallant" when he allowed Sallie to trample over him. But Ward had been much more than that, and she had never tried to find that out.

"No, no, he was a gentleman, he was," Jettie sobbed into Laura's shoulder, still holding the coat as if it would bring him back. Sniffing and trying to control her sobs, she offered her memory of him: "You know what he said when he found out about the baby? He said he was tickled pink. Tickled pink. Can you fancy that? Here he was, the most handsome man I ever did see, and he was tickled pink that I got his bun in the oven. He was just as proud as if I was that fluffed-up wife of his."

The words choked on sobs, but Laura heard them well enough to understand and feel a jolt she wasn't certain was horror or joy. Ward had actually fathered a child. She glanced down at the bent head on her shoulder and realized Jettie Mae wasn't any bigger than she. And she was going to have Ward's baby. The shock rippling through her was followed by something else, something stronger and more fierce.

Laura gripped Jettie's shoulders and forced her to stand up and face her. "You're having Ward's baby?" Even as she asked, her gaze swept downward to look for the evidence in the swelling beneath Jettie's starched apron, but it was too early yet. She took a deep breath and looked up in time to catch the maid's defensive expression.

"I thought he'd told you, he's that proud. But don't think I 'spect nothing, 'cause I don't. He took care of me, he did, and treated me like a real lady. He wanted to see the baby so bad . . ." Tears spilled over, and Jettie turned frantically away, her shoulders shaking with the sobs she had just fought off.

Laura touched her shoulder, trying to find some way to say the words the woman needed to hear, not knowing

what they were. "Don't you think maybe he's watching
from somewhere up above? Surely God wouldn't be so
cruel as to keep him from seeing his only child. I know
Ward would want that more than anything. And I know
what else he would have wanted." Laura said that firmly,
with resolution as the idea formed in her mind. She knew
beyond a shadow of a doubt that Jettie was telling the
truth about Ward's pride. Everyone had thought him half
a man since he had returned from the war. The child in
Jettie's womb proved them all wrong. If Sallie wouldn't
give him what he wanted, this woman had. That child
would have been every bit as precious to Ward as Sallie's
would have. There was only one thing that could be done
under those circumstances. She owed Ward's memory
that much.

Jettie brought her tears under control once more, and
wiping her eyes on the coat, turned to face the determined white woman who continued to touch her as if she
were a real person and not a piece of trash. She liked
the sounds of Laura's words, but she was suspicious of
any kindness beyond what was required. "You think he
really will know when this baby's born? Maybe he'll go
to that other place for planting this here seedling."

Laura's mouth twisted wryly at that thought. "Well,
then, we'll all go to join him when it comes time. There
aren't many saints on this earth. But I prefer to think a
man like Ward Breckinridge has done enough good in
his life to cover a few sins. And I think he would want
his child to have everything he would have offered had
he stayed here. The farm doesn't belong to me, and it
isn't worth much anymore in any case, but this is where
Ward's child ought to grow up. Sallie won't understand
that, but I can make her see that you ought to stay. I
don't think she'll have a lot of choice. She'll treat you
like a servant and won't pay you, but I've survived like
that for all these years. It's not a bad life if you learn to
get around her. It's better than looking for another man
to pay your way, isn't it?"

Jettie's suspicious expression gradually faded as she
felt the brunt of Laura's honesty. The hint of mischief
that had once lit her eyes flickered briefly as this speech
ended, and she offered Laura her callused hand. "You
got a wicked tongue, Miss Laura. Watch out someone

don' snatch it from yoah head. I'll take the notion into consideration"—her grin widened at this mimicry of one of Ward's favorite phrases—"and let you know what I think. This is a mighty fancy place for the likes of me, but you're right in one thing: it's better than what else I got to offer. There ain't never gonna be 'nother man like Mr. Ward in this world."

They both knew it was decided then, although Jettie's pride wouldn't allow her to admit it immediately. Combating the sadness and bewilderment that was gradually replacing her first despair, Laura shook the maid's hand and left Jettie to the privacy of Ward's study. She wasn't certain what was wrong with her, but the tranquillity she had been feeling since her return to Stoner Creek was evaporating, being replaced by a rage of emotions without logic or solution. Why on earth should she feel fiercely protective toward a black servant who was no better than a paid prostitute? And why should she be so furious with the cousin who had offered her house and home after all these years? And why did she despair over the passing of a man who had scarcely acknowledged her existence other than to use it to his own advantage?

Hurting, but not quite knowing why, Laura sought out Jonathan. He was her security, her shelter in the storm. If she could only talk to him, he would make her understand what was happening inside of her. Never had there been anyone she could talk to, really talk to. It would be good to have a man like Jonathan, who could listen when she needed him.

In searching for Jonathan, Laura stumbled across Cash, but he didn't notice her. In a room full of grieving relatives and whiskey-swilling, garrulous men, he stood like a beacon of peace, his head bent respectfully to hear the words tumbling from the woman at his side. That the woman who held his attention was her cousin Sallie should come as no shock, but Laura felt it like a blow to the stomach.

Not questioning why she felt this way, she turned from the parlor and sought the stairs. Cash had never made any secret of his admiration for the golden-haired Kincaid princess. All men coveted Sallie. That Laura had somehow thought that she and Cash were partners in the world outside Sallie's circle should have no bearing on anything. Cash had always been a private part of her life, a part no one but themselves knew or understood. But that didn't mean she had any claim on him. This feeling of gross betrayal was just another example of the confusion overwhelming her right now.

Laura found Jonathan in the foyer, saying his farewells to Ward's mother. At Laura's arrival, Mrs. Breckinridge nodded stiffly and swayed from the room, her heavy black skirts tilting over the wire-rimmed crinoline as she maneuvered through the doorway. Finding herself suddenly alone with the man she sought, Laura grasped Jonathan's outstretched hand with relief.

"Take me with you, Jonathan. I can't stay here. I just can't. Please."

To his credit, Jonathan didn't raise his eyebrows in shock or surprise. He merely searched her tear-streaked face and nodded briefly. "If you're certain, Laura. We can't shock the town any more than we already have. It would be best if we married discreetly as soon as possible, in any case. I hope you didn't have your heart set on a large wedding."

He coughed over his last words, taking out a large handkerchief to hold it to his lips, diverting Laura's attention from the argument that rose inside her to the more practical needs of the moment. "You're ill! You shouldn't have been out in that rain. You haven't had any sleep in days. If there were any room left in the house at all, I'd put you to bed right now."

Her gentle scolding brought a smile to Jonathan's lips. "Come home and pamper me there. I'll keep well enough until then."

The warmth behind his words held a promise Laura wasn't certain she was ready to accept, but hearing the noise and confusion behind her, knowing the hollowness that would be left when the crowd departed, she clung to the security of Jonathan's presence and took the cloak he offered.

Unaware of the man who had come to stand in the shadows of the parlor doorway, Laura swept out of the house in the protection of Jonathan's hold, braving the rain and the cold rather than stay within the confines of the brightly lit rooms of Stoner Creek. It was a farewell of sorts, although none of them knew it.

The man in the shadows gave a wry salute to the couple hastening into the weather and turned back to the welcoming glitter of the Kincaid salon. He'd had enough of shadows and cold and damp. The promise of a new day beckoned, and he would be there when the sun rose.

Jonathan laughed when Laura insisted that he drink a hot posset and take a hot bath and go directly to bed. He took the steaming mug from her hands, admired the flush on her cheeks caused by the kitchen fire where she had been boiling his bathwater, and bent a kiss to the moist curls on her forehead.

"I'll agree to your terms if you promise to accompany me. You are as exhausted and chilled as I am. I'm not looking to be mothered, Laura, and I trust you're not looking to be fathered. Come here and share this drink with me."

His touch on her shoulder spoke of what he meant, and Laura felt butterflies light in her stomach as she glanced nervously at the narrow sofa in front of the parlor fire. Jettie Mae's mother had gone home, and they were there alone, a fact she had not considered in her impulsive escape. It didn't suit her to be skittish about something that was inevitable, but instinct warned this was not the right time for what he had in mind. Jonathan had tried to hide his cough as they rode toward town, but it didn't sound a healthy cough to her. Obediently she followed him toward the old sofa, but she kept his hand in hers, where it was safe.

When she refused to share his drink, Jonathan sipped at it and regarded her burnished hair with a mixture of elation and confusion. Coming here with him meant that she was ready to take him as husband in every sense of the word, and he would scarcely be a man if that thought didn't excite him. It had been a long time since a feminine form had graced his parlor, and he had strong memories of a woman's arms around him in this place, arms that had clung to him as he carried her off to bed. But something in the way Laura's face averted from his and her hand held his stiffly between them warned that all was not as it should be.

"It's been a long and draining day, my love. I'll not press you for what you are not ready to give, but

wouldn't it be better if you learned to turn to me instead
of inside yourself at times like these?"

The concern in Jonathan's voice made Laura want to
weep, and she hated herself for the weakness. All her
life she had stood on her own. Why had she thought she
needed someone to support her now? But what choice
had she? She could return to being Sallie's personal servant, attempt to live alone on her income as a seamstress
if the town could ever forgive the scandal, or she could
marry this man who held her in respect and admiration.
Only a fool would choose other than the latter. She
straightened her shoulders and turned to meet Jonathan's
gaze.

"I don't think I want you to see what is in my eyes. I
have never let anyone know what is inside me, and I fear
to reveal myself now would be to frighten you away. At
the same time, I don't think I can go on living like this.
I'm not at all what you think, Jonathan. I think it would
be better if I gave back your ring until I have the courage
to be honest with you."

Jonathan had expected anything but this. As Laura
struggled with the ring on her finger, he stayed her hand,
clasping it firmly until she looked up to him. The emptiness in her eyes frightened him just a little, but he fought
back the fear. "I think you are suffering from nothing
more than the usual wedding-night shivers. I will admit
to having my own fears too. I'm nearly fifteen years older
than you, a gap of experience that looms wide at times
like this. You have barely begun to see the world, and I
feel as if I've seen everything there is to see. What happens when I grow old and crippled and you are still
young and beautiful? But there are worse things to worry
about when choosing a lifetime partner. If that is all we
have to fear, we are much better off than most."

Laura heard Jonathan's reassurances and wasn't reassured. He didn't understand. She was not certain that
she understood. She hadn't meant to say anything. The
fact that the words had escaped her without premedita-
tion frightened her more than anything else she had
done. She was not a creature of impulse. She thought
long and carefully over every move. She had considered
this marriage for weeks, and had consented only because
she had considered every other alternative and found

none. But that day with Cash had destroyed something inside her, some confidence that she had allowed to build, and she was too shattered to gather the pieces and put them back together again.

A tear rolled down her cheek, and Laura wiped it away irritably. "There is much more than the difference in our ages to worry about. That never concerned me. What concerns me is how willingly I have concealed the truth from you. I'm not a liar by nature, but I have gone to extremes I never thought possible to hide myself from you. That scarcely seems a promising basis for marriage. I think I have been using you, Jonathan, and I don't like myself very much. It might be best if I went to stay with someone else for the night. This is something that would be better discussed with clear heads in the morning."

Jonathan almost laughed at the sincerity in her voice. Setting aside his mug, he caught her shoulders and twisted her to face him. "The chilling honesty of youth; it's been a long time since I've heard it. Why must everything be black and white to the young? There is no such thing, you know, Laura. We're all shades of gray, no matter how well-intentioned we might be when we start out. Whatever awful secrets you can possibly harbor can wait until morning. Why don't you let me be the judge of what we should do tonight?"

With those words he took her in his arms and covered her protests with his kiss. There was a kind of desperation in his touch that warned and warmed Laura at the same time. She responded to it as well as she could, but it wasn't the same. She clung to his shoulders, parted her lips, met his tongue in the enticing dance that Cash had taught her, but she felt nothing more passionate than warmth and sorrow. She even allowed him to unfasten the buttons of her bodice in hopes that the touch of his hand would restore the ardor she had felt that wet day in the barn, but though her body rose to Jonathan's touch, her heart didn't respond. Where was the thunder she remembered? Where were the lightning and the fire and the clash of two bodies born asunder and determined to become one?

She had done the unforgivable, and now she must pay. Catching Jonathan's hand, Laura brought it to her lips and kissed the palm. When she had his full attention, she asked, "What would you say if you knew I had never been married?"

Jonathan stopped at once, his head coming up to stare deep into her eyes, and his soul gave a shudder at what he found there. The light was back, but it was a bitter light. His aroused body protested it didn't care, but he was a man of mind more than body, and he knew Laura expected more from him than an onslaught of the senses after this declaration. Thoughtfully he glanced down at the creamy skin of her breasts shimmering in the firelight, admiring the swelling foothills and the valley in between, aching to uncover the peaks. Instead, he pulled her bodice closed and began to button it.

"I'd say I have no business forcing you into a decision you're not ready to make. I'm no good at seduction, Laura. I want a woman willing to be my wife. If you're not ready for that yet, perhaps we had better talk."

Disappointment welled up in her. She didn't know what she had hoped, but it wasn't this reasonable response. Her skin still hungered to be touched, even if the fire and passion were lacking. Perhaps they were both tired, and the thunder would come later. Discouraged, Laura turned away and finished fastening her bodice on her own.

"I'm not a virgin, Jonathan. I know what to expect. I thought that would please you, but there's a little more to it than that, isn't there?"

He touched her hair and heard the little girl in her voice and felt the chill enter his heart. "Yes, there's a little more to it than that. I suppose that rogue Marshall simply had his way with you and then left?"

Embarrassed, Laura merely stared at the fire. "He was too drunk. He just left me with his hotel bill instead. No, it's worse than that. I consented to what I did. I even encouraged it. I thought I was doing it to protect you. Do you think madness might run in the family? Or perhaps what they say about bad blood is true?"

"Who, Laura?" he encouraged quietly, feeling that the truth lay there more than in anyone's blood or family.

Laura continued to stare intently at the fire while she hesitated. But now that the truth was out, he might as well know the whole of it. It would seal the decision she had made and release him from his foolish offer. Simply she replied, "Cash," and heard his intake of breath and knew that it was over, once and for all.

12

Despite Laura's protests, Jonathan slept on the sofa. She didn't argue long. They were both exhausted and emotionally drained and neither could be sensible after her stumbling revelations. She didn't feel better for having revealed her secret, the memory still haunted her, but she was relieved of the burden of the lie to a man she loved and respected. That the knowledge had destroyed any chance of a life with Jonathan was an unpleasantness that needed time to sink in.

When she woke the next morning to the smell of coffee and bacon frying, Laura dressed hastily and hurried to the kitchen to find Jonathan already there. In shirt sleeves and waistcoat he seemed less formidable than the intellectual professional she had looked up to and admired for so long. He gave her a small grin and gestured toward the set table.

"In long years of bachelorhood I have learned a few simple skills. Let me impress you for as long as I can. If you do not mind dining in the kitchen, have a seat."

"After four years of eating off my bedside table, the kitchen is quite unexceptionable, thank you. You were supposed to sleep last night, not wake early to impress me. How is your cough?" Laura adjusted her skirts over the wooden chair. After a year of wearing black, she had just become accustomed to the colors of her old wardrobe. But out of respect to Ward she had gone back to her blacks yesterday, and the dismal effect in this sunny kitchen seemed out-of-place.

"That is a subject we may discuss after we eat." Jona-

than carried the heavy iron pan of eggs to the table, then
poured coffee from the pot bubbling at the back of the
old cook stove. A platter of toast cooked hastily over a
wire rack in the wood-burning oven and another platter
of thinly sliced bacon completed his offering. He didn't
seem to notice Laura's slight grin at the informality of
pans sitting on the table. He appropriated a chair across
from her and motioned for her to help herself. "You
are not the only one with secrets. I've had the night to
reconsider my notions of honesty, and it's time we had
a long talk. After we eat."

That had an ominous tone to it and Laura glanced at
him sharply, but Jonathan seemed to be in a cheerful
mood, and she didn't question him further. At least he
didn't despise her for what she had done. She had been
young and foolish when she had run off after Marshall,
that was understandable, but what she had done with
Cash had no such easy excuse. Jonathan had every reason to think the worst of her. But this morning he appeared somehow relieved, and she felt anxiety begin to
build as they ate.

"I've always had an urge to travel, but what with one
thing and another, I'd thought myself tied to this place."
After demolishing the better part of his meal, Jonathan
sipped at his coffee and watched Laura pick at hers.

"I understand the feeling," Laura replied wryly. She
applied jam from one of the jars Jonathan's patients frequently used as payment for his services and waited to
see where this conversational gambit would lead.

"I thought you might." Jonathan gave up any further
pretense of eating his meal and settled for watching
Laura as she delicately spread the jam and nibbled at
her toast. "I've had a letter from a colleague of mine
who's looking for a place to locate. I'm considering asking him for an offer on my practice here."

Alarmed, Laura searched his face, but he revealed
only an expectant interest in her reaction. "You want to
leave Stoner Creek? Did you intend that before . . .
when we still thought of marriage?"

He reached across the table and caught her hand. "I'm
still thinking of marriage, but I'm thinking you need
more time. And I think I owe you more time. The truth
is, Laura, if we married and stayed here as I had assumed

you wanted to do, you could be nursing an invalid some-time down the road. I've tried to take care of myself, I know the proper routine, but last week, even when I knew I was next to useless against the fever, you made me feel as if I could go out and save the world again. I haven't felt like that in years, but you brought it all back to me, and I overexerted myself like a damn young fool. Do you understand what I'm trying to say?"

From the intense expression in his gray eyes, Laura was very much afraid she did, but she wasn't at all certain she wanted to hear it. She wrapped her fingers around his long, sensitive ones and tried to sort out his various messages. "Are you telling me that you are ill? That the cough isn't just a cold from exhausting yourself last week?"

Jonathan relaxed and sat back in his chair again. "You always were quick, Laura, thank you. Do you have any idea how difficult it is to admit weakness to a beautiful woman? But I was so certain that what I had to offer was better than what Ward and Sallie had to give, that I refused to let you see any reason to doubt my abilities. I knew if I was careful I wouldn't have to be an invalid for many years, if ever. And even if that time came, I have enough set aside to keep you comfortable, and you were better off with your own home than as Sallie's un-paid servant. But after this past week I've had to face my own faults. I want to be young again. I want to be strong. And I want to be the kind of person you obvi-ously think I am. My cynical attitude works for a selfish old bachelor, but an idealistic young woman would come to despise me, and more than anything else, I find I don't want you to despise me, Laura."

This was not at all the direction that she had imagined this conversation would take. Laura fought desperately to grasp what he was trying to say. She knew it was immensely important to finally recognize that there were more layers to people than she had assigned them, and that Jonathan was trying to show her what she hadn't seen before. Nodding her head slowly, she tried to rephrase his words into sentences that showed she understood.

"I do not consider you old or any more cynical than myself, but that is not what you are telling me, is it? You are saying you have consumption, like your wife had, aren't you? And that instead of working hard as we did last week, you must rest, but because of me, you can't." She watched his face to judge the correctness of her assumptions, seeing the pain flit across his features as she hit the mark, and the wry smile quirk his lips as she reached to take back his hand. "That is foolishness, you know. I would understand. You're too valuable to be lost to needless exertion. We could go somewhere else, if you like, where they won't even know you're a doctor. Then you could rest all you need and get better."

Jonathan tugged her chair around the table corner until he could reach the hasty chignon she had pinned up this morning. He ran his fingers along the slender nape of her neck and admired the directness and sincerity in her splendid eyes. "You're a very perceptive young woman, but I don't think you know what you want well enough to consign yourself to a life nursing an invalid. I have another suggestion to make, if you will hear me out."

Laura felt a moment's panic. Now that everything was out in the open between them and she knew he did not despise her, she was ready to fling caution to the winds and go wherever he wished rather than to lose him. She couldn't bear to lose this one friend she had come to rely on for everything that was good in her life. She caught his hand and slid it to her lips, placing a kiss in his palm as a plea not to desert her.

Jonathan closed his fingers around hers and smiled. "I really think I'm a fool to give up an opportunity like this, but let me be young and idealistic just this once. I have known love and passion. I know what we have is solid and dependable, but not the romantic dream of a young woman. I was willing to settle for the loveliest, most intelligent woman of my acquaintance and to hope that love and passion might come with time. I thought you had experienced the same, but now I know you have not. I would not deny you your dream, Laura. I think there is still something between you and Cash that must be worked out, and I am willing to step out of the way until it is resolved. Knowing the two of you, I feel confident that I will come out the winner, but I want you to be as certain as I am. But in the meantime, I want to make myself into the man you deserve to have for husband. I have heard that the hot, dry air of Arizona Territory has a healing effect on consumptives. I have always wished for an opportunity to explore the Western territories. I'm not sure they're the place for a gently born woman such as yourself, but I would see for myself. If you are willing to be patient with me, I want to come back a whole man."

Tears sprang to Laura's eyes as she watched the lined features of Jonathan's narrow face and heard the intensity of his request. She hadn't realized how close they had grown until she faced the prospect of time without him. Biting her lip, she tried to be reasonable. "There can never be anything between Cash and me, you have as much as admitted it. We are too much alike in too many ways, and come from worlds so far apart that we'll never meet. It's Sallie he wants, and always has been. I daresay she's the only reason he came back or brothers to stay. What happened between us was as accidental as lightning striking, and won't happen again. If you don't despise me for what I've done, let me go with you, Jonathan. I don't mind the travel; I grew up with it."

Jonathan smiled and brushed away a tear trickling down her cheek. She was unreasonably young and much too old at the same time, and if he stood and took her in his arms right now, there would be no turning back. So he stayed where he was and did nothing more than pat the back of her hand against the table. "I know, and when the time comes, I will ask you to go with me, but not now. You deserve a whole man, and I'm determined to give you one. Don't argue, Laura." He held up his hand to halt the protest forming on her lips. "Our only problem now is how to stop the gossip when I leave you here without the wedding ceremony they're all expecting."

He was going to do it, and nothing she could say was going to stop him. Laura turned her head away and pulled her hands back into her lap. She supposed he was right, but she had suffered enough partings to know this one could be permanent as well. On the heels of Ward's death, she wasn't certain she could handle it gracefully. She didn't want to be left alone anymore, and she fought back the wails of protest building inside her. Not Jonathan. Not solid, dependable Jonathan. Please, God, don't let him be taken away too. The thought that he could be going somewhere more permanent than Arizona Territory pressed far more desperately through her thoughts than her own disgrace.

"You needn't worry about that. I'll stay with Sallie and try to run the farm. There isn't a man in Stoner Creek who would be interested enough in me now that Sallie's a widow, to make gossip a problem."

She glanced up in surprise at the anger in Jonathan's reply.

"You'll not be returning to the farm. You'll stay here, in my house, where you can be your own woman and not Sallie's servant, if I have to marry you to make you do it."

A hint of a smile touched Laura's lips at the forcefulness in Jonathan's usually mild voice, and she turned back to him. "That will certainly end the problem of any man who might be interested in me. Wouldn't it just be simpler to take me with you?"

Jonathan drew his hand through his hair and gave her a wry grin. "I guess I want to have my cake and eat it too. All right, let me speak to a few people, explain my situation, and see if they won't protect you from the worst of the gossip, leastways. If I go, this house will need someone in it, and I'd just as soon it be you. I'll cough and look pitiful and the good people of Stoner Creek will rise to the occasion. Despite everything, there are good people here, Laura."

There were good people and bad people, just as in any place. There would be gossip, and there would be those who would pull their skirts aside and cross to the other side of the road before speaking with her. But Laura knew who her friends were, and though they were limited in number, they would not scorn her. She had always lived on the outskirts of society in any case. If she didn't live at the farm, she wouldn't even have to make the pretense of being part of them. She could survive, one way or the other. The sad part was that she was tired of just surviving. She wanted to live, and she looked at Jonathan wistfully.

"Are you certain you could not take me with you? I

won't even ask you to marry me. I promise not to be a hindrance."

Jonathan looked at the delicate curve of her pale cheek, the ladylike sweep of her thick hair, and the feminine and exceedingly slender curves hidden beneath the black cloth, and shook his head slowly. "That's too much temptation to offer a man, Laura. I want to protect you, not destroy you. I'm not doing such a good job of it so far. Let me make another stab at it. Wear my ring, live in my house, write to me as often as you can, and I'll be back before you know it. Maybe by then you'll be ready to take me as husband."

They were back to that again. Laura felt the heat rise in her cheeks and looked away. If she hadn't stopped him last night, if she had shown more passion . . . Perhaps she ought to try again now, before he set his mind to leaving. But he was already rising and preparing to go, and as much as she loved him, she could not make herself follow and go into his arms as a wife to her husband. She had offered herself to Cash for this man's sake. Why in heaven's name could she not offer herself to Jonathan for her own sake, and for his?

The awful truth of it burned humiliatingly through her center. Refusing to believe it, Laura rose and followed Jonathan to the parlor, where he donned his coat. She kissed him with as much vigor as she could summon and felt his response, but it wasn't enough. He smiled sadly, chucked her chin, and walked out after extracting her promise to send for her belongings. There would be no returning to the sticky web of Stoner Creek, but she could envision no future either.

Cash was the one who came bearing Laura's possessions in a few ragged trunks. She didn't want to think about how Sallie had come to call on her new neighbor for this duty. She ignored the question in his nearly black eyes as she thanked him for carrying the cases in, and she left Jonathan to deal with him as she retreated to the bedroom under the excuse of unpacking.

It was apparent that Jettie Mae had done the packing. Instead of the few crushed petticoats Laura owned besides the cast-off crinoline she was wearing, a new petticoat and crinoline that Sallie had decided didn't suit her gowns engulfed the first trunk that she opened. Sallie would never miss the garments, but she never would have considered packing them, either. The other trunks revealed similar surprises, and Laura was smiling by the time she had rifled through them. The only black Jettie had allowed her was the one she was wearing. And she suspected the only reason the gray had been allowed was for the extravagant lace trimming and the fine silk of the shirt, for it had once hung in Sallie's wardrobe too.

When Jonathan called her, Laura rose and entered the parlor with the smile still lingering on her lips. To her surprise, Cash was still there. The smile fled and her cheeks paled as she saw the expression on the faces of both men, but Jonathan smoothed the way with perfect calm.

"The youngest Chatham boy has fallen out of a tree and broken his wrist. I'm going to ride over there for a bit. Cash has some messages from Sallie for you, so I'll leave you to entertain him, if you don't mind." There was nothing in his look or voice to say anything more than his words, and he kissed her cheek before he parted, just as if she truly were his wife.

Laura scarcely saw him go. She was too busy avoiding the man filling the space of the small parlor. Cash was wearing a fawn frock coat today, with a gold-and-white-striped waistcoat and tan trousers. He needed only a gold watch fob and a silk top hat to complete the image of wealthy planter, but instead, he carried that light-colored Stetson and wore boots that showed evidence of having walked a field not too long before. It was touches like these that set him apart in her mind, reminding her that he was not all that he seemed. And neither was she.

Calling upon the ingrained etiquette of her upbringing, Laura gestured toward a chair. "Won't you sit down? I'll fetch some coffee if you'll wait a minute."

"Don't trouble yourself." His voice was as deep and warm and full of life as she remembered it. "I won't keep you a minute."

Laura forced her features to a polite expression of interest as she finally met his eyes. "I trust Sallie is not too disappointed in me. I know she will never understand, but I don't wish hard feelings between us."

Cash perused her face as he would a book, his gaze lingering on the telltale redness at the corners of her eyes, the shadows of her cheeks, and the slight quiver of her lip. "I don't suppose you'll explain any of this better than Doc. You belong at the farm, Laura. That's your home. Why are you running away this time?"

"You'll not believe me even if I could explain or understood it myself. Just take Jonathan's word and leave it at that. If Sallie's angry with me, she'll get over it. She always does." When she wants something, Laura added in her mind, but there was no sense in disillusioning Cash about the golden girl he envisioned. He would find out soon enough, and she suspected it wouldn't matter.

"She's too upset to be angry. Now isn't exactly the time to be deserting her. I don't understand you, Laura. I thought you were grateful to be home again. Would it hurt to stay at the farm a little longer, just until Sallie knows what she's doing? All you've succeeded in doing is causing a scandal. And now Doc says you're not getting married. I think you owe me a little more explanation."

If possible, Cash's eyes had darkened, and Laura could almost feel the anger in him. What right had he to be angry? Crossing her arms across her chest, Laura backed away from that all-knowing gaze and returned his glare with false bravado. "I cannot imagine why. Jonathan and I are both adults capable of making decisions on our own without the aid of anyone else, and you're certainly in no position to tell us what to do. I had hoped you would stand our friend in this, but no one is asking you to do anything. I will be happy to help Sallie in any way, but you can be certain that the Breckinridges will be much more efficient at operating the farm than I am, and they will be only too happy to step in. I will only be in their way."

A gleam of enlightenment began to shine behind the obsidian of Cash's eyes. "I see. You and Sallie's in-laws have never been on the best of terms, have you?" Cash offered a tentative smile as she stiffened and looked away. "And now Doc decides to be honest for the first time in his wicked life and leave you to your own devices. I'm sorry, Laura. I didn't mean to add to your troubles. Will you forgive me?"

She steeled herself against the tears threatening to erupt at the sympathetic tone of his voice. She didn't want his sympathy. She didn't know what she wanted from him, but it certainly wasn't sympathy. Clenching her hands together until her nails dug into her palms, Laura met his gaze. "There is nothing to forgive. I thank you for bringing my trunks. Will you accept some coffee now, or did you have other errands to do?"

She was dismissing him with all the grace and command of a queen—a tiny, irate, brokenhearted queen. Cash felt the tug of the bond between them, and he couldn't resist holding out his hand, tilting her fragile chin upward until he could read the flash of green and gold in her glare. "I know a gentleman would forget and never mention what happened between us, Laura, but we can both agree that I'm no gentleman. If that is what has come between you and Jonathan, I expect you to tell me, because Doc won't. I can make him understand what happened where a lady might be reluctant to."

Laura shook her head free from his touch, ignoring the painful longing inside her to be held by this man who cared nothing for her. "That has nothing to do with anything, Cash. And if you're no gentleman, I'm no lady, and I'm quite capable of doing my own talking. We're still betrothed, and we'll still marry. He simply has some foolish notion that he doesn't want me to be nursing an invalid. You might try to dissuade him of that, if you wish—otherwise, there is nothing else to be done."

Cash frowned slightly at the evasion he heard in her voice, but her words were sensible and what he wanted to hear, so he let it go. He gave a sardonic grin as he lifted his hat in parting. "I'll tell him I'll woo you and win you if he doesn't have the sense to take you with him. See if that doesn't get some action out of him."

He thought he was making her feel better, but as Cash placed his hat on his head and walked out the door, Laura felt worse than she had ever done in her life. Watching his straight proud back walk away from her, the Stetson tilted at a rakish angle over his ebony hair, she thought she just might die of the anguish and the shame burning through her.

Would she never learn from her mistakes? Or would she spend the rest of her life repeating them? Cash was not for her, would never be for her. Unless she wanted to be his mistress. That she even considered that possibility was the source of the pain that filled her breast as she closed the door after him.

13

Grinning to himself, Cash took the wide veranda steps to the old Watterson house two at a time. Inside the foyer of his new home, he threw his hat in the direction of the hall tree and whistled a note of greeting. His boots resounded loudly on the planked floor as he strode toward the newly resurrected kitchens at the rear of the house.

He hated this house. Built around a two-room log cabin, it had no style or grace, not to mention anything so prosaic as modern conveniences. He had ordered the new kitchen connected by a covered breezeway so his food wouldn't arrive cold at the table, but there was no indoor plumbing and the privy out back served as a deterrent to any large-scale entertaining. Trying to install anything resembling plumbing through the two-foot-thick log walls inside their plaster-and-clapboard casings was an undertaking he was not yet ready to tackle. He still had hopes of better things to come.

Which was why he was whistling as he strode through the breezeway to see if there was a cut of cold meat and some buttermilk to tide him over to dinner. He was a sight better off than he had been in his youth, so he couldn't complain, but he wasn't content yet. He wouldn't be happy until he had all his dreams properly in place, and at the moment they seemed to be stacking up nicely. There was still a chance they might come to nothing. The whim of a woman could never be relied on. But he had confidence in his own abilities. He would bring her around, one way or another.

As he chewed on the bread and cheese the cook handed him, Cash returned to his study and his desk and the ledgers that told him just exactly where he stood in everything but the one thing money couldn't buy. Swinging his boots up to the desk, he pored over the ledgers as if they were a Bible from which he took his lessons.

He wouldn't sell the California ranch just yet. He still had income from other sources to keep him in funds, despite the constant drain from the improvements on the Watterson farm. The town thought him wealthy, and he went to a lot of trouble to keep them thinking that, but there was a limit to everything. By anyone's standards, he had made good, but he intended to do even better.

Throwing back his head to rest on the high leather chair, Cash stared at a cobweb dangling from the distant ceiling. Energy charged through him, energy that he could turn to a number of different uses besides sitting in this chair and daydreaming. But just for a moment he wanted to savor the prize that awaited him if he played his cards right.

He was a natural-born gambler; there was no mistaking that. But he had learned to control the fever, knew how to play the odds, knew when to walk away. He had all the cards this time, and he gloated over them for a little while. He was young, healthy, with all his wits about him, in a country bereft of men, young or old. He had money to spend in an economy still torn and bleeding from the onslaughts of war. He knew the ladies liked to look at him. His mixed blood could be a blessing as well as a curse in that it gave him the darkly exotic look that women seemed to favor. Of course, the gambler's blood and the touch of tar that gave him these advantages also worked against him. They were the jokers in the deck that he had to watch out for. But on the whole, his wealth and his looks weighed heavier under present circumstances.

He reached for a cheroot and allowed a sardonic grin to lift the corners of his mouth. "Under present circumstances" said a mouthful. Before the war, the women would have looked at him as if he were a creature from the wild, a savage to be watched with curiosity but never allowed past the front step. His weren't the classically handsome features of the gallant white knights of Sir Walter Scott's tales, but the harsh, lined features of a rogue. But add the hint of gentlemanly sideburns, a stylish coat, and a polite bow, and he was suddenly acceptable, for lack of anyone better to compare him to. The war had put an end to the exclusivity of polite society.

Cash had only to consider his courtship of Sallie Kincaid Breckinridge to know the truth of that. He wouldn't forget the cool disgust in her eyes when he had first pushed his way into her drawing room. But that look had slowly disappeared as he had displayed his best manners, played the part of charming gallant, flattered her as she had been accustomed to being flattered. He'd had a few years' practice since he had seen her last, and she hadn't been prepared for it. But he had been prepared for her.

Just the thought of having Sallie Kincaid in his bed and Stoner Creek Farm as his home was sufficient reason to burn all his energy in their pursuit. He would know he had succeeded when he laid down that winning hand. Stoner Creek would belong to a Wickliffe, then, and his sons would work those lands. They would have what he had never had from this town—respect.

All that was almost within his reach. Glancing at the calendar, Cash marked the date. December 24, Christmas Eve. He pulled out the desk drawer to admire the Christmas gift he meant to present to the Widow Breckinridge. He knew it was too soon. Ward had barely been in his grave three months. But he would only show it to her, let her think about it. The glitter of that diamond would give Sallie plenty to think about in the next month or so while her brother-in-law argued over the allowance she demanded. Ward's brother wasn't the lovesick fool that Ward had been. He knew the farm didn't have any resources to meet Sallie's demands. And Steve Breckinridge wasn't about to dip into his own to supply his sister-in-law with the frills and furbelows that she required. But Cash could.

He reckoned it would take only another month before Sallie would surrender to the inevitable. Maybe not even

that long. She was bored with staying home, forbidden
the outlets of all the holiday partying out of respect to
her mourning. She couldn't fill her boredom with shopping, since she had already exhausted her quarterly allowance. Besides, she hated black and buying black.
Cash had already been the recipient of all these confidences, and he had relished them quietly, knowing just
how to use them.

When she heard his proposal, she would be watering
at the mouth. She wouldn't accept outright, pride would
forbid that. She was a Kincaid, after all, and he was
white trash. But he was rich trash, trash who could give
her all she craved, take her away to places where she
had never been, where they wouldn't take note if she
laughed and played all night long. And when it came
down to it, trash called to trash, and she would give in.

Cash used the heel of his hand to adjust himself more
comfortably in his tight trousers as his body responded
to the mental images he was creating. By the new year
of 1866 he would have Sallie Kincaid as his bride and
Stoner Creek Farm as his own. He'd never had many
Christmas presents, but this was one worth waiting for.

Remembering another gift hidden in his drawer, Cash
drew it out and considered it more thoughtfully. Anything too personal would not be proper and would be
refused, if he judged his little Laura rightly. But he suspected her Christmases had been as bleak as his in the
past, and he wanted to do something to brighten this
one. He could afford to be generous with all the future
held out for him. But she would never accept much more
than a token plus a little of his time. The ivory combs
would set off the golden highlights of her thick café au-
lait hair. She ought to have something pretty to show off
those thick honey lengths.

He didn't know if she would be going out to the Breckinridges' for Christmas dinner, and in any case, it
wouldn't be politic to present her with a gift beneath
Sallie's nose. There was time to ride into town and back
before dinner.

Were he a lesser man, he would be considering reliev-
ing the ache in his loins with the passionate little
"widow" who had welcomed him once before. But as he
saddled his horse, Cash only remembered that day with

a broad smile. Little Laura had the makings of a full-grown, sensuous woman, but she belonged to Doc, and Cash owed Jonathan Broadbent his life. The clever little monkey had known that when she had bedded him, known that he would not go back to her again out of loyalty to Jonathan once he found out about the engagement. So he knew better than to pursue her, but he could still hold fond memories. The thunderstorm had added to one of the most erotic experiences of his life.

Cash let the memory of Laura's face as he had last seen it return, and he frowned slightly at the image. She had not seemed well, and he was concerned about her, although she wouldn't let him express it. Surely by now the worst of the gossip had subsided. The whole town was talking about the violence of the Raiders and the outrages perpetrated in the name of justice by the Regulators. The fact that Doc Broadbent had gone to Arizona Territory to cure his consumption, leaving his fiancée behind, was a subject that had been hashed to death. There were those who said Laura Kincaid was no better than she should be for staying with Doc while the yellow fever was in town, but there were too many who had felt the benefit of her healing hands for this talk to go far. Jonathan had covered his trail well, building up a wall of protection around his young betrothed until the town had taken her in as one of their own. So it shouldn't be gossip that caused the drawn look under her eyes.

In the interest of returning all Laura's little favors, Cash presented himself on Jonathan Broadbent's doorstep that Christmas Eve, package in hand. He admired the scrubbed cleanliness of the small painted porch, the hand-tied wreath of evergreen, holly, and pine cones on the door, and the welcoming candle in the window. Perhaps Laura did not outshine her beautiful cousin, but she knew how to make a man feel at home.

Laura opened the door and gaped momentarily in surprise at the sight of the tall booted figure on her step. The cold wind had burnished Cash's dark cheeks to a brisk shine and blown his black hair into a tangle at his nape, but the elegance of his long navy coat and tight buckskins distracted from his wild appearance, rather like a wolf in sheep's clothing, she surmised.

"Cash! Is something wrong out at the farm? I wasn't expecting you."

He doffed his hat, and those penetrating eyes scanned her face, even as his normally taut features softened into a smile. "There's nothing wrong at the farm. Can't a fellow come to call just because he wants to? Are you going to let me in, Laura, or am I going to have to stand here and make a fool of myself on your doorstep?"

Immediately apologetic, Laura ushered him in. It was akin to inviting in a hurricane, but the fresh rush of wind and pent-up energy that was Cash Wickliffe added life to her sober walls, and she hid her nervousness at his presence behind her gladness. "Come in. Let me take your hat. Take a seat and let me fetch you something to drink. I've discovered Jonathan's secret hoard of liquor, if you'd like a bit of bourbon to take the chill off."

Cash threw his hat on the nearest chair and started for the kitchen at the rear of the house. "I found where he hides it when I was a kid. I doubt that his habits have changed. I can fetch my own; you needn't wait on me. Are you going out to the Breckinridges' for Christmas dinner?"

He threw this last over his shoulder as he reached to the top of the pantry cupboard and brought down the bottle hidden there. Making himself at home, he found a glass in the cabinet and poured a finger or two while Laura found cup and saucer and made herself some tea.

"I hadn't planned on it. Some of the ladies at the church are putting together a little dinner and entertainment for the children who lost their parents during the fever. I told them I'd help out, since I didn't have family of my own to tend to. Have you persuaded Sallie to invite you?"

Laura knew that was what was on his mind. Odd, how she had really known Cash well for only a few months, and then only in passing, but she knew how his mind worked. She smiled furtively as he threw off his fancy coat and sat down at the kitchen table as if he were the family she had just claimed not to have. She had forgotten this had been his home for some years. Jonathan had always had a tendency to collect strays.

"I didn't want to intrude, but I'll be there afterward. I reckon Steve will be more than ready for me to come along and take her off his hands before dark. He and Sallie aren't getting along too well these days."

Laura laughed at this understatement. Settling at the table across from him with her tea, she tried not to study the intensity of Cash's gaze or the strength of his rough fingers as they lifted the glass. This was Jonathan's friend, no more. She had to keep telling herself that, even as she felt the queasiness rise in her stomach. It had taken her some time to recognize it for what it was, and she hadn't had much time to contemplate what she was going to do about it, but she knew better now than to rely on anyone but herself to take care of her problems. So she answered Cash lightly, in the same vein as his words.

"It doesn't take much to please Sallie. I must say, I thought Stephen a better gentleman than that. All he need do is tell her how pretty she looks and why doesn't she wear that charming gray gown he remembers. Just offering her the excuse to discard black would make her deliriously happy for a few weeks, at least. Then he could offer to send her to Lexington to stay with the cousins for a while, and before anyone knew it, it would be spring. Stephen has grown greedy and blind with age."

Cash leaned his elbow over his chair back and shook his head over such cynicism from so prim and proper a little mouse. "You have a naughty tongue, Miss Laura. Sallie isn't quite that weak between the ears. She's shrewd, and she knows what she wants, and she knows how to get it. Honesty and directness are seldom the best policy when you're not in a position to wield them. And don't give me that disapproving look, Miss Kincaid. You know as well as I do that you've played the part of docile, obedient cousin for years, when what you really are is a sharp-tongued rebel. Now, don't let's quarrel. I've brought you a bribe to keep you docile and obedient for just a little while longer."

Despite the painful accuracy of his accusation, Laura couldn't help but laugh at Cash's wheedling tone. She took the small box he offered and with a smile stroked the pretty satin ribbon binding it. Cash looked more eager boy than bitter man as he sat there watching her expectantly, and it was much easier to fall into the spirit of Christmas than to brood over the dismal future ahead.

"I ought to save this for tomorrow," she teased, just to watch his black eyebrows draw down in a forbidding frown. How was it possible to know just precisely what it took to draw his ire? "But I won't."

"I should have brought you something shameful just for that," Cash warned, but the sight of the teasing glints in her eyes took any sting from his words. It was good to see the little imp back, if just for a little while. Sometimes it seemed a shame that they had to grow up and become serious, practical adults. But her reaction to his small gift kept him in humor.

"Oh, Cash, they're so lovely! You shouldn't have. Just look, they have the most exquisite little roses carved in the corner! I've never seen the like. Oh, Cash, I'm so ashamed I haven't got anything half so nice for you."

At the tears suddenly and unexpectedly welling up in those hazel eyes, Cash experienced a moment's panic. Never had one of his ladies gone so sentimental over something so prosaic as a couple of hair combs. You'd think he'd given her the crown jewels. He wasn't certain how to deal with this development.

Leaning over the table, he dabbed at her eyes with a handkerchief. "Lord only knows, Laura, if I'd known you would get all teary-eyed over a couple of combs, I would have just brought you a box of pretty pine cones and counted myself generous. If Doc were here, he would have seen you had a lot more than that, but I didn't think I had the right to act in his place, as much fun as it might be. I just wanted to thank you some for always making me feel welcome. There aren't many in these parts who will do that."

That sobered her instantly. Laura squeezed the long brown hand holding the handkerchief, then gently twisted one of the lovely combs into the hair behind her ears. "I don't know why you came back to a place like this, Cash, when you obviously have all the world at your feet. But that's not my business. I made a little something for you. Let me get it."

Touching the lovely ornate comb lightly to be certain it was in place, Laura hurried from the kitchen and came back bearing a neatly wrapped box. There had been few with whom she exchanged gifts in these last years, and she never had money for store-bought parcels, but it

seemed only natural to prepare some things for those
who meant so much to her. Knowing that Cash, despite
his wealth, had never experienced the truly lavish holidays she had known in her uncle's home, Laura wished
she could have come up with something a little more
elaborate, but anything else would have been inappropriate. She handed the package wrapped in a scrap of muslin and adorned with bits of ribbon and lace from her
sewing box to the man at the table.

"It's not so glamorous, but if you encounter many
teary-eyed ladies, it might be useful."

Not having expected any gift at all, Cash looked both
surprised and tickled at being remembered as he accepted the obviously homemade offering. "You didn't
have to give me anything, *pequeña*. You've given me
more than I can possibly repay, as it is."

Perhaps she really ought to tell him how much he had
given her, but Laura didn't think he would be appreciative of the news. It was better to keep it this way for
now. Perhaps someday the time would come, but that
time wasn't now. She simply shook her head in disagree-
ment with his platitudes and watched as he opened her
meager gift.

The hand-sewn and neatly monogrammed handkerchiefs that emerged from the wrappings brought an ar-
rested expression of longing and something else, some
deep memory that stirred in the back of Cash's dark-
lashed eyes as he gazed at the fine handwork. Not expecting such a reaction to her small token, Laura
watched his expression with surprise and the threat of
more tears. She had never been one overly given to ex-
pressing emotion, but lately she seemed capable of crying
at the slightest whim.

She shook off the notion and inquired quietly, "Is
there something wrong, Cash? I didn't mean to offend
you. That was all I could think of."

Cash shook himself from his reverie and touched the
elegant monogramming thoughtfully. "You couldn't have
found a better present, Laura. My mother used to make
handkerchiefs like these for me when I was a boy. I
haven't had any quite the same since. I probably wasn't
as appreciative of them as I am now. Thank you for

reminding me of so many things that I was in danger of forgetting."

Laura poured him another splash of bourbon and returned to her seat. "I shouldn't think I deserve thanks for disturbing old memories. The past is over and done and best forgotten. It is the future we must consider now."

"You're wrong, Laura." Cash glanced past her head to the narrow stairs leading to the unheated loft above. "I used to sleep up there. It was hot as hell in summer, and in the winter it was cold enough to give me chilblains. But every morning I'd get up to the smell of coffee and know I could come down and eat until I was full. I'd know Kate would be smiling and Jonathan would be waiting for me with whatever chore or expedition he had in mind that day, and I'd be so damned grateful not to have to chop tobacco or drag my father from the tavern that I would have done handstands and cartwheels if they had asked it of me. I have no intention of forgetting one minute of my past, Laura. The past is what the future is built on."

There was probably a good deal of truth to that, but her past was so flimsy and negligible that it didn't sound substantial enough to support any kind of a future, so she refused to acknowledge his accuracy. She had not thought about Cash spending years of his life in that drafty loft. It gave her an odd feeling to be thinking about it now. Looking at the man, knowing what they had done together, remembering the man to whom they owed more than loyalty, Laura felt the queasiness in her stomach grow stronger, as if the intruder there protested the shallowness of its protector, and she gave her cold tea a wry look.

"That is a solemn subject for a holiday eve. I don't think I wish to contemplate it right now. Will you be attending Christmas Eve services?"

Cash laughed at this change of subject and carefully tucked one of his new handkerchiefs into his pocket. "The good folk of Stoner Creek would fall flat on their faces if I walked through that door. Are you intending to persuade Jonathan to give up his agnostic ways to accompany you to church when he returns?"

Laura watched Cash's expression consideringly. "I'll

not ask him to do anything he doesn't want to do. I'm quite capable of attending church on my own. Don't change the subject. I asked if you wished to go. Sallie usually attends Sunday-morning services, but she's not given to coming into town at night. I rather enjoy the candles and songs on Christmas Eve. If you would like to go, I'd be happy to go with you. I really don't think anyone will rise up and stone you."

Cash gave her a scowl and rocked back on his chair legs. "I haven't been to church since I attended the colored services with my mother. They tolerated me because of my mother, but I was as out-of-place there as I will be in your holy heaven. Let's not push the good townspeople too far."

Exasperated, Laura clanked down her cup and rose from the table. "You're about as colored as I am French. If you don't want to go, just say so. I'm not going to pull your hair and drag you. But if you want to go, don't give me such idiotic excuses!"

A slow grin began to turn the corners of Cash's mouth as he slowly unfolded from the chair to tower over the steaming tempest he had conjured up in this very tempting teapot. "You're one hell of a lot more French than I am colored. I understand the French have terrible tempers and wicked tongues, and it's a damn sight for sure you didn't inherit yours from the Kincaids."

Laura had half a mind to punch him, but she had never done such a thing in her life and her reasons for wanting to do so now were mixed. Instead, she let herself be seduced by the shadow of his smile. "And it's a damn sight for sure that you didn't learn your language from your mother. It's your reprehensible behavior that earns you your reputation, Cash Wickliffe, not your lovely mother's antecedents. So quit hiding behind her skirts. Kincaids attend church. If you're going to court Sallie, you'll have to accompany her to church. Wouldn't it be a sight easier all around if the good folk of Stoner Creek were accustomed to seeing you within hallowed walls before then?"

Cash's grin faded as he studied her serious face. "You mean that, don't you? You expect me to walk into that church filled with the pious citizens of this county and

let you take the bricks and arrows they'd like to sling at
me."

"I think you've got that quotation a little confused,
but no matter. If anyone slings anything, it's much more
likely to hit you than me; you're a much bigger target.
Quit being a fool, Cash. The past is gone, whatever you
say. The war destroyed it all. Reverend Hammond will
be thrilled to welcome a wealthy parishioner. The church
roof is starting to leak over the sacristy. Christmas is the
perfect time for people to forgive and forget. Generosity
abounds. Come with me."

And at the end, Cash couldn't say no. Odd, how those
great green eyes could trap him, making him act against
his better judgment. He remembered a long-ago day
when he had followed this insistent creature rather than
stealing a horse and running. Even then, she'd had the
power to command him.

Looking down at the petite package in dull plumage
who dared challenge him as no other would, Cash had
to grin and give in. He could toss her into the air as
easily as a feather. Actually, he could toss her into bed
without much more effort. Never had he a better awareness of how easily he could overpower a woman as well
as he did this one, and it wasn't just physical strength
that gave him the advantage. He knew if he held out his
hand, she would take it. He satisfied himself with just
the knowledge, however; he didn't need to experiment.

But despite his strength, in the end Cash fell victim to
a conviction greater than his own, never quite understanding how she did it.

14

By mid-January the morning sickness had subsided sufficiently for Laura to feel normal again, if ever she could feel normal again. At the moment, resentment tinged any effort at rational thought. Why was it that she could spend all of her entire life in obedience and propriety, only to be caught the few times she slipped and made a mistake? How could life be so cruel as to punish her like this when all she had intended was good?

She resented the creature growing inside her, already rounding her stomach and causing her to let out the seams of her bodice. She resented Cash for planting it there. She resented Sallie for being the only woman Cash could really see. She resented Jonathan for leaving her to deal with this problem alone.

It was far easier to cast resentment far and wide than to sit down and deal with the problem directly.

She was pregnant and unmarried. The baby's father had his heart set on another, and her own intended husband was two thousand miles away basking in the Arizona sun. She had no money and nowhere to go. Hell couldn't be any worse than this.

Yet when Cash came whistling merrily up the walk one sunny morn, Laura merely wiped her hands on her apron and went out on the porch to meet him.

"You're supposed to smile in the sunshine, *pequeña*," Cash declared as his boots hit the wooden steps and his eyes came even with the haunted ones of the slender woman greeting him. "It's a glorious day. Shall we sit out here and enjoy it?"

Laura knew in her bones what came next, and she gratefully lowered herself into the cane-backed porch chair he offered her. Now was the time. If she were to say anything, it would be now. But she had only to look into the joy dancing in his dark eyes to know her lips would remain sealed.

"You've brought good news?" she managed to murmur as Cash chose the porch rail for his seat and propped his boot against the post in a graceful, if wholly ungentlemanly manner.

Cash sent her a winning smile. "All the cards are mine, Laura. Full house, flush deck. I suggested a quiet ceremony in Lexington and an extended honeymoon trip to New York, and she agreed without reservation. Will you come and stand up with us? I'll make certain there's someone to accompany you home."

Even though Laura had known it was coming, Cash's casual verification of her fears cut swiftly and painfully to her very core. Even the tiny being within her fluttered as if in protest, and her hand went unwisely to her waist to capture that brief movement.

Cash reacted swiftly to her shock, swinging his legs down and grasping her cold hand. "I'm sorry, Laura. Was I too callous presenting it to you that way? I thought you understood . . ." He stiffened slightly as a thought occurred. "You do understand? Sallie has accepted my proposal of marriage, despite my background, despite everyone's objections. Did you think she wouldn't?"

She heard the pain and the hidden anger and forced herself to smile and squeeze his hand gently. "I didn't think Sallie that great a fool, no. You just caught me a bit by surprise. Ward's scarce been buried four months. I didn't think even Sallie would be that hasty. A long engagement, perhaps, but I can see you're right. She'd be happier away from here." She finally raised the courage to meet his eyes. "I know it's what you always wanted, Cash. I'm happy for you, I really am. I know you'll take care of her."

"And who will take care of you, Laura?" Cash brushed the back of his hand against her pale cheek. "What have you heard from Jonathan? Is he ready to send for you yet?"

"The last I heard, he'd been in Arizona about a month. He said the railroads didn't go all the way out there yet, and the journey is a rough one. He says he's never seen anything quite like the land out there; it's the exact opposite of Kentucky and he's not at all certain I'd like it. I think he's hoping for an instant cure so he can come back here."

They both knew that wasn't possible, but it wasn't something that could be said out loud. Cash sat back down and braced his weight on his legs, swinging her hand loosely between them. "Anytime you decide to join the rascal, I'll be happy to give you the money. I don't suffer Jonathan's illusions about your fragility. In the meantime, will you be coming to the wedding?"

He had given her enough time to think and decide, and Laura knew of a certainty she could not bring herself to stand at the altar while her cousin bound herself to the father of this child growing within her. She might be strong, but she wasn't that strong. Yet. She would learn to be, somehow, but not right now. She had better things to expend her limited energy on.

"No, Cash, I don't think so. I understand why you're leaving Stoner Creek to do this. I think it best if you leave me behind too. Sallie won't miss me. She'll resent having to make excuses to me if I were there. You've chosen the best way. Go quietly and with my blessings, and by the time you return, you'll be awaited eagerly."

"It just for the gossip of it," Cash acknowledged wryly. "Well, if I can't persuade you to come to the wedding, let me persuade you to return to the farm. I'll bring over my servants to begin setting things to rights, and I need someone there to oversee the renovations. You would be doing us a favor if you could keep an eye on things."

It was tempting, very tempting. She could hide out at the farm, where no one but the servants would notice her growing girth, and she wouldn't have to make all the awful explanations she knew were coming. But she had hidden from herself and her home for four awful years in Cairo, and she knew that wasn't any solution.

Besides, the idea of living in the house that Cash meant to restore for Sallie poisoned her insides. Somehow she had managed not to hate Sallie through all these years. She didn't think it would be possible to be so objective when confronted daily with the proof of Cash's preference for her beautiful cousin. It wouldn't be a healthy situation at all, and Laura shook her head.

"I'm sorry, Cash, I've come to enjoy my independence

too much. I would feel like a child again to return there. I hope you'll understand."

She had returned for Ward but wouldn't for him. Cash reluctantly understood that. He wouldn't push her friendship beyond the bounds he already had. He squeezed her hand and let it fall.

"I understand, brat. But if I leave a driver at your disposal, will you ride out to keep an eye on things? I'll have men there to protect the property, so you'll be safe enough. I just figure you know better than anyone what needs to be done and how it should be done. I'll put you in charge of a bank account with sufficient funds to pay any workmen that you hire, and you need to pay yourself a salary for services rendered too."

Cash always knew what he was doing. Laura stared past him at the street and contemplated his offer. Sallie had little or no interest in refurbishing the house she had called home all these years. She just expected it to be there as it always was, without being reminded of the tedious details for its upkeep. And Laura knew the men who would love the job of repairing the house, men who desperately needed the money to support their wives and children. And she certainly couldn't complain of a little extra income for herself either. Sewing wasn't the most profitable business around.

There was only one hitch in Cash's plans, a hitch he knew nothing about. He had no reason to know that she had been contemplating leaving town, that his offer a moment ago of the funds to join Jonathan had given her a new surge of hope.

There were drawbacks, definite drawbacks to that hope. The child she carried wasn't Jonathan's, and she had not mentioned it to him. She didn't know how he would react to a pregnant fiancée appearing on his doorstep. And the journey itself was a dangerous one. How much more dangerous would it be to a woman in her condition? She didn't relish giving birth on a train full of strangers.

But to stay in Stoner Creek . . . Laura sighed and wished she were a million miles away on some desert island. She finally brought her gaze back to Cash's dark intent face, saw his probing look, and averted it with a casual wave of her hand.

"Do I have time to think about it, Cash?"

It wasn't what he expected, but he acquiesced easily. "Of course, Laura. It will be a week before we have all the loose ends tied. Is a week enough?"

A week, and they would be married, husband and wife, Cash's long, splendid body covering Sallie's tender curves in the act that had created his child growing inside her. The idea was too painful to contemplate.

Laura nodded absently, heard his farewells, and watched him walk away with full knowledge that the next time she saw him, he would be someone else's husband. She watched the way his shoulders strained at the tight coat, watched his easy stride, watched him mount his horse with the ease and strength of an equestrian, and all she could remember was how it felt to have him on top of her, inside her, holding her until the lightning flashed and thunder struck and there was nothing and no one else in this world but them. How had he forgotten so easily? Sadly Laura pulled her shawl more tightly about her shoulders and went back into the house, letting the prison door slowly close behind her.

Right or wrong, Laura chose to stay and oversee the renovation of Stoner Creek rather than run away and hide. With that decision, she saw no reason to notify Jonathan of her impending fall from grace. She not only feared to lose his friendship forever, but she equally feared he would drop everything and return to save her from herself. She wouldn't have that on her conscience for anything. She had got herself into this, she would get herself out.

Laura waited until Sallie and Cash had gone before sending for Cash's driver and going out to the farm. She supposed she ought to learn to hook up Jonathan's carriage and drive it, or at the very least learn to saddle his horse, but she didn't think the fourth month of pregnancy to be the best time to learn. Besides, traveling country roads in these desperate times without weapons or male assistance would be a foolhardy mistake. She had made enough mistakes for a lifetime.

When Laura arrived at the farm, Jettie Mae took one look at her, placed her hands on her hips, and started scolding. "You been a widow too long to 'splain away that belly, Miss Laura. When that man of your'n comin' home?"

It was only fitting that the first condemnation would be made by a woman who had already been there three times before. Laura gave a wary smile and glanced to Jettie Mae's growing abdomen. "He's just as unobtainable as your man, Jettie Mae. Now, I want to hear no more about it. Have you made arrangements for when that baby's due?"

The maid shook her head, gave a scowl as if longing to say more, but under Laura's steely gaze she relented. "I done asked that no-'count driver of Mr. Cash's if he'll harness up the wagon to take us back to town. My mama's been birthin' babies since she was no more than one herself."

Laura looked to the solemn nine-year-old in pigtails and ribbons holding the hand of her little five-year-old brother and shook her head. "Your mama isn't used to having a house full of young ones around. Maybe you'd better let these two stay with me. They'll be close enough to visit back and forth but far enough to give you and your mama a rest."

Jettie opened her mouth to protest, thought better of it, looked down at her two children who seemed delighted at the prospect of an extended visit with "Aunt Laura," who gave them cookies, and shrugged her shoulders. "You don' know what you askin', but I'd be grateful. They ain't used to bein' in town."

"I'll be glad of the company. Now, let's find paper and pen and start making lists of what needs to be done around here."

As it turned out, Cash had already made extensive notes and left them for her. Seeing the strong black scrawl across the page, Laura felt another grip at her stomach, but she refused to fall into the megrims again. She had work to keep her mind occupied. There was no point in dwelling on what could not be changed.

But as the days went by and Laura caught the suspicious glances of other women at church or at the store, and she sat and wrote her hollow letters to Jonathan, the ache widened and grew worse. She felt as isolated and alone as she had in Cairo. There was none she could turn to for advice or sympathy, and the only explanations she had of what was happening inside her body came from an old black woman who could neither read nor write.

While Jettie's children played with the rag dolls Laura made for them, she searched Jonathan's medical library for books on childbirth. What she found was either too technical to interpret or too condescending to take seriously. Imagine calling a woman's body a "delicate vessel" and her mind "too weak" to withstand the emotional stress of carrying a child. One tome recommended that she take to bed and remain in a darkened room with someone to wait on her every whim to minimize the dangers of this difficult time to both body and mind. Laura suspected that passage had to have been written by a woman who had borne one too many children under hostile conditions and was intent on getting even with husbands everywhere.

Whatever the case, Laura had no husband to pamper her, and she had to make a living of some sort if she were to eat. She had accepted the use of Jonathan's house on the pretext of looking after it for him, but she could not in all conscience accept his money to keep her fed. She had no trouble finding sewing jobs, but there was a limit to how much sewing could be accomplished in a day. Cash's generous allowance for overseeing the renovations allowed her to buy a few materials for baby clothes and pay for the extra groceries for Jettie's two children, but the two jobs combined left little time to pamper herself.

By the end of February the unpaved lanes to the farm were a mire of mud and snow, and work on the house came to a temporary halt. Laura tried to school herself to patience, but more often than not she found herself pacing the small interior of the house to stare at the snow and the rain from one window after another.

Her wide skirts still hid her pregnancy from the uninitiated, but one or two of the women she had helped during the fever stopped by to visit and offer seemingly general observations on the amount of milk they had consumed during their confinements or to offer beef broths they just "happened" to have left over. Laura was grateful for their discretion, but she knew her secret would be out soon enough if these few knew.

It was humiliating to an extreme to receive a deputa-

tion at the beginning of March from the church, offering
their understanding of her "situation" with Jonathan ill
and thousands of miles away. One woman offered her
sister's home in Louisville as a haven for Laura's "disgrace." Another urged obtaining funds from the Breckinridges to join Jonathan so the child could have a name.
All of them assumed the child to be Jonathan's, and
Laura held her breath in fear of one of them offering to
send word to him. None did, however, and she somehow
managed to dismiss their offers with murmurs of Sallie's
expectations and assurances that Jonathan would be
home in time.

Whatever words she used seemed to satisfy them, and
though a few still crossed the street rather than speak to
a fallen woman, others brought her baby linen their own
children had outgrown, and still another offered a cradle
she no longer needed. Staring at these items in the candlelight before going to bed, Laura finally began to accept the reality of what was happening to her.

She was going to have a baby. Glancing down at the
growing pear shape of her abdomen beneath the folds of
her nightshirt, Laura ran her fingers over the place where
the child kicked and felt a frisson of fear run through
her. A child without a father. She must have been mad
to do this.

She tried to imagine a tiny creature kicking and crying
in that cradle on the floor, but the exercise was too
strong for her mind. She had held other people's babies
before, but never her own. She had never even contemplated having a baby before, and she was afraid to contemplate it now.

Just one afternoon in a haystack with Cash had done
this. It seemed improbable that just that one act could
result in something so permanent as a child who would
share her life for these next twenty years.

The thought of Cash instantly returned the image of
Sallie—golden pretty Sallie who had refused to share
Ward's bed and had never borne a child. If one afternoon
with Cash had given Laura a child, chances were very
good that Sallie would return from her honeymoon carrying Cash's heir. That thought was too painful to bear,
and Laura turned away from it. Cash would be damned
almighty proud if he knew of his accomplishments with

two Kincaid women. She would have to make certain he
never learned who the father of her child actually was.

Jettie went into labor during the second week of March
while the wind howled around the chimneys and winter
dumped one last snowstorm on the Easter flowers just
starting to open their yellow heads. Laura had been
warned to stay away, and she entertained the children
during the day as the snow fell and blew and piled around
the house, but when one of Jettie's sisters arrived to an-
nounce the birth of a little boy, Laura couldn't stay away
any longer.

Wrapping herself in two shawls and Jonathan's heavy
woolen greatcoat and pulling on a pair of his boots,
Laura left the children with their aunt and set out in the
storm to see Ward's son.

She was quite mad to do it. She had abandoned crinolines for the warmth of several layers of petticoats, but
they dragged in the snow and quickly became wet and
cold about her legs. But when she arrived at the tiny
one-room cabin where Jettie's mother lived, Laura found
herself welcomed with open arms.

She unloaded the parcels of hand-sewn baby linen and
bundles of Jettie's favorite treats that she had baked
while waiting, and warmed herself by the fire while Mrs.
Jackson gently lifted the newborn from its nest in the
room's lone bed. Laura knew the "Mrs." was merely an
honorary title and the "Jackson" had been adopted from
her former owners, but Jettie's mother conducted herself
with the dignity of a society matron. She seldom said
much, but that was to everyone's advantage, for she
knew more than would be comfortable for half the
county, including Laura.

"Good as gold, this one is," the woman whispered as
she handed the sleeping infant to her visitor. "Just like
his daddy."

What was left unspoken flowed between them as Laura
carefully accepted the bundle and stared in wonder at
the tiny miracle she held. A shock of dark hair lay plastered against pale skin still flushed with the day's exertions. The infant's face was withered into a restless scowl,
and already he sucked a fist formed of perfectly sculp-
tured miniature fingers. It was impossible to trace any

sign of Jettie or Ward in this wondrous little creature, but there was no doubt that he was as white as Ward— or Cash, for all that mattered.

It was well known that Jettie and her sisters were, at best, half white, products of an institution that allowed white masters to use their female slaves as they pleased. Laura could only wonder how Jettie's mother had felt to be used in such a way by a man who had no intention of marrying her; she could never ask. Perhaps there had been affection in the relationship. Perhaps it had been a mutual arrangement. Whatever the facts, Mrs. Jackson had remained a slave until the day the military's proclamation reached Stoner Creek, and not a moment longer.

"His daddy would be awful proud," Laura murmured, gently touching the tiny fist. "We've got to see he's raised like his daddy would want."

No representative of Jettie's father had come to stand by her mother's side when Jettie was born, nor had the fathers of Jettie's children. They had been born without acknowledgment of anything but the sins of their mothers. To see Laura Kincaid standing there now, holding her cousin-in-law's child, admitting the family's responsibility, brought a silent nod of satisfaction from the older woman. Perhaps the war had brought an end to a way of life, but perhaps this was a signal that the new world being born would be a change for the better.

"He needs a name," was all she said as she watched Laura rock the child lovingly in her arms.

Laura didn't express surprise. The boy's father would be the one to choose a name. She wasn't a part of Ward's family, but the nearest thing this child would ever see. Stephen Breckinridge would have an apoplexy before admitting the child's paternity. Sallie would never know or care. But the child was a Breckinridge and deserved a family name.

"His daddy's full name was Ward Taylor Breckinridge. Don't you think Taylor Jackson has a nice sound to it?"

A rustle from the corner caused them to turn in the direction of the bed. Jettie stirred against her pillow and the candlelight fell on weary lines of her face. "Taylor Breckinridge Jackson," she announced firmly as she reached for the tiny bundle Laura held. "He's gonna be a gentleman one day."

The name would undoubtedly send shock waves through the community if it were known, but what went on at the black church was not generally known by the white population, and the infant's baptismal name would never be known to anyone else. For a moment Laura hesitated, wondering if there were some way she could steal this child and raise him as white, but Jettie's beckoning hand showed her the selfishness of that thought. For the first time, Laura began to understand the preciousness of the life growing within her.

She released the child with tears in her eyes. "You let me know if there's anything you need, you hear? When the weather turns nice, we'll go back out to the farm and fix up rooms just for you and the little ones. You can choose just how you want them decorated."

Jettie grinned at the thought and gave Laura a conspiratorial glance, but her attention soon wandered to the infant starting to grunt and root as she held him near her breast. Laura turned away from the intimacy of the moment and found herself facing Mrs. Jackson.

"You shouldn't get that girl's hopes up," she whispered disapprovingly as Laura tested the dryness of her coat beside the fire.

"I'm not," she replied defiantly. "That child belongs at the farm, and he can't live there without Jettie, and Jettie can't live there without her children. So that means they all have a home at Stoner Creek for as long as they like."

"That Mr. Cash gonna have something to say about that," the old woman warned as Laura donned her cloak. "You might get around Miss Sallie, but that Wickliffe boy ain't gonna stand no nonsense from nobody. He's a wild one. It would break his mammy's heart to know where he been and what he's done."

Laura didn't want to hear a list of Cash's indiscretions. She heard enough of the whispers as it was. She wasn't the only woman he had lain with since returning, although the others were considerably less innocent than herself. And she knew he gambled. He had made his money by gambling; he had as much as admitted that himself. But that was none of her concern. The child in Jettie's arms was, although she could not bring herself to say why that was so. She felt she owed it to Ward's memory, and to the memory of what once had been. That was enough for her.

"I know how to handle Cash if it comes to that." Laura heard the defiance in her voice and tried to mute it. "Don't you worry. Jettie and her family have a home for as long as I'm alive to say anything about it. And when I get through with Cash Wickliffe, he'll say the same thing. And I think it's about time those children got some education. I've been teaching them their ABC's, and they're just as bright as can be. Something's got to be done about teaching them."

Lucretia Jackson managed to look alarmed and secretly pleased at the same time. "You don' know what you talkin' about, chile. They ain't nobody gonna teach the likes of them. They may be as white as you to look at, but ever'body gon' know who they mother is."

Laura began to smile as she mulled over this impulsive decision. If she took the time to think about these things, she always discarded her ideas as impossible. But once they were out of her mouth, she wouldn't go back on her word. And she knew just the man to help her. "I can't do anything but teach them myself for right now, but just you wait. One way or another, they're going to school. They've got to know how to read and write to make their way in this world. Do you think Ward would want his son to grow up ignorant?"

Lucretia snorted rudely. "Do you think anybody else ever cared? You blind and fanciful, chile, but if you can do it, I won't stand in your way none. My baby's been sellin' herself to get along. I don' want her babies to do the same."

It seemed all women could do to get along in this world was sell themselves in one form or another, but Laura didn't say this aloud. Let Jettie's mother think her an innocent, as she probably thought all white women. She needn't know that Laura hadn't even had the sense to sell herself for money as Sallie and Jettie had. She had sold herself for pleasure, and somehow that seemed even worse.

Striking out into the cold wind, Laura huddled inside Jonathan's greatcoat and found her way back more by instinct than anything else. Eyes almost closed against the sting of flying snow, she pushed through knee-high drifts along the fence and down the trash-strewn alleys until she reached the back gate to Jonathan's home. This route was simpler and less open to observation than the main roads. She let herself in the gate and crossed the dark yard to the kitchen, grateful for the yellow play of light indicating someone had left the lantern on, and hopefully, the fire lit.

It took a moment to register the stranger sprawled insolently in her best chair before the leaping flames, swigging from the last bottle of Jonathan's bourbon. Shock numbed Laura from recognition as she glanced to Jettie's frightened sister huddling in the corner, then back to the bearded man in the rags and remnants of Union blue. At the sight of Laura, Jettie's sister grabbed her meager shawl and ran to escape through the open door behind her. The man merely turned his head and offered a lewd smile.

"Welcome home, wife. I heard you had a bun in the oven and I've come home to restore your honor. Isn't that what any Southern gentleman would do?"

15

"Marshall!" Laura could scarcely remember his name or face, but she could remember the insolence in his voice with a clarity and a shame she would never forget. Her cheeks burned with more than cold as she regarded his long frame and wondered how she had ever imagined herself in love with such filth.

The shreds of blanket he had wrapped around the soles of his disintegrating boots lay in dirty heaps upon her clean kitchen floor. The remainder of the blanket he had apparently used as coat, and it, too, lay where it fell when he grew warm enough to discard it. Scattered bread crumbs, bits of meat, and the smear of what she suspected was the last of her apple pie across his tattered shirt gave evidence of the meal he had just forced Jettie's sister to prepare. Laura eyed the bottle in his hand with disfavor, then glanced to the enormous black pistol holstered to his side.

Coldly she demanded, "What are you doing here?" although she already suspected the answer. It had been a filthy, cold winter with no immediate sign of ending. Marshall wasn't the sort to suffer in silence.

He waved the bottle and eyed the waistline of her skirt with interest. "I'm doing the honorable thing, of course. Your friend there was more than relieved to hear I'd returned from the dead. How thoughtful of you to wear black for me, dear Laura, when I can't even remember our exchanging vows. But that's all in the past. I'm here to right all the wrongs that have been done."

He lied. He was here to make himself comfortable for as long as he was able, but there was little Laura could say or do. Once shaved and made presentable, he would be easily recognizable as the beau she had followed and presumably married. What would she say? Could she declare to all and sundry that she had been living a lie all these years? Could she throw the brave Union soldier all assumed to be her husband out into the cold and snow? He had her trapped, and he knew it.

"You're here to cause trouble, Marshall Brown. I've got more of that than I can handle already. You're welcome to clean up and get warm and borrow some of Jonathan's clothes, but you better be gone by daybreak. I never want to see your face again."

He frowned and lowered his feet from the fender as he turned his gaze more fully on the woman he had last seen as a seventeen-year-old girl. She had not yet rid herself of the overlarge coat, but it fell open enough for him to see the fullness of the breasts behind that lace-trimmed bodice and to note the thickening of her waist that hadn't been there before. He grunted and took another pull at the bottle.

"Seems to me you ought to be damned grateful I showed up. Whole town's been whispering about the disgrace of a Kincaid giving birth out of wedlock. Well, we'll just tell them the kid's mine, that you been helpin' me fight those damned Confederate rebels that don't give up, and you couldn't say nothin' until it was safe. That'll take care of the gossip. I gave it plenty of thought while I was sitting here. You need a man around the house, and I need a house. Seems a fair exchange to me."

"You're a pig, Marshall. You've always been a pig. I can't stand to look you in the face. Did you really think I'd let you stay here after what you did to me? I could have come home if you hadn't stuck me with your hotel bill. It took me four years to save enough money to get back here, and I'm not going to let you ruin my life again. This is Jonathan's home. You can't simply take it over."

He shrugged. "Don't look to me like you got any choice. The doctor won't be coming back for a long time, as I understand it. When he hears your husband has returned, he won't be coming back at all, I speculate. No, this looks fine and cozy to me. You'll have to get rid of those damned kids in the loft, though. I don't need a bunch of darkies jumping around and keeping me awake come morning."

Laura stood frozen, rapidly running all her alternatives through her mind, discarding all of them. She could turn around and run back out into the night, but where would she go? And she couldn't leave Jettie's children to this brute's frustration. She would have to wake them and take them to their grandmother's, but then what? There wasn't room in that tiny cabin for her. She could run to Reverend Hammond or any of the ladies of the church, but when they heard she was running from the man they assumed to be her husband, they would turn her out again. A wife didn't run from her husband, and no one would encourage such a thing.

Besides, this was her home, and there was no reason she should have to leave it. Marshall would have to be the one to go.

"The children stay with me until it's time for them to return to the farm. If you don't like children, you can find somewhere else to stay. I will be more than happy to take up a collection at church to finance your journey home, and I've already offered you some of Jonathan's clothes. He scarcely needs his woolens in Arizona. I appreciate your offer to give the child a name, but the child isn't yours and I'm doing quite fine on my own."

Marshall gave her a baleful look as she shed her coat

and moved briskly around the kitchen, tidying up the mess he had created. "Damned if you haven't grown as hard and cold as that pestilential uncle of yours. Should have known a chit who would cross half the state on her own didn't have the soul of a woman. Now, that cousin of yours, she was a man's woman. A man likes a little softness to cuddle up with at night. Didn't take her long to find another, now, did it? And here you are, an old maid with no man at all. You're damned lucky I came back here."

Wearily Laura wrung out the rag she had used to clean the table. "Why did you come back here? This isn't your home."

"It's gonna be. I like it here, where a man can do what he wants and there ain't nobody to look down their nose at him. I've made quite a few friends out there, and they don't object at all to my claiming a Kincaid for wife. It could be right convenient sometime. But I'm tired of sleeping in the woods and filthy shacks. I've decided to set up headquarters here."

By that she understood he had joined the bands of roving soldiers terrorizing the countryside, and she shuddered, remembering that night out on the farm. Had he been there then? But no, those had been the ex-Confederates who styled themselves the Raiders. Marshall would be one of the Regulators, who took out their penchant for violence by hunting down the Raiders and "punishing" them by raping their women and shooting their children. Headquarters, my foot. Gossip central was what he was looking for.

"You're beginning to talk like the trash you've been associating with. If you think you're going to pass yourself off as respectable, you're out of luck. A decent man wouldn't keep his wife in another man's home."

Annoyed, Marshall staggered to his feet and hovered over her. Although he was not a tall man, he had the advantage of more inches than she. "You're beginning to rag my nerves, woman. I want a bath, and then I want a soft bed and some sleep. If you'll shut your everlasting tongue, I'll leave you alone. Otherwise, I'll teach you what happens to shrews."

This was utter nonsense. This was her home. He had no right ordering her about. But the meanness in the glitter of his eyes and the hand on his pistol caused Laura to think twice. The flutter in her stomach reminded her she had more to worry about than herself. Perhaps in the morning she would come up with some plan to remove him from the house. At this hour, in a raging storm, she didn't have much choice. And she certainly wasn't going to have him sleeping on her clean sheets in that condition.

Feeling the weight of the day bearing down on her, she slowly pumped the water and set it to heat over the fire. She dragged in the huge tin tub from the storage area between Jonathan's office and the kitchen and pushed it in front of the fire while Marshall watched with a satisfied expression. She disappeared into the other room to fetch towels and cloths and soap. After laying them out on the kitchen table, she went in another direction to rummage through Jonathan's wardrobe for suitable clothes. When she laid these out over a chair and disappeared from the room one more time, Marshall made no objection, but this time she didn't return.

Climbing into the loft with the heaviest blanket she could find, Laura was too tired to fool fear of his ire at her deception. If he had some fool notion that she was going to wait on him hand and foot while he bathed, he might as well shoot her and get it over with. She didn't have the strength to stand on her feet one moment longer. And in his state of drunkenness, she doubted that he could manage to come up here and drag her down. She would be safe for this night, at least.

She wished Cash would come home. Falling into a deep sleep, she dreamed of Cash holding an armful of babies and roaring in outrage at some objectionable sight just beyond her field of vision. Marshall appeared as some grinning jack-o'-lantern, and Ward sat a horse and strummed a harp, while Laura scrubbed incessantly at some floor. The night wasn't any more restful than the day.

Laura rose the next day to discover Marshall hadn't disappeared like her bad dreams. His filthy clothing lay scattered across the floor, and the cold bathwater sat where he had left it. The children stared at the jarring sight in the midst of Laura's normally orderly kitchen and grew silent, watching her with wide round eyes.

The baby felt achingly heavy in her abdomen this morning, and she couldn't bear the thought of wrestling with Marshall's maliciousness and keeping him separated from these children. Silently she found their coats and took them on an expedition through the snow to meet their new baby brother. They accepted this announcement with excitement and forgot the menacing disorder that spoke of long-ago dark nights when men had come and gone, leaving their mother to cry herself to sleep.

Mrs. Jackson seemed surprised to see them so early, but as the children drank the hot chocolate she gave them and exclaimed excitedly over the baby and the little presents waiting for them, she listened to Laura's hurried explanations with calm.

"Well, there ain't nothing much you can do," she finally admitted when Laura's words ran out. "Even if you could get out to the farm, which you can't with the roads being what they are, you'd be worse off with no man 'round to look after you. Leastways, here in town he can't do nothin' much. You a Kincaid, after all. Folks'll look after a Kincaid. You don' know he means you any harm. Might be a little sweet-talkin' will turn him 'round. That baby needs a daddy. Maybe this is God's way of sendin' one."

That was a depressing thought. She had turned away a sensitive, caring man only to be taken in by a violent brute. If anything, it was God's way of punishing her for her sins. Perhaps carrying this child she hadn't wanted wasn't punishment enough, since she had actually begun to secretly look forward to it. There had to be some way out of this trap, but she hadn't found it yet.

After lingering as long as she could, Laura finally trudged back out into the snow. It had silently been agreed between them that it would be best to leave the children behind. If this were going to be her future, it would be better to start it out on the right foot. And there was no use in endangering the children if Laura's surmise that Marshall was capable of violence came true.

The sun had come out and glittered on the new-fallen crust of snow with all the hope and promise of a new day. At any other time Laura would have felt joyous at this sign of spring just around the corner. But knowing what she faced when she entered what had once been the safety of her home kept her spirits dragging in the slush beginning to form in the roads. How could she bring herself to live the lie of life with Marshall?

Entering by the front door rather than face the mess in the kitchen, Laura felt the cold emptiness of an abandoned house. Life had fled with her dreams, but glancing into her bedroom, she also discovered Marshall had gone with them too. He had evidently made himself at home in Jonathan's wardrobe, selecting what he preferred over what she had given him. His discards lay in crumpled heaps upon the floor, but at least he was nowhere in sight.

Trying to keep her hopes from rising, Laura silently began to return the house to order. She tidied the bedroom first, making the bed rather than stripping it, as her first impulse told her to do. It would take more than Marshall's absence to convince her he wasn't returning, and she didn't intend to struggle with the burden of laundry until she was certain he wasn't coming back.

The kitchen was a little more difficult. She had given up the luxury of baths since her pregnancy made it impossible to carry heavy loads. The only way of removing the filthy cold water from in front of her fire was to lug it out one pail at a time. The procedure seemed to take hours, and when she was done, she could do no more than collapse on a chair and hold her aching back.

She was still wearing the clothing she had worn to bed the night before. She needed to find fresh clothes before Marshall took it into his head to return. The thought only made her more tired, and she closed her eyes and tried to absorb a little of the peace of the first quiet she had known in weeks.

A knock on the door woke her with a start, and Laura realized she had fallen into a doze as she hastily rubbed her eyes and tried to remember what she was doing. Brushing her hand through her hair to return some semblance of order to the heavy strands escaping their pins, she shook out her rumpled skirts, glanced at the limp petticoats with dismay, and hurried to answer the eager knock. Heart pounding with hope, she flung open the door, only to discover the preacher's wife waiting on the porch.

"Laura! I just heard the news, and I couldn't wait to come over and offer my apologies. You poor thing, suffering under this burden, knowing your gallant husband couldn't come out of hiding while he fought those terrible men. Why, you never even let us suspect he had returned. Tell me all about it. When did you know he wasn't one of the unfortunate casualties? I can hardly believe it!"

She chattered on as Laura led her to the parlor and offered her a chair. She seemed oblivious of the fact that Laura answered scarcely one question out of ten. Before there had even been time to put a kettle on to boil for tea, two more ladies from church showed up at the door, and Laura was becoming resigned to her fate. The fact was, she was too tired to fight.

Marshall had wasted no time in ingratiating himself with the townspeople, but then, he'd done a fine job of it five years ago when he had first entered her life. He knew how to play the part, there was no getting around that. Aunt Ann had always said that everything always comes around full circle, and that seemed to be the case here. Five years ago she had been madly, passionately in love with a handsome Northern gentleman to the extent of running off after him. Now he was back, claiming the marriage he had once denied. She now had what she had wanted then. The irony of it did not strike Laura as humorous.

After the ladies had finally left, tittering about leaving the "lovebirds" to their nest, Laura forced herself to return to the bedroom and set herself to rights. Even as she stripped to her chemise to wash, she listened for the sound of the door and jumped at every creak and groan of the old wood. Maybe she had been wrong about Marshall's character. Perhaps he was weary of fighting and wanted a home and family again. Maybe snowballs grew in hell.

She dressed carefully in a heavy brown velvet that had seen better days but still seemed presentable. Its major asset was the high-necked bodice and concealing folds of material. She carried the child low, but even the heavy

velvet could not entirely conceal the thickness of her
waist or her swaybacked walk. Still, the billowing crinoline hid much, and once she had her hair neatly tucked
into a net so she didn't feel like a disorganized hoyden,
Laura felt more in control again. It was just the weariness
of her pregnancy causing this inertia. She would try reasoning with Marshall once again.

She stoked the kitchen fire and prepared a supper
sufficient for two. She had no illusions about Marshall
not returning now. He would be here in his own good
time, and he would undoubtedly expect his supper
when he came. Perhaps she would win him over better
if she appeared quiescent. He could not really mean to
go through with this. She had no money or belongings
that he could covet. There was nothing for him here.

When he walked through the front door without
knocking, flinging Jonathan's coat and hat over a chair
and striking through to the kitchen with a bellow of
greeting, Laura felt one more illusion slip away. He
greeted her as if there had scarcely been a day since they
first parted, kissing her cheek as if he had convinced
himself he truly were her husband. When he flung himself down in a chair and waited for her to place his meal
in front of him, she contemplated dumping the kettle
over his head, but caution prevailed.

Instead, Laura studied him warily as she removed
the rolls from the oven and placed them on a plate,
then took down the large bowl from the shelf and
began to ladle the stew into it. He had obviously gone
to the barber and had his hair and beard trimmed until
he almost had the air of a respectable merchant. A
dash of gray through the dark brown of his hair added
to the distinguished look, and Jonathan's conservative
black satin vest and high collar and black tie heightened the illusion. But even as she watched, he loosened
the tie and removed the collar, and the illusion began
to crumble.

"Why in hell aren't you wearing something a little
more cheerful than that ghastly thing?" he asked as
Laura finally came to sit at the table. "I'm not dead, so
you needn't wear mourning anymore."

"Brown isn't the color of mourning," Laura answered
patiently, not really desiring the food she spooned onto

her plate but not knowing what else to do. "And I don't
have a large wardrobe to choose from. As you learned
some years ago, I don't have any money of my own. I
live in this house free of rent, but I have to buy my own
food and clothes, and what I can earn at sewing is
scarcely enough for one."

If that was meant as a warning, Marshall ignored it.
He poured himself a large tumbler of the whiskey he had
brought home with him and finished off a roll before
replying, "That's all right. I've got a hoard of silver plate
stored out in the woods that we can sell for now. And
something will turn up. I don't suppose you had the sense
to get money out of the brat's father. Seems that's the
least he could do before he ran away."

Laura gritted her teeth and counted to ten. Temper
would not get her anywhere. "Jonathan doesn't know of
the child. If you've kept up with the gossip long enough
to know he's in Arizona, then you know he's a sick man.
I'll not have him worried about me. Besides, he has no
wealth either. You've come looking in the wrong place
if you want a life of leisure."

Marshall grunted and gave her a sardonic look. "I figured that out five years ago. But this damned war made
me lower my standards some. A roof over my head and
food in my stomach will suffice for the moment. We'll
see about the rest a little later. I hear Sallie has found
herself another rich husband. I wonder how long it will
be before she gets tired of a colored boy prodding her
and starts looking for a real man?"

That was disgusting. Laura gave him a look of revulsion and rose from the table. "If you will excuse me,
I don't feel well. I'm going in to lie down for a while."

"Fine idea. I'll be in to join you shortly. You ain't
much, but at least you're cleaner than those whores they
have down at the hotel." He contentedly sipped at his
liquor as Laura turned around in the doorway.

"I'm not your wife, Marshall, and I don't intend to
act as one. I'm near seven months gone with child and
you'll not touch me in that way or I'll shoot you with
your own gun. Failing that, I'll poison your food. I
know everything in Jonathan's medicine chest back
there, and I know just which ones to use. So I suggest
you keep yourself happy with the charms of your

whores and satisfy yourself with my cooking. That's all you'll get from me."

Marshall chortled at her irate use of such language and gave her bloated stomach a wicked stare. "That's all right. You ain't much to look at like that anyway. Your cooking ain't much to brag about either, but I don't expect any of you Southern ladies to know anything about cooking without slaves. I'll bide my time for a while. We'll get along, you'll see. Just you keep your mouth shut about everything else, and we'll do just fine."

She didn't have much choice but to keep her mouth shut about everything else. Not wanting to know whether or not to believe his words, Laura merely nodded and went to fetch blankets. She was small and the parlor sofa would hold her comfortably enough. As if any bed could be comfortable for a belly that stuck out so far that nothing could hold it. Damn Cash, damn Jonathan, and damn Marshall Brown to hell. Never would she traffic with another man again. They weren't worth the effort.

16

"Excuse me for intruding, Mrs. Brown. I'm Dr. Peter Burke, Jonathan's associate. He told me to look in on you as soon as I arrived in town." He had also been told that this faded young woman was Broadbent's fiancée, but his glance to Laura's obvious pregnancy made him hesitate to mention that.

Laura interpreted the look just the same. Forcing a smile to her face, she gestured for him to enter. Although it wasn't quite April yet, the sun was hot, and she could see the perspiration on his forehead. "Jonathan told me you would be arriving soon, Doctor. It's a pleasure to have you here. The winter and spring have been harsh,

and without Jonathan's experience, there has been little
I can do to alleviate the inevitable illness.''

Burke entered the neat parlor and looked around at
the crowded bookshelf in the corner, the masculine solid-
ity of the furniture, and the other evidence that this was
still Jonathan's home, and he sent her a curious look,
but he settled into the chair indicated.

"Shall I fetch you some coffee, Doctor? There's still a
chill in the air despite the sun.''

He shook his head. "No, please, stay seated. You
should be resting. When is the baby due?''

Laura relaxed at this easy introduction of a subject
uppermost in her mind. "In another two months, if I
calculate correctly. I'm rather grateful that someone will
be available in case of complications. I know a reliable
midwife, but this is my first, and I'm nervous about it.''

"Would you permit me to examine you if I get my
bag?'' He studied the dark shadows beneath her eyes,
considered her slightness despite the advanced pregnancy, noted other signs that made him uneasy, and instantly offered his full sympathy despite the variety of
stories he had heard about this woman.

Laura glanced nervously to the door, wrung her hands,
and finally shook her head in defeat. "No, better not.
My husband will be home soon and will want his dinner.
Would you care to stay for the meal? We would be glad
of your company.''

Burke had seen enough women afraid of their husbands to know the symptoms when they were displayed.
His gaze carefully focused on the fading bruise along her
cheekbone, went to a flaming red scald at the base of
her palm, and finally rose to meet her eyes. A letter to
Jonathan was already forming in his head. "I thank you,
Mrs. Brown, but I have only come to request your assistance. Jonathan said he had an office behind the house
that I might be able to use until I could establish a place
of my own. Would it be too much to ask if you would
consider my renting it from you?''

Laura pulled her scalded palm into the cuff of her
gown and avoided the doctor's eye. He was younger than
Jonathan, about Cash's age, she surmised, but she could
read his every thought on his rather expressive features.
Perhaps the unruly lock of dark blond hair falling over

his brow only gave the appearance of youth. The intelligence in those sharp blue eyes belied any youthful innocence. She could feel the heat of the burn go all the way up her arm when his gaze rested on it. He couldn't possibly know Marshall had done that only this morning, in a fit of temper when she had burned his bacon.

"You are welcome to use it free of charge, Dr. Burke. This is Jonathan's home, and he may offer its use whenever necessary. I daresay now that Marshall has returned, we will be looking for a place of our own, and you will be able to live here instead of wherever you are staying. Have you been putting up at the hotel?"

"I've found a room at Mrs. Parker's that suits me nicely. Please do not think of abandoning this place on my account. I'm not married and I don't know how to cook, and Mrs. Parker's meals are preferable to most of the places I've ever known."

"She is eminently respectable, I agree. Would you care to see the office?" Anything to distract that piercing look. He reminded Laura of Cash in that respect. This man would correspond with Jonathan. She had to do something, say something, to keep him from writing about her plight.

"I would appreciate that. Is there an outer entrance so I won't disturb you with my comings and goings?" He rose when she did, and followed her through the kitchen.

"Of course. Jonathan keeps his carriage out here and uses the carriage alley. His horse is over at the livery right now, since I can't take care of it, but you're welcome to keep it here. We're only too glad to have a physician again. You'll find that all homes welcome you."

As he examined the layout of the office and examining rooms and Jonathan's small laboratory, he asked questions, finally concluding with the one Laura dreaded to hear: "Let me examine that burn on your hand, Mrs. Brown, while I am here. How did you come by it in such an awkward place?"

He didn't give her a chance to refuse, but took her hand firmly in his and pushed her cuff up. Laura allowed him to look and apply some salve, but kept her secrets to herself. "It was an accident, Doctor. I grow clumsier with each passing day. May I trust you, Dr. Burke?"

He gave her a speculative glance but returned to his work. "I certainly hope so. Jonathan and I have corresponded regularly after an article of his appeared in a medical magazine while I was still in school. His thoughts and mine run much on the same path, which was why I was eager to come here. I regret that it took so long for me to make the move."

"Then you know that Jonathan is ill, that he needs to remain in Arizona and rest, that he shouldn't be emotionally disturbed in any way. I, too, know how to read medical journals."

Burke applied a bandage and straightened to meet her gaze. "He tells me the tubercular lesion is not extensive and that he hopes to recover well enough to return for you within the next year. I shouldn't think he ought to make that kind of journey in vain."

Laura heard the disapproval in his voice, but that was the least of her worries. Turning at the sound of a door closing in the front of the house, she spoke hastily. "No, of course not. Things have happened rather quickly, and I've feared to disturb him. I'll write to him soon. But you do understand my position? I don't want him thinking he must play the part of gallant knight. It would be worse than useless. Do not jump to hasty conclusions before you've had time to learn the situation."

Marshall's voice carried easily and they both moved toward the connecting door to the house. Burke opened the door for her and bowed as she passed by. In a low whisper he replied, "I'll be patient, Mrs. Brown. Perhaps you'll come to trust me a little more in time. From what I understand, you are too intelligent a woman to do otherwise."

Laura pretended not to hear him as she greeted her "husband," who stood suspiciously in the center of the kitchen, watching them. "Marshall, this is Dr. Burke. I've just been showing him Jonathan's offices. He will be taking Jonathan's place for now."

Marshall immediately assumed his most genial smile and held out his hand. "Dr. Burke, it's a pleasure to meet you."

By the time the doctor left, Laura could feel Marshall's temper simmering, and she frantically searched for some means of escape. She had been right about Marshall's propensity for cruelty. Often it was a subtle cruelty such as eating the entire meal she had prepared before she could swallow the few bites he left her time for, or "accidentally" dropping the sewing she was working on into the fire after she had denied him the few coins in her purse. But there were other times, times when his frustration and fears and fury boiled to the top, and he unleashed his violence on her. She felt one of those times about to erupt now, and she was helpless to prevent it.

As soon as the door closed behind their visitor, Marshall calmly turned and smacked the back of his hand across her face. Laura staggered backward, grabbing a chair for support, holding her hand up to the pain, but refusing to cringe before his furious gaze.

"Why in hell did you tell that busybody he could use our place? I don't need him out there at all hours watching what I do."

She should have known that. Reason and logic didn't apply in Marshall's warped mind. She knew he still rode out at night with his vicious band of men, but it had never occurred to her to deny the only doctor in town the office that Jonathan had told him he could use. Hiding the patronizing defiance she felt as she watched the stupid cunning on his face, she answered as reasonably as she was able.

"I told you that this place doesn't belong to me, but to Jonathan. He offered Dr. Burke the use of it, not me. Once Jonathan finds out about us, he has every right to ask us to leave so Dr. Burke can live here. You had better contemplate finding another place to live."

Marshall hooked his thumb in his belt and gave her a considering look. "That farm of your cousin's looks fair game to me. You're supposed to be looking after it, ain't you?"

She had feared that he would discover that. She had not returned to the farm since the weather had turned, nor had she taken much of Cash's money for her services. Now that spring was here, the painters and the carpenters would be coming to her here in town when they needed supplies, but she had hoped Marshall would be too busy with his plotting to notice. But she should have known one of them would inform Marshall of where the money came from to pay them.

"Cash and Sallie will be returning soon. I haven't been

invited to live with them, and you can be certain that
Cash will not appreciate your inviting yourself." Keeping
the chair between them, Laura straightened, although all
she really wanted to do was sit down and cry. She
couldn't believe she had sinned so badly to deserve this
much punishment, but she could see no hope of escape
anytime in the future. The child, alone, would be with
her for a lifetime, a scar of shame for all to see. Why
must Marshall be added to the burden?

"No man could object to a free cook and housemaid.
That's what you did for the holier-than-thou Ward, didn't
you? And how else are you to keep an eye on those
thieving carpenters? Even your cousin couldn't expect
you to go out there every day in your condition. I think
that's the ticket. We'll already be installed by the time
they come home. There won't be any polite way they
can throw us out. It's bound to be a sight better than this
hovel. I'd suggest you start packing your things today."

Laura let the horror and humiliation wash over her at
his words. Closing her eyes, she swayed slightly at the
thought of living in the same house with Cash and Sallie,
feeling their sympathy, their irritation at her unwelcome
presence. She would rather die, but she knew better than
to say that out loud. "Dinner is almost ready," she murmured, and pushed herself away from the chair without
looking at him again.

In the weeks since the doctor's arrival, Laura had deliberately ignored Marshall's command to begin packing.
He had returned to her life little over six weeks ago, and
already she felt as if it were a lifetime. She had learned
how to avoid the worst of his wrath by never confronting
him directly, but sooner or later he would demand to know
why she wasn't ready. And then the violence would begin.

She placed her hand over the huge swelling of her
stomach and felt the kicks of life within. The baby wasn't
due for weeks. She didn't know if she could hold out
that long, although Dr. Burke had assured her the child
was doing well when she had managed to let him examine
her. But he had said she had better get more rest or risk
having the child come early. She had tried, honestly
tried, but the choice between going without rest or risk-

ing Marshall's wrath had only one clear-cut answer. She was too exhausted to even think clearly anymore.

The roads to the farm were open now, and the painters and carpenters were hard at work. She really ought to see what they were doing, but she had sent Jettie out in her place. Jettie hadn't wanted to go and leave Laura, but they both knew there was little enough that she could do. Marshall had the entire town eating out of his hand. He even attended church on Sunday without her, accepting the well-wishes of Laura's friends and their sympathy and understanding at her confinement. He'd had the nerve to tell them that the doctor had told her to rest and not accept visitors, so there were few to see the bruises on her face or the dark shadows growing beneath her eyes.

He had already gone out to the farm to look things over for himself. It was only a matter of time before he demanded that they remove to the privacy of its environs. Dr. Burke had been a constant visitor and a burr under Marshall's saddle since he had arrived. Laura knew the situation was growing explosive, but she could not commit herself to leaving the protection of town and imposing on the empty hospitality of Stoner Creek. With no friends at all within screaming distance, it would be akin to leaving the frying pan for the fire.

Ignoring the growing pain in her back, Laura stirred the beans over the fire and waited for Marshall's inevitable return at the end of another tedious day. With May just around the corner, it was at least light at this time of day, and she didn't have to stumble through the house lighting lanterns so he wouldn't fall over the furniture when he entered. Somehow, it seemed easier to face Marshall in the light, and Laura kept her gaze fixed on the spot of sunlight coming through the room's one window.

As the sunlight faded, so did her hopes. When Marshall came home after dark, it meant he was drunk. She had learned the pattern. When he meant to ride out and perpetrate some filthy act, he came home early and sober to eat. But when there was nothing planned for the evening, he felt free to drink himself under the table. Sometimes he was too drunk to lift a hand to her. Others, he was just nasty enough to use her for a punching bag.

The day had been warm, and spring lingered in the air

even with the onset of darkness. Laura felt nervous and restless as the night grew late. Marshall had once again ordered her to pack and be ready to leave in the morning, and once again she had disobeyed. The child inside her hadn't moved all day, and she covered her abdomen worriedly. Something was wrong. She could feel it in her veins.

Her backed ached with every movement. If Marshall struck her tonight, she wouldn't be able to stand, or get back up if she fell. She was terrified he would hurt the child. So far, he hadn't gone that far, but it was only a matter of time. He spoke resentfully of her size, used vulgar language when he mentioned the baby's father, and indicated he had every intention of using her for wife once the child was born. She had to make some decision soon, but there just didn't seem to be any escape.

Dr. Burke offered the only hope of understanding, but Laura couldn't imagine how he could protect her from Marshall. Like Jonathan, he was a man of intelligence and sensitivity, not a man prone to carrying a gun as Marshall did. He would have to be her last resort.

As a palliative to her anxiety, Laura started packing a small bag of necessities and some of the baby linen she had accumulated. Perhaps it would be better if she could hide from Marshall until the baby was born, at least. She could go to Jettie's mother, beg her to take her in, to find her a harbor in the other tiny cabins and cottages of former slaves and freedmen scattered throughout the country. None of the white community knew anything about the black society in their midst. Laura knew that much from her dealings with Jettie. Not a soul in town had any idea that Jettie's child belonged to Ward. Few even recognized Jettie as the nurse who had cared for Ward during his last illness. The black population might as well be invisible for all anyone else knew or cared. All she had to do was persuade them to hide her.

Knowing that was an impossible thing to ask of strangers, Laura kept on packing anyway. She had to do something or go mad. She couldn't just sit here and wait for Marshall to return and beat her senseless. The more she thought about it, the faster she packed. She had no way of knowing that this wouldn't be one of the nights when he was too drunk to stand and had to be carried home. She just knew she had to get out of here.

As it was, she was too late. While she hesitated over stepping out into the night to run to Mrs. Jackson, she heard Marshall's steps on the back porch. Laura's gaze fell to the telltale bag sitting on the kitchen table, and she made a step toward it, calculating how much time it would take to move her bulky body out of the kitchen and into the parlor before Marshall entered. Not enough.

The door swung open and Marshall found her there, hands on the bag, a guilty expression on her face. It didn't take a strong mind to know what she had intended. With a sneer, he made the single step across the room and backhanded her across the face.

"Run out on me, will you? Did you think me the same kind of milksop as your doctor friend? Where did you think you were going that I wouldn't come after you? Not to Burke's, if you're smart. He's been treating the coloreds and there's been some nasty words said about it around town. I ain't about to stop what's going to happen to him."

The pain in her cheek couldn't compare to the others she suffered, and Laura eased her weight back to her feet from the support of the table. "You told me to pack, so I packed. Burke has nothing to do with this."

Marshall smacked her again, harder. For good measure, he hit her again, watching in satisfaction as Laura staggered backward, her fingers too weak to grasp the sink board as she slowly slid to the floor. "Don't lie to me. You think you're Miss Holier-Than-Thou, but you ain't nothing but the same piece of trash as your cousin's rich husband. I bet you spread your legs for half the town before trapping that damned doctor, and he ran away when he found out. That's what they'll be saying soon enough if you try to leave here."

Pain exploded inside Laura's head with his blow, and she could scarcely hear his words or comprehend their meaning. Fearing he was more than capable of kicking her when she was down, Laura tried to cling to the sink and the red blur of consciousness.

When she didn't pull herself upright, Marshall chortled and knelt beside her, grabbing her hair and shoving his whiskey-soured breath in her face. "I mean to be a man of position around here, wife. And you're going to help me to it. Now, you got your choice. You do what I say without complaint, or I make you learn what it's like to have nothing." One thick hand went to the bulge of her abdomen. "And I can start right here."

In her struggle to get away, Laura fell backward, hitting her head against the corner of the cabinet, feeling blackness swarm up around her as her senses reeled. But her instinct for self-preservation was fully roused, and she fought for consciousness, grasping a table leg and protecting herself as best she could with its bulk.

He was smothering her with his foulness, and she was far beyond understanding what he wanted. The pain in her abdomen worsened, and there was a burst of moisture between her legs. Panic-stricken, Laura struggled to pull herself up by means of the table leg.

Unbalanced by her movement, Marshall bumped drunkenly against the table, knocking it a few inches across the floor, jarring the pewter water pitcher Laura had left there earlier. Water splashed over the side of the table, drowning him in a sudden deluge as the pitcher rolled and fell to the floor. Laura scarcely noticed the water pouring around her, most of it striking Marshall, who half-covered her, but she clung to enough consciousness to grasp the significance of the pitcher. Without giving a thought to what she did, she grabbed the rolling pitcher and swung it with what strength was left to her.

There was nothing satisfactory about the dull thud it made against Marshall's pate. She felt only relief when he fell to the side instead of on top of her. He groaned and gagged as if he were about to be sick, and had she any thought at all, it would be to pour one of his bottles of whiskey down his throat and drown him. But she was operating simply on instinct now, with no thought at all.

Pulling herself up by the table leg, Laura grabbed the bag and continued on the path she had set herself earlier. She clung to enough consciousness to remember her goal as she staggered through the back door and toward the alley to safety. It never occurred to her to stop at the nearest house and ask for help. Head shattered from Marshall's blows, pain spreading rapidly through the rest of her, she knew only to move her feet toward Jettie's mother, the midwife.

17

Someone kept screaming. She wished it would stop. It hurt too much. The pain swallowed her and sent her back arching upward and she couldn't move her hands to stop it. For a moment the screams stopped and the pain subsided slightly, except for the ache in her head. Voices murmured around her. Mrs. Jackson, of course. Reassured by recognizing some of her surroundings, she drifted briefly, then the screams began again, and the pain returned, or perhaps it was the other way around. Laura was beyond knowing. Pain washed through her, pushing to escape, bearing down harder until she didn't think she could survive, and the screams reached a new crescendo.

More voices as the ripping pain subsided into dull aches. A male voice. Panic began to grow, and she tried to pull herself from the stupor that numbed her senses, but she could feel the pain beginning again, and the scream slipped out. Her voice was hoarse with it. Her voice. Her screams. God, what was happening to her?

Strong hands touched her in places where only one man had before, and a cold rag was placed across her aching head as her body raged on without her. A soothing voice spoke in her ear, while a man's curt words ordered someone about from somewhere at the end of the bed. Somehow Laura found reassurance in that curtness, and the coldness against her bruised cheek helped. But then the pain began, and she couldn't stop it. It rocked her body, and this time it wouldn't stop. Spasm after spasm shot through her, and she couldn't fight it, couldn't turn away, couldn't run anymore. With a wail, she let go, let it take control, and blessedly unconsciousness came to claim her.

The dull throb in her head prevented Laura from opening her eyes immediately. She could feel sunshine. The warmth prickled over her bare arms along with the hint of a spring breeze. She was afraid to wake, afraid the pain and misery would return, and she clung to sleep for protection. She dozed awhile longer until she realized something was wrong, something was different, and she stirred restlessly, seeking the reason without wanting to know.

She felt lighter than she had in months, as if some terrible burden had disappeared. She still ached, but it was nothing compared to the pain that she remembered. She moved again and realized she was not in her own bed but on a straw mattress. She had never slept on a straw mattress in her life. Not that she remembered anyway. The thought jarred her one more step toward waking.

"Here, honey, take a taste of this. Just a drink, Miss Laura, and you'll feel better. Let me hold your head, honey."

The soothing voice continued to murmur insistently, and Laura obediently lifted her head and sipped at the cool drink. She thought it was water, but the taste was odd. She did feel better, and she rested her head gratefully on the pillow afterward, hoping to find sleep again. A persistent noise somewhere nearby made her toss and turn, however. A mewling sound. Was there a kitten in here?

The noise grew louder, and more voices murmured in consultation. Then the first voice returned to her side and an arm came behind her, forcing her to sit up enough for more pillows to be placed behind her head. The pillows were old and hard, and she shifted restlessly against them.

"This little one done want his breakfast now, Miss Laura. You just a mite bit of a thing, but you got enough where it counts for this little fella. Here, let me help you hold him. He'll help himself, he will."

Laura murmured a protest as she felt her gown being unfastened, but her arms closed instinctively around the heavy weight placed in them. Warm skin brushed her breast, and instantly she felt the soreness. When an eager mouth closed over the nipple, she cried out and jerked awake.

A dark head of hair rested against her breast, but it wasn't Cash who suckled there. Laura's eyes opened wide with surprise as she cautiously studied the stranger pulling eagerly at her, flailing helplessly with tiny fists until he had what he wanted and settled comfortably to nursing. Cash's son. The miracle of it held her in awe, keeping thoughts at bay as she slowly explored the long sturdy body in her arms. Babies were supposed to be tiny, but this one had long legs that kicked when she touched them, and long fingers that curled compulsively around hers when she tried to examine their tiny, perfect fingernails. And a healthy appetite. She winced as he tugged harder, and wondered that she was cursed with still another demanding male.

Lucretia chuckled at her expression. "Try him on the other side, honey. It will be a while before the milk comes in enough to satisfy a boy as big as that one. Dr. Jon done himself proud with that one."

At the mention of Jonathan's name in connection with Cash's child, Laura winced again. Obviously Mrs. Jackson had not accepted Marshall's lies, but she had no reason not to believe the gossip. Those thoughts were enough to bring back what she had tried to forget, and Laura closed her eyes against the heated pain that memory returned.

"I have to get out of here before Marshall finds me," were her first words. They came out more as a whisper than the direct command she had meant them to be.

"You ain't goin' nowhere for a while, honey. That boy there done took it out of you. You need plenty of rest, the doctor says. Don't you fret none. Your man ain't gonna find you anytime soon."

If he wanted to, he would, but maybe he wouldn't want to. Grasping that possibility, Laura gave herself up to the sensations of the warm little body in her arms. Her son. It seemed incredible to believe. After all these months, she finally held her son in her hands.

He gradually quietened until she knew he slept, and under Mrs. Jackson's instructions she lifted him to her shoulder and rubbed his back. His dark head rested trustingly against her neck, and she felt his warm breath against her skin, and her heart was won without a fight.

Tears caught in her lashes as Lucretia lifted him from her shoulder and placed him in the box she had padded with an old blanket. Laura didn't want to let him go. She had never been given the chance to love someone so openly, and it seemed unfair to have to let him go, even for a minute. She was happier when the old woman moved the box closer to the bed where she could watch him sleep and reach out to touch the dark shock of hair against his pale head.

"You got a name for him?" Mrs. Jackson moved around the room, taking a pot from the side of the small hearth and pouring coffee.

For the first time, Laura registered her surroundings with clarity. The little cabin was filled with sunlight from the open door and windows. A small fire burned in the grate that served as the cabin's only heat and kitchen. The smell of coffee perfumed the air, and she accepted the cup offered gratefully. She realized she wore only the summer nightshift that she had packed in her bag, and wondered who had found the strength to change her. She couldn't remember taking off her clothes.

That thought was followed quickly by the sound of a male voice greeting someone on the front step. A vague memory of the prior night returned, just enough to make Laura blush heatedly as the familiar form of Dr. Burke entered the low doorway.

"Well, Mrs. Jackson, it seems our patient is doing much better this morning." He set his bag down on a rickety table and accepted the coffee his hostess handed him. Sipping it, he studied the woman watching him warily from the bed. "Good morning, Mrs. Brown. I didn't expect to see you up and so lively already. You had a rather rough night of it. How do you feel this morning?"

Her head ached. Laura could feel the swollen side of her face. She ached in other places she had no intention of mentioning. All told, she felt like hell, but she merely sipped her coffee in imitation of him and answered, "About as expected, I should say."

He made a noncommittal grunt and set his cup down.

Crossing the space between them in a stride, he tilted her face up to the light. "Mrs. Jackson, I'd recommend you keep her away from a mirror for a week or two." His fingers probed the bruises gently.

Laura shook her head away. "Don't worry about mirrors. I can't stay here a week or two. I need to leave as soon as possible. I couldn't risk traveling before, but I can't risk staying now. I need to get to Lexington, at least. I can pay the fare if you'll just get me to the train station."

She would have to use Cash's money to pay the fare, but she would pay him back somehow. It was more important that she protect his son than worry over the honesty of taking his money. She closed her eyes and steeled herself against embarrassment as Burke's exploring fingers examined her. He was very good at making his touches impersonal. It was nothing like it had been when Cash touched her. Perhaps that was why Jonathan's touches had not incited the same flames. Or perhaps it was only the forbidden that made her ache for more. Well, she had had enough of the forbidden. From now on she was taking the safe route.

"You'll not be going anywhere for two weeks, at the very earliest, Mrs. Brown. Your body needs time to recover from its exertions, and your son shouldn't be exposed to the rigors of travel. If it's your husband you are afraid of, I'll summon the sheriff to protect you."

Laura laughed, although it came out more a croak. "You must come from more enlightened places than Stoner Creek, Doctor. The sheriff will do nothing to keep a wife from her husband. In fact, he's more likely to incarcerate you and Mrs. Jackson for preventing Marshall's access to me."

Burke stepped back and gave her battered face a stare. "You are being slightly hysterical, my dear. Any thinking man need only look at you and know it's best to keep you safe from the man who assaulted you. Let me press charges against him, and he will be locked up and you needn't worry about him."

A sudden flashback of that horrendous day when the men of town had stood in front of the courthouse and watched as Watterson nearly beat Cash to death with a

whip brought more hollow laughter to Laura's lips. Let
him think her hysterical. She knew without even trying
what would happen should he be fool enough to take out
a warrant against Marshall. Her eyes opened and she
lifted a glare to the man standing there, thinking himself
all-powerful in his skill and knowledge.

"Let me try to explain one more time, Dr. Burke. Do
not think me unappreciative of your offer, but you will
have to understand: a wife is a husband's property
under Kentucky law. He can do anything he wants to,
and no one can interfere. The Emancipation Proclamation did not include wives, as far as I recall." At the
disbelief lingering in his eyes, she made her meaning
more explicit. "If your neighbor chose to burn his own
house down, would you have the right to stop him?"

Put in those terms, he understood. Shaking his head,
he tried again. "I find it hard to believe that in this
day and age, no one would come forward to help you.
You command a good deal of respect in this town. No
one seems aware of your husband's propensity for violence—"

Laura cut him short. "He's not my husband. He's a
brute and a villain and there is nothing I can do about
it. The sheriff is a man. All the town fathers are men.
And they will all believe Marshall before they will believe
me. They will say what you just said. She's just hysterical. Having the baby caused her to lose her senses. She'll
be all right in a little while. Just give them time. Marshall's a fine man.

"I've lived here far longer than you, Doctor, and I've
heard the excuses a thousand times before. They turned
their backs when men beat their slaves, and they turn
their backs when men beat their wives. It's all the same
thing. And you're in no position to argue with them. If
you're not careful, you'll end up on the wrong end of a
noose. There are ignorant people in this county who resent a white doctor treating any but white people. If you
insist on wandering into houses like this one, you'd better
start wearing a gun."

Burke looked startled, then angry. "Now, wait just
one minute, Mrs. Brown . . ." He stopped, remembering
her declaration that she was not married, and amended,

"Miss Laura. I'm a physician. My business is to heal the sick, whatever color they might be. No one is going to tell me whom I can or cannot treat. I'm certain Jonathan never turned anyone away."

Wearily Laura closed her eyes. "No, but he never went to their houses, either. He knew the town. If someone came in his back gate while no one was looking, then no one could complain. But he did not flagrantly display his disloyal tendencies. Ask Mrs. Jackson. Jonathan is a good man, but he's been around long enough to learn caution. How many babies have been lost because Dr. Broadbent couldn't come out to help you, Mrs. Jackson?"

The old woman's face was a mask of indifference as she replied, "Not none of them, Miss Laura. Warn't nothin' he coulda done for them anyways."

Even Burke had the sense to know differently. He had only to look at the woman lying on the straw mattress to know that it was his hands that had saved her, and that she would have been lost had she been left to the cares of an old woman without his skills and knowledge. It wasn't just conceit, but the woman's own admission when he had arrived last night. Burke's idolization of his older mentor slipped to a more reasonable regard. Jonathan was only human, after all.

"That docsn't resolve what we have here. If Marshall isn't your husband, then you can press assault charges and the sheriff will have to abide by them."

Laura was growing weary of his insistence. "It's all the same, Dr. Burke. The whole town knows I left to marry Marshall when I was still a child. He's behaved as my husband these past weeks, claimed my child as his, and no one is going to doubt his word. It's easy enough to prove people are married, but how does one go about proving they aren't?"

"Well, I am not about to stand helplessly waiting for him to come kill you. There has to be something that can be done."

"Take me to the train station as soon as I can travel." The words whispered wearily from Laura's lips as her eyes closed and her head fell back upon the pillows. She couldn't carry the burden any longer, and she slept.

The doctor and the midwife exchanged glances. The woman on the bed was too small and frail to bear what she already had. It seemed a miracle she was alive. Yet she still kicked and protested and demanded her way. Burke looked down upon the healthy, sleeping infant, wondered briefly who the father was, then packed his bag and nodded to the old woman.

"I'm going to the sheriff, no matter what she says. And I'm writing to Dr. Broadbent. There has to be something done to protect her."

As if Jonathan's name had penetrated her consciousness, Laura stirred and murmured, "Cash. Tell Cash."

Lucretia's eyebrows momentarily raised, then lowered. When the doctor turned to her for explanation, she shrugged. "Her cousin's husband. They be good friends, but he gone No'th for his weddin' trip. He'd be the one to tell, for certain."

"There has to be some way to get word to him. I'll find out." Restoring his hat to his head, Dr. Burke strode out.

Laura woke when her son woke and slept when he slept. By the next day she was feeling well enough to be irritable. Her entire jaw ached, and though the swelling seemed to be down, it felt stiff and painful when she tried to eat or speak. Marshall had obviously split her lip also, and anything hot scorched across the cut. There were bruises on her breast that made her moan when the babe beat at them, but she hugged him closer and calmed his angry hands with soothing words, and he soon turned to more important matters as he drained her filling breasts.

"That boy done gonna be up and walking afore you," Lucretia muttered as she watched his eager pull. "You never did say what you gonna name him. Boy's gotta have a name."

Laura had had time to think about that, but she'd never had any real hope that she would ever see this day. Now that it had come, she felt as defiant as she had the night Jettie's child had been born. "Jonathan, of course. Jonathan Marcus Kincaid."

Lucretia's eyes narrowed at that. "They ain't gonna

call him Kincaid. And your daddy's name was Mark, not
Marcus. That sounds like that fancy stuff Cash's momma
done used on him."

"It doesn't matter what anybody thinks." Laura stroked
the dark head on her breast lovingly. "I'll call him Mark
and everyone will think he's named after my father." She
turned anxious eyes to her protector. "Do you think you
could take him over to your church and have him baptized? If something happens to me, I want him to have
a name."

"Ain't nothin' gonna happen to you," Lucretia answered scornfully. "You a Kincaid. You be fine."

Lucretia had been a relation of Jemima's, the cook at
Stoner Creek before the war, and Laura knew full well
that kind of talk. She had spent enough time in Jemima's
kitchens listening to the lies and the laughter and the
sorrow, and she knew when everything was hopeless, the
lies prevailed. She wasn't fooled by Lucretia's assurances.

"No matter. I want him baptized, and if anything hap-
pens to me, I want him taken to Cash and Stoner Creek.
Cash will take care of him. If Marshall comes, you hide
Mark and get him to the farm. Don't worry about me.
I'm big enough to stand on my own; Mark isn't."

The old woman looked skeptical but nodded to the
wisdom of this decision. If she had any thoughts about
Laura's assertion that Cash would take care of her son
rather than her cousin Sallie, she didn't speak them
aloud. White people had their own brand of trouble. She
wanted no part of it.

18

"I've come to bring my wife home. I know she's in there, so stand out of my way, old woman."

Laura had waited for that voice with dread for days now. In her mind, she had practiced what she would say and do when the time came, but her mind wasn't the same as reality. Panic raced through her veins, and she glanced down to the sleeping innocent beside the bed. She had been practicing standing, creeping slowly about the perimeter of the small room, but she wasn't swift enough to pick up her son and run. Placing a kiss on her fingers and caressing his head with it, she pushed the box beneath the bed and out of sight.

At least she had a gown on today. She hadn't been able to pack petticoats, and the ones she had worn that night were ruined, but it was better than greeting the light of day in her nightshift. Laura swung her legs over the bed where she had been resting and braced herself on the nearby table to rise. It would be better if she got far enough away from the house to keep Marshall from waking the infant.

Marshall looked red-eyed and belligerent when Laura came to stand in the doorway. He must have been on a week-long drinking spree to look so disheveled and sick. She gazed upon him imperturbably as she brushed past Mrs. Jackson to step into the street like a mother quail distracting the enemy from her young. The children who were inevitably playing in the dirt had disappeared at the first sign of trouble. She was rather grateful for their discretion.

"I've come to bring you home, Laura," Marshall said stiffly, coming toward her. "It's not right you staying here in a colored shack."

Laura edged slowly from the door, aware that eyes

watched all around her, but in this section of town they weren't eyes that she knew. There wasn't anything Mrs. Jackson could do, and the old woman stood silently by, backing toward her door as Laura eased away from the house and Mark.

"I'm not well, Marshall. I'm not even supposed to be out of bed. I can't do your cooking. You'll have to hire someone in." She had planned that, dug through her brain for any protection she could derive. It wasn't much, but it would help if she had someone on her side, someone who could see what he did to her, and for what little reason.

A brief anger flitted across his face and disappeared as Marshall put on a contrite expression. "I'm sorry, Laura. I won't hurt you no more. I was drunk and lost my head, but I won't do it again. I promise. The sheriff has offered me the job of his deputy, and I'll have a little money to bring in. I can pay for some help for a little while. Just get the baby and let's go home."

All Laura could think was that it was a damn good thing she had talked Dr. Burke from going to the sheriff. Tensing her shoulders, she took another step or two down the road. "The baby died, Marshall. You killed it." She said that out of pure meanness, to get even with some of the hurts he had caused, but he didn't even flinch.

"That's all right. We'll have another one. The whole town's whispering about you being down here. They're asking ugly questions. It's time you came home."

Facing Marshall, Laura didn't see the two men hurrying down the street behind her. Her entire attention was on Marshall's wicked, lying, weasely face. He couldn't meet her eyes, couldn't look at the damage he had done to her. She didn't know how bad it was, had refused to look at a mirror, but she knew from the colors of the bruises on the rest of her body that she couldn't be a pretty sight. She wanted to shoot him, wanted to find a loaded pistol and put a bullet between his eyes, but they would hang her for that, and her son needed a mother. Somehow she would have to kill him. But not now. Not in the bright light of this brilliant spring day.

"You'll have to send someone to fetch me, Marshall. I can't walk that far. And you'll need to stop and get

Mrs. Perkins before you bring me home. She'll help me. I'm not going to be alone with you anymore."

The men hurrying up behind her gasped as Marshall's mask suddenly dropped, and he grabbed Laura, twisting his hand in her hair with a curse, swinging her to face them, so they could see the bilious yellow and green bruises marring delicate cheekbones. If he meant to hold her hostage against their attack, he underestimated his enemy. Before Marshall could so much as raise his voice in warning, the taller of the two men strode forward, wielding the whip in his hand. Bringing it down across Marshall's neck without touching Laura.

Laura gasped at the crack of leather and tugged away from Marshall's weakening hold. Her eyes opened in disbelief at the sight of Cash's dark face livid with fury, and she could do nothing but stare as he lashed out again and again. Marshall fell to his knees and tried to roll away, and Cash's mouth became a malevolent scar across his face. As soon as Marshall tried to rise, Cash coolly flicked the whip across his back again.

"Crawl, Brown. I want to see you crawl. I want all the brave citizens of this town to see you crawl until your hands bleed. I want you to know what it's like to be broken and humiliated, and I want them to know what happens when a man behaves like an animal. Start crawling, Brown, or I'll bleed you into a bloody pulp."

Laura nearly fainted as the whip lashed again, slicing open Marshall's coat and drawing blood. A hard arm caught her up, and she gratefully grasped Dr. Burke as he looked on, doing nothing to prevent the fury unleashed by Cash's hand. Heads began to peer out of doorways, and Mrs. Jackson crossed her arms in satisfaction as Marshall hurriedly obeyed the command to crawl. Each time he tried to rise, Cash struck again, taking satisfaction in the blow.

"Doctor, you have to stop him," Laura murmured, horrified, but somehow elated at the scene. Each blow of the whip felt like a vengeance for her suffering, and she could not bring herself to interfere.

"Mr. Wickliffe seems to be an intelligent man. He won't kill him. I daresay before he is done, the man will have second thoughts about coming around you again."

Laura closed her eyes as Marshall tried to escape down

an alley and Cash struck him down again. A crowd was beginning to gather at the end of the street. This alley ended in a larger thoroughfare, not one of the macadamized roads but a brick street used by whites as well as blacks. She could feel curious eyes turned in her direction, but for Cash's sake she remained where she was. Let them know why he did this. Let them fully understand Marshall deserved every blow. And since Cash was now a member of her family, the only male member, they would allow him to get away with it.

As they disappeared around the corner, Laura let her shoulders slump and she turned away. She had not known Cash had returned already. She had once hoped to be gone before he returned. That hope was lost forever, and the scene that was yet to come sat threateningly on her shoulder like some evil bird. "I had better see to Mark, Doctor. Perhaps you ought to go after Marshall."

"I would prefer to leave him rotting in the gutter." His hard tone caused her to look up, and he patted her hand soothingly. "I'll not, of course. Mrs. Jackson, perhaps you will help me get our patient seated." He glanced to the woman waiting stoically in the doorway.

The older woman stood aside and let them enter. Apparently she had already rescued Mark from beneath the bed, and she held him out to Laura now. "There won't be no need of you hidin' this young 'un now. He'll be fine."

If "now that his daddy's home" didn't come out in words, it laced her tone. Laura gave a weary nod of acknowledgment and lifted her sleeping son to her shoulder. "I don't know how to thank you. If you hadn't been here . . ."

"Folks gotta look after one 'nother. Jettie Mae's the one told me when that Wickliffe boy come home. You always got friends in these parts to look after you." She gave Dr. Burke a second look. "And you, Doctor, best looks to yo'self. If Dr. Jon ain't comin' back, we need you in one piece. There's goin's-on hereabouts you don' know nothin' 'bout."

Burke bowed formally at this warning. "I take your meaning, Mrs. Jackson, but I can't stop doing what I was meant to do. If you'll see to Miss Laura, I'd best go attend to Mr. Brown."

For lack of anywhere else to sit, Laura returned to the
bed and rested with her back against the pillow, keeping
a firm hold on her son. She knew Cash would be back,
and there would be no hiding from him now. She could
only pray that he would assume her child was Jonathan's,
as everyone else had before Marshall came to town.

She didn't have long to wait. Cash entered the open
doorway without knocking, his eyes flashing fury and his
face still contorted with rage. One glance from him sent
Lucretia scurrying from the room, slamming the door
behind her. Laura clung to her son and watched him
calmly, knowing the storm would break over her head
but not harm her.

"Why didn't you tell me?" were the first words out of
his mouth, the first words she had heard in over three
months from him.

"It wasn't any of your business," was her calm reply.

Cash strode across the room and pulled back the blanket covering the infant's head. His hand stilled momentarily as it encountered the small black head, and then
his fingers automatically lifted to stroke the soft fur of
hair. "Mine," he announced firmly, without question.

She wanted to deny it, wanted to jerk the child from
his hand and hide the truth, but she had known from the
very first that she could not. Her only hope had been
that he wouldn't guess. She could tell the truth to Jonathan when the time came, but she had hoped there would
never be any need to speak it to Cash. She should have
known that was a fool's game.

"Mine," Laura answered softly.

Cash jerked as if she had smacked him, then reached
with both hands to claim the infant, pulling him from her
grasp, holding him expertly as he examined tiny fingers
and toes in the same way she had done when first confronted with him. The infant woke and squirmed and
stared with sightless eyes at his father, then gave a wail
of protest when discovering a stranger's rude touch. The
look on Cash's face softened, and he almost smiled as
he guided the flailing fist to his son's mouth and watched
him grow quiet.

"He's big, isn't he?" he asked in wonder, rocking the
tiny bundle in his arms.

Laura could have spent the rest of her life denying her

feelings toward this man who came and went through her life like a summer storm, but in that instant she could not deny the overwhelming emotions welling up in her as she saw her son with his father, and read the love on Cash's face.

"Dr. Burke says he's larger than most. He must take after you."

That admission brought Cash's head up, and his dark eyes met hers and held them. "There was time. You could have told me. Why didn't you?"

What explanation could she give that he didn't already know? "It was what I wanted," seemed to be the only truthful reply.

His face hardened again, and his words were crisp. "I thought you smarter than Sallie, but I suppose it runs in the family. I'm taking you with me back to the farm. My son belongs with me."

If she had ever dreamed of the day when Cash found out about his son, she would never have dreamed this reaction. Laura stared at him incredulously, all the arguments against such insanity racing through her mind, but Cash's stubbornly determined expression warned who would prevail. She was weak, weaker than usual, mind and body and soul debilitated by the horrors of the last few months. But still she couldn't give in without a fight.

"Don't be ridiculous. You and Sallie are newlyweds. You don't need a dependent relative hanging about your necks like an albatross, and you certainly don't need to ruin your marriage by bringing home your . . ."

She hesitated momentarily over the word, and Cash's furious frown cut her off. "Don't you dare say it, Laura." He shifted the child in his arms and held him protectively. "We've both made mistakes, but there's no reason to take it out on this child. You're going back with me. I'll not leave you here prey to that villain out there, or any other. We'll discuss how to go on after you've had time to rest and recover."

"But Sallie . . ." Laura's mind rebelled at the thought of returning to the farm and Sallie, but right now she knew she needed its safety. Torn by confusion, she allowed Cash to walk over her protests.

"The farm is mine now, to do with as I wish. Sallie is the last one with a right to complain if I bring you and our child home. She needn't know the boy's parentage, if that's what worries you. I'll not treat her that cruelly."

That wasn't exactly Laura's greatest worry, but his sensible words caused her to nod in relief. It would be weeks before she was herself again. By then perhaps she would have found a solution. She had to find a solution. The idea of living under the same roof with Cash and Sallie, knowing they retired to the same big bed together every night, would drive her insane if she thought about it at all.

Seeing her acceptance, however reluctant, Cash held his tongue. There was no need to tell her more just yet, no need to tell her Sallie carried his child too. She would discover that fact soon enough for herself. Sallie made no point of concealing it. Her complaints were so vociferous that he had been relieved by any excuse to return to the farm and escape her constant company. He had not thought the urgent wire from the doctor would have this conclusion, and he was still shaken by the sight of Laura's delicate beauty marred by the fists of a filthy beast, but he was glad to be back. Carefully he released his son into Laura's hands.

"What is he named?"

Laura hesitated, but Lucretia had taken him for his baptizing just yesterday. Avoiding Cash's eyes, she answered, "Jonathan Marcus. Everyone thinks he's Marshall's, but I can't bear to call him Brown."

Cash's dark eyes gleamed briefly as he gazed upon mother and son. "I didn't think you knew my full name. I'm honored that you would reward me in such a manner, pairing my name with an honorable man like Jonathan."

The emotions of the last hour had taken their toll, and Laura closed her eyes and leaned back against the pillows. She couldn't bear to watch his face, to feel the warmth welling up inside her knowing he was looking at her with affection, with the same affection he had shown the young child she once had been. Perhaps he thought of her as the younger sister he had never had. Whatever it was, it was not what she needed from Cash. From anyone else, yes, but not from Cash.

Softly she replied, "I always admired your name, as I always admired your mother's courage. It seemed only fitting. I call him Mark, though, so people think he's named after my father."

Cash's voice took on a wry tone. "Wise choice, *pequeña*. You rest now. I'll be back shortly with a carriage. I'll send someone to pack your bags later."

She was really doing this, really agreeing to accompany Cash back to the farm and Sallie. She must be out of her mind. She had heard of medieval priests who flagellated themselves to cleanse their souls. Her soul ought to be as pure as the driven snow if she lived through this. She pretended to sleep and felt Cash lift the child and return him to his box. She heard him speak in a low voice to Lucretia outside the door and felt certain money was being exchanged. She ought to feel bought and paid for, but she merely felt tired. Maybe tomorrow she would wrestle with the demons of her conscience.

19

"Laura, I decleah, you're no better than that sassy darkie downsteahs in the kitchen." Sallie flaunted the elaborate train of her fashionable lilac shot-silk taffeta as she swept around the room fingering the various personal effects Jettie Mae had helped Laura unpack.

Laura occupied herself studying the effect of Sallie's half-crinoline and the way the cascades of lilac material were drawn up behind her to create a devastatingly rich effect that had not yet reached these backwaters of fashion. Cattily Laura observed the flatter skirt in front would not long conceal Sallie's spreading waistline. That thought triggered a deep pain, and Laura turned her face to the wall. It did not take much imagination to wonder why Sallie's usually svelte figure had grown more voluptuous these last months.

Laura's refusal to reply did not deter her cousin. Picking up one of Mark's tiny gowns, Sallie sniffed and wrin-

kled her nose. "The least you could do is write to Dr.
Broadbent and tell him to come and marry you. The
scandal is simply *enormous*, Laura. I can scarcely hold
my head up and go to town."

"Then go back to New York, Sallie. From the sounds
of it, you preferred the society there." Laura wasn't up
to being polite. She didn't want to be here. She didn't
have to suffer her cousin's condescensions any more than
necessary. As soon as she recovered her full strength,
she was going to take her life back into her own hands
again.

"I never saw so many fashionable people in all my
life," Sallie agreed heartily, with a trace of wistfulness.
"They make the folks 'round here look like red Indians."

Laura noticed the exaggerated Southern accent came
and went with Sallie's moods. From some of the things
she'd heard these last days, it seemed Sallie's Southern-
belle pose had made quite a hit in the Northern environs
where Cash had taken her. It was becoming increasingly
obvious that Sallie had wished to stay when Cash had
insisted on coming home. The differences did not bode
well for the new marriage, but Laura had never expected
Sallie to make Cash happy, not in the way a good wife
makes a man happy. No, they both had what they
wanted, and neither required the loving relationship that
Laura craved. And would never have.

Tired of her self-pitying thoughts, Laura responded
just to keep Sallie talking. "Tell me all the places you
saw. Was New York as large as they say?"

Sallie's eyes widened in remembrance as she turned
toward the bed. "You never saw such a hotel! It filled a
whole block and towered up to the sky, and everything
was plush velvet and hushed voices and there were the
cutest little boys in red caps right at your fingertips every
minute to help with bags and everything. I felt like a
princess. And Cash had these friends who'd made some
kind of investments or such out in California, and they
took us to the most dazzling restaurants! Imagine all the
crystal that must go into those chandeliers! And silver
glittering all over the tablecloths. I never thought the
North had such graciousness, but they beat us proud.
Maybe Cash will take me back when the harvest's in. I
never did have time to order some winter gowns. I

couldn't possibly go back to wearing what that little dressmaker in town sews. Why, I bet she doesn't even have one of those new machines that stitch so much nicer! Did you see this? Did you see how fine a stitch holds these ribbons?"

If Laura had seen the expensively laced ribbons on Sallie's clothes once, she had seen them a dozen times in the last two days. The lilac had discreet black ribbons covered with black lace down the neatly fitted sleeves and around the cuffs and bodice, and Laura would have given her eyeteeth for anything half so elegant. As soon as she was able, she intended to duplicate the style herself, but the idea of sewing on all that lace and ribbon without the new sewing machine made her fingers ache to think of it. Still, she knew she could do it, and better.

"You never went to town for your gowns anyway, Sallie. And haven't you forgotten something?" It was a reminder of a subject that Sallie had not yet broached with her, but one that needed to be discussed.

Sallie gave her cousin a suspicious look. Laura's face was no longer puffy from the bruises, but the discoloration was ghastly. She had made no attempt to dress her hair, but merely wore it in a long braid down her back as if she were still a child. Sallie frowned at the sight and went back to playing with the pretty china pieces on the mantel. "I can't imagine what I've forgotten. Cash promised to give me anything I wanted. And I want to go back to New York."

"Sallie, Cash isn't Ward, and he isn't going to take you anywhere if your belly's big with child. You're going to have Cash's baby, aren't you?"

The china figurine fell to the stone hearth and shattered. Sallie glanced at it and stepped away. "What's that to say to anything? You had one. If you can do it, I can."

Ugliness crept in and found a lodging beside her heart as Laura glanced at the broken figurine. Uncle Matthew had given her that china doll when she had been only a child. She had carried it to Cairo and back, carefully wrapped in dozens of linens and petticoats. And now it lay shattered like all of her dreams. She closed her eyes against the pain and hate and steeled her voice to be calm.

"You were married in January. When's the baby due? September? October? Are you planning on waiting until the baby is born before going to New York, or do you want to have it on the train?"

Sallie picked up a hairbrush from the dresser and flung it at the wardrobe door. "On the train! Dammit, why should I be burdened with this miserable brat just when life is getting to be fun again? Do you know how hard it is to live day after day in this ratty house, watching things fall apart, watching all the brave boys die and go away, watching an invalid grow older and weaker every day? It's torture! Pure, unmitigated torture! And I'm never going to do it again."

If Sallie thought she had a sympathetic audience, she'd better think twice. Laura watched stoically as Sallie stalked the room, fingers clenched with rage.

"A baby! Who thought the beast would stick me with his brat so soon? That's all he talks about. 'Sallie, don't you think you should stop drinking wine now that you have the child to think about? Sallie, shouldn't we go home now that there's a baby to consider?' He never gives a damn about what I think or how I feel. All he cares about is flaunting his masculine prowess in getting me pregnant before we're scarcely wed!"

Oh, well, Laura could sympathize with that. Cash had been crowing over little Mark since he'd brought them home. Discreetly, perhaps, but crowing just the same. She'd known it would go straight to his head if he ever learned he had gotten both Kincaid women with child. Actually, to give him credit, he'd probably be the same were she Jettie Mae, but that was beside the point. Cash had a soft spot for babies and no patience with the women who bore them. Of course, Sallie was enough to try any man's patience, but that was no reason for him to ignore Laura as well as his wife. Cash had been altogether too circumspect in his avoidance of this room.

Which suited Laura just fine, she told herself. Just watching her cousin stalk the room like a cat in a cage was sufficient reason to count herself lucky. Never again would she allow a man to tie her down. Let Sallie suffer the disadvantages as well as the advantages of holy wedlock.

"Sallie, you've been a married woman, you knew what

to expect. You have no one to blame but yourself. You're going to make yourself sick if you don't settle down. Having a baby is no picnic, but you'll get through it if you just take care of yourself. Have you called on Dr. Burke yet?"

"No, and I'm not going to. It's embarrassing enough to have a husband touching me whenever he wants. I'm not going to let some complete stranger into my room." Sallie drew herself up proudly, though she seemed to cringe slightly as her words came out, and she turned away with a flush of color on her cheeks.

"Embarrassing" wasn't exactly the word Laura would use to describe Cash's touch, but it would not do to dwell on just what word she would use. "Exciting" came instantly to mind, but there were others, and they were best left unsaid or unthought. "Sallie, you're being a prudish old grandmother. Doctors are the modern way of doing things. He's very nice, and he's from the North. You ought to like him."

"Well, you can have him. You certainly ought to find *somebody*." With that sarcastic comment, Sallie swept out of the room

Laura sank back against the pillows and stared at the familiar ceiling of her old room. She hadn't come very far, after all.

Cash came in after the evening meal, his cheroot still in his hand as he dismissed Jettie Mae and turned his eager gaze to the woman and child in the bed. At his request, he'd been given permission to enter after his son was fed, and he had come so quickly that Laura was still patting the infant over her shoulder, bringing up milky little burps.

She looked up in surprise, then hesitation as he came forward, his gaze fastened eagerly on the child in her arms. She didn't understand his fascination with the baby. Other men passed out cigars and went on about their business, but from what she'd heard, Cash didn't seem able to sleep, think, or talk of anything else. Before she was even awake in the mornings, he was at the nursery when Mark began to wriggle and cry with hunger and wet. He popped in at lunch when he should be out in the fields, often carrying some little trinket he'd found in town to amuse Mark. And every evening, after dinner, he came to examine his child for changes since lunch and to play with him until he slept.

Had Cash been her husband, Laura would have been charmed. As it was, she worried herself to sleep each night with this unexpected behavior. She hadn't planned on staying at Stoner Creek. She wasn't certain where she was going, but she couldn't live forever under the same roof as Sallie, not while Cash stood between them. She wasn't at all certain of her feelings for Cash, and she didn't want to be. He had stood her friend too often to deny him, but she couldn't bear to be in the same room with him right now. The longing was too deep, too primeval to resist for long. She had been glad when he had been satisfied with visiting only the nursery. She didn't know how she felt now that he had finally come to see her.

"You make a beautiful mother." Cash stroked a straying strand of hair from Laura's cheek before lifting the child from her shoulder.

"So does Sallie," Laura replied wryly before she could stop herself.

Cash grimaced and balanced the babe in his arms, admiring the sleepy features of his son rather than meet Laura's eyes. "I didn't think it would be long before you found out. I'm sorry, Laura. Had you only told me . . ."

She pulled her bed jacket more firmly closed and tied the ribbon. "Don't be ridiculous. It's Sallie you've always wanted. I knew that. What kind of friend would I be if I forced you into something you didn't want because of something I did?"

Cash looked mildly startled as he finally faced her. "You did? I rather thought it took two, my dear. And did the bruises on your pretty face not shame me, I would shake you until your teeth rattled for not telling me while you had the chance. The child is as much mine as yours. Did you not think I had some right in the matter as to how he would be raised?"

"No, I did not. He is mine. I carried him for nearly nine months, not you. You had next to nothing to do with the whole affair. Men are free to go from woman to woman without ever sharing the consequences. Why should you be any different?"

The infant squirmed restlessly at the increasingly angry voices around him. Cash bounced him lightly in his arms and whispered soothing words, then spoke more softly when he replied. "You know damn good and well I don't care what other men do. I was practically raised an orphan by a man who thought I was good only to be his donkey. Do you think I want my child to be treated like that? What do you think would have happened to him had that Brown character got his hands on him?"

Laura flinched, but continued to meet his gaze steadily. "I'd not let that happen, and you know it. I am quite capable of taking care of my own child, and I mean to do it, Cash Wickliffe. I'm not staying here forever."

"You can go anywhere you want, miss High-and-Mighty Kincaid, but my son stays here!" Turning on his heel, Cash stalked out of the room, carrying the infant with him.

Laura stared after him in dismay. Never had she dreamed she would enmire herself so deeply by carrying Cash's child. She should have married Jonathan and gone with him to Arizona. She had been a fool not to. Jonathan had been a fool to leave her. Settle the differences between herself and Cash, her foot and eye! There would never be an end to those differences now. They would always be there, staring her in the face, speaking to her through the lips of her son. She would never be free of him. She would never be free again.

Laura's thoughts were far less dramatic when Dr. Burke finally gave her permission to take the stairs and return to civilization again. Weeks of captivity had given her an eagerness for almost anything but the four walls of her room. She dressed carefully in the gray silk she had taken in again to suit her new figure. She had added some black braid in a V over the bodice and taken in the wide sleeve and used the extra material to make a cuff like Sallie's. It could never be confused with a fashionable gown, but Laura felt like a new woman wearing it.

Jettie Mae had been left to preside over the nursery, and Laura had to smile to herself at the notion of Ward Breckinridge's child lying in the same room with Cash Wickliffe's. The thought tickled her fancy, and she wore a slight tilt to her lips as she entered the immense foyer at the foot of the stairs. She looked around eagerly for someone to talk to, only to discover Cash standing in the parlor doorway, arms crossed over his chest as he watched her come down.

"It's about time, *pequeña*. I thought you meant to grow to the bed like moss to a stone. Are you joining me for dinner tonight?"

The thought made Laura's stomach tie in knots, and she found an instant distaste for food as Cash's dark gaze swept over her. But he did nothing more than hold up the door frame as he waited for her reply.

"I was looking for Sallie. Is she not here?"

Cash shrugged and stood up properly. "She's been invited for the evening to her former in-laws."

"And you didn't go with her?" Puzzled, Laura said the first thing that came to mind before she stopped to think. She could have bitten her tongue off as she realized the dark irony behind Cash's words and now watched the bitterness flash briefly in his eyes.

"They're not up to white trash this evening. Maybe some other time. Don't you think it's just a little bit humorous that I can sit down at table with some of the richest men on both coasts, but I can't get past the front doors of my own neighbors?"

He hid the pain very well, but the bond between them was such that Laura could feel it just the same. She winced and held out her hand. "That's quite all right. We can be outcasts together. Will you take me in to dinner or shall I find someone else?"

Cash snorted inelegantly and wrapped her fingers around his coat sleeve. "We can invite Jake and Mort from out back and Jettie Mae to join us, and we'll be right at home with our own kind, my dear. Fallen women and trash, what a party that will make."

"If you're going to be mean, I'll not eat with you. This is my first night out of that wretched room, and I want everything to be pleasant. So please warn me in advance if you intend to get drunk and I'll go get Jettie for company."

Cash sighed and relented. "All right, Laura, I'll behave. Have I told you yet how beautiful you look without that extra color on your cheeks? You were never meant to be a high yellow, my dear."

He was teasing her, of course, not meaning a bit of what he said, but Laura still flushed at the casual words. She had no right to take them in any other way but brotherly ribbing. "I was never meant to die of starvation while listening to idiots, either. I expect sensible conversation tonight. I want to hear what you really saw in New York and not how gorgeous the gowns were."

Cash chuckled and obediently led her to the dinner table. He liked intelligent women. He had married an intelligent woman. If she was also one of the most selfish bitches imaginable, he could learn to live with it for what she brought him. But occasionally it would be pleasant to converse intelligently with someone who was not out to skewer him for what he was worth.

And this adorable little monkey he had known since childhood fitted that role quite nicely.

20

"Cash, I will have your head for this if it is the last thing that I do," Laura muttered through clenched teeth as they walked toward the sundries store in the middle of town.

"That's a nasty temper you're developing there, *pequeña*. I thought it was a perfectly reasonable thing to do. You have no need of the place, and Burke does."

"My name is Laura, Miss Kincaid to you, you filthy savage." Too furious to control her temper, Laura politely smiled at the preacher's wife passing by and pretended for all the world to see that she wasn't ready to assassinate the man walking beside her. At midweek the street was fairly empty, but she well knew the eyes peeking out from behind lace curtains in upper-story windows. Should she throw a screaming tantrum in so public a place, it would be all over the county by nightfall, a fact that Cash undoubtedly had counted upon when choosing this time to reveal his treachery.

Cash sent her a sidelong look and chose discretion over temptation. Solemnly he opened the beveled-glass door for her. "Miss Kincaid, if you will. I shall be down at the feed store when you are ready."

Laura stepped up to the entrance and turned, her gaze nearly level with his now. "You had no right to tell him to move into Jonathan's house. That was my decision to make."

"Shall I tell him to move out again?" he asked maliciously, meeting the flashing fury of her eyes with equanimity.

Before she could reply, Eliza Breckinridge, Steve's wife, joined Laura on the stoop in front of the store. Ignoring the man on the walk, she turned to Laura and patted her hand. "Laura, how good it is to see you out and around again. Sallie didn't tell us you were better. Did she tell you about our little soiree Friday night? You will come, won't you? It will be just like old times with you and Sallie together again. You know you're just like family and you'll always be welcome."

Laura would have smiled at Eliza's generosity in pretending her disgrace had never happened had she not felt the stiffening of the tall man in front of her. It did not take a lifetime of experience to interpret his reaction. Cash hadn't known of the soiree and Eliza was pointedly not inviting him. In fact, she was quite capable of inviting Laura merely to spite the upstart white trash who thought he could buy his way into the circle of bluebloods.

Quelling her irritation, Laura gave a polite nod. "So generous of you, Eliza," she murmured politely, "but I cannot leave Mark for any length of time as yet. Perhaps you and Steve would stop by someday for a visit. Sallie would be delighted to have you."

That safely threw the ball back to Eliza's corner. The other woman made polite murmurs, pressed Laura's hand, and without even a nod of recognition to Cash, sailed out into the street, her tartan skirts rustling in the dust.

Anger gone, replaced by some deep, hollow emptiness, Laura turned to enter the store. To her surprise,
Cash entered with her, not taking her arm as he had
earlier but remaining protectively near as she searched
the shelves for the threads and supplies she required.
After the animosity she had hurled at him earlier, she
found his behavior strange, but she could not object
when he was available to reach the scissors she needed
on the top shelf when the shopkeeper seemed undisposed
toward bringing out a ladder to help her.

He paid the man cash from his pocket, although Laura
had been prepared to pay with her own small store of
coins. Not arguing with his pride, she hurried after his
long strides as they left the shop and headed for the feed
store.

"I can pay you back, Cash. I do not expect you to pay
for my needs."

He sent her a disgruntled look and kept on walking.

"Cash, damn you, we have to talk. Will you slow
down!" Determined to take this opportunity to clear the
air between them, Laura tried to keep pace.

"Your language is inappropriate, Miss Kincaid. Why
don't you look at the pretty bonnets in the milliner's
while I make my purchases? I'm certain you can't be
interested in horse feed."

"I don't want bonnets. I want a moment of your time,
and I'm sticking like a bur until you give it to me."

He shrugged as his long stride carried him up the steps
to the feed store. "Suit yourself."

A man shoved open the screen door and stepped out
onto the long wooden porch, gesturing to someone behind him. "Put it in the wagon, Charlie," he called, before turning and discovering Cash in his path.

Clad in open-neck shirt and loose-woven trousers instead of his formal coat and tie, Cash still had an aura
of stateliness bequeathed to him by his well-bred if disreputable parents. Beyond that, the thick length of black
hair on his collar and the cold harshness of his tanned
features were well-known everywhere in the county. No
one could mistake him for any other than who he was,
and the elderly planter confronting him now was no
exception.

So when he deliberately spoke to Cash's face, there

could be no denying the intended insult. "Boy, help Charlie haul those sacks down to the wagon!"

Cash halted in mid-stride, one foot on the porch, the other on the step below. Insolently he blocked the man's path and the path of the black boy behind him. Leaning one arm across his bent knee, he smiled mirthlessly. "Hello, George. Nice day, isn't it? You do know General Fisk and the Freedmen's Bureau say we can't hold slaves anymore, don't you? I thought maybe that news hadn't got out your way yet."

"Damned Yankee upstarts can't tell me what to do," the man growled, finally focusing on Cash's face. "And neither can you. Now, get out of my way, Cash Wickliffe."

"That's Mr. Wickliffe to you, George," he repeated Laura's phrase of earlier with an ironic twist, then turned his attention to the boy. "Charlie, is he paying you a fair wage? You know he has to under the law. And if he doesn't, you can leave him anytime. There ain't no call for you to haul around sacks twice your size unless that's the way you want it."

Rising to his full height again, Cash lifted the hundred-pound sack from the boy's back and flung it toward the wagon as if it were a feather pillow. It landed with a loud thump and a corner seam began to spill grain. Taking Laura's arm as if they were about to make a grand entrance into a ballroom, he skirted past the startled man and boy and entered the musty dimness of the feed store.

Despite Cash's cool control, Laura could feel the anger seething in him. His fingers would leave bruises on her arm, of a certainty. She was glad when he finally placed his order and paid for it, leaving it to be delivered later. She felt the tension inside him would explode should a single wrong word be said or someone look at him cross-eyed.

Cash's long, even strides slowed to a more sedate pace as they started back down the street they had just traversed. Laura felt as if he were daring anyone to cross his path, and she didn't dare broach the subjects she had followed him to discuss. Frustrated, she ground her teeth and wondered if it made any difference at all what she thought. Others were so involved with their own problems, what would they care about hers?

Her silence must have jarred Cash's attention in some way, for he finally bent his regard to her tight-lipped expression. She was wearing the old-fashioned bonnet he had seen her wear a thousand times before, its ungainly brim hiding all the subtlety of her delicate beauty. Her long-sleeved gown and heavy petticoats were too heavy for this early-June day, and without an instant's thought he swerved from their direction to stop at the window of the previously maligned milliner's.

"The hat with the turned-up brim and the spray of pink roses, don't you think?" he asked out of the blue.

Laura stared at him as if he had lost his wits; then, deciding this was better than having her arm ripped off, she turned to admire the dainty confection. She didn't have to look to know which one he spoke of. She had admired the hat weeks ago, before Easter, but she would never have enough money to own a hat like that. Neither had anyone else in the county, obviously.

"It's lovely, and Dorothea would be delighted to have it taken off her hands, I would say. But will Sallie wear anything not from New York?" She had to throw in that word of caution. The coldness between husband and wife was too obvious, and she greatly feared Cash would get his hopes up about the effectiveness of such a gift. After a day like today, Sallie's rejection of his gift could be disastrous.

Cash ignored her warning and steered Laura inside the shop. The milliner instantly appeared at the sound of the bell and smiled in delight at Laura. "Miss Laura, welcome back! You're looking lovely today. I daresay Mr. and Mrs. Wickliffe have been taking good care of you." She threw Cash a shrewd look.

Not raising an eyebrow at this blatant flattery, Cash pointed to the object of his attentions. "We want that hat in the window. How much will it be?"

Already aware of customer reaction when she stated the price, Miss Dorothea hesitated, then offered a simpering smile. "Why, don't you worry 'bout that, Mr. Wickliffe. I'll just bundle it up so you can carry it off and send you the bill later. Would you like anything to go with it? I have in some of the loveliest lace mittens . . ."

This time, Cash did raise a brow, but he followed it with a slow smile as the stout lady reached into the window for the hat. "I like your style, Miss Dorothea. Let's have a pair of those mittens and some of those ribbons over there on the counter, and I want you to make up one of those little bonnets with all the frills around the outside. Green would be a good color, I think, green and gold. Use your own judgment in the decoration."

The milliner frowned briefly. "Mrs. Wickliffe doesn't wear green much. She favors blue. Would you prefer it—?"

"Green, Miss Dorothea," Cash insisted firmly. "Spring green, like new leaves."

She nodded hurriedly. "Yes, sir. Shall I send word when it's done, sir?"

Laura kept her mouth closed in amazement as they concluded this transaction. She was well aware that Cash had paid hard money for everything he had bought this day. Her uncle and Ward had never carried money with them. The merchants had always sent the bills at the end of the month. She seriously suspected a slur to Cash's character implied by the merchants' demand for payment up front. Cash's generous reaction to Dorothea's offer of credit indicated his awareness of the insult too. But why on earth did he insist on a green bonnet? Sallie hated green.

Laura hurried after him, allowing him to assist her into the carriage without her usual protest. When Cash climbed up on the other side, tilting the springs with his greater weight, she couldn't confine her curiosity any longer.

"Why, Cash? I know Dorothea is thrilled, and she's a good lady and I'm happy for her, but Sallie will throw a tree-topping rage when you present it to her. Do you like making her mad?"

Cash merely nodded at the bandbox at her feet. "Put it on. I want to see what it looks like. And throw that mangy article you're wearing out in the ditch. I wouldn't give it to a goat."

This command finally blew the lid off Laura's long-simmering rage. "How dare you! What do you think I

am, Cash Wickliffe, to say such things to me? I know
I'm not pretty like Sallie. I'll never be pretty and
I don't want to be. It certainly hasn't made her any
happier. And I can't afford the best hats and gowns,
but I do the best with what I have, and there is nothing wrong with this perfectly good bonnet. It belonged
to—"

"—Sallie once," he mimicked in tandem with her
words. "And I'm certain a decade ago it looked just fine.
On Sallie. But you're too small and delicate for that kind
of monstrosity, which is why she gave it to you in the
first place. I'm not a blind man, Miss Kincaid. I know
my wife for what she is. I've always known. To my regret, I've not always used my knowledge, but that's beside the point. Now, throw out the ugly bonnet and put
on the new hat. I want to see your face when you spit
fire at me."

"I will not." Laura crossed her arms and stared stubbornly ahead. "You have no call to order me about. I
don't belong to you. I'll buy my own clothes, and as soon
as I find another house, I'll take care of myself."

"That you will not," Cash informed her firmly, bringing the carriage to a halt at the side of the road before
turning toward her. "And unless you want me to forcibly
remove that piece of trash, you will humor my whims in
this too. You are entitled to my support as any other
member of my household. Do you want the entire county
clucking their tongues and shaking their heads when they
see Sallie gowned in all her finery and you trailing along
behind in ragpicker's attire? Is that how you plan to get
even with me, Laura? It's certainly a more subtle method
than most, but I had not thought it of you. I thought of
all the people in this damned county, you were the one
friend I could rely on."

Tears started to her eyes, tears of frustration and rage
and something else, and Laura jerked her head away
from that long dark face and glared out over the fields.
"Go ahead, play on my sympathy, Cash. You're stronger
than I am. You don't care when they whisper behind
your back, but I do. It hurts, and I'm tired of it. I
just want to live my life in peace, give Mark a life of
respectability. How will it look if you start buying me
gifts and parading me about while Sallie stays home

growing big with your child? Use your head, Cash. Before long they'll start taking another look at Mark and tongues will be wagging all over again. As it is, they don't know whether to call me Kincaid or Brown, and they're none too sure if Mark is Jonathan's son or Marshall's. I really don't think I could bear it if they add your name to the list.''

Cash grabbed the back of the bonnet and with a single rip loosened the ribbons and heaved it into the road. He was left staring at a gleaming cascade of golden brown caught in a net, and he wished he had ripped off that last hindrance too. But he had gone far enough for one day. He had not seriously abated his anger with the first move. The second would only unleash something else entirely.

"I will assume for now that you object to having three men on the list and not to my name in particular, although you might correct me if I'm wrong. And you're right, I don't give a damn if they all know Mark is my son. But for your sake I'll forgo my claim in public. But not in private, Laura. He's my responsibility as well as yours, and I mean to see that he has everything I never had. And I can't do that if you go wandering off in search of your damned independence. You can do as you will, wander as you like, but Mark stays with me. Is that understood?"

"No," Laura whispered, but she knew he wasn't listening. Already he was turning the horses back to the road, and she could see her bonnet lying crumpled and muddy in the field beside them.

She didn't understand him. She never would. She'd spent a lifetime ignoring what lay behind the faces that people present to the world. How could she ever hope to plumb the depths of a man like Cash Wickliffe?

She couldn't, and there was no use in trying.

With the bandbox lying untouched between them, Laura stared at the road straight ahead, while Cash silently whipped the horses into a trot.

21

The sultry heat caused the short hairs around Laura's brow to stick to her skin and curl as she hurried up the back stairs from the kitchen to the upper story, where the sound of an infant wailing drew her. She dried her hands on her apron as she ran, wondering if it would have been better to bring Mark outside with her while she supervised the laundering. The heat upstairs could easily be worse than that outside by now.

Jettie was already changing the infant's diaper when Laura arrived. She flashed a knowing smile as Laura began to unfasten her bodice. "Won't be too long and this one gonna be bigger than you are. You'd best let me start feeding him something more solid or he'll eat you up."

Laura acknowledged the truth of that statement with a nod and a wince as Mark grabbed hungrily at her breast. The odd sensation of his insistent pull kept her attention otherwise transfixed, however, and she scarcely noticed when Jettie slipped from the room.

A fresh breeze drifted through the open window, lifting the loose hairs at her nape where she had pulled the heavy mass of her hair up and pinned and tied it with a scarf to the top of her head. She looked no better than the black laundresses below, but comfort was more important than appearance on wash day.

From the veranda outside she could hear the low rumble of Cash's voice and the sharp reply of Sallie's soprano. They had been sniping at each other for days now, and she wished it would end. June was only half over, and it promised to be a long, hot summer. Tempers would explode often enough as the heat increased. With Sallie's pregnancy to add fuel to the fire, it promised to be one potboiler of a season.

Mark made a protest as Laura tensed with a renewed explosion of anger from the couple below. She made an effort to relax and concentrate on the babe in her arms, admiring the thick dark hair Jettie kept telling her would wear off, watching the intensity of the infant's expression as he drank his fill.

Laura wished she had a better memory of Cash's face as he had touched her there, but that day was a jumbled blur of emotions and sensations, none of which were perfectly clear any longer. She remembered the thunder, the sense of safety in Cash's arms, the feeling of belonging, but they were all twisted up in the act that had created this child in her arms, and she couldn't sort one from the other. Obviously what they had done together did not bring the peace she had felt at the time. It was all a chimera, a seductive sense of false security that was part of the attraction between men and women, or Sallie and Cash wouldn't be harping at one another as they were now.

A door crashed below and Laura could hear Sallie's quick light footsteps on the stairs as she stormed to her room. From the far end of the hall came the sounds of drawers being jerked open and slammed shut, the squeak of wardrobe hinges, and Sallie's enraged cries for her maid. Then the repeat of angry footsteps as Sallie took to the stairs again.

Laura sighed and switched Mark to her other breast. If Sallie didn't watch out, the child she was carrying would be born with a temper as terrible as hers. She wondered what Cash had done to provoke it this time. It didn't take much. Just his presence sometimes sent Sallie off into a rage. If she had hoped for another Ward Breckinridge as husband, she had certainly lost that round. Cash wasn't about to cater to her every whim. No more than necessary, leastways.

Remembering the violent arguments that occasionally erupted from Sallie's bedroom, Laura tried to shut the sounds from her mind as she did at night. She didn't want to imagine Cash in Sallie's bedroom, demanding his husbandly rights. She didn't want any of this. She had to get out, if only to save her sanity.

She had finally written to Jonathan, explaining everything. It had taken her weeks to pen the tale and scratch and scribble and rewrite so he would understand that she was fine, that he needn't trouble himself, but could he use some company? Cash would be furious when he found out, but she had to think of herself, since no one else would.

Perhaps Cash thought her no more than a useless doll without feelings of her own; that was the only reason Laura could find for his callous behavior. Did he truly think she wouldn't feel anything when she saw him and Sallie together, heard their fights, watched their hurt, proud faces as they parted in anger? She wasn't a piece of stone, and she wouldn't be treated as one.

Caught up in these reflections, Laura didn't hear a sound until the click of the door opening made her jump. Mark wailed briefly as he lost his grip, then settled down again as Laura adjusted him and glanced cautiously toward the door to the hall

She felt her heart stop as she discovered Cash leaning against the door frame, arms folded across his half-open shirt. She tried to avoid looking at the shadow of dark curls above the taut cotton, but the hungry gaze focused intently on her and their son held her still. As Cash's eyes drank in the sight of her beside the window, tension slowly seeped from the taut outlines of his shoulders as he relaxed in the quiet of the peaceful scene.

Ever since the episode in town, Cash had conspicuously behaved with propriety as far as Laura was concerned. Her words had chipped at some hard part of him that he had considered inaccessible, but they had brought a vague awareness of her position, and he was doing his best to treat her with the respect she deserved.

But sometimes there was a weakness in him that could not be averted. Right now was one of those times. He had not come up here expecting to find Laura. She had been busy with the wash below when he had last seen her. He had meant only to steal a moment of peace in the nursery with his son, the one being in this world who accepted his presence unequivocally and with joy. To find Laura in here with him disrupted the oneness he had felt in previous entries into this private world.

But even at odds with himself over this intrusion, Cash couldn't tear away his fascinated gaze. He knew very little of art, had admired a few landscapes in the museums in New York, but he knew the picture spread before him now deserved immortalizing in oil.

Laura had always called her hair a mousy brown, but it glimmered in the sunlight from the window, the frail wisps capturing and refracting the light around her face, spilling like molten gold to her bare breast. Her skin had the same glow, as if sprinkled with diamond dust, and he regretted that the day he had known all of her had been a dismal one, hiding the beauty that now unfolded before his eyes. Color suffused her cheeks beneath his steady perusal, but Cash couldn't bring himself to tear his gaze away just yet. This was how motherhood should be, he told himself, but the hot surge in his loins spoke another message.

When the babe's attention finally wandered from her breast to his surroundings, and Laura lifted him to her shoulder, the spell broke and Cash lifted himself from the wall. "I'm sorry. I didn't mean to intrude."

Awkwardly Laura tried to close her bodice while bouncing the wide-awake infant on her shoulder. "You could at least turn your back." The words came out more softly than she had intended. She wanted to scream at him to go away and never come near her again, but a deeper instinct wanted to encourage him to come forward and admire what they had wrought together.

Being more base than gentleman, Cash responded to his own deeper instincts. He stepped forward and removed the infant from her hold, allowing her to turn away and cover herself.

"He must grow an inch a day," he murmured as he dangled the child admiringly. The babe kicked his long legs and gurgled happily at the sound of his father's voice, then promptly brought up a stream of milk when Cash attempted to put him over his shoulder. "Ugh. Are all babies so disgusting?"

"You haven't seen the half of it yet." Laura shakily fastened enough buttons to cover herself, then went to the washbowl to get a rag to help clean him off. Cash had never made her this nervous before. She didn't know what was coming over her.

"Oh, yes, I have. I came up here the other night when Jettie Mae was scolding like a magpie. You must have been exhausted not to have heard her. I think I would have thrown the kid out with the bathwater if I'd been left to clean that mess."

Laura chuckled as she wiped at the milky streak down Cash's cotton-covered back. "I heard about that. I think I'm indebted to Jettie for life for that one, according to her. I do hope you're paying her adequately. I'm not at all sure she's worth a cent, but I couldn't do without her."

"I think Jettie Mae is one of those subjects we have yet to discuss, but I'll not turn her out if you say she stays." Cash flinched as his son made another belching noise, but this time his dinner stayed with him and he relaxed.

Laura giggled softly at this reaction. "I've seen you with blood streaming down your face, and drenched in sweat and rain, and you never flinched. Is your son so scary as all that?"

"Blood doesn't smell like he does. I feel like I ought to go take a bath. Maybe I ought to go back to California and not come back until all these monsters are grown up. Sallie wouldn't object to that."

Cash didn't surrender the infant when Laura held out her arms, but walked to the window and stared blindly out. Laura didn't want to hear what he had let slip. She wanted to go back to the genial banter of before, but for whatever reasons, they were too close for that.

"Sallie's spoiled. You knew that when you married her. The only way anyone can get along with her is to agree with her. Uncle Matt sometimes threatened not to buy her the new hat she wanted if she didn't behave, but I don't think that threat is very effective anymore. What is it she wants now?"

Cash shrugged. The damp spot on his shirt clung to his skin, emphasizing the ungentlemanly width of his shoulders. "She has some birdbrained notion of spending the summer at some resort. I've told her I have too much to do here to attend her, but that's scarcely a deterrent. Isn't it considered improper for a lady to appear in public in the latter stages of pregnancy?"

Just the topic was highly improper, but the two of them had never stood on formality. Laura wrung the rag out in the bowl. "You're asking me about propriety? I'd suggest you find a better authority. But I daresay she wants

to go with the Breckinridges; they used to go every summer. If Eliza and Steve's mother think it's all right, then
I guess you can't find a better authority. It's cooler down
by the springs. Maybe it will take some of the edge off
Sallie's temper."

Laura would have said more, but the nursery door
slammed open and Sallie stalked in, rage coloring her
cheeks. "Who the Sam Hill do you think you are, Cash
Wickliffe? That's my carriage and my stables and I won't
be denied the use of them! You go down there right this
minute and tell those black devils of yours that I want
the carriage hitched, and I want it now."

Cash stood still, staring out the window a minute
longer, until the infant on his shoulder began to squirm
uneasily under Sallie's strident tones. Then wearily he
turned and handed the babe to Laura, not taking his eyes
from the squirming bundle as he spoke to his wife. He
touched a thick black lock tenderly when he replied.

"The carriage and the stables are mine, Sallie, bought
and paid for with my money, just as I paid the mortgage
on this land and the upkeep on this house. I don't want
my money going to destroy my child. You can't ride in
your condition, and I'll not have you taking the carriage
out without someone to handle the horses and look after
you. You're going to have to grow up sometime, Sallie."

Laura rocked Mark in her arms and glanced uneasily
toward the door to her room. She wanted to escape this
ugly scene, but Cash blocked her path. She felt relief
when he advanced toward Sallie, obviously intending to
escort her from the room, preferably to a more private
place for confrontation.

As if fearing he would do exactly that, Sallie retreated
farther from the hall door toward the center of the nursery. Sending a scathing glance to Laura and the infant,
she sneered. "Your child! That's all I ever hear about—
your child! I suppose you expect me to stay home and
toddle about like dear obedient Laura. You gawk over
that brat as if it were your own. Well, you can have it,
and I daresay you can have my dear cousin too, if you
want. She doesn't seem overly particular in her choice of
men. In a few years she'll be just like that snotty maid
she hired behind my back, popping bastards once a year.
You all think I'm too dumb to notice, but I'm too smart

to care. Why don't you try dear Jettie Mae too, while you're at it, Cash? Ward seemed satisfied with her services."

At Laura's startled look, Sallie laughed proudly. "You thought I didn't know that, didn't you? Well, I know a lot more than I let on, a *lot* more, if you take my meaning." She turned her vicious gaze back to Cash. "And you're going to let me go to the Springs whether you like it or not, or I'll tell the world what I know."

Cash leaned wearily against the closed door and crossed his arms over his chest, giving his wife a searing look. "Tell the world whatever you like, Sallie. I don't give in to such tactics. Had you told me it would be cooler at the Springs, as Laura suggested, if you had even said you would be going in the company of the eminently respectable Breckinridges, I wouldn't have objected in the first place. Whatever you might like to think, it is only your welfare that concerns me. But now you're going to have to make a few promises before I let you go."

Laura held her breath as she watched Sallie's fleeting expressions. Sallie could not possibly know as much as she liked to pretend. She was shooting arrows in the dark. But even her speculations, if dropped in the proper places, would cause gossip and scandal. Laura didn't think she could bear any more of that.

But it was Cash whom Sallie intended to hurt, and he wasn't responding as calculated. Laura let out her breath in relief as Sallie's expression turned from furious to shrewd.

"What kind of promises?" she asked cautiously.

"Nothing difficult. I don't want you riding. If you go to the Springs, you'll stay at the Springs until I come after you. You are to listen to Mrs. Breckinridge and take her advice at all times. I intend to speak with the lady before I let you go, telling her I'm placing you entirely in her charge and instructing her to let me know if you don't behave. If you mean to act like a child, I'll have to treat you as one."

There was an unhealthy glitter in Sallie's eyes by the time Cash finished his speech, but she fluttered her eyelashes and touched a cool hand to her dangling curls and offered a slow smile. "La, but I thought you meant *real* promises. The Springs is the most proper place in the world; I wouldn't *dream* of doing anything untoward there. But then, I could hardly expect someone like you to know these things, could I?"

With that cutting retort, Sallie gathered up her skirts and approached the door, daring Cash not to let her by.

He gave her a hard stare, then unfolded himself and with a mocking bow opened the door for her.

Before leaving, Sallie turned and gave Laura a blithe smile. "He's all yours, dear cousin. I've got what I want." Then, sweeping her skirts around her, she rustled from the room.

The bleak look in Cash's eyes as they met Laura's startled gaze quickly turned hard and cold. "She's generous with her favors," he said with heavy irony. With a formal nod he strode out, leaving Laura with the impression of an angry boy grown into the wide-shouldered, slim-hipped body of a powerful man.

22

The house without Sallie settled down to a stable if somewhat dull routine. Cash spent his days in the fields, doing the jobs most planters assigned to overseers. The evenings he spent pouring over books and ledgers and technical journals, learning those things men like Ward had learned at their daddies' knees.

Laura kept out of his way. There was a stiffness in Cash now when they happened into each other that she did not like, and she found it easier all around to avoid him.

The task wasn't difficult. With Jettie acting as her right hand and Cash's open purse to ease the work, Laura slowly returned the once stately house to the gleaming magnificence she remembered. Neglected wood was scrubbed and cleaned and polished with beeswax. Old draperies were removed and salvaged for scraps for maids' rooms and workers' cottages, while new ones were measured and basted and fitted and sewn by a team of women Laura knew to be expert at handwork.

Once carpenters and plasterers and painters were done in the rooms under renovation, Laura moved in with wallpaper samples and material scraps, working with the furniture she and Jettie decided worth keeping. Old pieces not worth refinishing were passed out to those who could still find a use for them, usually under Jettie's guidance.

It was summer and Jettie's eldest was called to help her grandmother with the gardening and canning, but when the children were all together and racing through the bushes on a warm evening, Laura gave them a speculative look and began to make further plans.

Since Sallie's departure, Laura's reluctance to remain at the farm had mysteriously waned. She had even dared wear the new hat to church now that Cash seemed otherwise occupied. By blithely explaining that Sallie hadn't felt the hat suited her, she dispelled all speculative looks. Everyone had found new gossip to worry over, and the ninety-day wonder of Laura's disappearing husband came to an end.

The escalating war between white planters and the Freedmen's Bureau kept everyone occupied as the hot summer grew hotter. Since Kentucky had remained part of the Union, the commonwealth's slave laws hadn't been abolished as they had in the South. The martial law during the war had successfully undermined much of the intent of the slave statutes, but with the war over and Lincoln dead, rebellion threatened to sprout anew over the issue of Negro freedom.

Laura heard some of the stories firsthand as Stoner Creek's former slaves trickled back, looking for a roof over their heads and food in their bellies. Jemima was one of the first. Her husband, Henry, had been killed serving in the Union Army during the war. The army had issued a proclamation declaring the families of all soldiers to be free, and like many another, Jemima had left for the city.

Now she was back, a smaller, more bitter version of her old self. Laura listened to her tales of the city spilling over with unemployed, uneducated laborers with no means of finding food and housing. Even house servants like Jemima found themselves no better off than as slaves. There was no one to protect them if their employers didn't pay them, and nowhere else to go if they objected to their treatment. Those who found the courage to try the courts found themselves facing hostile judges and juries, and the constant lynchings of "troublemakers" deterred all but the most foolhardy.

Jemima's tales of woe strengthened Laura's resolve. The house servants had been more family to her than the Kincaids ever had been. She had never learned to think of them as animals or pieces of furniture that came with the property. Perhaps she had never given them much thought either, but she had spent precious little time in the past worrying over anyone but herself. She had finally been given the instruments of change, however, and she was determined to wield them well.

If Cash meant for her to stay here like a useless ornament, he would soon discover she had a mind of her own.

Laura started quietly enough, inquiring at the local private academy about discarded schoolbooks. The promise of a generous donation from Mr. Wickliffe made them exceedingly willing to comply and to go so far as to obtain more books from other schools in the district.

Supplied with the essentials, Laura and Jettie put their heads together and decided one of the basement storerooms had sufficient room for a few tables and chairs. It would be cool in summer and warm in winter and there was access to the outside through the old basement kitchen, so no one could complain about the noise of the children coming and going.

Unpacking a carton of slates Jettie had obtained and into whose source Laura did not feel compelled to inquire, she continued the question of where to get the best price for chalk before she realized Jettie had become unnaturally quiet. Glancing up, Laura found the maid inching nervously toward the door, and she hastily looked over her shoulder to where Jettie's gaze was fastened.

Cash had come quietly into the room and stood now tapping his coiled whip against his knee-high boots, his expression anything but pleasant as he gazed around at the incipient schoolroom. His attention slowly focused on Laura as Jettie made some mumbled excuse about "burning bread" and fled.

Nervously Laura debated standing up to him and launching an offensive, but she didn't have that kind of courage. When all was said and done, this was his house, and she had never once sought his opinion on the use of it. She returned to unpacking the crate.

"I don't disappear when you close your eyes." Cash spoke softly, but the hint of threat still lingered in his words.

"I didn't think you would." Laura sighed and sat back on her heels but didn't turn to look at him again. She didn't need to. She could see him as clearly as if he stood before her, knew the exact manner in which his unruly hair brushed the stiff collar of his shirt, the way his dark eyes pierced her, the frown on his chiseled lips. She could see the brilliant white of the shirt she had carefully ironed herself just yesterday, knew how it looked against the stark gray of his waistcoat and the navy of his frock coat. He must have gone to town today instead of out in the fields.

"Do I get some kind of explanation?" Again the soft voice, but the boots sounded a little closer.

"I didn't think you would be interested." Shrugging lightly, Laura disentangled her skirt and attempted to rise. She automatically took the hard brown hand held out to her, and regretted it immediately. The shock of his touch coursed through her, but Cash seemed perversely unaware of that fact as he kept his grip even after she stood in front of him.

Laura politely tried to slide her fingers from his, but Cash appeared motionless, staring at her as if she were a phantom who had materialized unexpectedly. Not until she jerked did he release his grip and step back, the cold, distant look returning to his eyes.

"I'm interested. Now, tell me what is going on."

He certainly didn't sound as if he wanted to know, but Laura knew her obligations. Crossing her fingers behind her back for luck, she answered hesitantly, "I spent some time last winter teaching Jettie's children. They seemed so eager to learn, I thought . . . Well, it just seems a criminal shame that they can't get some education. They're not horses, you know. They have minds. They need to be taught."

Cash's gaze drifted to the toddler Jettie had left behind. Now four months old, Taylor Breckinridge Jackson was a sturdy youngster with a propensity for trouble even before he learned to walk. Awakened by the sound of voices, he had crawled from the box where Jettie had placed him and was even now rocking against one of the rickety chairs scavenged from the attic.

Cash's eyes narrowed as he watched the infant butt his head against the chair leg. He was across the room in a single step as the chair tilted and the babe tumbled over on his well-padded bottom. Taylor's wail halted abruptly as he found himself swung in strong arms and fascinatingly close to the beamed ceiling. His hand waved in circles as he tried to catch a cobweb while Cash returned his attention to Laura. "This one belongs to Ward, doesn't he? He's the reason you're determined to see Jettie's children educated."

"One of the reasons, yes." Laura stuck her chin out and met his stare squarely. "What other chance does he have?"

"About as much chance as I did," Cash responded crudely, reminding Miss High-and-Mighty Kincaid of his origins. If she were deterred by the reminder, she didn't flinch.

"Less," Laura said coldly. "At least you had an educated mother. Jettie can't even read and write. What chance do you think Taylor has in this world with a mother like that?"

"The same chance as our son will. I'll send them both to school when the time comes. You needn't wear yourself into a wraith for Ward's sake." The next words came out of his mouth without planning. "He was Sallie's husband, for pity's sake. Did you love him that much?"

Laura stared at Cash with incredulity. "You too? What is it with people that they can't stand to see a single woman without pairing her up with every man in her life? If we count Ward, that makes you number four, doesn't it? How does it feel to be only number four?"

A wry shadow of a smile crossed Cash's face as he lifted the toddler to the ceiling to satisfy his curiosity, but his gaze followed Laura and not the child's enthusiasm. "Sarcasm doesn't become you, *pequeña*. We both know where we stand in the lists. There are times when I wish I had been number four; the guilt wouldn't be nearly so great.But there are other times . . ."

She didn't dare interpret the look in Cash's eyes as his words drifted off. She felt his meaning in the pit of her stomach, felt the raw ache of memory, and coward that she was, she turned her head away.

"There is no guilt involved," she said firmly to the wall. "What's done is done and I'm not at all certain that I would do it any differently if we could go back in time." She turned back and reached for the child who was now wiping his face with disgust at the cobwebs covering him.

Cash shifted the bundle back to her. "I would," he said enigmatically before turning toward the door. Before Laura could question his words, he continued, "If you're going to have a school, hire a damned teacher. You're not one of the servants."

He strode off, leaving Laura to stare after him in frustration and bewilderment. She would never understand what went on in his head, but she was beginning to like it too well for her own good.

23

Despite Laura's growing ease with the situation, she still fought a restless frustration she couldn't define. She refused to admit she found satisfaction in the delight of Cash's eyes when she ordered his bath and had it ready for him when he came in from the fields. She desperately ignored her anticipation of those times when Cash would come to the nursery while she was there, and they could laugh at their son's multitudinous talents together. If his hands brushed hers when she gave him the baby, she tried not to recognize the shiver of pleasure that coursed through her. He was her cousin's husband, and that was all that could be between them.

So she had no right to feel disappointment or anything else when her birthday arrived without any sign of recognition. Sallie had never bothered to acknowledge it since Uncle Matt died, and Laura didn't expect one of her cousin's irregular and flighty letters to mention some-

thing other than the fun she was having. As far as Laura
knew, no one else knew of the importance of this date
to her but herself, so she had only herself to rely on if
she wanted to make a holiday of it.

But she could treat herself for a change. She knew
Cash would be furious that she rode out alone, but she
didn't see any other choice if she were to have this little
holiday she planned for herself. If she waited until a carriage and driver could be found and readied, the kitchen
was likely to catch on fire and the cattle in the side field
would get loose and trample the garden and Taylor
would pull down the draperies and smother himself and
everyone else in sight. If she wasn't there to watch it
happen, they would have to struggle along without her.

Refusing to give in to self-pity, Laura cantered along
the shady lane, enjoying the wind in her hair and the
anticipation of spending a few hours with friends she had
neglected these last months. She had a few coins in her
pocket. Perhaps she would indulge in something completely frivolous. Cash had not attempted to buy her anything else after her tirade over the hats, but she still
craved something new once in a while. Perhaps she could
strike up a deal with Millie, the seamstress, to take in
some hemming and whatnot to give her a little spare
money.

She dreamed of making enough to buy a sewing machine, but that was an impossible dream. What coins she
could earn would have to go to buy clothes for her and
Mark. It was enough that Cash paid for the roof over
their heads and the food in their bellies. He couldn't be
expected to provide everything. Her pride wouldn't
allow for that. But if she could set a little aside every so
often . . .

While Laura was bargaining with the milliner over new
hat ribbons and persuading Millie to part with a few sewing jobs, Cash was riding over the corn field observing
the gathering of thunderclouds in the west. He knew the
danger of this weather well. When the high buildup of
summer heat and humidity hit the cold wind riding in
those clouds, anything could happen. He had seen barn
roofs whip off the walls and fly into the trees, oaks as
old and sturdy as the mountains rip from the soil and
topple across the horses huddling beneath them. Hail as

big as his fist could tumble from those clouds, or nothing
worse might happen than a drenching and welcome rain.
It never did to second-guess Mother Nature.

Ordering the horses into the barns and field hands into
securing anything that might catch a breeze, Cash called
it a day and turned his mount toward the house. Jemima
had told him about the special birthday dinner being prepared, and he wanted to add a little surprise of his own.
He figured Laura was too damned proud to accept anything but a trifling token of his appreciation, so he would
keep the biggest surprise as a casual afterthought. But
he meant for her to have some little gift at the table from
him. He wasn't accustomed to giving or receiving gifts,
but he remembered last Christmas as if it were yesterday.
He had enjoyed the experience, and he wanted to see
her smile like that again.

A flash of lightning split the distant sky as Cash rode
into the stable. The thunder followed as he unstrapped
the girth and removed the saddle. The storm was still a
few miles off; he would have time to inspect the grounds
for any possible leaks or loose ends.

As he came out of the stables and gazed up at the
towering edifice of the house, his heart swelled with
pride. The mansion gleamed with new coats of paint
around the now-sparkling windows. The shutters had
been restored to their former pristine condition, and the
grounds had been manicured to picture-book perfection.
He was well aware that it was Laura's patience and endurance and talent that had wrought these changes, along
with a generous helping of his money. He had given her
instructions, and she had carried them out beyond his
fondest wishes. 'Twas a pity that he couldn't say the same
of his wife, but he and Laura understood one another,
and they both knew what Sallie was and forgave her for
it. He was a lucky man, if he only had the sense to
remember it. To come from the filth of a tobacco-road
hovel to this . . .

But sometimes there was a creeping sense of failure
that Cash couldn't quite rid himself of. He had a wife
who had brought him the farm he coveted, but even Sallie's name couldn't bring him the respect he had hoped
would accompany his acquisition. He had worked to gain
a wife who would stand at his side and make other men's

heads turn, but it had never occurred to him that she would refuse his company once they were married. She had complainingly done her duty as his wife as a lady was taught, but she had offered none of the solace he had hoped to find in his marriage bed. Once she had declared herself pregnant, they had silently but mutually agreed there was no point in continuing that part of their marriage. Now he had everything he had hoped to gain, but he found little satisfaction in it.

Actually, he felt as restless and unfulfilled as he had when he took that steamer up the Ohio a little less than a year ago. Now, besides a ranch in California, he had a horse farm in Kentucky and a beautiful wife, but still he wasn't satisfied. It was a fleeting feeling, one he successfully buried in hard work, but every so often it came back to nag him, as it did now as he observed the airy draperies Laura had created blowing through the open upstairs windows.

Blowing through open windows. Cursing, Cash strode hurriedly toward the house. What in the name of Jehoshaphat were they doing in there that no one had closed the windows? Even a blind man could see that a storm was in the making, and those windows went into the nursery. He'd wring Laura's neck if she were down in that blasted schoolroom of hers and ignoring what was happening outside.

A streak of black lightning nearly toppled Cash as it whipped between his legs when he tried to enter the kitchen. A dog's furious bark and the slamming of something hard to the floor accompanied by more screams of outrage identified the departing creature as a cat. And if Cash did not miss his guess, Franz the Second had just chased it out of the parlor.

Closing his eyes, Cash resisted temptation and strode toward the usually peaceful parlor. Hearing the sound of his boots, two young maids hastily began righting overturned tables and sweeping up shattered glass. They stared at him in terror as he surveyed the damage, but it wasn't the broken lamps or beheaded figures that he was noticing. It was the absence of something important.

Cash gritted his teeth and demanded, "Where's Miss Laura?"

The one maid looked as if she might faint. The other stared at him soundlessly, clutching her broom as if for protection. Cursing silently, Cash spun at the patter of light feet behind him. Jettie Mae's mischievous grin did nothing to relieve his ire. "Damn your impudent hide, woman, where is she?"

Jettie shrugged. "Gone to town, I done suspect. Ain't she allowed a little time to herself after the goin's-on 'round here?"

If this were an example of what happened when Laura turned her back, Cash didn't want to answer that question. Remembering his reason for entering the house, he ordered the windows closed and strode back into the approaching gloom of the storm. Damn Laura's will-fulness to hell. He had told her not to go out alone. Now here it was, ready to storm, and she was probably half-way between here and town and about to get drenched. He just hoped to hell she hadn't reached town yet. There was something he'd been meaning to tell her but hadn't found the courage or the words to say.

As he remembered another time when Laura had been riding alone before a storm, Cash's sense of urgency climbed to new heights. He'd be damned if he'd have her sharing another barn with a stranger.

By the time he reached town without a single sign of Laura, Cash's temper had reached explosive proportions. He had only signed on to run a damned farm, not a full-blown circus. If he had to spend his time rounding up strays, he might as well be back in Texas. He kept his near-panic buried beneath fury, where it belonged.

The first fat drops of rain began to fall as he rode past the dry-goods store. Following instinct, Cash turned his mount down the alley to the doctor's house. He still thought of that renovated carriage house as home, and very likely Laura would do the same.

Instinct served him well. Laura's horse was tied to the barn door, and riding around to the front, Cash caught the flash of green that was Laura's favorite shopping gown. Closer, he could see her standing on the wide front porch Jonathan had installed for his wife, and for a moment he thought she was standing alone, debating the wisdom of riding out into the rain.

But heaven forbid that any Kincaid would do something so simple and innocent. As Cash halted his horse in front of the house, the lithe figure of the young doctor stepped from the shadows of the door to greet him. Cash had the sudden urge to swing first and ask questions later, but he had learned some control with the years. Swinging down from his horse, he stepped onto the porch steps, and ignoring Burke's outstretched hand, glared at Laura.

"What in hell do you think you're doing out here by yourself? Haven't I told you—"

"Say one more word, Cash Wickliffe, and I'll shove you off this porch. I'm tired of being cursed at and ordered around and treated like a half-wit. Why aren't you back at the farm stabling the horses and battening down the doors before this storm?"

Burke stared at the petite woman with hands on hips glaring at the tall man who dwarfed her even when he stood a step below her. He had always thought Laura a timid, quiet woman, as so often abused women seemed to be. She had a haunting smile and lovely eyes, and more than once he had wondered if she might truly be eligible, but never had he imagined her unleashing this kind of temper. She did it in a perfectly ladylike soft voice, which made it all the more effective as a tirade.

"What do you think I have the damned farmhands for? And if you hadn't gone traipsing off to who-knows-where, that's where I'd be now. Haven't you got the sense God gave a goose, woman? There's a storm out there, and a featherbrain like you could blow away in it."

The young doctor considered interfering at this insult to a lady, but a second glance at Cash's dark face gave him second thoughts. He didn't know the man well, but that wasn't a look of just anger etched into the weathered lines around Cash's eyes and mouth. And he didn't yell as many another man would have. There was the sound of concern behind his words, and almost a look of fear in his eyes. The fists clenched at his sides began to relax even as Laura spoke, so it wasn't Laura they were meant for. Perhaps he'd better not consider that notion too closely. Burke stepped back a foot or two, out of the scene of battle.

"If I had a stick, I'd hit you. Did you think I rode

out just because I saw a storm coming and thought it would annoy you? All I wanted was a little time to myself. Is that too much to ask? Just a few minutes to . . ." Laura's anger was rapidly turning to tears, as it so often did. Frustrated, she broke off before she could reveal what she had no intention of revealing. She was twenty-two years old today, and what did she have to show for it?

Cash's anger didn't abate at the first sign of her distress. Carried away by the danger she had unwittingly placed herself in, he stepped up to the porch and grabbed her shoulder. "When are you going to learn to put a little trust in me?" he shouted as her tears disappeared and she backed away warily. "Marshall is back. Did you ever stop to consider he might return? He's deputy sheriff now. What would you have done if you'd run into him again?"

Horrified, Laura could only stare, watching Cash wipe the grim look from his face with the same stroke that he used to brush the wet hair from his face. Weariness replaced the anger as he finally acknowledged the other man witnessing this confrontation. Stiffly holding out his hand, Cash said, "I apologize, Burke. It looks as if we're in for a bit of a blow. Do you mind if I stable our horses until it goes over?"

The summer storm blew over as quickly as promised, but another kind lingered in its wake. Later, watching Cash Wickliffe lift his wife's slender cousin into the saddle, hearing the laughter that sprang to her lips as he made some insulting sally, Burke couldn't help but wonder at the fallacies of the human heart.

Did they really think that hurling anger and insults would hide the deeper emotions just beneath the veneer?

24

Already shaken by the emotions she had been submitted to this day, Laura broke down into real tears when confronted by the small birthday party awaiting her back at the farm. Dismayed at this turn of events, Cash turned to the other women in the room for help, but Jettie May only laughed, jiggled Taylor on her hip, and gave him a taunting look he didn't wish to interpret. Jemima grinned and gave Laura a big hug which seemed to lessen the tears. The other maids and servants who had helped prepare the surprise shifted noisily from foot to foot and gave each other embarrassed grins, leaving Cash to shoulder the rest of the burden.

When it came time for Laura to open her gifts, a bottle of last year's grape wine was brought out and served all around. Laura started with the smaller presents first, knowing instinctively that the large, awkwardly wrapped package was from Cash. She exclaimed over hand-carved beads and embroidered handkerchiefs, and cried out in surprise at the hand-beaten metal tussie-mussie holder one enterprising lad had created. One of the kitchen maids provided the flowers to fill the ornament, and Laura proudly pinned it to her bodice before reaching for the final gift.

Cash went back to the sideboard and the wine while she opened his present, and turned around only when her exclamations of happiness filled the air. Eyes bright again with tears, Laura unfolded the exquisite rose-pink figured silk and sifted it gently through her fingers, luxuriating in the sensuous feel of the expensive material, smoothing it against her cheeks to better appreciate the quality. Her eyes lifted to meet Cash's, and she had to turn away or feel the hot burn of tears down her cheeks again.

He had not smiled or said a word, but the intensity of his dark eyes gave him away. She couldn't say any of those things that ought to be said; his feelings were much too close to the surface, and he wouldn't appreciate her releasing them in front of the company. For whatever reason, Cash liked giving her this gift, and he wanted her to have it. She ought to protest, but she couldn't. With a soft "thank you," Laura carefully refolded the material and returned it to its paper.

The thought that they were entitled to no private moments or exchanges of feelings struck oddly hollow as Laura considered it later. Cash was her friend, had always been her friend. There had never been a need for reticence between them before. Why did they feel the need now? But it was there, a strain of distance that kept them from saying what they really felt, from venting any emotion other than anger. It was odd and ought to be unnecessary between old friends.

Vowing to right whatever had gone wrong between them, Laura sought Cash out later that evening. Coming down from the nursery after settling their son in for the night, she found him sipping at a glass of something in his study while poring over his ledgers. He looked up at her entrance, and the frown marring his forehead instantly disappeared behind a mask of indifference.

Nervously brushing down the brown taffeta she had worn to dinner, wishing she had one of Sallie's new flatter crinolines so she didn't feel so separated from him by the circumference of her hoops, Laura launched into her crusade for better understanding.

"I know I didn't thank you enough for the silk, Cash. I . . . I don't have a gift with words. You're my friend. I ought to be able to let you know how much I appreciate your thoughtfulness, but it's so hard to know how you will take it, that I—"

Standing, Cash interrupted. "How would you thank Ward if he had given the gift?"

That brought Laura's head up with a snap. She examined Cash's face for expression, but found none. Aside from the fact that it would never have occurred to Ward that Sallie's mousy cousin would covet beauty, she knew immediately how she would have reacted. Could Cash possibly guess? Or did she dare explain?

"Ward was like a brother to me." Laura tried to express herself so he would understand, but he stood there so impassively, she couldn't tell if he was even listening. When he said nothing, she stumbled on. "I . . . I suppose I would have kissed him on the cheek. He would have expected it. I don't know."

Cash finally relented at the helpless wave of her hand. "I suppose it is something to know that you don't look on me as your brother. And we'd better not try that kiss-on-the-cheek business. I'd have to lift you up so you could reach, and things could get a little awkward. So I think I'll settle for your thanks, especially since I imagine I embarrassed the hell out of you."

Green eyes flashed with sudden laughter at this acknowledgment. "You'd better learn to mind your language if you expect to be invited into the finer homes. Do you have any idea how much you have sworn at me this day?"

"Oh, I suspect I have an idea or two. You want a chance to get even? I've got another surprise up in the sewing room. You can use all the foul language you know when you see it."

Laura's eyes widened as she contemplated the suddenly mischievous laughter behind Cash's words and pondered what it meant. With Cash, it wouldn't do to speculate. Without a word, she gathered up her skirts and crinoline and hurried toward the door.

She heard him strolling along behind her, his long legs easily keeping up with her hasty footsteps as she ran up the stairs and toward the back room where she kept all her bits and pieces of cloth and thread. On rainy days she had spent hours in here bending over the drapery sewing with the other women, but usually she was too occupied in other parts of the house to spend as much time here as she liked. Besides, sewing draperies was dull. She wanted to create exquisite confections like Sallie had worn home from New York. Her hands itched to try out her ideas on the rose silk even now. Panic struck her as she imagined Cash filling the room with his idea of appropriate materials and threads. It wouldn't do. It wouldn't do at all.

She burst into the room and gave a sigh of relief as everything seemed as before. In the dim light she sought

familiar shadows, seeing nothing out of place. Behind
her, Cash approached bearing a candle. The single flame
flickered over parts of the chamber as he solemnly
handed it to her. He remained in the doorway as she
circled the room, finally discovering an unexpected object in her way as she approached the table.

Lowering the candle to examine the stumbling block,
Laura gave a cry of mixed surprise and grief. Her hand
smoothing the polished surface of the tiny table, she sat
in the chair next to it and stared at the gleaming metal
machine waiting for her touch. Gilt letters gleamed back
at her, and she traced them with her fingertip. Singer.
She knew that name. It had haunted the back doors of
her dreams ever since she had seen one in the hands of
a traveling salesman on the steamboat back from Cairo.
She touched the silver wheel, moved the candle to discover the pedal ramp near the floor, and cried silent
tears. This couldn't possibly be for her. They must cost
a fortune. But she wanted it so badly, she could weep
for the thought

"Oh, hell, Laura, are you crying again?" Cash stalked
across the room and whipped the candle from her hand,
setting it blasphemously on the narrow table. When she
squawked and moved to remove it before wax could mar
the gleaming surface, Cash caught her hand, then sat
down on the larger table behind him. "It's a damned
machine, Laura. A little wax won't hurt it. What are you
getting so excited about?"

He knew. He knew and he sat there pretending innocence. She wanted to pound that muscular thigh swinging
so precariously near to her. How could he act so casual
when he was waving the moon under her nose, tempting
her to who knows what wickedness? Tears streamed
down Laura's cheeks as she lovingly brushed her fingers
over the marvelous machine. At this moment she would
do anything he asked just for the opportunity to see it
work.

"The draperies are almost done," she whispered.

That was a far distance from the subject at hand, but
Cash managed to follow the crooked path of her thoughts.
"Yeah, well, I should have thought of it sooner, I admit,
but I'm not much at knowing what kind of gadgets a
woman needs. But the salesman showed me how it sewed

all that lace on just as quick as a wink, and I thought maybe you'd like to play with something like that. You can charge whatever fripperies you need down at the milliner's to fix up that silk into something fancy. I didn't think you'd let me buy you the gown, but surely you can't complain about the makings."

Propped casually against the big table, Cash watched her closely, but Laura prayed he couldn't see her in the darkness. Her every thought had to be written across her face. He had bought it for her, not to ease the task of renovating his house. For her. Sighing, she caressed the machine again. "I doubt that you could have found a better way to keep me here, Cash. When Sallie returns, she'll take over running the house, and I can just stay up here and sew whatever you require. I'll not ever need to come out again."

Cash snorted inelegantly. "I'd suggest a trip to the privy upon occasion. Don't be such a sap, Laura. You've worked yourself half to death to make this place a home. Don't think I haven't noticed. You deserve some token of appreciation. If I'd known you'd go all sentimental over a piece of machinery, I would have bought you a new stove for the kitchen. Now, come on, it's late. You can play with your new toy in the morning."

He stood up and held out his hand and Laura took it reluctantly. Her glance returned to the machine, but the warm masculine hand gripping hers was a decided distraction. His fingers had never fully lost their calluses and none of their strength, but there was more of a gentleman's smoothness to them now that he spent more time supervising than laboring. For a brief moment she wondered how they would feel against her skin, but she hastily dropped his hand and swept toward the door.

"You are right; it is late. Mark will be up early. If the weather holds, could I have a carriage in the morning? I'll need to pick up some new threads and maybe just a bit of lace and ribbon. Did the salesman leave instructions? I've never seen one used."

Her brisk words had the desired effect. He had been contemplating asking for that kiss on the cheek. She had firmly set him in his place. Slowly following her out, Cash wondered why he felt so elated and so disappointed at the same time.

*   *   *

When Cash returned from town with the mail, Laura eagerly followed him into the study. She still hadn't received a reply from Jonathan, and she had sent off for a pattern from the lady's magazine she had borrowed from Millie. While she waited for the pattern to arrive, she was practicing using the machine on new muslins for the maids. She had never seen anything quite as amazing, and she was dying to experiment on something more challenging.

As Laura sifted through the odd bills and advertisements, she scarcely noticed Cash's expression as he picked up the letter addressed to him. There was nothing in the lot from Sallie, hadn't been for weeks. Laura didn't find that at all surprising, and she didn't think it bothered Cash greatly. He had passed her Sallie's few ventures into literary expression without comment when they came. There had been nothing personal in them to hide. Obviously they had been written on rainy days in boredom to relive the glory of summer parties and evening musicales, not for the benefit of asking how things fared at home without her. Upon occasion she complained of her growing girth and the need for more gowns and shawls to disguise her size, but whatever Cash sent her in return apparently kept her satisfied.

Cash's growl of fury sent Laura rocking backward on her heels. She glanced up in time to see Cash crumple the letter and heave it toward the nonexistent fire. Without a word of explanation, he stormed from the room, and a moment later she could hear him screaming for a groom from the front porch. Cash never yelled at the servants like that. Daringly Laura bent to pick up the discarded letter.

Smoothing the battered linen paper, she deciphered Mrs. Breckinridge's spidery scrawl. Biting her lip, Laura read the letter once, then returned to the pertinent passages, scanning them again to make certain there wasn't some mistake. Surely Sallie couldn't be so foolish . . .

Shaking her head as she found no error in her interpretation, Laura crumpled the letter again and looked for a flint to light a fire. Cash had every right to go screaming off in haste, but there was no reason anyone else need know of it. She lit the piece of paper and watched it burn in the grate.

If Sallie wanted to scandalize society by carrying on while six months pregnant, that was nobody's business but hers and Cash's. Laura couldn't imagine what kind of affairs a woman could have in that condition, but Mrs. Breckinridge's outraged accounts left plenty to the imagination. Even if it all came to nothing, it sounded as if Sallie was doing her best to lose that baby. Sometimes the workings of her cousin's mind eluded Laura.

Right now, Laura's concern was all for Cash. Looking out the window, she could see the horses being readied and the carriage brought around. She didn't want to be Sallie when Cash found her, but she didn't want to be in Cash's shoes right now either.

If all society scorned him even as Sallie's husband, what would they do when they thought him Sallie's cuckold?

25

The fire reached the barn roof, igniting the newly baled hay in the loft and silhouetting the circle of men and horses against the night sky as they admired what they had wrought. A woman's hysterical screams became anguished cries of pain, but the men mounting their horses gave no evidence of consternation. The light from the fire briefly illuminated the slight sway of a human form dangling from a tree limb nearby as they turned their mounts toward the cover of the trees.

The screams became a whimper as a man rose from the ground and adjusted his baggy trousers. The woman left in the grass had nothing but a torn calico gown to cover her nakedness, and the bright yellow material emphasized the darkness of the breasts and limbs left exposed by the jagged rips.

A man with a rifle stepped from the shadows of the trees, and the rapist swung suddenly at his approach, reaching for the gun that should have been at his hip, realizing belatedly that it had fallen to the ground. Fear filled his face as he recognized the new arrival.

"Now, Brown, you're gonna get yo'sef killed if you report any of this," the rapist warned hurriedly, backing off in the direction from which his comrades had already departed. "They just uppity darkies that needed teachin' a lesson. You ain't got no call to interfere."

The newcomer chuckled and shifted his rifle to a less threatening position. "Andy, you don't think I'd go standing in the way of your fun, do you? I like me a little dark meat on occasion myself. No one's going to be reporting this little incident to the sheriff, so there won't be no cause to pull you in. But you've got some other problems brewin' if you don't take my advice. You remember that doctor back in town?"

Losing his need for caution, the other man picked up his weapon, and shoving it in his waistband, strolled arrogantly toward his horse with the new deputy sheriff at his side. "The one that got you the hidin'?" He snickered.

"That was that white nigger, and that's another story." Irritably Brown cut off the chuckles. "I'm talkin' 'bout that damned Yankee doctor who's been treatin' the niggers."

The other man gave him a suspicious glance. "I seem to remember your bein' a Yankee yourself. What's that got to do with anything?"

Marshall caught the bridle of the man's horse and placed his finger protectively on the trigger of his rifle. "Don't believe everything you hear. I got a reason for what I'm doin'. The doctor's filed a complaint against you, Andy, and the sheriff's going to have to act on it. You're going to have to hightail it out of here, if you know what's good for you. Or you can join up with me, and I'll look after you until we get this damned town straightened out."

The man called Andy hesitated. The new deputy sheriff didn't come from these parts, and Andy was automatically suspicious of strangers. But Brown was married to a local woman, from all reports, and he had good reason to loathe the doctor and the breed of men he represented. Speculation raised its ugly head as Andy considered the stories circulating about this hard man some called deputy and others called bastard. Brown wasn't all that he seemed to be, and Andy's eyes gleamed in the fading light of the fire.

"Maybe you and me and the boys got a thing or two to talk about after all . . . Sheriff." Andy put his boot in the stirrup and threw himself up on the horse, then waited patiently for the other man to join him.

The silence of the house was almost funereal with Cash gone. Turning out the few downstairs lamps before going to bed, Laura glanced around the darkness uneasily. She had never stayed in this house alone before. It was a rather eerie experience, as if the house had anticipated this moment and meant to make the most of it. She shivered and rubbed her hands over her bare arms. She was being ridiculous. Jettie and her children slept in the back bedroom, Jemima had the room next to the kitchen, and several of the maids had beds in the basement. The house wasn't empty. It was just her imagination

Carrying a candle, Laura slowly traversed the stairs to the upper story, listening for the creaking of the roof and the old elm outside. Perhaps she could go into the sewing room for a while and experiment with some scraps of lace and ribbon to see how well the machine stitching held on different kinds of material. She had already discovered there were a number of tasks she would still have to do by hand to make gowns look right. She would hate to have to sew all that lace on by hand if the machine couldn't do it.

Deciding she was only postponing the inevitable, Laura reluctantly turned into her own room. In another day or two Cash would be back with Sallie, and the little world she had created for herself would come tumbling back down again. Cash had already been gone two nights, and it felt like years. She knew she was spinning impossible fantasies, but she didn't seem able to stop it. The bed staring at her now seemed cold and lonely, but it was the same bed she had slept in the better part of her life—the same bed she would sleep in for the rest of her life if things continued as they were.

She had to leave, that was all there was to it. No, that

wasn't all there was to it. Lifting the candle again, Laura turned toward the nursery door. Entering, she let the flicker of light glow over the sleeping infant in the cradle. He hadn't lost his full head of dark hair, and as he lay there now so peacefully, she could see the image of Cash as a youngster. Life had cruelly taken a beautiful child and twisted and beaten at him until he was the hard, cold man he was today. Perhaps not exactly cold. She had seen Cash with the children, knew he had the capability to love, but he made no effort to exert it. He stayed aloof, turning his energies to the farm and the animals and ignoring the people around him, as they had ignored him all these years. She couldn't take his son away, deny him that chance of love.

Sighing at the complexity of people, Laura blew out the candle and padded silently back to her own bed. She had taken this path enough times to know it by heart. At least Mark was sleeping through the night now. He was eating enough solid food to begin weaning him over the next few months, but something in her fought at the notion of losing that one small bit of intimacy she possessed. Weaned, Mark would be independent and on his own. She wouldn't be needed anymore.

Not wanting to face where that thought led, Laura wandered to the window and looked blindly out. Once Sallie returned, she would have to leave, that was all there was to it. Perhaps she would stay long enough to help during the latter stages of pregnancy and the birth. Sallie would be totally impossible until then. But then Laura would have to go. Perhaps with another infant to dandle on his shoulder, Cash wouldn't object so mightily to parting with Mark. And perhaps having a baby would change Sallie into the loving wife she ought to be. Perhaps the moon would fall into the sea too, but that was another thought that didn't bear close examination.

A gleam of light where there usually wasn't one caught her eye before she could turn away from the pane. With a wry twist of her lips, Laura wondered if perhaps that was the moon falling into the sea. But there was no sea and no moon, and the flicker developed a companion, and another, and another.

A sudden bolt of fear shot through her. The night the Raiders had visited wasn't that far removed from her

memory to be forgotten. She remembered torches, big
flaring torches, and she remembered the way they
scorched the summer-dry grass and ate toward the house,
and panic began to twist at her insides.

She stared a little longer, making certain she wasn't
observing some natural phenomenon that her earlier fear
and imagination had conjured into something else. But
the flares were moving purposefully now, and their goal
seemed very specific. She couldn't see the tobacco field
through the branches of the elm, but she knew their direction. With a quiet scream of outrage she flew back
into the hall.

She woke Jettie first, warning her to gather the children and find safety. Then she ran down the back stairs
to Jemima, sending her after the maids in the basement.
She didn't know where any of them would go, but they
ought to at least be alert if the Raiders started for the
house.

She knew little of the men in the old slave cabins out
back. Cash had always dealt with them. But she knew
the grooms and the stableboys in the barns, and she ran
to them next. Maybe if she could rouse enough people,
they could chase the intruders away. She quelled the
growing fear that it would be too late.

Half-dressed grooms and stableboys staggered out of
the loft and back rooms as Laura screamed for help. At
the shout of "Raiders!" they awoke more fully and began
reaching for pitchforks and scythes. It was scarcely the
arsenal needed, and frustrated, Laura ordered them to
go wake the others while she opened the gun cabinet.

She could smell the smoke as she left the barn, and a
glance over her shoulder revealed flames licking at the
night sky. It was too late. She knew it was too late.
The fire would roar through the ripened tobacco like dry
tinder. She didn't stop to test the wind. It almost always
blew from the west, and the tobacco field was to the west
of the house. She ran harder.

Jettie had already ordered the hysterical maids to
begin unloading the guns from the cabinet. The cabinet
had been locked and no one had known where Cash kept
the keys, so they had broken the glass, and it crunched
underfoot as they grabbed rifles and pistols and ran to
the men beginning to gather outside.

Laura knew a sense of futility as the field hands grabbed the rifles, then stared helplessly from them to the burning tobacco. Cash had hired ex-slaves as well as white soldiers returned from the war. The slaves had no knowledge of firearms and were terrified of retaliation by the murderous Raiders. The soldiers knew how to handle guns, some of them even knew how to ride the horses being led from the barn, but their willingness to fight swung on which army they had fought with.

Had Cash been here, he could have whipped them into a fighting force of some sort, but there was little chance that they would take orders from a woman with no position of authority that they knew of. Watching the flames leap higher and wider and begin to roar toward the house, Laura nearly wept in frustration. After all their hard work, everything that had been sacrificed, they couldn't lose it all now.

Stoically accepting the loss of the main cash crop, Laura ordered the men unfamiliar with firearms to start organizing a bucket brigade to protect the house and outbuildings. Jake Conner grasped this opportunity to take charge, and Laura gratefully left him to browbeating the frightened men and maids into taking up buckets and shovels and forming a line of protection. Then, turning to the head groom, she ordered him to horse any man willing to ride, and before anyone could guess her intention, she took the first mount saddled.

Put to shame by the sight of a woman bearing a rifle and riding defiantly toward the fields, the others followed suit, whatever their personal opinions might be. Those sympathetic to the complaints of the Raiders about the loss of their slave property and the injury done white landowners by the hiring of black workers now faced the prospect of not only losing their jobs by refusing to fight but also losing face by allowing a woman to fight for them. Whereas their stubborn, narrow-minded opinions might allow them to lose their jobs for a cause, their stiff Kentucky pride wouldn't allow them to face the scorn of a woman. And in the company of a group of men eager for a fight of any sort, they easily fell into the mood of their fellow workers.

It wasn't much of a fight. At the sight of the armed band of men riding toward them, the Raiders melted back into the darkness from whence they came. They specialized in picking on the helpless, issuing their warnings in the form of raping defenseless women and lynching unarmed men, succeeding in their cause through terrorism, not open battle. Laura watched in disgust as the torches were pitched into the field and their tormentors rode off without a single shot fired. "Worms," she spat out loud, causing several of the men closest to her to turn and look.

The field was too far from the creek to save. There was nothing she could do to recoup Cash's hard work, but the house and the people in it were of more importance. Giving a signal to the head groom, Laura directed the men back to the valiant efforts at the mansion.

The wind was picking up, the precursor of a storm, and Laura gave the darkened sky a hopeless glance, unable to determine the distance or the speed of unseen clouds. Very likely the wind would blow the flames to destroy everything before the rain came to save them, but she could always hope.

Terrified of sending the children out into the night while the Raiders were still abroad, Laura had Jettie and some of the younger maids round them up and keep them on the front lawn, some distance from the house, assigning a few young boys shotguns to protect them and to signal if anything went wrong. Then, turning back to the bucket brigade, she fell into line with a kitchen pot and began the tedious task of hauling water toward the creeping line of flames.

The stench quickly became unbearable as the wind carried the thick tarry smoke into their faces. They coughed and continued to carry water. Jemima's cousin Jake had the strongest men digging trenches across the back lawn, trying to stop the fire that way. Laura had no idea of the efficacy of such measures, but it was increasingly obvious that their puny efforts with buckets had little chance of saving anything.

She worked until she thought her arms would fall off. One of the maids swooned and had to be carried away. The smoke billowed around them until white became black and they could barely see each other through the gloom. The wind whistled through the trees, throwing the branches violently back and forth, sending the leaping flames in all directions. Someone screamed as sparks ignited her cotton clothing. A splash of water doused the flame, but fear became more rampant, and the brigade of water carriers became more cautious in approaching the fire.

Carriages and wagons began to arrive from neighboring farms. Laura could only wearily think the fire must be worse than she imagined for the flames to be seen that far away. Someone grabbed her shoulders and tried to drag her away, but she shrugged him off and followed the rut she surely must have worn in the grass by now. She had to save Stoner Creek. It was all she had.

A collective gasp went up as a gust of wind blew flames into the dry mock oranges circling the lawn. The green leaves took a moment to ignite, but already dried by summer heat and the scorch of fire, they soon turned into torches that soared ten and twelve feet into the air. The old bushes with their hundreds of dead branches were no major loss, but the danger of the leaping flames came that much closer to the house.

Thank God that Cash had had the sense to keep all the truly combustible materials away from the house, Laura murmured to herself as she found herself tracing a new path to this latest peril. The stables were the biggest danger, but they were on the other side of the house, still out of reach of the wind and fire. By the time the fire got there, everything else would be gone, and the stables would be meaningless.

She wept as the flames swept from the bushes into the overhanging branches of a young birch. She had kept that tree watered all summer so it would survive, but there were too many dead branches from previous neglected summers. The wind whipped the flames right through it and out of their reach. She heard the crowd cry out as the birch fell into the leaves of the stately old elm, but she couldn't bear to watch any more. There was no way humanly possible to reach flames that high. Only heaven could save them now.

This time when someone caught her shoulders and tried to lead her away, Laura stumbled after him. She hadn't realized she was sobbing until a handkerchief appeared in her hand. Useless fragment that it was, it couldn't possibly hold all the tears and memories that poured from her now. Gone, all of it, soon now. Her wonderful sewing machine would be a heap of scrap. Mark's hand-carved wooden cradle would be ashes. The lovely rose-pink silk would never become more than kindling. But it wasn't just the material things that would be lost; she would lose all that had connected her to this land, to these people. She would be the same homeless five-year-old she had been when they had first brought her here.

The rain began to patter in large splashes, and Laura was aware of the heartfelt prayers rising all around her as people turned their faces to the sky. But it was already too late; she could feel it somewhere inside her. The flames were licking at the roof now, not steadily, but with increasing intensity.

Cries could still be heard from the direction of the field where the men beat off the dying flames in the tobacco crop. Most of the action had turned toward the house. People still poured water on outbuildings in hopes of keeping them wet enough to hold out until the rain came, but the roof of the towering mansion was beyond their help. It hadn't been built for easy access.

The rain, when it came, fell in a great deluge. Screams of joy split the air, and children danced through the downpour in hysterical reaction to their elders' relief. As it became obvious that the rain would do more in a single minute than hours of human effort, the bucket brigade slowly subsided, falling back to watch the guttering flames eat along the roof and shrubbery.

They began to pull together in little groups, the white neighbors gathering about their wagons and murmuring among themselves, some already starting to break away and head for home and dry clothes. Several attempted to pry Laura away with them, but she shook her head and asked them to take Jettie and the children. None refused her request, although she obviously meant Jettie's children and those of the servants as well as her own.

The black field hands and hired help gathered in nervous little groups more for protection than anything else. There was anger in the air, a tension that too often had only one outlet, and they were aware of their position as targets for much of the hatred that had caused this disaster. Jemima clucked and hushed the weeping among the house servants, but Jake stood warily silent to one side, clutching one of the rifles that had been handed out so freely earlier.

Several of the white field hands were wiping their brows and cursing among themselves. Some of them still clutched guns; others were making their way back toward the cabins where they kept their belongings. Laura had no idea of which of them would be loyal to Cash and which might cause trouble. She just knew that trouble was brewing, and someone had to put a stop to it.

She gave a last glance to the roof. The fire was out now except for a few sparks still smoldering in dry pockets. The attic should have received the most damage, but the rain pouring in would soon drench the rooms below. The charred outline revealed only one corner had been seriously damaged. Perhaps something could be done to save the rest. It could have been worse. The house and its contents still stood—if no one decided to take this opportunity to rob the place.

Laura found the familiar silhouette of Steve Breckinridge moving toward the horses. There was no love lost between Steve and Cash. Steve had once hoped to acquire some of the lands that Cash had snapped up with Sallie. But he had come out to help in this time of need. Perhaps he could be persuaded to linger a little longer.

Laura ran after him, catching him by his shirt sleeve before he could find his horse. He turned and glared down at her warily, but covered in soot and wet to the bone, she scarcely produced a threat of any sort. He caught her elbow and supported her as she tried to get the words out.

"I can't do it alone, Steve." Appalled at the way these words almost sounded like begging, Laura straightened her weary shoulders and tried again. "Cash isn't here. I don't know those men . . ."

He caught her meaning quickly enough and nodded. "You should have left with the women. I'll take you with me. Ma and Eliza are still at the Springs, but one of the maids can look after you."

Laura shook herself free, angry that she couldn't make herself clear. "No, I can't go. There's no one here. Don't you see? I've got to take care of the house. And the horses. There's no one to look out for them. Help me."

Exasperated, Steve looked from the petite scrap of wet hair and cloth to the gathering of nervous and expectant servants on the front lawn, then up to the damaged mansion. With a curse, he tried to pretend he didn't know what she was saying. He owed Cash Wickliffe nothing. But little Laura had never done anything to anyone. Except act like a stubborn mule.

"You're a damned fool, Laura, always were. Why worry about what isn't yours? Come home with me and let them take care of themselves."

"And I always thought you a gentleman." Voice dripping with scorn, Laura lifted her chin and turned her tired feet back toward the lawn and the waiting servants. She would do it alone and damn them all to hell.

In a moment heavy boots squashed through the puddles behind her and a loud masculine voice began shouting orders over her head. Almost collapsing with relief, she tried to throw him a grateful glance, but Steve was already marching off in the direction of the idle field hands.

Following in Steve's footsteps came the remaining farmers and neighbors who had lingered to see how the disaster would end. If a Breckinridge could help a Wickliffe, then it certainly behooved them to do the same.

Laura stopped and closed her eyes, and with the rain beating down her cheeks, turned her face to heaven and gave grateful prayers of thanks.

26

There were workers hammering a temporary cover over the hole in the roof and carpenters and plasterers running in and out inspecting the damage to the interior when the carriage pulled up through the muddy ruts created in the front lawn by the prior night's traffic. Laura was vaguely aware of the activity around her as she led the maids through upper-story rooms attempting to salvage what she could after the drenching from the storm. The whole house reeked of smoke, but the fire itself had done little more than burn through the attic to scorch the ceilings on the inside. The rain pouring through the roof and gathering in the attic and seeping through the plaster and down the walls had created the greatest disaster, causing entire sections to cave in, soaking everything in sight, and coating the rooms in shattered chunks of plaster and filth. The arrival of a lone carriage scarcely commanded her attention.

The hysterical screams and the curious male voice that followed brought her back to reality quickly enough. With a jolt of recognition, Laura picked up her skirts and flew toward the stairs. Cash was home.

He was bellowing staccato questions at the men who rushed in upon his arrival, while Sallie whimpered and looked helplessly at the muddy footprints trailing through house and hall and at the strangers staring from disarranged rooms and doorways. Laura's arrival focused both their attentions on her, and she slowed her mad rush to a more ladylike speed. She'd had no sleep to speak of and had only managed to change from her drenched clothing into a dry cotton gown that had been buried in the back of her wardrobe and survived the downpour. She was conscious that she looked little more than a dirty

servant at the moment, but there were more important
things on her mind than appearance.

Cash cursed and started after her as Laura stumbled
on a particularly large piece of plaster on the stairs, but
Sallie's faint scream and swoon forced him to stop and
catch his wife. Laura recovered her step and watched
with a wry twist of her lips as Cash carried Sallie into
the parlor and ordered it cleared of drying objects so he
could lay her down. When it came to attention, there
never had been any competition between them. Sallie
had it all.

Apprised of Cash and Sallie's arrival, Steve Breckinridge strode in from outside. Finding Laura in the hall
and glancing to the parlor where Cash bent over Sallie,
Steve made a grimace and ran a weary hand through his
hair. He wasn't as good-looking as Ward, but there was
a stability to him that could be relied on. Laura touched
his sleeve and drew his wandering attention back to her.

"You'd best go home and get some sleep, Steve. I
can't tell you how much I appreciate your staying.
Without you . . ." She shuddered to think what could
have happened. The possibilities were limitless and all
unpleasant.

"Well, that's what neighbors are for, I reckon. I hope
Wickliffe is man enough to handle Sallie as well as this
mess. I sure wouldn't want to be in his place."

Cash was beside them before they knew it, his expression grim and hard as he heard these words and acknowledged the man who spoke them. Breckinridge had not
once crossed the portals to Stoner Creek since Cash had
taken up residence there, and both men were well aware
of that fact as they faced each other. Their dislike for
each other dated back to childhood, but neither man
made mention of the fact as they stood amid the ruins
of last night's disaster.

"I trust I owe you thanks for helping out with whatever
in hell happened here. If I can do anything for you . . ."
Cash's gruff offer went unfinished, since he was in no
position to know what he had left to offer.

Neither man extended a hand to the other, Laura
noted with annoyance. She wanted to kick Cash, but she
understood he had been rejected enough not to want to
suffer it again, not now when everything was crumbling

around him. Instead, she turned to Steve, prying at the stony wall between them.

"They've got coffee and hotcakes ready in the back. Won't you have some before you leave? I hate to send you out hungry."

The offer of hospitality should have come long ago and from other lips than Laura's, but at least it was said. Steve glanced down at the dark shadows beneath enormous green eyes, then back to the tall hard-eyed man looming protectively near her. With a nod to both of them, he agreed. "I'll go out the back way and grab a cup, if you don't mind." He glanced back to Cash, then into the parlor, where maids were waving smelling salts beneath Sallie's nose. "You might want to send Sallie over to our place while things get righted here. You too, Laura. We'll be happy to have you."

It wasn't enough, but it was a step. Laura saw the slight relaxation of Cash's shoulders. Cash hadn't been invited to join them, but under the circumstances, it wouldn't have been appropriate. The fact that Steve hadn't openly rejected their meager hospitality was sufficient for now. She gave a small sigh of relief as the two men parted formally, without open hostility. She would take whatever small favors came her way for now.

After Steve disappeared into the back, Cash returned his gaze to Laura, and his grim expression dissolved into concern. "I'll find someone else to tell me what happened. I'll get Sallie back into the carriage, and you go with her. Where's Mark?"

If Laura hadn't been so exhausted she might have taken some satisfaction in noting Cash thought of her before Mark and Sallie, or that he had so much confidence in her care that he hadn't worried about Mark until now. But exhaustion made it too difficult to think beyond his immediate command. Shaking her head slowly, she answered, "Jettie should be bringing him home shortly. I've got to stay here. Send Sallie away. Her room's a disaster."

Cash's lips tightened at her refusal, but after the ordeal she must have been through, he couldn't argue with her. Seeing the tall black man at the back of the hall, he signaled him to step forward. "Jake, is there a room anywhere that the ladies can rest in?"

Jemima's cousin stepped hesitantly forward, but seeing
Laura nearly wilting on his employer's arm, he nodded.
He was unaccustomed to being in the house or dealing
directly with his employer, was only here now at Jemima's command and as a result of chaos, but he had been
in the army and didn't shirk his duty now. "The rooms
on that side ain't too bad, suh." He jerked his head
toward the east side.

"Good." Gesturing toward one of the maids in the
room with Sallie, Cash pointed at the stairs. "Take Miss
Laura and Mrs. Wickliffe to my room. When Jettie
comes, have her take Mark up to them. Under no circumstances is Miss Laura to be disturbed for anything
else for the rest of the day."

Laura struggled to protest. There was too much to do,
too much that couldn't be left to untrained servants to
understand, but Cash wasn't listening to a word she said.
He was already walking off, shouting orders to every
unfortunate who wandered close enough to hear him. It
was really more than she could do to fight him. The
house was his, not hers. Why fight at all? Closing her
eyes and swaying slightly, Laura gathered enough
strength to climb the stairs.

She did manage one small rebellion, however. Refusing the use of the large suite where Cash slept, she ordered a couple of workmen to locate a dry mattress and
take it into the sewing room. Farthest from the fire, it
had come through the night unscathed, although it was
one of the few rooms that had not yet undergone renovation. Still, its shabbiness suited her, and Laura gave a
sigh of relief as they hauled in one of the mattresses from
the children's room.

There were still things that needed to be done before
she could rest. Cash had been a fool not to take Steve
up on his offer to house Sallie. She could hear her cousin
complaining all the way down the hall, and Laura knew
from experience that Sallie wouldn't be quiet until she
had what she wanted. It was more or less like dealing
with a spoiled child. Steeling herself, Laura walked down
the hall to Cash's chambers.

She had never been in them for more than the time it
took to measure the windows for new draperies. Being
on the east side, the room received only the morning

sun; in the afternoons it was cool and restful in here with the curtains drawn. She had consulted Cash on the hangings of the massive tester bed, but he had shrugged and said he didn't care, so she had chosen the brown-and-gold design herself. She thought it went well with the expensive Aubusson rug her uncle had installed in here with its dominant shades of ivory and gold. The airy design of the wallpaper had been a little difficult to find, but the brown fern fronds had seemed more masculine than the usual roses and nosegays, and she was quite proud of her creation. Cash had never said a word about it.

But Sallie wasn't so reticent. Propped against a half-dozen pillows, she querulously pointed at the heavy velvet draperies on bed and window and ordered them removed. At sight of Laura in the doorway, she struggled to sit upright. "I can't live with these monstrosities around me. Have them clean my things and bring them in here. I vow, Laura, how could you let him ruin this room like this? It looks like a mausoleum. What's been going on here? Did lightning finally strike us down? It's a pity he couldn't have been here. I'm sure God meant it for him."

Since there was only one "he" she could be referring to, Laura held her tongue. It wasn't her place to come between husband and wife. "The draperies in your room are drenched and reek of smoke. I don't know that they can be saved. I can have someone take down the bed hangings in here, and perhaps the curtains in my room will dry fast enough. I'm not certain there's enough to cover all these windows, though. Maybe if we just open these up you won't notice them so much."

"Oh, never mind. Just leave them alone. I'll see to it myself just as soon as I get a little rest. Get out, all of you." She made a commanding gesture, shooing the maids from the room .When Laura turned to go also, she stopped her. "Not you, Laura. Stay. I need someone to talk to. I need someone here when that beast comes in."

Laura gave the wall a curse, then smoothed her expression into impassiveness and turned back to her cousin. Sallie had truly come down in the world if she needed her to talk to. She more likely had some request that she didn't wish the maids to hear. And from the sounds of it, it was a request that Laura didn't want to carry out. She wasn't about to take sides in this family argument. It might become obvious too quickly that her sympathy was on Cash's side.

"The heat must be making you miserable," Laura said quietly, heading for the washbowl and the cool water someone had just filled it with. "Why don't you lie back and rest for a while? I'll fix you a cool compress."

"I don't want a cool compress." Sallie sat up and flung one of her pillows at the far wall. "I don't want this rotten child. I'm sick to death of the heat and the company out here in the middle of nowhere. And just when I was beginning to enjoy myself a little, that miserable cur had to come and drag me back here. My God, what does he think I can do in this condition? I'm having his brat, for pity's sake, what more does he want? And if he thinks I'm going to hang around this place after it's born, he'd better think again. I don't need him to get me out of here anymore."

That didn't sound at all promising for this marriage or the child's future, but Laura could remember days during her pregnancy when she had felt like throwing herself off a cliff or shooting someone. It came with the territory. Sallie would calm down later, when she had a little one in her arms. Laura poured a glass of water and offered it to her cousin. Sallie really didn't look well. There was a puffiness around her eyes that had never been there before. Stripped now of her voluminous petticoats, she looked almost fragile. Blue veins lined the skin of her swelling breasts above her chemise, and her abdomen appeared abnormally large for the sixth month of pregnancy. Laura made a note to herself to call Dr. Burke as soon as possible.

"This is your home, Sallie. The people here love you. You're just tired because of the baby. Drink this and get some rest. Things will look much better when you wake. Cash will straighten out this mess."

"Cash is the reason for this mess." Suddenly breaking into tears, Sallie wiped at her eyes with the back of her hand and collapsed into the pillows, sobbing almost soundlessly as she buried her face in the down-filled cases.

Whatever the mess Sallie referred to, Laura could almost be assured that Sallie was as much the reason for it as Cash. The night sky might as well have married the sun for all they would ever be together on anything. But they were both too headstrong for Laura's poor powers of persuasion to help. She could only sit at the side of the bed and wipe her cousin's forehead with a wet cloth and wait for the crying jag to come to an end.

"You don't know what it's like being married to a man," Sallie finally whispered into the pillow.

No, she didn't, but Sallie didn't know that. She was merely dismissing Laura's early "marriage" from her mind, assigning her the role of younger cousin she had always assigned her. That Laura had a life of her own never occurred to Sallie. Laura said nothing to correct her.

"They only think of themselves. All they want a woman for is to ease themselves between their legs. Even Ward wanted that. It's disgusting, Laura. Disgusting. And this is the result!" Sallie made a gesture of derision to her swollen belly. "*His* child! Not mine. Not ours. His. Because he put it there. Well, I don't want it, and I won't have it. I won't!"

Laura heard this tirade with uneasiness. Sallie was spoiled, yes, but usually she was rational. Denying the child she carried wasn't rational. Laura didn't know how to respond. She made soothing noises which Sallie ignored.

Triumphantly Sallie pointed to the chest one of the grooms had carried up. "I've got my escape in there. I won't ever have to put up with a man in my bed again. I've found a real gentleman, a proper Boston gentleman, and he won't ever make me do those disgusting things again. He promised, Laura. He said he only wants to make me happy, that he'll take me anywhere I want to go. He just enjoys looking at me; he doesn't need any of the rest. I knew there were real gentlemen out there somewhere. These awful hillbillies around here are uncivilized degenerates."

Laura's uneasiness began to build, but there was nothing she could do or say without being wrong. If that was the kind of life Sallie wanted, she should have sought it before she married Cash, before she got herself with

child. It was too late now, her head said, but deep in
her heart she wanted to tell Sallie to go find her Boston
gentleman and leave Cash alone. Only Cash would be
crushed by such a rejection, so she said nothing.

Sallie sighed and sank back into the pillows, squeezing
Laura's hand. "I knew you would understand. You may
not be pretty, but you're smart, Laura. You don't have
any man telling you what to do. But I have to have
someone to take care of me, and I've finally found him.
I'm going to ask for a divorce, Laura."

The ugly word resounded through the quiet room even
after Sallie fell asleep. Laura remained where she was
for some time after she knew her cousin slept. Divorce.
Such a thing had never occurred to her. She had no idea
of the ramifications of such a scandalous act. She had
never known anyone who had been divorced before. She
felt quite certain that such a woman would be kept outside of polite society, so she never would have the opportunity of talking to such a person.

At the sound of Jettie Mae's voice coming up the
stairs, Laura finally rose and drifted from the room, but
Sallie's words remained in the back of her mind. They
played there all day, even after Mark had been fed and
everyone left her alone to sleep. She couldn't sleep. She
dozed to the sounds of male voices and the pounding of
hammers on the roof and footsteps running up and down
the hall. Throughout the cacophony, the refrain still
wove in and out of her dreams. Divorce. Cash and Sallie
could get a divorce.

Cash would be devastated. What would happen to
Stoner Creek? As Laura finally slipped off into sleep,
she envisioned a weeping Cash turning to her for comfort. She would open her arms and take him in, and
together they would find that ecstasy they had once
shared in a barn in a thunderstorm.

The crash of a dropping tool jarred her from dreams
of thunderstorms. Laura lay there staring at the gray
gloom of a strange room, slowly orienting herself to this
new situation. She had learned at an early age to be
adaptable. She could gauge from the lack of light that
she had slept all day. She knew she was in the sewing
room on a crude straw-stuffed mattress. She could hear
voices, and her inner ear sought out the one she most

wanted to hear. And finding it, she filled with enormous guilt and fear.

She wanted Sallie to divorce Cash. Because she wanted him for herself. She, Laura Kincaid, the nondescript dependent relative, longed to be the woman on Cash Wickliffe's arm. And in his bed.

Shuddering, she realized just how far she had fallen. She would have Cash in her bed even now, with Sallie in the other room, if he wanted her. She would do that for him if he asked it of her.

It was a humiliating thought. Her only saving grace was that Cash scarcely knew she existed. And she would have to see that it stayed that way.

27

"Just get the damned thing covered so we don't drown in our beds. We'll worry about the walls this winter." Cash shoved his hat on his head and strode angrily toward the door. The workmen waiting for his orders exchanged glances and raised their eyebrows behind his back. This wasn't the same man who had made them go back and redo a ceiling earlier in the summer when it wasn't completed to his satisfaction. They shrugged and turned to their ladders and lumber. A temporary roof would keep out the worst of the rain, but there was no promise that it wouldn't blow off or rot before spring. But if that was what the man wanted . . .

Well aware of the exchange of glances behind him, Cash strode out into the humid August heat with a simmering fire inside him to match anything the weather could throw his way. He'd be damned if he lost everything he'd worked for to a yellow-bellied bunch of scoundrels like those renegades under Marshall Brown. He had enough contacts to know his enemies. Raiders hadn't done this, no matter what Laura thought. Marshall's marauders had.

Cash ground his teeth and calculated his losses. The tobacco was a serious setback, particularly after he'd expended so much cash on the damned house. But there were still the corn and hemp, and he had several promising yearlings that would bring good money in a postwar economy starving for horses. It was just that it would take a year or two to see real money out of the foals in the field now, and corn and hemp wouldn't bring the same prices as tobacco. There would have to be economies.

Not that he could make Sallie understand that. The thought of his wife brought a grimace to Cash's already grim expression. He almost wished he had ignored Mrs. Breckinridge's scandalized hints and left Sallie to make a fool of herself with that man-milliner she had taken up with. That kind of fop was scarcely a threat, and it would have kept Sallie out of his hair awhile longer. She was raising holy cain and keeping the house in a constant uproar at a time when he really didn't need the aggravation.

What he really needed to do was find Brown and wring his neck. Cash derived great satisfaction just from contemplating the thought. A lynching suited him right down to the ground.

It hadn't taken long to verify his suspicions. A few nights down at the tavern drinking with some of his old gambling buddies had pried loose enough tongues to get the name of the culprit. Cash had half a mind to join the crusading vigilantes calling themselves the Regulators, who had slipped him the information. But he had a loathing for acting outside of the law that had something to do with the women and children in his protection.

Gaining his horse, Cash swung up into the saddle and set out to supervise the cultivating of the burned-out field. He couldn't use that field for tobacco again for another few years. Perhaps he'd try a crop of winter wheat.

But thinking of the fields and what he would do with them didn't keep his mind from dwelling on the topic of women and children. He had one child in this world and another one coming. For their sakes he had to recoup his losses, if nothing else. The respect he had hoped to gain for his family seemed highly elusive, and although he had hoped Sallie would aid him in his goal, he knew now that she would only work to destroy it. Her demand for a divorce was the hysterical whim of a pregnant woman, Laura had assured him, but Cash wasn't so certain. If it weren't for the child, he'd be mighty tempted.

But there was the child she was carrying to consider, and the effect of the scandal, and Cash pushed temptation to the back of his mind. He knew enough about the law to know Sallie couldn't obtain a divorce on her own and that he would have to accuse her of adultery before the wheels could even be set in motion. Knowing Sallie, adultery would be damned hard to prove. Snorting at that cynical thought, Cash turned his horse down the row the men were working. Even a daguerreotype of his wife and that man-milliner in bed wouldn't prove the case. They would probably both be fully dressed in their finest garments.

He had a need for a woman. He had fully intended to be faithful when he had said those vows at the beginning of the year, but the very few times Sallie could be persuaded into bed were scarcely sufficient to last him through the nine months of her pregnancy and whatever time she would demand afterward. Perhaps if he thought he would be welcomed with open arms after such a drought, he might have the stamina to make it. As it was, the torment seemed purposeless. Sallie would undoubtedly prefer it if he took his needs to the hired women in town.

Cash certainly could understand why Ward had taken that rascally Jettie Mae to bed. But Jettie had shown no interest in enriching herself in Cash's bed, and to be perfectly truthful, he had no interest in entertaining her there. And as much as he wanted a woman, he couldn't bring himself to return to the whores in town. Sallie hadn't exactly been a joy in bed, but she had been clean and lovely, and he had no desire to return to a woman who had been used just minutes before him.

Cash did his best to ignore the images of another woman who had welcomed him into her arms, a woman more responsive to him than any other he had ever known. Instead of fading with time, the images came

more frequently now, but he was certain that was only
due to his unanswered lust. Laura was a gentlewoman in
every sense of the word. She would be horrified if she
knew he thought of her in such a manner. And if she
ever learned of his thoughts, she would leave, taking
Mark with her.

So he had to keep his thoughts to himself. Maybe after
harvest he could go into the city and find one of those
married women who liked to court danger. He'd found
enough in the past to keep him satisfied. A few good
romps and he would be himself again. Then he could
turn his full attention on bridling Sallie and regaining his
lost profits.

One of the hands in the far pasture finally caught his
eye, and something in his frantic wave sent Cash cantering dangerously across the rutted field. Even before he
slid out of the saddle, he knew what he would see, and
his heart sank deep into his boots. Not the horses, God,
please not the horses.

"Well, that's what happens when you hire those ignorant darkies to do a white man's work." Dignifying the
dinner table with her presence for the first time since her
return, Sallie didn't even waste a smug look at her husband sitting opposite. She daintily cut into her chicken
without giving him a glance.

Laura gave the brooding fury on Cash's face a hasty
look and tried desperately to think of a way of diverting
the confrontation, or at the very least escaping from it.
The news of the knifing of one of Cash's prized yearlings
had tension crackling throughout the household. Sallie
did no one any good by tightening the screws.

"No black man I know of would kill a horse. It's tanta-
mount to killing a baby. Only a white man would commit
such a heinous crime." The calm with which Cash uttered
these words revealed the depth of his fury. It took every
ounce of his self-control to continue sitting at the same
table with his wife after that remark.

Through thick lashes Sallie gave her husband a shrewd
look, then, exercising a pleasant smile, turned to her
cousin. "Didn't I hear the new deputy sheriff's mighty
interested in you, Laura? P'raps we ought to ask him

out to investigate. Someone has to put a stop to these depredations."

Laura's heart froze, and she heard the sudden intake of Cash's breath. She had hoped Sallie wouldn't have heard about Marshall, or that she would ignore the gossip, as was only polite, but that had been wishful thinking. Sallie might pretend not to know about such scandals as Laura's running away to marry Marshall or Cash's whipping Marshall through the streets, but Sallie wasn't stupid. She knew everything, and what she didn't know, she could put together. Sallie simply used only that knowledge that could be used to her advantage.

"I'll not have that piece of white trash put one foot on my property. Don't take your sour grapes out on Laura, Sallie." Cash had quit eating and was making inroads on his wine as he sat back in his chair and waited impatiently for dinner to be done.

Sallie finally raised her head and deigned to give him a glance, even if only a mocking one. "How droll. Little Laura has finally found a protector. I should have known it would be my husband; she's coveted everything else I own."

Laura felt her meal curdling in her stomach. The black storm in Cash's eyes did not bode well for either of them, but she feared the flash of lightning in Sallie's gaze even more. Sallie was dangerous in her unpredictability. No one could guess her target until the final shot was fired.

Before Laura could open her mouth to object, Cash intruded with bored mockery.

"I beg your pardon, my dear, but you own nothing, least of all me. Now, I suggest you put your claws away before I take it in mind to cut them."

His last words held a dangerous edge as Cash rose from his chair and with one final glare stalked from the room.

Laura quietly folded her napkin and started to follow his example. The sound of Sallie's contrite voice was almost not enough to stop her, but years of obedience took precedence, and reluctantly she turned around to face the stunningly lovely woman at the table.

There was a bitter smile on Sallie's lips as she met the accusation in Laura's eyes. She lifted her wineglass in toast to Laura's look. "You could at least say 'I told you so' like anyone else, but you ever were the grimly polite sort. Don't you think life might have been much simpler if you had just once pulled my hair and scratched my eyes and fought for what you wanted?"

Laura briefly studied the question, but seeing the pain and emptiness in her cousin's eyes, she just shook her head. "Not when what I want hurts too many other people. I can't be that selfish, Sallie."

"But I can, you mean." Sallie emptied the glass and carefully set it down, watching the glass and not Laura. "Well, as Ward would say, I'll take that into consideration."

When she said nothing else, Laura hurried away, heart thumping erratically. She didn't want to know what was going on in Sallie's head when she talked like that.

In the days that followed, Cash's refusal to spend any more money on repairing the fire-damaged house caused Laura a great deal of concern, but Sallie took it in stride. It was as if she had already turned her back on Stoner Creek and was looking in a new direction. Laura tried to persuade herself that Sallie was finally thinking about the arrival of the baby to the exclusion of all else, but her cousin's behavior was not that of a new mother feathering her nest. Rather than ordering children's gowns and cradles and tiny blankets and booties, Sallie was browsing through ladies' magazines and ordering the latest patterns and sending for swatches of material to be compared to the pictures in the books. She had already ordered a bolt of blue taffeta and insisted that Laura sew it to the dimensions of one of her New York dresses, but Laura had ignored her request.

Laura returned to the sewing room that now served as bedroom for both herself and Mark. The nursery had been damaged by water, and Cash's reluctance to deal with it had made it simpler to work around the nuisance. She certainly didn't mind keeping the infant with her, but once Sallie's baby was born, life might grow a little more complicated.

Taking the restless infant to her breast, Laura sat in the rocking chair and stared out over the stable roof. She wasn't accustomed to looking over the farm from this angle, but she liked seeing the rolling hills of emerald with the horses gamboling in the pasture. Except now

Cash had men patrolling the fence lines, watching for trouble.

It was like living in an armed camp anymore, and she didn't like the feel of it. Her mind drifted back to the letter in her pocket, the long-awaited letter from Jonathan. He was coming home. She had feared that he would say that. Despite all his assurances that he was perfectly healthy and capable of making the trip, she had hoped and prayed that he would just send for her. But she should have known better.

Now she dreaded Jonathan's arrival. He would understand that she would have to wait for Sallie's baby before leaving. But this time he wouldn't understand if she insisted on staying after the new arrival. Neither would anyone else. And she couldn't stay, not after discovering her feelings about Cash. She wasn't precisely sure what they were yet, but she knew enough to recognize their unhealthiness. Cash was a married man and she wasn't an adulteress. For her own good, she had to leave. But for Cash's good . . .

That was the stumbling point. Whatever her feelings for Cash might be, they included a large dollop of concern and protectiveness. It was as if, once having saved his life from Watterson's whip, she must spend the rest of her life looking after him. Cash certainly wasn't a man who needed protection from the normal run of things. She was fully convinced he would know how to deal with the Raiders and return the farm to profit and any of those other things that life threw his way. Her concern was for something more elusive, something she had seen in his mother's eyes, knew existed in Cash's soul, something that was in great danger of dying if things kept on as they were.

Laura didn't like the way he was going to town every night and coming home drunk. When she took his clothes for laundering, they smelled like cheap perfume and whiskey, and she knew of only one place where that combination could be found. He was selling his soul to the devil, and she didn't know how to stop him. But she did know depriving him of his son wasn't the way.

The time would have to come when some decision had to be made, but that time wasn't now. Sallie's baby wasn't due for another three months. Anything could

happen in three months. It would just be nice having
Jonathan's sensible head to help search for some solution. She would look forward to his arrival and not borrow trouble by imagining the worst.

As she rocked, Laura heard a fumbling at the door.
She hadn't bothered with a lamp in the early-evening
gloom, but it was full dark now. Mark was peaceful in
her arms, occasionally making sucking noises, but essentially asleep. She didn't want to disturb the calm she
found in his company. Questioningly she turned her gaze
to the door and murmured a quiet welcome. Jettie Mae
was the only one with enough temerity to disturb her at
this hour.

When the door opened to reveal the tall silhouette
outlined against the lamp in the hall, Laura felt a tug of
panic. But he came in without a word, shutting the door
behind him, and she tried to still her trembling nerves.
Cash had never harmed her; she had no need to fear him.
She need only fear herself and the emotions hovering too
near the surface as he approached.

"I didn't know you were still awake," he whispered
quietly, coming to a halt just before her chair. "I just
wanted to see if everything was all right."

And she knew he spoke the truth. She had heard him
countless times in the nursery in the middle of the night,
checking to see if the baby still breathed, roused by some
unexplained noise. Cash slept lightly, and lately she
doubted that he slept at all. She hadn't heard him return
from town. Perhaps she had dozed off a little herself.

"We're fine. He's asleep. Would you like to hold
him?" It was too late to be embarrassed at his finding
her here with her bodice unfastened and the child at her
breast. He certainly had to know how his son was fed.
She was counting on the darkness to conceal anything
else.

When he leaned over the chair, Laura could smell the
whiskey on his breath, but he didn't seem drunk. His
arm was strong and sure as it balanced on the back of
her chair and he touched a wondering hand to the child's
face, not inches from her bare breast. Laura held her
breath, but Cash merely pushed the blanket back to better inspect his son's satisfied expression.

"He's lucky to have a mother like you." The words

were said so low as to be scarcely audible, but Laura heard everything he said and thought with a sensitivity attuned to him. She lifted Mark so Cash could take him, but said nothing to acknowledge his remark.

"There's a chair over by the table," she offered as Cash lifted the child from her arms. This evening visit was highly improper, but as long as he was here, she wouldn't turn him away. She would never turn him away, she acknowledged wryly to herself.

Cash brought the straight-backed chair around and lowered himself to it, sprawling his long legs in the narrow space between Laura's rocker and the window. With deft hands he removed his son's blanket and placed it over his shoulder, then laid the infant's head there, rubbing his back gently as Laura had taught him to do months ago. The scene was so homely that Laura almost cried at the sight.

"He's grown so big," Cash murmured, loud enough to be heard this time.

"He doesn't take after my side of the family, that's for certain," she said with a hint of irony. Cash's chuckle and swift look in her direction caused a commotion with her insides, and Laura hurriedly sought a distraction. "He's already crawling, and the other day I could swear he was trying to pull himself up like Taylor does. He'll be running before we know it. You'd better construct a cage before that happens. I can tell right now we're going to have our hands full with the two of them egging each other on."

Cash smiled in the darkness and allowed the soft Southern lilt of her voice to wash around him, comforting him with the familiarity and the commonplaceness of tone and topic. He needed this tiny oasis of calm, and the odd thing was, he felt as if Laura knew it. There was no other good reason for her to accept the irregularity of his presence here.

"I'll lasso them both and keep them corralled until they're manageable. I take it Jettie and her young ones are going to be a permanent fixture here, so I might as well get used to it. If this next one's a boy, we'll just have to hire a lion tamer to keep them in line."

Cash's jocular words hit a note too close to one of her worries, but Laura didn't find it appropriate to introduce the subject. If Sallie's baby wasn't a boy, how would they make it understood that the new baby was a sister, and not someone Mark might grow up to love as a man does a woman? That was one more reason Cash would have to understand why she had to leave, but she wouldn't intrude upon his reverie right now.

Instead, she found a different subject to quietly introduce. It was no less worrisome, but certainly more pertinent. "Cash, I hate to bother you, but I wish you would talk to Sallie. I've tried to persuade her to call in Dr. Burke, but she refuses to see him. I'm afraid something isn't right. I'm not a midwife and I don't have much experience, and I could very well be wrong, so don't go getting yourself all shook, but I would feel better if she saw a physician."

Cash removed the infant from his shoulder and stared down into the sleeping face illuminated by the moonlight through the window. Tiny lashes swept over fair skin, and a rosebud mouth pouted open and exhaled a milky breath. He didn't smile, but chucked the fat little chin and held a pudgy hand. He wanted to ignore Laura's quiet request, but it was something he had thought about himself. Her speaking of it made it imperative.

"I'd hoped you could persuade her to it. She isn't listening much to me these days. Are the Breckinridges back from the Springs yet? Maybe they could talk her into it."

"They won't be back until September. I don't know which is worse, forcing her into being examined, or hoping we're wrong and letting things go on as they are. I'll have Lucretia come out. I think Sallie may accept a midwife more than a male physician."

Cash nodded agreement. "I'll do that; you don't need to trouble yourself. I never did thank you for what you did the other night. I've heard various versions, but they all amount to the same thing. Your timely warning probably saved lives as well as the house."

"The wages of insomnia, or an uneasy conscience, I'm not sure which. I only wish I could be stronger. If you had been here, you could have caught the culprits."

Cash gave her a curious look, then stood to place the child in his cradle. He tucked Mark in, then turned back to the woman who had stood when he did. He didn't touch her, but remarked upon the similarity of her creamy skin in the moonlight to that of the child. Laura had skin made for touching, but he knew better than to break a sacred trust.

Keeping his hands curled at his sides, he replied, "If I had been here, I would have done just as you did. It was more important to stop the fire. The criminals will still be there when I'm ready to go after them. Go to sleep now, Laura. I won't let anything happen to you. I promise."

With that, he walked out the door.

Laura watched him go, and felt the tear sliding down her cheek as the door softly closed behind him. Why did his words go straight to her heart, when she knew in her head he only meant to be reassuring? He would never know they touched her somewhere deep inside, somewhere where she was alone and unprotected.

28

For the first time in the weeks since the fire, Cash smiled and joked with the staff, taking their ribbing about his age with easygoing camaraderie, thanking them gracefully for their thoughtfulness, but Laura noticed the smile didn't quite reach his eyes, and he kept his gaze averted from her. She had a curious hollow feeling in the center of her stomach when he finally left for his study, leaving the servants to clean up the remainder of the birthday dinner.

She had hoped to return some of that joy they had shared on her birthday a little over a month ago, but though there had been laughter and surprises and friendship today, something was missing. Perhaps she only felt that way because Cash had scrupulously avoided giving her any more of his attention than the rest of the gathering. Perhaps it was just her own selfishness demanding recognition that made her interpret his reactions that way. Everyone else seemed perfectly satisfied at the way things had turned out. She could hear Jemima singing in the kitchen and two of the children giggling as they cleaned out the ice-cream bowl. Sallie hadn't bothered to descend to the dining room for the celebration, but then, she hadn't bothered much to share her company since her return. So there was no real reason for this empty feeling.

But it was there, and Laura couldn't rest with it. It was as if Cash were sending off a plethora of signals that she couldn't interpret fast enough to create anything but noise. She wasn't a telegraph operator. She would have to ask him for plain speech.

After seeing to the remains of the birthday dinner, Laura took off her apron and gathered up her deliciously full new batiste skirt and petticoats. Cash had given her the means to make these things. She had wanted to return his thoughtfulness in the only way open to her. If she had failed, she wanted to know why. It was that simple, or so Laura told herself as she approached the closed study door.

The draperies in here were pulled wide to reveal the vast expanse of rolling lawn just outside the window. The desk that Ward had once used was now buried beneath files and ledgers, old pieces of harness, and assorted paraphernalia that Cash had brought in for various reasons. Books had begun to pile up around the desk as Cash sorted through them for information he wanted and then left them, as if he had returned to them more than once. It should have been the picture of utter chaos, but to Laura it looked like a room well used and appreciated, and she felt happy here.

She found Cash seated in his leather chair and facing the window away from her, but it was another sight that caught her attention. Framed in the window, a familiar sturdy little body rolled on the cushioned window seat, gurgling happily at the sights outside the glass. Laura caught her breath, and the sound brought Cash swinging around to face her.

He was holding the gold brocade vest that she had made for him, the one with his initials discreetly embroidered on the material. Beside him lay the leatherbound volume on animal diseases that Dr. Burke had brought as his contribution to the party. As Laura looked closer, she could discern all the other odds and ends that had been lovingly made for him by people he had hired and housed and kept on despite the uproar and protest around him. Her words caught in her throat, and, embarrassed, she turned to watch Mark in the window.

"I didn't think you'd miss him for a while." Cash's voice was raw and aching, and he carefully turned his head aside as he folded the vest and set it on the desk with the other things.

It suddenly dawned on Laura that he had been crying. The shock nearly took her breath away, and when she recovered, she wanted to run and throw herself at his feet and comfort him, but then he rose with the same graceful assurance that she associated with Cash, and she locked the thought away. He bent to lift his son and to sit in the window where Mark could better see out.

"I didn't miss Mark. I was looking for you. You worry me sometimes."

Cash jerked his head back in her direction, but his features were lost against the glare from the window. Still, she could hear the slight edge of laughter behind his reply.

"You're a caution, Laura Kincaid. Haven't you got enough to worry about in this madhouse that you need worry about a renegade like me?"

"I don't worry about most things. It doesn't pay. I just do what I can and hope for the best. But I guess my livelihood depends on you, so you worry me. Foolish, granted, but some things can't be helped." Laura kept her voice light, but she could tell by the set of Cash's head that he wasn't buying it.

But politely he allowed the little lies to pass. "I've never had a birthday party before. How did you know it was my birthday?"

Laura was quite proud of her sleuthing in the matter, but she shrugged nonchalantly. "Dr. Burke said the date should be on your marriage papers, so I just told Sallie that you wanted them put in a safe place and asked her where they were. She had them right in her desk, and your secret was out. I just wanted to return the favor you gave me. I can't buy you a sewing machine, but the least I could do was give you a little recognition."

Cash made an indecipherable noise, then propped his long legs on a chair and set the restless child in his arms loose to crawl on the floor. "A long time ago, my mother used to make me a new shirt for my birthday. I can vaguely remember that. Then she wasn't well enough to make anything, and I was lucky to get beans for supper. After that, I decided birthdays weren't what they were rated to be, and forgot about them. I'm not so sure that isn't the right attitude, after all. Looks to me like I've reached this one without doing anything humankind couldn't live without."

"You're a remarkable fool, Cash Wickliffe, but if you want to sit here and feel sorry for yourself, far be it from me to interfere. I just wanted to make certain I hadn't offended you in some way. Excuse me for intruding."

Laura swept around and stalked toward the door, but before she could reach the knob, Cash was behind her, catching her shoulders and turning her around. She wasn't prepared for his sudden proximity. Her defenses were down, and when his arms closed around her, all she could do was stare. And then his mouth was on hers, and nothing else mattered anymore.

Just the touch, just the momentary forbidden touch, was enough to recreate an earlier time, to explode old myths and forge new, very tentative dreams as their mouths molded together and opened to each other. They moved apart quickly, mutually, but the damage was done, slight as it seemed at the time. Laura touched the burning bruise of her lips as Cash turned his back and gripped his desk.

"That wasn't your fault, Laura. I get crazed sometimes. Everyone needs a warm body to hold occasionally. This just seemed like one of those times."

Pulling her hand from her mouth and gripping it behind her back, Laura leaned against the study door and tried to think of something to say, but her mind wasn't functioning. Her heart was, though. It was thumping loud enough to be heard by the woman upstairs. Not that Sallie cared, she told herself callously, but Laura cared. She cared too much.

"I'm sorry I didn't think of that sooner." Laura tried

to force the lightness back to her voice. "Everyone ought to get a birthday kiss."

Cash's smile was grim as he turned back to face her. "And you always see that everyone gets what he wants. Laura, didn't anyone ever tell you that saints reside in heaven? When are you going to learn to live for yourself?"

She stared at him in astonishment and growing anger. "You're a fine one to talk! What do you think I was trying to do back in town? And who was the one who brought me out here anyway? Why did you bring me here, Cash? What earthly purpose did you think I'd serve out here now that you've got everything you want? I'd suggest you think about that, Cash, and then let me go when the time comes."

Before he could make any reply, Laura grabbed the doorknob and rushed out. She wasn't certain she had any of the answers she had sought when she came in, but she had more questions than she could possibly face. Flight seemed the only practical alternative for the moment.

Cash rode into town after that. He was in town every night now, and tongues were beginning to wag. Laura watched him go from the sewing-room window. Jettie Mae had returned Mark to her without her usual sly looks or comments. It didn't matter. All Jettie's innuendos were true. The lust that had flared up between Cash and Laura one summer's day was not a fleeting thing, but the brand of the devil.

Turning back into the room, Laura considered going in to Sallie and easing her conscience somewhat by seeing if there was anything she could do for her cousin. Although in the latter stages of pregnancy Sallie couldn't go into town or do much visiting, she still had enough visitors to know by now that Cash was frequenting every tavern and brothel within a thirty-mile radius. The notion didn't seem to bother her, but Sallie wasn't inclined to show that kind of hurt.

With that thought firmly in mind, Laura could find a new perspective for the afternoon's incident. Cash was trying to retaliate, to make Sallie see how much she had hurt him, and Laura just happened to be in the way. He had recovered himself quickly enough when he realized

Laura was more vulnerable than the whores in town. That was all it had been. Just a momentary aberration.

But one that had revealed to both of them what should have remained disguised: she hadn't protested his kiss, but participated fully. That knowledge would be between them forever after.

And it burned like acid all through Laura's gullet as she thought about it. She couldn't stop thinking about it. She felt the pressure of Cash's hands on her back, knew the scent of his skin as his head bent over hers, had the heat of his lips branded to hers. Her body knew where such pressures led, and she craved the ultimate result. It was humiliating to no small degree that she had no more moral responsibility than the creatures of the field.

So she didn't go to Sallie until later that night, when the screams and commotion began in the room down the hall and she couldn't ignore the inevitable anymore.

Sallie had continued to refuse to see Dr. Burke, but she had allowed Lucretia to come and stay. The old woman had warned she was carrying twins and needed bed rest, but Sallie had continued to traipse up and down stairs, wreaking havoc wherever she went, asserting her authority by making demands that sent servants scurrying hither and yon. After one or two brief fights, Cash had stayed out of her way, working in the fields until dark, going to town until morning. No one had the means to make Sallie remain in her bed when she wanted to do otherwise.

Lucretia had warned this might happen, but Laura hadn't been prepared for it to happen so soon. Too soon. Pulling on her robe and running for Sallie's room, she mentally calculated the months. Seven. The babies couldn't come now. They would never live.

But nature wasn't governed by the laws of man. Sallie sat screaming in the bloody puddle of her bed while Lucretia and Jettie Mae hurriedly pulled at the sheets and tried to remove them from under her. A nervous maid hovered in the corner with clean linens, her eyes wide and terrified at the frantic activity. At the sight of Laura running in, braid flying, chenille robe flapping about her ankles, the maid's face turned gray and she nearly fainted.

Laura grabbed the linens from her and gave curt commands. "Send someone into town for Dr. Burke. Send someone else to look for Mr. Wickliffe. He's probably at the tavern, so don't send someone who can't get in. Do you hear me?" At the maid's terrified nod, Laura shoved her toward the door. Hysteria wasn't needed at a time like this.

Sallie's hysterics were sufficient. Laura helped strip the bed and remake it, then applied herself to holding Sallie's hand and calming her while Lucretia examined her. Once the initial pain and its results were disposed of, Sallie quieted. Clutching Laura's hand, she smoothed the covers over her swelling abdomen.

"It will be over soon, won't it?" she asked with a certain amount of satisfaction.

Uneasily Laura murmured soothing sounds. It would be over too soon. The chances of a seven-month babe surviving were next to nil. Sallie didn't seem in the least concerned.

"I'll have my figure back in no time. Eliza told me how she did it. And if I don't nurse, I'll be just as firm as before. No one need ever know I've had a child."

Laura caught Jettie's look and frowned, shaking her head to silence her. Sallie was just running on out of nervousness. Her looks had always been important to her. It was only natural that she find this topic to distract her from what was happening.

Sallie screamed again as another contraction took control, and Laura bit her lip. The pain shouldn't be this great this soon. She glanced to Lucretia who was keeping a stoic face as she finished her examination and washed her hands in a nearby basin. The old woman muttered a few words to Jettie and sent her off to fetch the necessities. When she turned back to meet Laura's questioning gaze, she shook her head but said nothing.

Breathing a little harder, Sallie tried to find a more comfortable position. "You never lost your figure, Laura, but then, you never had much of one to begin with. I think maybe nursing even helped yours a little, although you'd better be certain to wear your corset from now on. Don't think I don't know that you go without one when you wear those dowdy house gowns of yours. It isn't proper. Mama would turn in her grave if she knew."

That was a topic she could deal with, and Laura tried to smile. "Why should I accent what I don't possess? You're just jealous because you can't go without one. I bet you'd give anything to be rid of the hot, tight old things."

"Don't be ridiculous." Sallie gave a supercilious sniff. "A woman should take care of her best assets. A trim figure and a bright smile will win you any man you want. You'd best take a lesson from me, Laura, if you mean to catch Cash after I'm gone."

Laura nearly fell from her seat at these words, but Sallie's grimace of pain prevented immediate response. She clutched her cousin's hands tighter as the pain seemed to roll over and take possession of her, and Laura tried not to panic when she saw the bright spot of red forming on the clean sheet where there shouldn't be one yet.

It took Sallie a while longer to recover from this one, and Laura patted her head with a cool cloth and gave her a sip of water as she rested. Cautiously, making certain that the pain wasn't immediately returning, Sallie adjusted her position again, not bothering to look at Laura.

Laura thought she had forgotten their earlier topic, but she was quickly disillusioned as her cousin continued as if they had never been interrupted.

"Don't think I don't know about the two of you. You've been making sheep's eyes at Cash since you were a tot. And every time I turn around, the two of you are together cooing over that brat. I wouldn't be surprised if the brat doesn't belong to Cash; there's a certain resemblance. He's like an ungoverned stallion, spending his prowess on any mare in heat."

Laura tried not to flinch as Sallie turned her shrewd gaze in her direction. She merely moved to wring out the cloth in the bowl. "Don't be ridiculous, Sallie. You're overwrought. This will be over in a while, and you won't remember any of the silly things you've said. Cash likes children. He'll be so tickled when he sees yours, that he'll give you anything you want."

"The voice of experience?" Sallie snickered. "Prim, prudish Laura. Heaven only knows what he saw in you, but he came after me soon enough when I let him, didn't he? But you can have him back now. He's served his purpose. You can do me a favor, though."

This time the contraction took longer, forcing Sallie to arch her back and scream louder, cursing frantically as wave after wave struck at her insides, beyond her ability to control. Lucretia's lips tightened and her eyes looked unhappy as she watched for some sign of the impending birth. More blood spilled to the sheets, but there was no indication that the child was any closer to making his entrance.

Sallie dozed fitfully for a while, moaning occasionally as smaller pains struck and subsided. Conscious of the words said and unsaid between them, Laura remained grimly silent, grateful for the loyalty of the woman who had to have heard them. Lucretia was certain to have suspected Mark's paternity from the first, but she had never mentioned the subject. Laura would be forever in her debt.

When Sallie woke, it was to another contraction, and she gasped, grasping for Laura's hand as she struggled. Beginning to panic, she tried to speak, but Laura hushed her, soothing her brow with the cooling cloth, giving her something or someone to grip.

The August heat was abominable, even this late in the evening. Not a breeze stirred through the open windows. The mosquito netting lay limp and unmoving as Sallie rose up and fought against the pain encompassing her. The smell of blood slowly began to permeate the room as the candles guttered low and Lucretia moved to light new ones.

Jettie returned with bowls of hot water and towels, retreating to a far corner where she could be called upon as needed. But as the hour grew later and the struggles intensified, it became obvious there was nothing she could do, nothing anyone could do.

In a moment of brief respite, when a slight breeze entered the room to warn of the coming dawn, Sallie fought for breath and pulled Laura closer.

"Promise me you'll persuade him to give me a divorce. That's all I ask. I'm getting out of here, Laura, if it's the last thing I do."

It was the last thing she did. After giving birth to two stillborn babes in a puddle of blood, Sallie slipped into unconsciousness, and soon after her spirit departed from her body, finding that other place where men were always gentlemen.

Laura held the tiny lifeless infants to her breast and cried.

29

The gray light of dawn brought Dr. Burke. The infants had already been cleaned and wrapped and tucked in a wooden box, and Sallie's lifeless body had been washed and prepared for the coffin that would be made later that day. When Burke arrived muttering harried excuses at having been called to another birthing earlier in the evening, Laura greeted him at the bedroom door and led him back toward the stairs.

"I don't think there's anything you could have done, Doctor. It was too soon." Tired as she was, Laura had a hard time refraining from adding, "Sallie did it to herself." It did no good to place blame. Nothing would bring back her cousin or those two tiny infants who would never have a chance in this world.

Exhausted himself, Burke still heard the ragged edge of Laura's voice, and catching her arm, he kept her from escorting him down the stairs. With eyes of concern, he noted the strained lines about her mouth and the emptiness of her gaze. "Where is Mr. Wickliffe? He ought to be here. You've got to get some rest before you collapse. You have Mark to think of."

As if his name called to him, Mark emitted a wail of neglect that echoed down the hallway. Laura gave a wry smile. "He won't let me forget. You need some rest yourself, Doctor. Shall I tell Jemima to fix you something to eat before you go?"

A vile curse broke the dawn silence outside, and the front door flew open with a crash as a large form stag-

gered against it. Oblivious of all the gazes swerving in
his direction, Cash turned his face up the stairs to where
Laura's slight figure could be discerned against the darkness. "Why is Burke's carriage here?" he demanded
without preamble.

"Let me." Patting Laura's hand, Burke gently turned
her back toward the bedrooms and away from the stairs.

Shamefully Laura allowed him to maneuver her that
way. She didn't want to be the one to break the news.
She couldn't bear to see the light in Cash's eyes go out
forever, as she knew it would. This was no longer her
affair. Her grief was private and separate, and it was
time she acted upon it.

Cash's roar of pain and outrage filled the house not
moments later. Had he been sober, he might have dealt
with the news more sensibly, but drunk, he let all his
emotions show, and the echoes of his anguish rang
through silent halls long after he grew quiet. Laura felt
the tears roll down her cheeks, but she continued her
path toward her room. It wasn't her place to comfort
Cash. Sallie had made her cousin's place in Cash's life
too uncomfortably clear.

Jettie took Mark after Laura fed him, and Laura fell
exhausted into her bed. Every word that Sallie said
slipped in and out of the byways of her mind, mixing
with her sleep, haunting her dreams. Images of Cash as
a stallion mounting mares gave her cause to shudder in
her dreams. Sallie holding her breasts up to be suckled—
not by her child, but by some unseen creature—formed
unwanted pictures in her mind. She didn't see herself,
but felt the piercing pleasure of possession make her
womb ache, and she tossed restlessly into another dream.

Gradually, as Laura regained consciousness some hours
later, clearer thoughts replaced the cloudy veil of sleep,
but they were no less troublesome. Sallie was the only
family she had. As far apart as they had been, she still
mourned her loss, for with Sallie went all the memories
of her past: of the summers on Stoner Creek with Uncle
Matt and Aunt Ann and the barbecues with Sallie laughing and flirting with all the neighborhood gallants, the
parties, the holidays, the happy moments that they had
shared. All of the past was gone now, snuffed out with-

out a protest, and she was left rootless, with nowhere to turn.

And the guilt, the overriding guilt as Laura thought of Cash and how she could almost be glad Sallie was gone. The guilt was worst. How many times had she secretly hated Sallie for taking Cash away when she needed him most? How many times had she thought she would be better for him, wished Sallie would go away and stay away so she could have his attention? The thoughts were far more sinful than the action she had once taken in chasing after Marshall. And now she was paying for them.

And Sallie could possibly be right. If Laura played her cards right, she might attract Cash's attention and hold it long enough for him to turn to her, even to marry her. In his grief he would seek any source of comfort, and there was this physical attraction already there between them. Sallie knew about men; she must have seen it too. The possibility was there, and Laura hungered after it as she had once hungered after a home of her own.

But it would be wrong. Laura didn't even need to think about it to know that it was wrong. She felt it deep down inside of her. Perhaps people made marriages out of physical attractions, but she had already seen the ruins of Cash and Sallie's marriage and knew what could happen. And inside herself she knew she didn't have even a quarter of the attraction that Sallie had possessed. If Sallie couldn't make it work, no one could, particularly not Laura.

She didn't know where that left her, except alone. There was always Mark. She comforted herself with the thought of his sturdy little body pressed to her breast. She would have years of watching him grow, of his laughter and his pains. She didn't need any more than that. She had almost missed that opportunity. She was twenty-two years old and not likely to ever marry. To have Mark was like a miracle, one not to be ignored. She would make a life for them. She knew she could.

Below, she heard the murmuring of many voices and knew the neighbors were beginning to gather. She strained to hear Cash above the others, but there was an ominous silence in that direction. The few male voices that she heard had no resemblance to the smooth, commanding voice she knew so well

She wondered if she could sit this one out, if she could just hide in her room and let everyone think her so overwhelmed with grief as to be bedridden. It would be so much easier than going down to face all those people after all that Sallie had revealed to her. Laura felt as if her adultery were written across her face. Not that what she and Cash had done was actually adultery, but it might as well have been. The result wasn't much better.

But she was a Kincaid, and more was expected of her. She wouldn't allow dead Kincaids to overshadow her now as they had when alive. She would do what was expected and more. Afterward she would wonder what to do next.

Jettie and Lucretia already had Sallie laid out in one of her prettiest New York gowns, the two infants cuddled in her arms as if they belonged there. Her golden hair framed her face in smooth curls as it had for so many years, not as it had looked last night when drenched in sweat and tears. Laura could scarcely bear to look, but for the sake of appearances she approached the parlor table to offer her farewell. The room grew silent as she touched a hand to the face of the little girl who had never breathed life, and someone hurried up to lead Laura away when her knees almost buckled under her.

But that was the last time Laura gave in to grief. There hadn't been time to dye a gown black, so she had to meet her guests in the old gray silk she had once trimmed with black as a widow in Cairo. The neighbors didn't care what she wore just now. They simply wanted to hear the details of Sallie's death as they had gossiped about her actions when she lived.

When it became apparent that Laura had no intention of castigating Cash for not being there when his wife died, they lost interest in her and sought each other for the speculation running rampant about Cash's whereabouts. Laura merely thanked them for coming, gave endless gratitude to those who filled the kitchen with their offerings of food, ordered refreshments served to those who lingered, and consulted with the preacher and his wife about the time of the services. She would be all that was proper and nothing more.

Cash's absence niggled at the back of her mind as she

made her way through the guests, but there wasn't time to worry about it. Steve Breckinridge and some of his cousins arrived, assuring Laura that Eliza and Mrs. Breckinridge had been summoned from the Springs and would be here in time for the services. There were words concerning Sallie's burial next to Ward, and Laura agreed without a second thought. Sallie and Ward belonged together. Both had been thoughtless creatures of an earlier time. It seemed only right that they should lie together through eternity.

Laura wondered if she ought to search Sallie's trunk for some sign of the man that Sallie meant to run off to. He really ought to be notified if she meant anything to him at all. But she didn't have the heart to search Sallie's things just yet. Maybe another day.

As the number of neighbors arriving and leaving slowed to a trickle, Laura threw an anxious glance about the rooms in search of Jettie or her mother. Finding the maid, she worked herself around the back of the room, past the lingering knots of people come to pay their respects and staying to gossip. Catching Jettie's arm, she led her back into the hall, and finding still more people there, they slipped into Cash's study.

"Where's Cash?" Laura demanded as soon as they were alone

Jettie rolled her eyes expressively. "Where you think he is? Done passed out in the barn with one of his horses. Jake got the animal out so he don' step on him, but it might do a damn sight more good if it walked over that man's face."

At that moment Laura could only agree. But Cash had to be made to see to his responsibilities. She wasn't going to do it alone. Callously she ordered, "Go throw a bucket of water over him and have Jake get him dressed in something suitable. I don't care if he sits in the corner unconscious, he's going to sit with Sallie tonight."

Jettie grinned and nodded and raced off to do what she had been waiting to be told to do. Laura walked out of the study and straight into an open set of arms.

She gasped and looked up to find Jonathan's concerned gray eyes staring into hers. At that moment Laura almost lost it all, all the pride and determination and stubbornness that had been keeping her going all through the day. She nearly fell into his arms when they closed around her, and she choked on her sobs as he patted her back.

"Hush, now. It's going to be all right. You've been doing just fine, Laura. Don't let go now. Why don't you find some of that excellent coffee I remember Jemima used to make. I heard she's back here now."

It was just what she needed. Sniffling, Laura accepted his handkerchief with almost a laugh of remembrance of other handkerchiefs he had held for her. She needed to be told what to do right now. Her mind wasn't functioning clearly anymore at all.

"When did you get in? Nobody told me. Come back to the kitchen with me. We can't talk with all these people around." Laura hurried down the hall, forcing Jonathan to fall in step with her.

"I got in last evening. I sent a telegram from Lexington to Burke, but he must have been out when it arrived. Don't curse me too roundly, Laura, but I ran into Cash while I was looking for a place to stay. He was with me last night when everyone was looking for him."

Laura didn't know whether to laugh or cry at this discovery, and she threw Jonathan a sharp look. The only place they could have met was at the hotel, and she knew perfectly well the kind of women that stayed in that hotel. He didn't manage to look the least bit sheepish when he caught her look. In fact, Jonathan was looking quite handsome with his newly acquired tan and his brown hair lightened with a streak of Arizona sun. She smiled faintly at his answering smile.

"Won't you go in the parlor and tell everyone that for me? That's all anybody wants to hear. Where was Cash when his wife was dying? If they thought she was crying for him, they've got Sallie all wrong."

"I can imagine." Jonathan stopped in the kitchen doorway while Laura embraced the old black woman at the stove. Others of the kitchen maids came up crying, and Laura spoke with all of them, saying a reassuring word, employing a light smile, giving them the strength that she scarcely seemed to possess herself. Jonathan had spent this last year thinking about the woman he had left behind. He remembered her as frail and helpless, a wounded doe he had wished to take in and make better.

But there had been episodes even then that had made him realize that she wasn't the hurt creature he needed to protect. Perhaps, in some way, she did need someone to look after her, but not in the way he had his first wife. The evidence of that was right here before his eyes. Laura could never quiescently accept his love and help, she would have to return it threefold.

And there was the cross between them. Jonathan didn't want to dwell on that right now. He wasn't certain if he had returned just in time or too late. Only time would tell. He accepted the black coffee that Laura handed him, and allowed himself to be lulled into complacency by the welcome in her eyes.

"This is better than I remembered." He sipped at the scalding brew without a qualm despite the heat of the August day outside and the baking ovens within. After Arizona, he could handle heat. It was the humidity making his shirt stick to his back that made him grimace. "Maybe we'd better go back in the other rooms. You're likely to melt if you stay in here for long."

Laura hadn't noticed. Sending a nervous glance over her shoulder to the back door, where she hoped Cash would be making an entrance soon, she unwillingly accepted the offer of Jonathan's arm. Cash wouldn't be in any shape for anyone to see him right now, not even his best friend.

Sensing every nuance of Laura's behavior, Jonathan halted and glanced back toward the kitchen door, then returned his gaze to Laura's worried frown. "Cash isn't taking this too well, is he? Shall I go find him?"

"He's not likely to appreciate your interference. I have one of the servants looking after him. Perhaps it's better this way."

Jonathan looked up at the people gathering near the doorway wishing to say their farewells, and he shook his head. "You shouldn't have to do this alone. I'll go get him. Now isn't the time for me to monopolize you, in any case. We'll talk another time."

Laura nearly cried out a protest at his departure. Everything seemed so much easier when she had someone at her side, sharing the burden. If only she could let the burden go, pass it around so that everyone in the room held a piece of the weight, but she couldn't. She had never learned to share. Holding her chin up, she approached the crowd of guests prepared to make their parting condolences.

Cash finally came downstairs an hour later when the worst of the crowd had departed for their homes and suppers. His eyes were bloodshot and his thick black hair still looked damp from scrubbing, but he appeared sober and respectable, much to the disappointment of his audience. He said no word to Laura and avoided the bodies laid out in the center of the room, but took his place near the parlor door to accept the arrival and departure of Sallie's mourners.

Someone handed him a cup of coffee, and he accepted it with a nod, but for the most part people were content just to observe and not to approach him. He stood silently aloof just far enough that the guests could escape without speaking to him if they desired. And the few remaining mourners so desired. They departed hastily, giving him slight nods and hurrying off to gloat over the fact that they had finally seen the absent husband.

A few of the Breckinridge cousins remained in place of Eliza and Steve's mother, who had not yet returned, and Laura ordered trays brought in with a cold collation from the kitchen. Telegrams had been arriving all day. She wasn't certain who had been thoughtful enough to notify all the cousins and distant aunts and uncles throughout the Bluegrass, but they apparently all meant to make an appearance on the morrow. She had never thought of the rest of the Kincaids and Aunt Ann's family as being of any relation to her, but she supposed in some way they were. There would be people arriving she might have seen only twice in her lifetime. She wasn't certain she could live through another day of this.

Without realizing he'd moved, Laura found Cash at her elbow, pushing her toward the door. She looked up at him in amazement, but his expression was black and unreadable.

"Get out, Laura. You've had enough. I'll frighten everyone else off for the rest of the night. It's a pity I can't do the same in the morning."

It was amazing how their thoughts had taken the same direction. Laura managed a weak smile. "I don't suppose if I load a shotgun, that will help?"

"Don't. Just don't, Laura. Go to bed."

Cash shoved her out the door to the interest of the two Breckinridge cousins, and Laura fled before this audience. She didn't know what was the matter with him, other than he'd reached some breaking point which she threatened to push him over. Now wasn't the time to rear back and argue.

Maybe, in the morning, they could talk.

30

The morning brought chaos and torment and Laura had all she could do to walk numbly through the hours, greeting people she didn't recognize, arranging accommodations for those who would stay, seeing that everyone was fed, while waiting for the hour when Sallie would be carried to the cemetery and laid to rest for eternity.

At various and sundry times someone would come up and insist that she sit and rest and eat, and ever obedient, Laura would comply, but it never lasted long. She didn't have the tongue to gossip, and her protector would eventually wander away, and soon she would be submitted to the onslaught of demands all over again.

It didn't matter. She was much better off keeping busy, not thinking, just doing what was asked of her. Cash didn't circulate among the guests, but she was aware that he was there, clearing the room so Sallie could be laid in her coffin, talking to someone about the gravestones he wanted made, keeping his distance from the aristocratic relatives swarming through the damaged mansion. There wasn't a chance for them to exchange a word or two, and Laura couldn't help but feel it was better that way.

She didn't want whatever Sallie had seen between them to be noticed by any other. Cash's reputation was notorious and her own didn't bear close scrutiny. The gossips would have a field day if they began speculating about the relationship between the new widower and his wife's cousin. Before the day ended, they would have Cash murdering Sallie and Laura carrying his child. She was sick and tired of all the gossip, and Cash didn't deserve that kind of treatment. She would do everything in her power to keep him from being hurt by any more filthy tongues.

When Steve Breckinridge dragged his wife and mother to Cash's side to offer condolences, Laura nodded in satisfaction. Now was the time for people to recognize that Cash was not a fiend, but a bereaved husband and father. He would need their support in the weeks to come. She said as much to two distant cousins as she directed them toward Cash. It would take time, but they would have to recognize him for what he was.

The people from town arrived in time for the funeral, and led by Jonathan, they gathered around Cash in a show of support as they made their way to the cemetery. He didn't seem aware of their presence, but stood alone in the midst of the crowd as Sallie and his children were laid in their grave. Being the next nearest relative, Laura stood nearby, but she had an aunt on one side and a cousin on the other, and they kept her sheltered. Suddenly she had become a Kincaid to be recognized.

Returning from the grave site, there was much speculation as to what would become of the farm now, but Laura had never had any doubts about that. Under the law, the farm became Cash's when he married Sallie, and by rights, after all the money and hard work he had put into it, it could belong to no one else. She was the one who would have to leave.

Her various female relatives broached the topic later that evening, when Cash had disappeared from the crowd. Once Laura had firmly convinced them that the farm was Cash's, she was offered homes with several relations, but she couldn't bring herself to make that decision right now. None of her relatives had chosen to live in Stoner Creek, and to move away would be to deprive Cash of Mark. Somehow she would have to discuss that sensitive subject with Cash before making any decision.

But when she next saw Cash, he wasn't in any condition to discuss anything. Long after everyone else had

retired to makeshift beds in the rooms that could be
termed habitable, Laura still lay awake on her narrow
mattress. The muffled sounds from the front hall drifted
up to her, and, ever vigilant, she was up and into her
robe before anyone else could be roused.

Jonathan was just closing the front door gently behind
him when she appeared on the stairs. Braced across his
shoulders was a sadly disheveled Cash, and Laura gave
a small gasp as she saw the gash across his cheek. Wordlessly she ran to Cash's other side and helped Jonathan
guide him into the study, where a leather couch would
provide a bed. Leaving Jonathan to examine him for further injuries, she ran for warm water and bandages.

From the fumes of whiskey rising from him, it was
easy to judge that Cash had been drinking, and his unconscious state could as easily be from the drink as any
blows to his head. But Laura bit her lip in anxiety as
Jonathan finished cleaning him up and bandaging him.
She could see dull bruises forming in several places along
the tanned expanse of Cash's chest and ribs, but since
Jonathan didn't seem inclined to wrap them, she had to
assume they weren't serious. Only the gash on his cheek
and a stab wound in his upper arm appeared to need
treatment.

She waited silently for Jonathan to finish, then turned
her questioning gaze to him as he stood up. He took the
blanket she held and covered Cash, then gripped her
elbow and led her out.

"Let him sleep it off, that's all you can do. He'll be
sore in the morning, but I wager Cash has suffered worse
in his time. Go on back to bed and don't worry about
it."

Pensively Laura drew her brow down and removed her
arm from Jonathan's grasp. "What happened? Do you
know?"

Jonathan shrugged. He had seen Laura in her nightdress before, but she still looked helplessly young with
the long braid down her back and her slender figure
wrapped in the old robe. He didn't want to lay any more
burdens on her frail back, but it was better she hear the
story from him than the gossip from some other

"He was gambling down at the tavern. apparently he's

been losing as much as he's been winning lately. Did you know that?"

Laura shook her head. "I only hear whispers of where he's been. I'm supposed to surmise what he's been doing from that. He's been like this since Sallie returned from the Springs. I don't know what's got into him."

"Drink, mostly. He was drunk when he accused another man at the table of cheating. That started the brawl. He did a pretty good job of finishing it, too, but someone hit him over the head with a chair from behind. I'm going to stay here and wake him every so often to make certain he's all right, but his head is harder than a rock. He'll be fine."

Laura threw an anxious look toward the study door, but recognizing her place, merely nodded and took Jonathan's advice. She had no right to do anything else.

Cash wasn't available in the morning to wave farewells to the departing company. Laura was urged to join them as friends and family took carriages and wagons back to the train station, but she murmured polite words of staying with the Breckinridges and seeing that the farm was set to rights before she could go anywhere. They accepted her excuses, made open invitations, and left without anyone offering to stay with her.

Had it been Sallie, they would have all offered to stay, Laura thought cynically as she returned to the house. But she couldn't be counted on for cheerful company, and not knowing what else to do with her, they left her alone. With Cash. And a houseful of servants.

This state of affairs couldn't last, but she needed to talk with Cash before coming to any decision. And Cash wasn't in any shape to decide anything at all. Cursing her inadequacy, Laura set the servants to cleaning up the aftermath as she waited for Cash to arise from his slumbers.

Jonathan had made himself at home on the parlor sofa until the guests had started to depart. Then he, too, had gotten up, and murmuring words of reassurance in Laura's ear, left for the day. She was grateful for his presence and his aid and wondered for the hundredth time why she had ever turned down his offer of marriage.

When Cash finally stumbled from his study, Laura had

his bed made up and fresh water carried to his room along with a tray of black coffee. He grimaced at her through a swelling eye and didn't argue when she sent him upstairs.

But he was back down shortly after, dressed for the fields, his wide-brimmed hat pulled down over his face to disguise the worst of the bruises. At any other time Laura would have given him wide berth, but there was a topic that had to be discussed, and she wasn't going to let him escape any longer.

"I need to talk with you, Cash." She stood in his path, ignoring his grim expression and the inches towering over her.

"No, Laura, you don't. I'm not fit for talking to. I'll be moving back to the Watterson place tonight. When there's time, I'll bring in some lawyers to make arrangements. You just stay here and do what you have to do to keep the place together."

Stunned, Laura allowed him to escape around her. She was half-tempted to race after him, but it would be fruitless to try to argue when he was in this mood. She doubted if she would get any sense at all from him. But a slight panic began to run through her veins as she contemplated his words.

She wasn't certain what she had envisioned, but it had never included Cash leaving Stoner Creek Farm. Vaguely she had contemplated leaving with Jonathan. She had also considered inviting some perfectly respectable widow to come here and live and act as chaperon. She had thought of finding her own house in town. Dozens of thoughts had flitted through her head, but none had been like this.

Perhaps she hadn't heard him right. Or understood his intent. The thought that perhaps she ought to hire lawyers of her own passed through her weary mind, but that wasn't the kind of thing a lady was brought up to do, and it wasn't the kind of relationship she wanted with Cash. She wasn't certain what kind of relationship she wanted with him, but it certainly wasn't one that involved lawyers. On the other hand, she didn't want to be indebted to a man who intended to spend the rest of his life drinking and gambling away the only home she knew.

Uncertain of where she stood or of what Cash wanted,

Laura couldn't order further work done on the house. She greatly suspected the cash flow that had once renovated Stoner Creek had dried up. She had managed to salvage some of the draperies and bed hangings, and they were already back on the beds and windows. Mattresses soaked by the rain had been taken out and dried and aired and returned to the beds if still usable. Scorched and stained wallpaper would have to be ripped from the walls and whitewash applied until something else could be provided. Laura turned herself to that task next, refusing to sink into the grief and uncertainty that hovered around her.

She was helping Jettie Mae feed the children in the kitchen when she heard Cash's boots on the front stairs that evening. She couldn't drop what she was doing and run after him, so she waited patiently for him to make an appearance of some sort. She hoped he would call her to his study and explain things to her. If they could just talk, they could work something out.

Instead, Cash appeared in the doorway with satchel in hand, hat on his head, prepared to walk out. Laura stared at him in incredulity and couldn't speak a word as his gaze sought her out.

"If you need me, I'll be at the Watterson place tonight. I'll be going into town tomorrow. I'll set up an account for you at the bank there so you can buy what you need without having to ask me for it. We'll work out some kind of arrangement once I know the law and what I can do. Have Jake keep an eye on that foal in the far stall, and in the morning have someone take a look at that elm and see if it shouldn't be taken down. It looks like the fire killed it, and I don't want it falling on the roof."

Laura choked on the words crowding her throat. Cash was looking at her, but he wasn't seeing her. He looked like some stranger just stepped off the riverboat with his broad-brimmed hat and light-colored coat, his cravat abandoned and sticking out of his pocket. She could see the bronzed base of his strong throat through his open shirt, and she had the urge to place her fingers there, but a caress wasn't what she had in mind. She wanted to strangle him.

There were ten dozen things she wanted to say to him. She wanted to scream and rage. She wanted to cry and plead. She wanted to heave dishes at his head and fall on her knees and catch his legs. But he had staged this confrontation in front of a room full of servants, and she was left speechless. She didn't even know how to argue.

In the face of her silence, the servants remained mute. Cash gave them little time to recover their speech. He stalked out without another word, slamming the back door after him.

It was over. He would be returning to California soon. Laura read it in his face. Here she had been worrying herself silly about how she could stay close so he might see his son, and he was planning on moving two thousand miles away. So much for her understanding of men. When would she ever learn?

Quietly she said to Jemima, "Put some of that chicken in a basket with a pot of those green beans. If the biscuits are done, put them in there with whatever else you have that he might eat. Send someone over to Watterson's with it when you're done. He has to eat something."

Jettie Mae looked as if she might speak, but Laura quelled her with a look. She didn't want to hear any more opinions this night. She'd had one too many forced on her already.

Lounging on the old horsehair sofa that had come with the house and hadn't been worth giving away, Cash propped his boots on a barrel of molasses he'd ordered stored here and tried not to look too closely at the empty house around him. It echoed hollow in the nighttime darkness, and he wondered if he believed in ghosts. He could think of plenty that might come back to haunt this place, including the lost spirits of his parents.

The smell of fried chicken still wafted from the basket on the floor, although he had demolished most of the contents already. He had wondered how he would eat after he burned his bridges and walked out. He should have known Laura wouldn't let him starve. He wasn't certain if the basket were a pagan sacrifice to keep the devil away or just Laura's innate kindness; whichever, he felt better for it.

Sinking his head back against the sofa, Cash contemplated the cobwebs on the ceiling reflected in the light of the one small candle that he had found. He felt as hollow inside as this house. He knew he was doing what had to be done, but it pulled at his gut to do it. There for a little while he had come to learn what a home was about. He'd almost had that once with Doc and his wife, but then Kate had died and Jonathan's had become a bachelor household, and the memory had lapsed. Laura had brought it all back again. Laura, not Sallie.

It wouldn't do to think like that. He should never have married Sallie in the first place, he knew that now, but it was too late. Far too late. He'd been fulfilling a childhood fantasy, believing in rainbows when he had married Sallie. It hadn't taken long for the fantasy to crumble, about as long as it took a dreamer to wake from sleep. The stark reality of waking hadn't kept him from falling asleep and dreaming again, but this time he knew the difference.

Cursing, he fished a cheroot from his pocket and lit it. He'd had a life in California that he could have made something of. It had been pure stupidity to return here and imagine that he could crush his past and rise to the Bluegrass gentry by the simple expedient of wealth. That had been made plain enough to him. He wouldn't repeat that mistake.

The only question now was what he would do for the future. He blew a smoke ring and tried to think through that question. Emotions kept jumbling the usually clear logic of his mind. He saw Sallie and his stillborn children in the coffin, and unbidden tears filled his eyes. Sallie of the laughing eyes and golden hair, gone, because of him. He cursed and sought safer topics, settling on the gurgling laughter of Laura's son, only to realize he was allowing his heart to guide his thinking and not his head.

It would be a damned sight better if he had never known the Kincaid women or Stoner Creek Farm. Then he could just pull up his few roots and move on. But the weight of the yoke was in place and he couldn't shake it.

Grimly he turned his thoughts back to the vicious attack by Marshall's marauders and his plans to terminate the danger once and for all. There was something he could sink his teeth into. To hell with women and babies and homes. Action, he understood.

Champing down on his cigar, he began to make plans.

31

"He's down at the tavern drinking every night; almost got himself kilt just the other day. Don't see as how he's any problem at all. Wouldn't've minded having a taste of that wife of his, but now she's gone, there ain't nothin' left but your wife, Brown. Where's the sense in raiding the place again? Just go in and take what you want."

Marshall sent his cohort a furious look and turned back to his bottle. He didn't like anyone getting too close to his plans, particularly not a loudmouthed bastard like Andy. If he hadn't needed the manpower of Andy and his Raiders, he would have left them alone, but he needed real thieves and murderers, not the puling country bumpkins who got their jollies wearing sheets and pulling their pants down for every female that crossed their paths. Andy was a true son of Satan, and he helped attract more of his kind. Filling their own pockets was all that mattered to them, not the damned Kentucky politics that kept the other splinter groups of marauders going.

"Keep your tongue in your mouth where it belongs, Whitlow, or it'll get the pox before your cock does. I owe that son of a bitch, and he's going to pay before he dies. That's all you need to know. I'm keeping your pockets lined, ain't I?"

Marshall drank deeply of the whiskey, ignoring the filth of his surroundings. Only he knew he would have to break that devil's spawn they called his wife before he could collect the debt owed him. Once that was done, he wouldn't need these murdering bastards again.

He could see himself now, the glorious Union hero who put period to the depredations of the notorious Raiders. They might even name a school or somesuch after him one of these days. After he rid himself of Wickliffe and claimed his rightful wife.

Seeing the Stoner Creek mansion from the master's chambers was going to be a distinct pleasure, and the sooner, the better.

"Before I do anything, tell me what your intentions are toward Laura."

"What in hell business is it of yours?" Grumbling, Jonathan turned away from his former ward to pour himself a drink. He had no intention of making this easy for Cash. It was time the man woke up and faced the truth.

"I'm making it my business." Cash took the bottle from Jonathan's hand and refilled his own glass. It was too early in the afternoon to be drinking, but he needed fortification of some sort. This was closest to hand.

"If you don't know the answer, Wickliffe, you haven't got the sense I gave you credit for. The only question here concerns *your* intentions. Laura might not be given to many words, but she's never lied to me. I think your intentions are of most importance to her right now."

Cash glumly accepted that fact. Jonathan would know what had happened between them. He could in all probability place the blame for the separation between his old friend and his wife's cousin purely on his own shoulders. Steeling himself to the inevitable, he replied, "I'll support Mark, you know that. That's why I'm here. I just want to make certain Laura gets everything that's due to her, but I want some rights too."

"You gave up your rights when you married Sallie. Most of the town thinks Mark is mine. I'm fully capable of taking care of both of them. You can leave town with a clear conscience if that's what you're after."

Cash wasn't certain what he was after. He glanced around the cold hotel room where Jonathan was staying. He'd seen many of these in his day and he wasn't looking forward to going back to them. There was always the ranch. He could install some cute little Mexican maid, and after a while maybe he'd even teach her to speak English and marry her. Anything was possible.

Grimacing, he sipped his drink. "That's not what I'm after. I don't know why I'm even talking to you. I'll just do what I should have done in the first place and let

Laura decide. But there's a few things I've got to take care of first."

Jonathan watched as Cash rose from the chair and strode toward the door. When it became apparent more information wasn't forthcoming, he spoke. "You can't go proposing marriage to her now. Her cousin's barely cold in the grave."

With a snarl Cash turned and gave his former mentor a look that defied argument. "Marriage is the last thing on my mind. Do you think I want to destroy any more innocent lives? I'm going to give Laura what she wants—freedom."

The door slammed as he stormed out, leaving Jonathan to carefully regard the silent wooden panel. Perhaps Cash had the right of it after all, but he felt fairly certain that Laura wouldn't agree.

Sighing, he went downstairs and headed for Burke's office. If he was going to have to stay in this forsaken place, it wasn't going to be at that hotel any longer.

If he were the right sort of cad, he'd sign over the farm, consider he'd done his duty, and walk off leaving Laura to deal with the problems of Marshall and the lost tobacco and the damaged house and the crop that needed to be harvested. But Cash still retained too much of his mother's conscience to consign Laura to that fate.

He would solve the problems that he had caused and hand the property over free and clear of any further obligation. He had already poured a fortune down that drain—what difference did it make if he dropped a few more coins? He didn't need that much money any longer. It hadn't accomplished anything he'd wanted to do anyway. If he couldn't have what he wanted, money wasn't going to make the difference.

Not daring to contemplate what he wanted, Cash screwed his face into a frown and strode down the street. Several of his white field hands had already quit, refusing to work any longer side by side with the black men he had hired. He'd heard the epithets thrown in his direction. Nigger-lover was the least of them. His mother's origins had been dragged through the mud and splattered against him in more ways than he had thought humanly possible. He had to give them credit for imagination.

The short-term solution would be to fire the black hands and hire only white, but that wouldn't last in the long run. Most of the whites thought working in the field like slaves beneath their dignity. They would quit at the first opportunity. And if he left for California, leaving Laura in charge, they would grab that excuse to quit. They would never work for a woman. He needed to build up a strong and loyal force that would stay under any pressure. It sounded impossible, but there were enough unemployed people in the state to eventually find the ones he sought.

Marshall and his bunch were the worst problem. By spending enough time drinking with some of the so-called vigilantes who hated Marshall as much as the Raiders, he'd been able to learn enough of both groups to stem some of the worst offenses to his workers. The vigilantes didn't interfere much when they heard of a planned lynching of a Negro worker, but to keep Cash's interest, they would pass on the information to him if it involved one of his people. But even though he'd been able to prevent any immediate mayhem, his workers were getting nervous. Several of them had families to be concerned about, and they were talking of moving north. Cash couldn't blame them, but they were good workers and he didn't want to lose their labor if it could be prevented.

So he had to put a stop to Marshall Brown and his gang's terrorist activities. He knew it was they who had robbed the train last month. The sheriff hadn't even bothered to try to locate them, he was that terrified of the scoundrels. Being sheriff didn't pay enough to lay his life on the line, or even to figure out that it was his deputy masterminding the gang. Cash cursed and wondered how he could trap the murderous band on his own. Without thought, his feet turned in the direction of the tavern.

Finding murdering thieves was a sight better than thinking about the woman waiting for him back at the house.

Laura smiled in delight and invited Jonathan in, ushering him into the front parlor and calling a maid to serve them iced drinks. Although August was almost gone, the weather hadn't eased, and the humid heat had everyone's tempers on edge, while clothing became permanently glued to their backs with the stickiness of perspiration. The dim front parlor was the coolest room she could offer, but with the draperies pulled to keep out the sun, it had a stifling closeness to it.

As they took their seats, Laura had time to admire Jonathan's newfound healthiness. A hint of gray streaked his hair along with the glints of sun, but it only made him look more distinguished. Without the harried look of worry to line his face, he appeared younger, and he smiled more easily. Whatever he was doing in Arizona, it served him well.

He cocked the corner of his mouth in a slight grin under her observation. "Do you approve? There aren't many women in the territory yet to burnish my pride, so I'm relying on you to provide the necessary polish."

Laura had forgotten how much she enjoyed Jonathan's company. He was so easy to be with, unlike Cash, who drove her to the pits of despair. She tried not to think about the heights of ecstasy she knew he could also produce. "I approve. I was just thinking that you must be doing something right out there. You look wonderful."

"Thank you, madam." He made a grave bow with his head. "It's all for you, I hope you realize."

Laura wasn't that vain. With a laugh she countered, "And because you've found some fascinating research that keeps you so occupied that you don't worry about anything else. Tell me about it. Your letters don't give enough detail."

With a sheepish grin at her accuracy, he agreed. "I didn't think you'd be interested in the details. Little specks under a microscope and sick cows can't be very appealing to a lady."

"But they might be interesting to me. Sick cows? However did you get involved with cows?"

"Because they seem to be affected by tuberculin toxins too. Pasteur's theories on the causes of disease offer so many possibilities . . . The scope is incredible. If someone could only make some breakthrough, show that the microbes we see in our microscopes are the reasons people and animals get sick, then maybe we will understand better why Jenner's vaccine works and we can develop one for every disease known to mankind."

The excitement crept into Jonathan's voice without his noticing, but Laura heard it, and smiled, but a part of her wept inside. He was happy, and she was glad for him. He had found what he needed. But what he needed wasn't her. That was a purely selfish thought, and she shoved it aside as he talked with increasing enthusiasm.

But as they finished their cool drinks and a maid came in to ask if they would like to be served lunch, Jonathan reverted to his original reason for being here. Rising and taking Laura's hand as she extended the invitation to stay, he shook his head.

"I would like to stay. I would like to share all my meals with you, if I could. But you haven't given me that permission yet, and I don't think now is the right time to press for it. I just want you to know that my offer still holds, Laura. I'll be delighted to take young Mark as my son and you as my wife. The nights can be lonely in Arizona, as I imagine they must be for you here. When you are ready to decide, I want you to let me know. I'll be around until you do."

Laura watched him go with a wrenching of her heart. Jonathan was a good man, the kind of husband every woman dreamed of. But he deserved better than she had to offer. Why couldn't she love a man like that, who would take care of her every need and smother her in love and protection? Some part of her must be deranged. Perhaps it ran in the family. She should try to overcome it, accept his offer, turn her back on the lush Kentucky fields that were her home and follow Jonathan's sanity to an arid land, cleansed of the corruption of the past. And perhaps she would. It seemed the only sensible thing to do.

But her heart wasn't in it. Turning away, Laura went in search of lunch. She needed nourishment if she were to tackle the task of directing the elm tree's removal.

The thunder began to roll late that afternoon. Laura threw a nervous glance toward the gathering clouds on the horizon and lifted her face to the wind. It came from the west. It was late in the season for the wicked winds that could tear a tree from its foundations, but Kentucky weather could never be counted on to do anything normal. At least she didn't have to worry about the tobacco that wasn't there any longer.

That wasn't much of a silver lining, but it was the only one she could conjure up as she went about the tasks of ordering the horses inside and battening down the house and barns. The house was the weakest point if a true gully-washer moved in. The wind could rip that piecemeal roof right off the beams, and there was no tile to keep the water from dripping through the cracks in the sun-dried wood. This seemed to be a year for momentous thunderstorms. She didn't want to think about what this one would bring.

No wind came with the approaching storm. The sky gradually darkened, but it was as if the clouds trapped the summer's heat on the ground, and the trees and grass bent under the weight of the humidity. Cash had appointed Jake as his second in command, but the men grumbled under the black man's orders, their tempers already riled by the heat and irritated further by the pressure of the clouds. Jake lost his temper and snapped at them, and several more threw down their pitchforks and hoes and walked out.

They weren't the first to leave, and Laura watched their departure with gnawing anxiety. She threw a glance to the corn ripening in the distant field. If the storm didn't flatten it, it would be ready for harvesting before long. Cash would need all the help he could get to bring that corn in. And she didn't like being left with only a small band of men to protect the house and outbuildings in case the Raiders decided to return.

Surely they wouldn't return so soon after Sallie's death. But a thunderstorm had no respect for the dead. Ordering someone to chase the chickens back into their house, Laura started for the stables to make certain the horses were all in. Cash would never forgive her if any more of his precious horses were lost.

The evening meal was consumed in tense silence. Mark cried and pounded fretfully at the mashed potatoes on his plate. Laura picked him up and comforted him, but there was little she could do to satisfy his complaints any longer. Her breasts had begun to dry up after Sallie's death. She missed the closeness as much as the child, and she hugged him tighter with an inward cry of loneliness.

She wished Cash were here, even if only to rail at him and hear his furious replies. It would be some outlet for this frustration building inside her. She didn't think the storm had anything to do with the emotions winding like a spinning top in her breast. It almost hurt her lungs to breathe, so tight was the cord wrapping around her. She didn't know where she was or which way to turn half the time. She didn't like behaving like a weather vane, but she seemed to have nothing to hold on to any longer. It was a crazy, spinning feeling, as if she had been caught up in tornado winds and was swirling around, waiting to be dropped. She was terrified of her own emotions, and she wasn't certain that she could keep a handle on them much longer.

Knowing she was reaching some breaking point, Laura hastened up the stairs after the meal, seeking the privacy of her room with only Mark for company. She let him crawl about the floor as she pumped the pedal of the sewing machine, pouring all her energies into this motion as if it would solve the tension bursting her seams. The material couldn't fly through her hands fast enough, and she kept glancing toward the window, waiting for the storm to break.

But the window faced the wrong direction and Laura could see only the occasional flash of light, indicating the storm was moving closer. Lightning would be streaking the western sky, but from this angle she could see only its reflection. That was what the whole of her life had been like. She lived in the reflection of other people's lives. She wanted to race outside and confront the lightning and dance in the face of it. She was a person too. Why weren't the tumult of the storm and the ecstasy of the sun for her? Why must she muddle along in the shadow of everyone else, everyone's cousin but no one's friend or wife? It wasn't fair.

Kicking the iron stand when the thread knotted and jammed, Laura stood up and pulled Mark from the draperies where he was clinging in his effort to see out the window. The wind was rising now; she could see the trees tossing their mighty heads. A horse neighed in its stall, but the sound was caught and carried off before she could

even register it fully. She remembered another night
when torches had lit the fields, and she shuddered.

The howling of the wind was worse in the hall when
Laura opened the door to Jettie Mae's knock. The cracks
in the unshingled roof gave entrance to strange noises,
and the remaining branches of the elm rattled against the
wood. The men had been able to trim out only part of
the branches before heat had taken its toll and they had
quit for the day. The tree was too near the house to cut
down and take apart on the ground, they had told her.

Jettie grimaced at the sound of the rising wind. "You'd
better get downstairs. It sounds like dis old house gonna
rip apart any minute now."

The house had stood up to thousands of storms in the
past, but Laura was eager for any excuse to escape her
lonely thoughts. Gathering up Mark and his bedding, she
followed Jettie down the back stairs to the kitchen, where
the house servants had gathered to sip coffee and whisper
among themselves.

They grew silent when Laura entered, but Jemima
filled a cup for her and a new subject was found, and
soon the younger maids were giggling among themselves
while the adults exchanged desultory conversation over
the events of the last few days.

The hurried knock at the back door was almost lost in
an abrupt change in the wind, but someone heard it and
a chair scraped back as someone else ran to answer it.
The young girl gave an abrupt scream at the terrified
face in the doorway, then fell back as the large black
man rushed into the cozy kitchen.

Seeing Laura, he gasped almost incoherently, "They
back! They back in the cornfield!"

Laura paled before Jake's wild terror. And then it occurred to her what he was saying, and rage replaced any
fear. The Raiders weren't going to satisfy themselves
with waiting for the storm to demolish the cornfield, they
meant to take credit for it themselves.

Rising from her chair, she handed Mark to Jemima
and calmly ordered, "Get the guns, Jake. We're going
after them."

32

The wind tore at Laura's hair as she ran outside with the rifle in her arms. The ancient long-barreled Kentucky weapon was almost as tall as she was, but it was slender and lightweight and she knew its deadly accuracy. She scarcely paid attention as Jake ran after her, holding a heavier shotgun. While Laura ran for the stables, he ran for the cabins, intent on waking the men within.

What she was doing wasn't fully sane, Laura realized, but it didn't stop her from yelling at grooms and stable-boys and hauling out the horses. She took the first one saddled, a large mare with the strength and endurance Cash favored in his animals. She would go mad if she stayed in the house while those criminals destroyed the fields and their lives. She wouldn't waste away without a fight, as so much of the countryside was doing. While she had a home to fight for, she would fight.

Mounting a man's saddle in long skirts was a hindrance, but Laura didn't care if her petticoats were rigged up over her ankles. There was no one hereabouts to notice. The rain finally came down, hitting the barn roof in a pounding wave as she rode out. She was soaked through before she could leave the stableyard, but she didn't falter. There were no torches to guide her this time, but she knew where the cornfield was. Through the gathering darkness and the gray veil of rain she could discern the trees marking the fence line. Checking the gunpowder pouch she had tied to the saddle and kept dry beneath her skirts, she kicked the mare in the right direction.

The men gathering in the paddock stared at Laura as if she truly were insane, but as maids came rushing from the house with the rest of the farm's arsenal, they grabbed guns and horses and headed out after her. Good jobs and good food weren't that easy to find. They knew which side their bread was buttered on. If that frail, meek little lady could ride against the murderous Raiders, they'd damned well better do the same.

Laura paid scant attention to the horses beginning to pound the ground around her. She had never known such fury in her life. Marshall had done his best to maim and kill her and her child when she had been in his care. If Cash were right, Marshall must be bent on finishing the job now. Well, this time she wasn't eight months pregnant. She would give him the battle he was looking for. The coiled tension inside her ached for release; a fight was just what she needed.

The wind jerked at Laura's skirts and made the horse skittish, and she had to haul on the reins with superhuman strength, but she kept it galloping forward, even when lightning struck somewhere ahead and thunder cracked through the air. Never before had she carried murder in her heart, and the feeling terrified her, but she let the emotion out, letting it take over and carry her along beyond sense and reason. By the time she reached the cornfield, she was as elemental as the winds and rain, flying into the countryside bent on havoc.

Before she had even found the targets, shots rang out. They were there, and she was going to get rid of them. She was conscious of the destruction already wreaked, the trampled corn that had once towered well over her head and now crunched underfoot, but her entire being was focused on the sights and sounds ahead.

Finding a black shadow rearing his horse away from the oncoming army of field hands and grooms, Laura took aim and fired. The smell of sulfur disappeared quickly into the wind and rain, and she let the others surge around and ahead of her as she stopped to reload. Blasts from a shotgun brought a scream of pain and the frightened whinny of a horse. One down, she thought in satisfaction as she jammed the shot down the barrel and caught up the reins again.

And then she was ripped from her horse, screams of black rage ringing in her ear as she was jerked against a masculine body and hauled across a man's thighs. Laura started to struggle, using every ounce of her pent-up fury, but the sudden awareness of the familiarity of the arms around her depleted the fight in an instant. Cash.

He cursed her with every vile epithet she had ever heard, and some that had never scorched her ears before. Riding away from the fight, Cash dropped Laura on the grassy stretch beyond the field, leaving her standing in the drenching rain to find her own way back to the house as he reared his horse in the other direction to return to the brawl.

She could hear the shouts and cries of angry men even over the furor of the storm. Unaccustomed to riding or rifles, many of the field hands would be resorting to knives and fists by now. She had done a horrible thing by leading them on, but it was too late to regain her senses now. Even as she thought this, a fierce gust of wind ripped at one of the outbuildings, lifting the tin roof and crumpling it like a piece of paper, flinging it in the direction of the pond.

Terrified, Laura glanced to the sky for some sign of the twisters that often fell from a storm like this. Although the temperature had dropped to the point where she was shivering, no hail came from the clouds, and she heard nothing of the deadly wail that signaled a tornado. Still, it was no night for man or beast. Lifting her skirts, she began to run through the muck and gray rain toward the lights of the house.

Men might die tonight, and it was all her fault. That thought ran senselessly around and around in Laura's head as she ran, stumbling, falling into the wind, hitting the ground on her hands and knees, and struggling up again. The distance to the house was not great, but it seemed to swim on into eternity as she battled the forces of wind and rain and the fear in her heart.

A mighty blast rocked Laura back on her heels as the sky ahead flared brighter than day and the hair on her arms and head stood straight up. The hideous stench of smoke and electricity scorched the air even as another loud crack followed, and she gazed in horror at the charred elm sundered in two and falling toward the house. She screamed, but in the chaos of the storm, all sound became one, and she staggered under the impact of the crash.

Mark! Screaming, weeping, tripping on her skirts and

petticoats, Laura crossed the remaining distance to the house. She might as well be dead if anything had happened to Mark. She wouldn't live another minute. Breath rasping in her throat, she stumbled up the stairs.

The air was filled with the odor of hell, but the thunder seemed to be moving away as she wrenched open the door. Oil lamps still burned in the kitchen as she fell in, and a steadying hand grabbed her before she could hit the floor.

"Jemima! Where is everybody? Are they all right? The tree . . ." She gasped for air, unable to say anything else.

"They down in the basement, chile. I just come up to see what done hit us. Lawd Amighty, you a sight! You'd best get yo'sef up them stairs and into dry things while I warm up this coffee. Where them men? They be needin' to dry out too."

Laura brushed off the cook's hovering attentions and wrung her skirt out on the brick floor as she tried to gather her wits about her again. "Send someone up to see if the lightning started any fires. The men are still out there. Cash is out there. There's going to be wounded. We need bandages, hot water . . ."

She was thinking out loud, but the worried old woman was responding as quickly as she talked, throwing wood in the stove, pulling out pails and bowls. At the sound of Laura's voice, Jettie had appeared at the top of the basement stairs. Other voices were right behind her. Feet were beginning to scamper in different directions. A quiet panic began to fill the kitchen, but a fire was stirred, water was being pumped, and footsteps echoed on the floorboards overhead.

Laura scarcely had time to ascertain that Mark was safe and sound asleep in the schoolroom below and that the lightning had set no fires before the first sound of horses thundered into the yard. Fighting a growing panic, she ran down to greet them.

There were shouts, but she couldn't understand them over the howl of wind and the pounding of rain. She didn't recognize the man who nearly fell off the first horse, but she identified the slight man remaining in the saddle of the second horse as one of the grooms. He grabbed the loose reins, and giving her a tip of his head, steered the nervous animals back toward the safety of

the stables. Laura caught the injured man as he staggered, guiding him with an arm around his waist to the
safety of the lighted kitchen.

Jemima clucked and muttered as the man was depos-
ited on the kitchen bench, but more horses were riding
in, and Laura didn't linger to hear her complaints. This
time Jettie Mae joined her in the drenching rain as she
ran out to sort the wounded from the wet.

They came in erratic shifts, the terrified horses kicking
and shivering and swarming in the yard as experienced
and inexperienced riders alike strove to bring them under
control while they clung to the reins with weariness and
pain. Some staggered in on foot. Others came with
bodies draped over the saddles in front of them. Little
by little the less injured dragged the animals to their
stalls, while Laura and Jettie sought out the wounded.

There was no opportunity to ask what had happened.
There was no opportunity to think at all. Laura worked
mechanically, helping Jake pull a man from a saddle,
using her small body as a crutch to support a leg-shot
man on the way into the relative security of the kitchen,
catching a loose horse that threatened to tear down the
paddock gate. There was little point in seeking the kitchen
herself. She was too wet and filthy to tend the injured,
and there was no sense in sending one of the frightened
maids out in the rain and wind in her place. With Jake
and Jettie at her side, she could manage.

But she kept searching for some sign of Cash. Laura
knew it had to be Cash who had hauled her from the
field. She still felt his hard arm crushing her ribs, knew
the rough brush of his cheek against hers when she had
fought with him, even if the throaty sound of his voice
hadn't reached her ears. He was out there somewhere.
As the panic in the yard started to subside and the rain
slowed to a steady downpour, Laura began to consider
going out to look for him.

All in all, she would have been better off if she'd given
in to that mad urge, she decided a moment later when
the stallion raced into the yard, sides heaving as he
reared and plunged and steadied under the curse and
insistent tug of his rider. Cash was off and striding in her
direction before a groom scarcely had time to grab his
reins. Laura's heart quailed, but she held her place, until

a hard arm reached out to grab her, and she gave a slight scream of surprise when he lifted her off her feet.

"I ought to wring your neck. What in hell did you think you were doing? You could have got your head shot off. My God, Laura, I'm going to tie you to a bedpost until you learn some sense. What in hell have you been doing? You look like a drowned rat." His ranting continued on as he dragged her into the lighted kitchen, shaking her slightly, until water sprayed from them like wet dogs.

Cash dropped her on the kitchen floor and as a puddle of water spread from Laura's dripping skirts, he gave her a black glare that seared her soul.

"Get upstairs and out of those clothes before you catch pneumonia." At her mutinous look Cash took a step forward and caught the sagging cotton of her soaked bodice. "Upstairs, Laura, or I'll strip you down right here."

The menace in his voice she understood. He had never spoken to her like that before, but she'd had enough experience with Marshall to know when to run. Fighting her fear, Laura turned and fled from the room.

Cash felt the scathing looks on the faces of the others in the room as he watched her go, but he wasn't in any humor to cater to their sensibilities. Swinging on his heel, he stormed out in the same fury with which he had entered. As hard as he had tried, he had failed tonight. Although he had brought down a few of the miscreants, Marshall's band was still essentially intact to strike another night. Cursing Laura, the storm, and his own ill luck, Cash strode toward the stables and the men seeking to dry themselves. He would hang before he let Brown and his bunch win again.

As soon as Cash left, Laura hurried back down the stairs to the kitchen. Jettie had already disappeared to change her own clothing, and Jemima caught one sight of her mistress and turned her around again.

"Mastuh Cash catch you down here, he gonna whip your hide good. You get some of this here hot water and get yo'sef back up them stairs. You ain't gonna do a lick of good by makin' yo'sef sick."

The kitchen had begun to clear, with the less injured taking themselves off to their cabins or the stables to dry out. Several of the more severely injured were lying on makeshift pallets around the fire, nearly naked and covered in blankets. She wasn't certain who half of them were. Cash must have brought his own reinforcements. Jemima was right; she didn't belong here.

But she couldn't let Cash order her around. She wouldn't be bullied anymore. Brushing off the cook's admonitions, Laura replied, "The tree came through the roof. Rain is pouring through the attic again. I've got to get someone to help salvage some of the furniture. Is there anyone who can help me?"

Jemima rolled her eyes and placed her hands on her hefty hips in exasperation, but there would be no budging Laura if the set of her chin was any indication. She would start moving furniture by herself if someone didn't help her do it. "I'll find someone. You get yo'sef on upstairs, now."

Laura did as told, but not to change. There was little point in ruining another gown working in the steady trickle of rain through the newly plastered ceilings. The elm had obviously crushed the temporary roof, and she suspected it had torn through weakened timbers on the side of the house. Bricks were lying inside some of the rooms, and glass was shattered throughout the whole west side. The room that had once been Sallie's had tree limbs coming in through the windows.

She began pulling at the smaller items of furniture in the rooms that had just been restored from the fire. Sallie's room and furniture had been too damaged by the fire for restoration, so she stayed out of the chaos in there. But all the other rooms on that side had been gradually returned to some semblance of normal.

The wind was dying to a more natural speed as Laura dragged a washstand through the hall to an empty bedroom on Cash's side of the house. A couple of the maids ran up the stairs to help her, and together they began pushing a mahogany lowboy out from under leaking plaster. Some of this furniture had already been drenched once, and there were warped and cracking stains in the veneer. But Laura was determined to retrieve what she could from the desolation of this night.

Some of the older boys who hadn't been allowed to ride out joined them, and Laura left them to haul furni-

ture while she and the maids turned to the task of stripping draperies and mattresses and rugs. Most were damp,
but not totally ruined yet. The water hadn't had time to
go all the way through roof and attic and ceiling. The
house had been made solid once. It would stand up
through this catastrophe too, Laura vowed.

Cash's voice roaring up from the kitchen brought Laura's head up and froze the servants around her. Furniture
had been left willy-nilly up and down the hall where the
boys had dragged it, and there was damp drapery hanging all over the cherry stair rail and dripping from bed-
posts in every room. Laura flinched at the damage that
was being done to the wood beneath, but the maids
didn't know better and she couldn't be everywhere at
once. She needed to install a clothesline in the basement
and hang everything down there. But that thought had
no sooner formed than the sound of boots slamming up
the stairs scared it out again.

"Out! All of you out! I'll not have the damned roof
caving in on you for the sake of the lousy furniture. Get
downstairs where you belong." Drenched from head to
foot, his black hair plastered to his head, and his shirt a
second skin against his chest, Cash shoved through the
chaos in the direction of Laura's frozen stance. His eyes
flashed fires of destruction, and his bronzed face was
seamed with fury as he focused his attention on Laura,
oblivious of the scampering of servants beating a retreat
around him.

"I thought I told you to get out of those clothes, Laura
Melissa Kincaid!" He shoved aside a ruined velvet bedroom chair, and before Laura could evade him, his arm
grabbed her waist and hauled her from her feet for the
second time that night.

Laura screamed in rage and beat her fists against his
shoulders as Cash carried her down the only clear path
left to him. She hadn't realized how cold she was until
she felt the furnace of his body against hers. Their clothing ought to steam from the heat generated by the con-
tact, and she clutched desperately to his soaked shoulders
as he shoved open the door to his room.

"Put me down, you maniac! I won't be hauled around
like a sack of flour." Panic and anger began to mix as
they entered the darkened bedroom. She hadn't dared

haul any of the wet furniture in here, and the room remained relatively intact. When Sallie had taken over Cash's old room, he had moved into this adjoining sparsely decorated suite. The bed was plain and unadorned, the furniture simple and without the elaborate carving of the other rooms, but it was boldly Cash's, from the riding boots lying in the corner to the abandoned deck of cards on the dresser. Even after he had moved out, Laura hadn't dared to enter this sacrosanct interior.

But she was here now, and not liking it one bit. She ripped from his hold as soon as her feet hit the floor. "Who do you think you are, you big oaf? That furniture has been in the family for ages. I'm not going to let it be ruined by a leaky roof! Aunt Ann loved that dresser! I can save it. Let me go, Cash." She tried to rush past him, but he grabbed her again, shaking her into silence.

"To hell with the furniture, Laura! You're what matters. Look at you! You're shivering in your shoes and your fingers are blue with cold. Get those clothes off now or I'll rip them off, I swear I will."

Laura's hands grabbed for the buttons of her bodice as Cash made a menacing step forward. He had threatened her earlier and she had run in terror, but she wasn't going to give in this time. Boldly standing up to him, she met his black gaze with a glare of her own. "Look at the pot calling the kettle black! You've got an eye that won't open from that drunken brawl over nothing and nobody, and you condemn my saving the furniture? And you've ripped open the gash on your cheek again. It needs bandaging more than I need drying out. And I'm not any more likely to catch pneumonia than you are, standing there in your mud-filled boots. Get the hell out of my way, Cash Wickliffe. You're no example for me to follow."

"The hell I'm not! If you had any gumption at all, you'd be in my bed now, and Sallie would be weaving her spells on some poor besotted fool elsewhere. But you're a craven coward, Laura Kincaid. You couldn't stand up to me then, and you can't stand up to me now. You're too afraid someone will notice you if you say what you think. You keep your mouth shut when you ought to be screaming bloody murder. Well, it's about time I changed all that. Get those clothes off, Laura, my patience has come to an end."

"You can't talk to me that way. No one gave you any right to talk to me that way. I've only tried to do what's proper, that's more than you can say. Cash Wickliffe, *get your hands off me!*" Laura screamed as he shoved aside her hands and began ripping at the buttons of her gown.

"Tell me now you're not Sallie. That's what you always say, isn't it? Poor drab little Laura, never fitting in her cousin's shoes. But I know better, don't I, Laura? Of all the men in this county, I'm the one in a position to know that you're a hundred times better than Sallie could ever hope to be. And I'm not going to let you make a martyr of yourself for your damned dead Kincaids."

His words slammed against her ears with the violence of the storm outside. Laura couldn't absorb them all at once, but she could absorb the wrenching strength of Cash's fingers as he pulled at the frail material of her soaked gown. Meeting violence with violence, she grabbed at the linen of his shirt and jerked. A button went flying across the room.

"See how you like it, Cash! See how you like being pushed and shoved around and told what to do every minute of the day. How does it feel when a woman fights back? Tell me, Cash! How does it feel?"

She had little luck with ripping the strong material, but she could jerk at the buttons until they loosened and she could find the man beneath. The room was too dark to see his bruised torso, but she felt the heat of him scorching her hands as his fingers sought still another purchase. She gasped as her bodice fell away to hang limply from her shoulders, but she was too furious to fight his advances on her person. She meant to tear him limb from limb first.

"You tell me, Laura. I've been there before. You're the pampered one. You're the one who's never had to lift a pretty finger unless you want to. You're the Kincaid. Everybody looks out for you, don't they? Why didn't you go with your folks back to the city? They would have wined you and dined you and found you a man if you wanted one. But you don't want one, do you, Laura? You're afraid of men. You're afraid of everybody. You were so afraid of Brown riding in here that you led a band of innocent farmers right into his hands. I ought to strangle you for that alone."

He'd found the ties to her skirt and petticoat and sent them cascading to the floor as he spoke. As Laura suddenly felt the cold draft of the wind blowing against her wet legs, she loosed her hold on Cash's shirt and tried to step back in panic. She had no reply to his accusations. She needed none. Before she could offer any protest at all, he'd swung her free of her encumbering attire and stalked toward the bed.

33

"Cash!" Her scream of panic should have echoed through the house but for the distant roar of thunder and the pounding waves of rain overhead.

Cash merely bent to rip at her soaked and ruined shoes.

Laura kicked and struggled to right herself, but the electric air had undergone a subtle change. The heat of Cash's hand scorched her skin as he jerked off her stockings, but there was no pain in his touch. The hard hand grasping her knee did not bruise or threaten. She barely suppressed a gasp of unexpected pleasure when Cash finally rose to stand beside the bed, and she could see the broad expanse of his bronzed torso beneath the shirt she had partially ripped from his shoulders.

She wasn't going to allow such traitorous longing to overcome good sense. Garbed only in the thin chemise plastered to her skin, Laura tried to push past Cash's powerful body to escape the trap closing in on her. "Damn you, Cash Wickliffe! I'm not some toy to be tossed around as if I haven't got a lick of sense in my head. Get out of my way, you brute!"

His arm lashed out to catch her before she could make good her escape, and with his unoccupied hand Cash reached to jerk down the bedcovers. "Anyone with the sense God gave a goose would be down in the basement on a night like this. You had fair warning."

Laura screeched in outrage as he heaved her between the cool sheets. When he sat beside her to remove his boots, she scrambled to her knees and launched herself at his broad back. Her teeth sank into his shoulder as Cash threw one boot to the floor, and he howled in fury as he swung around and carried her back to the bed again with his greater weight.

His face hovered not inches from hers, but Laura was beyond fear now. All the pent-up rage and pain that she had carried with her for years exploded beneath this final indignity. Without caring whom she hurt, she tore at Cash's bruised chest, ripping at his shirt and scraping her nails down his skin. "I'm not going to let them take it all away! I won't, I tell you! This is my home, and they're not going to take it away from me. I'm going to fight them, Cash. I'm going to fight them, damn you. Get off me!"

With a curse, Cash shoved himself upright and reached for his other boot. Rage and whiskey still flowed through his veins, but he retained enough sense to know the source of the heat beginning to build like a fire in his middle. "You'll have to get through me first, Miss Kincaid," he warned tersely.

"I will." Flinging her legs over the side of the bed, Laura prepared to put her words into action. She wasn't running from him. She never meant to run from another situation again. But she wasn't going to sit here and take his abuse either.

"No, you won't." Throwing all good sense to the winds that seemed prepared to thrash the house into splinters, Cash grabbed Laura by the waist and hauled her back to the bed beside him. Heat emanated from every point where they touched, but he was a gambler and accustomed to playing with fire. He had no idea what he meant to do with her. He just knew he wasn't going to let her escape again.

Rage served much better than this other feeling slowly seeping through her muscles, and Laura struggled to regain her freedom. She had no breath left for words, but hit at his shoulders and wriggled in his embrace and tried to lash out with her feet. But she had no defense against the kiss with which he covered her mouth. She surrendered to it without a fight.

The rage with which they had fought each other now found another outlet. Instead of fighting against each other, their hands and bodies fought together, ripping at hampering clothes, straining for some solace neither seemed to recognize.

It all happened too fast. With the rain pounding against the roof and the wind whipping at the windows, they rubbed together and made fire. Perhaps the wind whipped the flames higher. Laura would never know. She knew only what her body told her, and that message said their only chance of survival was together. Right or wrong, she wrapped her arms around Cash's shoulders and arched upward into his embrace and found succor in the fierce penetration that joined them.

The piercing brand of Cash's possession came back to Laura with all the familiarity of yesterday. The rightness of it made her cry out and reach for more, and all was lost as they struggled feverishly to find that oblivion they had known once before. Laura's tears fell to the pillow as the uncontrollable waves of pleasure took over her body, and then there was nothing more she could do but let Cash carry her where he willed, until he, too, succumbed to that explosion of helplessness.

Lethargy sapped any remaining fury from them. Curled against Cash's bare shoulder, with his arms wrapped around her, Laura listened to the fall of rain, heard the steady drip as it leaked into the other rooms, and fell asleep without moving from the shelter she had found.

Cash pulled the blanket around her nakedness and held her close to his warmth. Tomorrow was the time to judge and condemn what had happened here tonight. Tonight he only knew he had come home.

They woke again in the predawn silence. Perhaps it was the sudden absence of rain or the forewarning of autumn's chill that sent them huddling for warmth. Laura snuggled closer into the encompassing heat of Cash's arms, then lifted her mouth to greet his lips when they moved across her face. The gentle touch of his hand on her breast was sufficient to send a shiver of desire careen-

ing through her, and with a sigh of relief she fitted her
hips to his and found his need to be as great as her own.

The fierceness of earlier had evaporated. This time
they were slow to touch and explore, to gentle and caress, taking their time to absorb each new sensation. For
Laura it was a voyage of discovery, and she couldn't help
the tears of happiness that fell when they could no longer
stay apart.

Cash filled her with a joy she had never known, a
joining of two spirits that made their bodies sing with life
and love and pleasure. For two people who had spent
much of their lives alone, just on the outside of the
human warmth and closeness of families, this miracle
knew no bounds, and they clung together for the pure
beauty of the blending and not just the physical pleasure
of their bodies.

They dozed again, waking only when the room was
filled with light despite the draperies on the windows.
For once, neither felt any urge to escape the haven of
safety of their bed, and Laura smiled contentedly as she
snuggled down beside Cash and his hand caressed her
hair.

"Happy birthday, Laura," Cash whispered against the
thick tangles of golden brown.

"Happy birthday?" She turned a quizzical gaze upward
to the underside of his unshaven chin, smiling to herself
at the intimacy of this angle.

"Merry Christmas," he answered inanely, as much to
himself as to her.

"You are touched in the head. The rain must have
given you the fever." Laura wriggled closer against him.
He certainly burned like a furnace, but the way his hands
closed about her didn't feel in the least irrational.

"Oh, no. For the first time in my life, I'm perfectly
fine. I've never made love before. Last night was the
equivalent of all the birthdays and Christmases I've ever
dreamed of. You're quite a package, Miss Kincaid."

Laura smiled and pressed a kiss against his shoulder.
Reality was beginning to return. She could feel it creeping up somewhere inside her, but she ignored it for the
pleasure of the moment. Cash's foolish words were a
soothing balm to her damaged pride. His touch was an
invitation to forget the past. She wanted nothing more

than to lie in Cash's arms for the rest of her life. Somewhere outside, a defiant mockingbird began to sing, and her smile could no longer be contained to her lips. She pressed closer against him and spread her kisses wider.

"Well, you're rather a pretty package yourself, Mr. Wickliffe. I particularly enjoy this peculiar shade of yellow over purple here on your ribs. And the green is quite spectacular. I've always admired a man who isn't ashamed to wear colors." She traced her fingers over old bruises and new, kissing each as her fingers moved to each new injury. The silken black hair on his chest made her nose tingle, and she rubbed it against him to stop the itch.

Cash caught his fingers in the thick tangle of her hair and drew her upward. Her skin was pale, but with a translucent glow that made his heart stop and then start again with an insistent pound. In the morning light her eyes were a brilliant green, and he swore they were twice the size as usual. They cut right through him, but he couldn't resist the smile on her lips.

"I'm not likely to indulge your fancy for colors anytime soon, *pequeña*. They hurt like hell."

"Shall I kiss them and make them better?"

Her eyes danced with mischief, and Cash discovered a new delight in this give-and-take of closeness. Whores got up afterward and held out their hands for money. Sallie hadn't been much better. But Laura . . . Ahh, Laura wanted a man's heart. He closed his eyes against the pain and indulged himself a while longer in the pleasure of her slender hands riding across his chest and belly, creeping ever closer to the place where he most needed those skillful fingers.

The rattle of footsteps on the stairs followed by Jettie's insistent cry of "Miss Laura!" down the hall brought them both to their senses with a jerk.

Laura pulled the sheet over her breasts as Cash swung his legs to the floor. Her eyes grew wide with this first sight of his full male nudity, but she wasn't allowed to indulge her curiosity for long. He reached in the wardrobe and grabbed a clean pair of trousers, pulling them on as he whispered orders.

"Go through the other door, Laura. I'll hold her off."

She knew what he meant without further explanation.

Wrapping the sheet around her, more for protection from the chill than from Cash's view, she grabbed her gown and petticoat and hurried toward the door connected to the adjoining bedroom. Over the years, doors had been knocked indiscriminately between half the upstairs rooms to indulge the then current needs of the owners. Married couples, new parents, the elderly requiring constant attendance—each had been reason enough to knock still another door in a wall. Laura was grateful for this eccentricity now.

"Miss Laura!" Jettie's voice held a hint of panic at discovering Laura's bed untouched.

Laura and Cash exchanged a glance of frustration, desire, and growing awareness before she finally dashed into the other room, out of sight. Their brief idyll was over. Reality was already intruding.

While Laura escaped, Cash swung open his door and yelled at the maid, "What in the hell is the ruckus all about? Is the house on fire?"

Jettie stopped in her tracks at the sight of Cash's half-dressed form. Her bold gaze swept over the disheveled black mass of his hair and his unshaven jaw to the discolored bruises of his torso, then back to the glitter of his eyes. With a questioning lift of her eyebrows she answered, "Mark is wailing for his mama, but she ain't in her room. What you done with her?"

Cash had to stifle his amusement at the maid's knowing look. Jettie Mae wasn't like any house servant he had ever known. She was more sister and mother rolled up into one. He lounged against the door frame and crossed his arms over his chest. "What have I done with her? I haven't been able to do anything with her for years. Considering the wreckage of these rooms up here and the fact that most of them were pouring rain just a few hours ago, I daresay she's found a safer shelter. Have you checked downstairs?"

Jettie gave him a look that should have quelled battalions, then flounced around and headed for the stairs. Cash held his breath as he heard Laura trip over something in one of the overcrowded rooms, but Jettie kept on going. She might be uneducated, but Ward's former mistress wasn't dumb.

When she was gone, Cash wanted to spin around and

run after Laura, but he steeled himself against the impulse. He was a grown man who knew the responsibility required of his actions, not an impulsive young boy heedless of the results. What he had done last night was unforgivable. Laura would realize that soon enough. He would have to start repairing the damage.

Cash could dress faster than Laura, and he was out and gone before she could see him again. She felt an odd quiver of fear that he hadn't lingered to say a word or two before he left, but she couldn't let her suddenly vulnerable emotions overset the work that had to be done. Cash had said things to her last night that she needed time to consider. She wasn't at all certain that he had meant what he said, or that she had heard him aright. They had both been beyond reasoning. Remembering just how far beyond reasoning they had been, Laura caught her breath and hurried to find her son. This was something that needed more than time to figure out.

Quieting Mark, gulping a hasty breakfast, answering as many questions as she was able before she had time to survey the damage, Laura submerged the new sensations bubbling inside of her in the immediacy of work. She stepped outside long enough to view the devastation visible from the house, then, shaking her head, returned to the chaos reigning within. There was only so much she could deal with at one time.

While Laura worked her way through the damage to the house, Cash rode the fields in hopes of finding something to salvage. The back of the field where the poorest corn stood had been ravaged by the rain and wind. With careful picking there might be enough to feed the animals through the winter. The rest of the field, however, was a total loss. Marshall's marauders and the ensuing battle had trampled it into muddy porridge for the birds. There was nothing left to save.

Counting his losses, Cash pushed back his hat and turned his face to the sky. The wind had blown away the heat and humidity, and a clear sunny day with a crisp breeze met his gaze. It was the kind of day to pack a picnic and take your girl and go fishing. He longed to do just that, to forget Stoner Creek and Marshall and the past, throw responsibility to the winds, and get on with his life.

But he couldn't. He couldn't just chuck it all and go to Laura fresh and clean of all that had happened. Her cousin was dead and in her grave scarcely a week now, and he had put her there. Her home was destroyed, and he was the man responsible. If he had never returned, Laura would be married to Jonathan now, having babies and doing good works, and none of this would have happened. It was time to pay for the damage and get the hell out of here.

The lawyer looked at him as if he were crazed. Pulling on a fat cigar, he checked the gold watch in his pocket, glanced out over the courthouse framed by the window, then looked over his client's head as he smoked.

"You can't be serious. A woman ain't got enough sense to keep a fire burning without a man's helping her. If you want to shuck it all, sell the place, that's my advice." Smugly he lowered his gaze to take in his unorthodox client. He had known Cash Wickliffe since he was a boy, and he could still see the boy in him now. Those dark eyes glared with a rebel's fire, but his whippet-slim body now claimed a man's muscular grace. The lawyer tapped his own paunch as he waited for Cash's reply.

"I'm not giving the farm to Laura, but to her son. He's the last of the Kincaids. It should be his decision to sell the place when he comes of age, not mine. All I'm asking you to do is draw up the deeds."

"But as the boy's mother has no father around to claim him, Miss Kincaid will be the one responsible for the farm until her son reaches his majority. Now, surely you don't want that, Cash. Appoint Jonathan guardian. They say he's the daddy, in any case, even if our new deputy sheriff disputes the matter."

Cash clenched his hands against the pure pulsating rage building in him. He was the father, and he wanted the whole damned world to know it. But he kept his silence. That was Laura's choice to make, not his. None of this was his any longer. Even Mark, he realized with a longing regret. He had given up his claim to Mark when he married Sallie. He couldn't use him as an excuse to tie Laura to him any longer.

"Just write up the deed, Will. I'm not worried about

Laura's being able to handle it, so neither should you be. I'll be back in the morning."

Swinging on his heel, Cash strode out. One bridge burned. How many more to go? The new deputy sheriff was an excellent starting place.

34

"Look Jonathan, the only way I can salvage the place is to sell my ranch in California, and that's just sending good money after bad. You know how Laura is about that farm. She's going to be distraught. All I'm asking is that you be around to help her, just for a little while. I don't know what decision she will make, but it will be her decision, not mine. I've interfered where I don't belong once too often. I don't care if she burns the place down. Hell, I'd rather not see the place ever again. But whatever she does, she does it on her own."

Jonathan watched Cash's restless strides up and down the small parlor with a mixture of dismay, anger, and hope. But Cash hadn't come here for emotion; he was struggling with enough of his own. That in itself was a good sign, but Jonathan kept that thought to himself. The cool gambler who had won his fortune in hard work and an ability to keep his thoughts to himself was slowly crumbling to human stature. Perhaps there was some justice in this world after all.

"I'm not the one you should be telling this to, Laura is. You're not planning on heading out without telling her what you plan to dump in her lap, are you?"

Cash ran his hand through his already rumpled hair. "I can't go back there tonight. I've got a score or two to settle. I thought I'd wait until I had the deed in hand tomorrow. But I hate leaving her there alone. The place is a wreck. I know she can handle it, but I don't want her to have to do it alone. Just go out and hold her hand, Jonathan. You were real good at doing that before."

Jonathan drew himself up angrily and pointed his finger at the door. "Out! Out of my house, Cash. I'll not be party to whatever it is you're planning. You get out of this house and go tell Laura to her face what you're going to do. And when you're done with her, if there's anything left of you, I'll gladly pour you on the boat and step in where I should have stepped in long ago. And if you so much as make one move toward her again, I'll have you nailed to the wall. Do you understand that?"

Cash tightened his jaw and faced him. "I can't do that, Jonathan. I did that before, and I'll not do it again. If she needs me, I'm going to be there this time, but I've got to give her time. Don't you see that? The whole damn town would come down around our heads if I did anything else. And I sure as hell can't give her time if I'm underfoot every day. I'm a man, Jonathan, not a stick of wood. I've been so damned honorable this past year that I don't know myself. But it can't last, hasn't lasted. I've got to put some distance between us."

Jonathan didn't want to hear that. It was the last thing he wanted to hear. Shoving his hands in his pockets, he glared at the man his former ward had become. "Tell that to Laura."

With a curt nod of understanding, Cash put on his hat and left. Talking to Laura wouldn't resolve anything, he knew, but he relied on Jonathan's support. If the only way he could get it was by going back to the farm and talking to Laura, he would do it, but he wasn't going to like it. Neither was she.

Laura hid her sigh of relief when she heard the familiar sound of Cash's boots on the front porch. It was nearly sundown and supper had already been put away, but she had left something warming for him on the stove. She had feared that he meant to return to Watterson's without coming by. She wouldn't have been responsible for her actions if he had.

Her emotions were still in the same disarray as the house, but avoiding the cause wouldn't solve anything. She needed Cash to help her think. She needed to know his feelings. If what had happened last night meant noth-

ing to him, then she would somehow have to struggle to
cope as she had once before. But she couldn't prevent
hope from burrowing into her heart as she listened to
him climb the stairs and go to his room to wash. What
little she could remember with any coherence of the prior
night hadn't sounded like she meant nothing to him.

Even if her hopes came true, even if he felt the same
as she, there were obstacles in the way. Laura knew that.
But they would be much easier to surmount together.
That's all she asked, that they face them together. She
was so tired of facing the world alone. Last night had
been a revelation, and she didn't ever want to go back
to being alone again. She was willing to sacrifice what
little freedom she possessed in a gamble that together
with Cash she would know more independence than she
had ever known in her life.

He was making a gambler of her too. Laura smiled to
herself as she heard him unconventionally using the back
stairs. When he discovered her in the kitchen, Cash
seemed somewhat taken aback, but he lifted the lid of a
pot on the stove to examine the contents hungrily.

"Mind if I eat first?"

"First?" With an amused lift of her eyebrows Laura
sought out silver and plates. She had sent the servants
off for a well-deserved rest, wanting Cash all to herself.
"Kitchen or dining room?"

Glancing around at the usually bustling kitchen, Cash
shrugged with a nonchalance he didn't feel. "I've eaten
in kitchens before. Makes no difference to me."

Finally sensing some of his nervousness, Laura bit her
lip and laid a place at the old pine-board table the servants used. She had dozens of questions, but with Cash
in this mood, she wasn't certain she had the right to ask
them. She didn't know her place in his life right now.
She wasn't his wife, and she had no intention of being
his mistress or housekeeper. So she waited for him to
show her what he expected.

Except Cash had long since developed the habit of
waiting for her to speak first. He had not trusted himself
to say what he thought in her presence. He relied on
Laura's innate caution to keep them both out of trouble.
Now that there was no longer any reason for them to
keep their thoughts to themselves, he couldn't seem to

break the habit. Laura had been born to this polite world of social inhibitions. She knew the rules; he didn't. So he waited for her to speak.

They managed to exchange a few words as Cash sat where she placed him: he, offering to help her with the pot; she, asking if he wished the salt. The commonplaceness of the exchange didn't lighten the tension rapidly building between them. Laura picked up the polishing cloth and the silver she had been working on while Cash started to eat. She kept an eye on his plate, asking if he wanted more of the potatoes, offering to fetch more iced tea.

He watched her work, admiring the glint of her hair in the light of the oil lamp, enjoying the sensation of being able to watch her without reservation. She had long lashes that swept over her cheeks when she looked down, and her cheeks were gradually acquiring a rosy hue as she became aware of his scrutiny. Her hands were long and slender, quick and efficient in everything they did. For a long time he had known that the slender package of femininity that she came in was only a dainty disguise for the diamond within. He didn't give a damn whether she came in blond or brown, tall or short. He no longer cared if other men's heads were turned by the woman on his arm. Sallie had cured him of that. If he wanted attention, he could buy that without much trouble, as he had bought Sallie. But what he wanted couldn't be bought.

And what Cash wanted was the woman beneath all the slight femininity. He needed Laura's strength, her caring, her passion. He had been a fool to believe that he would be happy by buying respect. He couldn't buy respect. He had to earn it. And he wanted to earn Laura's. No one else's mattered anymore. But first he had to give her the freedom to make her choice.

"Laura."

Her head lifted expectantly, and Cash found himself drowning in the luster of her eyes. He didn't know how he was going to do this. Jonathan had been a fool to send him back here. Last night rushed back to him so clearly that he knew he could just reach out for her and she would be in his arms. And bed. That thought jarred him back to the kitchen.

"I think it's best for you if I go away for a while. I'll sleep over at the Watterson place tonight. I'm having the farm put in Mark's name, where it belongs. I'll have someone bring you the deed when it's ready."

Laura stared at him, not at all certain that she heard him right. Giving her head a shake to clear the cobwebs, she inquired politely, "You'll do what?"

Cash knew that tone. The polite little girl who said "yes, sir" and "no, sir" while boiling with fury used that tone. The same little girl who had once loosed a killer dog on a man she had decided needed to die. He preferred it when she unleashed that fury and let it out, as she had last night, but then, they both knew what had happened last night.

Sighing, running his hand through his hair, Cash rested his forehead in his palm and tried to gather his defenses. "You heard me, Laura. and you know I'm right. You're grieving now, and you haven't had time to think about what you want for the future. I forced something on you last night that you shouldn't have to contend with right now. And if I stay, I'm likely to do it again. Jonathan will be here to help you. You'll have to decide how much you want to spend on repairs. I wanted to leave the place in better shape, but as it is, I'd better just leave." He wore a look of desperation when he looked up. "I'm trying to do what's best, Laura."

Laura thought she had spent the best of her fury last night, but she was wrong. Cash was perfectly able to kindle it all over again. Why had she ever thought that she could get along with this mule-headed man? She must have clouds for brains. He had gambled and lost and now he was just going to walk away, as if she were a deck of cards to be thrown on the table. But this deck of cards could talk.

Shakily Laura rose from the table, holding her hand against the wood to balance her rage. "What's best for whom, Cash Wickliffe? For me? For the boy upstairs who needs a father? For the servants who need to know they'll have jobs come next year or they'll starve? Who do you think you're helping by running away, Cash? I'll tell you who—yourself! You are the only one who benefits by your departure. You can forget the trampled corn, the crumbling house, old grudges, and cantankerous neighbors. You can forget those rotten thieves who would bring the whole world down to their stinking level. You can forget that grave out back and all the dreams that died with her. You can just ride away and be free again, leaving me to deal with all of it. You're a coward, Cash Wickliffe, and if you walk out of here tonight, I never want to see your face again!"

Cash stood up when she did and took her words like blows to the stomach, but when she was done, he curled his knuckles against the table and leaned forward to lash back. "You didn't even wait to hear how far I meant to go or how long I meant to stay. You couldn't wait one second to condemn me, as your neighbors have been condemning me for years. It never occurred to you to listen to my side of the story, did it? If that's what you think of me, then fine, it's a good thing we have it out right now so neither of us gets any fancy notions. Perhaps you have some right to hate all men, Laura, but I thought I'd given you some reason to think differently of me. It seems I was wrong. I'll send Jonathan to you with the deed in the morning. It's been good knowing you."

Reaching for the hat hanging by the back door, Cash slammed it on his head and walked out.

Laura held herself still against the urge to run after him and beg that he take her with him. He hadn't even offered to take her away from all of this. She should be used to that now. Marshall had left her here alone. Jonathan had gone off to Arizona. Cash had left once, but he had returned. Why had she thought he might take her with him if he ever left again? That must be one of those fancy notions he had talked about. He was right, she had been developing fancy notions. Far better that he left before they grew to any greater proportion. But, oh, how she wanted to run after him and beg him to take her with him. He didn't even have to marry her. She just wanted to go and to never look back.

Tears creeping silently down her cheeks, Laura left the polish where it sat and made her way up the back stairs to Mark's room. She didn't even want to think what would happen if another baby came of their lovemaking. Lovemaking. What a foolish word to use to describe what they had done. They had made lust and rage and tears, but she didn't see any love anywhere. They were too much alike in some ways. It was much better that he left now, while she still retained enough sense to see that.

But he had said last night that it was the first time that he had ever made love. Why did it tear at her insides to know that if he could leave her after that, he must say it to every woman he took to his bed?

Feeling the bitter bile scalding his lungs, Cash reined his horse back in the direction of town. He had known it would come to this. It would have been better if he could have gone quietly, without those words said. Then he might have had some hope of returning someday, some hope that she would be ready to make the choice he would ask of her. But as it was, she would just add one more stick to her pyre of hate, and he might as well bay at the moon for all the good it would do to talk to her.

When he reached town, he wasn't certain why he was there. He should have gone back to the Watterson place and got some sleep. Lord only knew he hadn't had much of that in some while. He had sat in enough filthy, smoky saloons these last weeks to cure him of any itch to become a drunkard, whatever the damned town might think.

Getting drunk tonight had a certain appeal to it, but the oblivion he wanted couldn't be found in a bottle. He wanted Laura's soft round arms around him. He wanted to kiss that sassy mouth of hers until she loved him back as she had the night before. He wanted to seek the haven of her body, find those heights he had never before explored, and then lie in her arms until morning, content to know that all was right with the world as long as he could have her until eternity came.

That was a damned fool notion for a man of his age, but he had a right to dream. If he didn't, he might as well go out and put a bullet through his brain. Right now that didn't sound a half-bad idea, but he'd much rather put bullets through the worthless brains of Marshall Brown and his gang. For what he had done to Laura alone, Brown should be skewered to the wall and used for target practice. Preferably with red-hot brands first.

Allowing the violence to build and replace his earlier despair, Cash reined in his horse at the tavern. He still

had those old scores to settle, and he'd found out more
in this place than any other. Some of Brown's gang had
loose tongues when oiled with cheap whiskey.

Using the caution he had learned when making his way
through Indian country a decade ago, Cash slipped into
the tavern through the rear door. It was Friday night and
every rowdy in the county was here. From the sounds of
it, they were well into their cups and reaching that deadly
point when fists fly and knives appear. Usually he preferred to get out of here before then. Men in that state
weren't the most reliable sources. But he had nothing
better to do with his time, and the violence in him craved
the trouble that brewed.

Cash remained in the shadows at the back of the room,
surveying the occupants. Brown never came in. He was
too well-known and apparently too clever to openly associate with these scoundrels. Most of his band and the
others that called themselves the Raiders were just ignorant farmers with grudges to grind, or soldiers returned
from the war with nothing better to do than fight. The
Raiders cursed the Union Army, sang hosannas to John
Wilkes Booth, and poured the vitriol of their bitterness
on every black head that crossed their paths that week.

But some of them were born thieves and murderers,
and Brown had somehow managed to gather these renegades into the hard core of his band. Those were the
men Cash knew had to be caught and hanged, but they
were too wary to show themselves in places like this. The
men here tonight had homes of their own somewhere
and returned to them occasionally, if only to beat their
wives and plant another acre of corn. They knew exceedingly little of Brown's plans, but just enough to keep
Cash worried.

Picking up a bottle of whiskey, Cash leaned a chair
back in the corner and pulled his hat down over his face.
That was signal enough that he wanted to be left alone.
In any case, the men around him were too far gone in
drink to pay him any mind. He took a swig just to warm
the night chill from his bones and watched carefully to
see who was here.

But it was the voices through the wall that finally cap-
tured Cash's attention. He'd known the storeroom in the
back was occasionally used as a trysting place for the whores

from the hotel out to make a little extra on the side. He suspected a wayward wife or two might use it for meeting lovers. On the whole, he had avoided that little niche, more out of disgust than respect for anyone's privacy. But tonight he began to feel he'd made a mistake in ignoring the people using that room.

He'd heard a woman's whining voice and a slap and had ignored it when he first came in, but now he realized there were only men's voices coming through the wall behind his head. And one of those voices sounded distinctly familiar.

The horror washing over Cash as he finally followed the gist of the conversation fueled the fury he had carried in with him. His fist curled around the bottle neck nearly snapped the glass in half as he clenched his jaw and listened closer. He closed his eyes and forced himself to remain seated instead of going in there now and ripping the bastard's head off. He had no intention of being hanged for carrying out the justice the sheriff was too damned scared to mete out himself. But he sure as hell would see it done one way or another.

But he was going to need help for this one. This time he was going to get Laura out of there before he went after the bastards. And then he was going to personally single out Marshall Brown for himself.

He'd always wanted to start a scalp collection.

35

"Look, I don't want to be one of those damned vigilantes any more than you do. But the sheriff has been sitting on his rear for the last year or more, ignoring the atrocities, and now he's letting Brown run the county. He's so confident, he really thinks he can bring this off. I am not making this up, Jonathan, I swear! He just thinks all he has to do is shoot me and call it protecting his 'wife' and the whole town will buy it when he moves onto the farm and takes over. I don't think he's quite sane. Or maybe he's saner than I am. He just might get away with it if we don't do something. All I'm asking you to do is go get Laura and Mark out of there. Take them to Lexington. They'll be safe enough there until this is over."

Jonathan paced the parlor. Roused from sleep, he had merely pulled his trousers on over his nightshirt and had made no attempt to comb his thinning hair. With his unshaven jaw, his appearance was more disreputable than Cash's after a night on the town. "I don't hold with breaking the law, Cash, and you know that. We're not any different from those madmen if we go after them ourselves. It's too dangerous."

"Hell, Jonathan, I'm not asking you to go with us. I'm just asking you to look after Laura. If Brown's gunning for me, it's too dangerous for me to be seen with her." Irritated, tired, still racking his brain for the best solution to a myriad of problems, Cash struggled to keep his temper down.

Jonathan sent him a sharp look. "And you really think that Laura is meekly going to pack her bags and come away with me?"

"If you went to her right now, yes, she would. She's so mad at me she'd bite the nose off my face if I got within reach. You'll have to wait for morning, though, and she may have cooled off a little by then. You'll just have to persuade her."

Jonathan looked away. He had no intention of trying to visualize the fight that had brought Laura to such fury. He knew her as a quiet, sensible woman who could be relied on in times of trouble. Cash had obviously succeeded in plumbing some other depth to her that no one else had ever reached. He could not remember ever seeing Laura in a rage. But biting Cash's nose off would certainly be a just reaction to his high-handed ways.

Smiling to hide the hurt, Jonathan nodded slowly. "I'll persuade her, but you're going to have to listen to me for a change. You can't do this on your own. You've rubbed too many people the wrong way too many times. If you're going to learn to get along in this place, you've got to learn to work with people, not against them."

Cash made a rude noise and rubbed his eyes. "What

makes you think I intend to get along in this place? They hate my guts and I return the favor. All I want to do is make the place safe for Laura. It's not going to be easy getting enough men together after that last fiasco, but I think I've got an idea that might solve that problem, if Brown carries out his plan as he said he would."

Jonathan stopped before the dark man sprawled across the couch. "You're doing it my way or not at all, Wickliffe. Get up from there and find Steve Breckinridge. Along with you, he's the biggest man in the county right now. And I'm not talking about height. If you want to get rid of this villain, you're going to have to work together and not against each other."

Cash squinted upward into the light behind Jonathan, not quite believing he was hearing this. "Breckinridge? Of all the people in the county, he's the one who hates me most. Besides Brown, perhaps. And maybe a few others. I'm not a very likable person."

"I'll damn sure swear to that." Jonathan swung around and crossed the room to put a distance between them. "But aside from that, you've got a common cause. Breckinridge is an old-fashioned gentleman who feels it is his obligation to look after a lady. And he considers Laura practically one of the family. On top of that, he despises Brown and wouldn't want him for a neighbor. This doesn't have anything to do with you. He'll see that quick enough."

There might just be some sense in that, although Cash wasn't readily prepared to admit it. "And what am I supposed to do with God Breckinridge if he agrees?"

Jonathan snorted at this reference he had once used against Steve's father. He ought to have known better than to say such things in front of Cash. As a child he had been like a sponge. It made him old to think about it. "Breckinridge will twist the sheriff's arm until he screams to go with you. That will make whatever idiocy you have planned as legal as it gets around here."

"You sure have a damned lot of confidence in my abilities, Broadbent. The sheriff would be just as happy to see me swing as to back me up." Even as he said it, Cash was wondering if it could be done. It would be pleasant to have the law on his side for a change, especially if he could hold a gun at the sheriff's back all the way.

"You can do whatever you put your mind to, Cash, I never doubted that for a minute." Jonathan watched Cash straighten his shoulders and stand. Cash had always possessed strength and intelligence; what he lacked was the confidence a father could have given him. It was a damned shame to let a child's life go to waste for the sins of the father. He hoped he had instilled enough knowledge in the boy for the man to carry on.

Reluctantly Cash held out his hand. "All right, you win. I'll go talk to Breckinridge, if you'll just go get Laura. Have her out of there before I go back to remove the servants. I'm not up to any more words with her right now."

Jonathan hid his grin. Cash would rather face the devil himself than Laura right now. It was amazing what one little woman could do to a man. Perhaps this would work out better than he had hoped. Only time would tell. "You'd better stay here for the rest of the night. You're going to need some rest before you tackle the world."

That was the truth. Gratefully Cash accepted the offer.

Cash wasn't feeling half so grateful when he set out to meet with Breckinridge the next morning. He had always resented the man's easy wealth and arrogance and the family ties that made him royalty in this part of the woods. But it was just those qualities that he needed now to turn the tide in his favor. For Laura's sake he would quash his resentments, but he wouldn't have to like it.

He wasn't feeling any better about the decision when he found himself in Breckinridge's study some while later. Seated on a glove-leather chair that had probably come across the mountains from some Virginia antecedents, Cash studied the shelves of books lining one wall and waited for an answer from the man standing at the window. He wished he'd brought a cigar, but that gambler's ploy of cool aplomb wouldn't necessarily work under these circumstances. Steve wasn't even watching him.

"If you're right, Wickliffe, and I'm not saying you are . . ." Steve finally turned to face the room. "You're talking about a lot of lives. These men are dangerous. If we corner them, they'll strike to kill. They're not likely to give up just because we have them surrounded."

Cash heaved an inward sigh of relief. He was with them, then. Crossing his leg over his knee, he leaned back in the chair. "I know that. And even in its current state, Stoner Creek is a formidable fortress. Once they get inside, there will be no getting them out. I've already considered that possibility. I'm open to suggestions, but I just don't see any other alternative. We've got to catch them in the act before they can be brought to justice."

Steve leaned back against the wall and crossed his arms over his chest as he stared at the man calmly sitting across from him, preparing to throw away his life's earnings. "I really think you're a little touched in the head. It is with much regret that I acknowledge that you have the right to do with your property as you see fit, and Stoner Creek is your property. But have you given any consideration as to how this will affect Laura if what you plan comes true?"

For the first time in their conversation, Cash's jaw tightened with some sign of emotion, but his voice reflected nothing in reply. "I think she would rather live her life without fear, at whatever cost."

Steve nodded agreement with this philosophy but hedged his agreement slightly. "She's a woman. They don't always think like us."

"Then it's me she will hate when all is said and done. That's not a concern of yours."

Cash's taut tones signaled the conversation had come to an end. Steve straightened and held out his hand as Cash rose from his chair. "I've been wishing for some way to hang those scoundrels ever since they tried to get at Ward. I'll be in to see Ben today. If he ever wants to hold another office in this county, he'll be ready whenever you are."

That was all Cash wanted to hear. Shaking Steve's hand, he departed with one last question: "Where's the best place to buy blasting powder?"

"Don't be ridiculous, Jonathan. I can't go off and leave the house looking like this. There's too much work to be done." Laura brushed a grimy hand against her cheek, leaving a smear of dirt as she tucked a straying hair back into her kerchief.

Jonathan thought she looked totally charming, but the glare in her eye didn't quite suit the picture. "The house is Cash's. Let him do the work. I'm getting you and Jettie Mae and the children out of here. For once in your life, Laura, listen to someone with a little sense and go pack your things."

Laura watched him with growing suspicion. It wasn't like Jonathan to be this firm with her. "You've been talking to Cash, haven't you? What did he say?"

"He said he wanted you out of the house. There, now you know it. So go get your things and let's be gone. We can have the servants pack up the rest later. I just don't want to be here when Cash arrives."

Neither did Laura, but still she hesitated. "I can't imagine Dr. Burke will be pleased to be inundated with women and children. Your house wasn't exactly built for company."

"Burke can go sleep in the hotel. Or with that widow lady he's been seeing. I'll bunk at the hotel too. I'm not setting tongues to wagging again."

Laura bit her lip and searched Jonathan's honest face. She didn't know what this was all about. Cash would never order her off the farm. She knew better than that. But Jonathan wouldn't be here if something wasn't happening that he thought she needed protection from. And if Cash were returning here . . . Well, it was time to move on. Last night had made that clear.

"All right, Jonathan, perhaps it is time I made some decision about my future. I can't live on Cash's charity forever, but neither can I live on yours. Perhaps when you see Cash next, you can ask him how much he will sell the sewing machine for. I could borrow the money down at the bank and pay him back little by little. I can turn garments out much faster with the machine, so I should be able to make the payments and support myself too."

Jonathan stared at her with growing wonder, but there wasn't time for argument. She had been brought up in the heart of one of the wealthiest families in the commonwealth. She was every inch a lady, from her dainty shoes to her refined speech. By all rights she ought to be gowned in satin and sitting in her front parlor with her feet on a little stool and nothing more strenuous than a piece of embroidery in her hands. If she wanted to make her living sewing for others instead of taking her proper place in society, far be it from him to argue.

Satisfied that she had made herself clear, Laura went in search of Jettie Mae. She felt a certain relief at jettisoning the monstrous responsibilities of the farm. Not knowing where the money would come from, she couldn't undertake the repairs that were desperately needed. And the task of salvaging all the rugs and draperies one more time was beginning to wear on her energy. What would become of all the furniture beneath that leaky roof, she wasn't prepared to say. She just knew that it was more than she could handle right now.

She refused to admit that Cash's walking out had anything to do with this feeling of being overwhelmed. She had never had any right to count on him, so she couldn't blame him for how she felt. She had only herself to blame, and only herself to find the solution. And walking out suited her just fine right now. Let him go back to California. The whole damned place could fall down and return to honeysuckle and Virginia creepers for all she cared. She would have a life of her own.

She wasn't happy with the idea of being alone again, but it was better than sitting in the house and weeping. She couldn't put Jonathan and Dr. Burke out for long. She would have to find a place of her own. But first she had to get packed and out of here.

Jettie Mae looked at Laura with curiosity when told to pack and prepare to leave, but she did as told without argument for a change. She had been promised a home at Stoner Creek for the rest of her life, but even she could see that the house wasn't the safest place to be anymore. If Laura left, she wasn't hanging around for long. Without a man here, this place would be fair game to every animal in the county, and there were plenty of them. If Mr. Cash weren't coming back, they'd both do well to skedaddle.

As the wagon with all her meager worldly goods pulled away, Laura didn't turn to look back. She'd come home a year and a half ago thinking she would probably die in lonely spinsterhood in this place. She was a little wiser now. Not much, perhaps, but a little. She knew the solid man beside her would marry her and take her away to another world if she wanted. And she knew she would be safe with him if she did. But she would never be completely happy. That was something many a young girl never understood. Marriage wasn't the source of all happiness. Happiness came from within. She could make her own happiness. She didn't need Jonathan to do it. And he didn't need her. She wasn't certain what she required to be happy. Perhaps people were never meant to be completely happy in this world. She only knew that the only intensely happy times she remembered were in Cash's arms. So it little mattered where she went or what she did, she would never be completely happy again.

Unlike Laura, Jettie Mae sat in the back of the wagon and watched the mansion disappear behind a veil of trees. The glass remaining in the upper-story windows glinted in the sunlight. The faded brick stood stark and naked against the blue of the sky without the elm to shade it. The unsightly gash in the once-proud tile roof appeared as a spreading blight with the singe marks from the fire spreading out around it. It had been a lovely house once upon a time. With a little love, it could be a lovely house again. But love was a commodity in short supply these days. Jettie saw the bleak emptiness of the windows and nodded to herself as her children waved good-bye to the shadows on the porch.

The last of the Kincaids had gone. The house would die of loneliness now.

36

Laura held a cool hand to her aching head as she rested for a moment in the darkness of Jonathan's parlor. Jettie's children were running up and down the loft stairs in celebration of their return to town. Taylor was entertaining Mark with a pot and spoon in the tiny kitchen. And that was only the chaos on the inside. Outside, Laura knew from experience, a storm of curiosity was beginning to build.

She could handle it. She had done it before. She just needed a moment's rest before the preacher's wife showed up at the doorstep with a covered dish to ask if she could be of any help. Undoubtedly she would bring along one of the church ladies. And before long they would ascertain that Laura had no intention of marrying Jonathan, and the gossip would begin to swirl all over again.

What did it matter? Had she stayed at the farm with Cash, the talk would have been far worse. At least in town it was evident that Jonathan and Dr. Burke stayed discreetly at the hotel. Should she have stayed with Cash without benefit of marriage, she would have found herself the victim of cold shoulders all over again. Dear lord, if she had married Cash, she would have found just as many cold shoulders, only the reasons would be different.

Only then it wouldn't have mattered, because she could have been happy with just Cash. She didn't need anyone else. Well, she had burned that bridge behind her. There was no use crying over spilled milk.

Reluctantly smiling at the state of mind that had brought her to these old chestnuts, Laura relaxed a second longer before tackling whatever task awaited her now. She didn't hear the sound of Jettie's bare feet or cotton skirts until the other woman was in the room.

"That Mr. Cash done gone and lost his haid," she announced without preface.

Laura let that sink in quietly awhile as she closed her eyes and tried to imagine what catastrophe had wrought that statement. She was finding it to be quite easy to accept madness when that was all that surrounded her. One could always adjust to anything. But Jettie was waiting expectantly for a reply, and Laura finally obliged with a sigh. "What has he done now?"

"He's lettin' that Breckinridge fella have all his horses and he's loadin' everythin' else up in wagons. They ain't gonna be nothin' left there atall."

Laura was certain that made some kind of mad sense if she just had time to think about it. "And how do you know that?"

Jettie shrugged her thin shoulders beneath the loose cotton. "You don' wanna know."

Now that Laura thought about it, she really didn't. The farm was ten miles out in the county. By all rights, there wasn't a soul but the people on the farm who ought to know what was going on there. But she had already learned that the network of black lives intertwined along the back roads and the hidden parts of town was a formidable telegraph without need of wires. There wouldn't be a white man in town who knew what Jettie was telling her right now.

That notion made Laura stir uneasily. Trying not to frown, she dismissed Jettie's unspoken question easily. "I daresay he's selling off everything with any value to recoup his losses. I can't say I blame him. He put a fortune into that farm, and all he got was burned-out tobacco and trampled corn in return. Let him sell the whole damn farm. I don't care."

Laura wasn't certain that Jettie accepted this explanation, but at least she left without argument, probably to pass on this information to the network to do with it as it would. Cash would undoubtedly be unpleasantly surprised when a few strange black faces showed up shortly to ask if he needed any help with the loading. She doubted if he would begrudge the others that would appear to scavenge whatever he threw in the trash. He knew what it was like to live on the edge of nothing. There was certainly plenty in that house for everyone.

But she didn't like the feel of it. She wished she didn't know Cash so well. It would be much easier to just sit here and resent his high-handed appropriation of all her family's possessions, but she knew better. Cash could very well be in need of funds to return to California. He had bought and bred the horses himself and he would sell them with impunity. But he would never touch the family treasures handed down by generations. Why was he loading them into wagons?

She had to know. She just couldn't sit here and let the world collapse around her, as restful as it might be. When she was old and gray she would rest. Right now she was going to see what the Sam Hill Cash was up to.

Remembering the time Sallie had flung that phrase at them, Laura smiled. Sallie had been a pure caution. She would have to remember her cousin's good points and try to keep them alive in some way. There wasn't anything wrong with being lively and flirtatious and beautiful. Sallie had just used her advantages to get what she wanted, as men had done through time immemorial. Sallie had been the clever one, not Laura. She wished the twins could have lived so she could tell them when they grew older. Instead, she would have to carry the tales of his lovely aunt to Mark, so he would know of his proud heritage.

But right now he was more interested in spoons and pots. Rising from the chair, Laura quietly headed for the bedroom and her riding habit. Jonathan had gone to settle in at the hotel. No one would miss her for a little while. She'd have accomplished what needed to be done before they came looking for her.

Laura had thought she'd seen the last of Stoner Creek, but she should have known better. Riding her horse up the lane, she stared up at the imposing mansion rising out of the trees and wondered how she had ever called it home. It didn't even look familiar any longer.

It looked even less familiar when she rode up to find the half-dozen wagons scattered about the lawn, more or less filled with the house's contents. Cash had been busy. There wasn't much time to linger and examine the fur-

nishings. Night came faster this time of year, and the sun
was already well down near the horizon. Tying her horse
to the hitching post, Laura wondered where everybody
was. The lawn seemed unnaturally quiet in the heavy air.

Her boots clicked hollowly on uncarpeted floors as she
entered the front hall. Off to the right she could see the
piano and the recently recovered couch still in the formal
parlor. In the smaller family parlor much of the older
furniture remained. She hadn't really done much redeco-
rating in there, thinking the children would only destroy
it. The pieces were shabby and scarred by dozens of kicking feet and restless bottoms, and she smiled at long-ago
memories of restless afternoons in the presence of the
low murmurs of Aunt Ann's gossiping friends.

The rest of the rooms were much the same. The good
pieces, the valuables, the smaller pieces were all gone,
most likely to the wagons, even the china from the china
cabinet. Laura hoped Cash had someone responsible
packing that. There were a few pieces of battered and
peeling silver plate left in the pantry, along with the old
china and pewter and whatnot, enough to make the place
look used but poor. Laura pursed her lips wryly. It had
never really occurred to her or Sallie or Ward to sell the
silver or china or crystal. They were part of the house.
And of course it had never occurred to them to sell the
house.

But it very much looked as if it had occurred to Cash.

Striding more purposefully now, Laura started for the
back and the stableyard. She supposed he would be stripping the tack room by now. He had that right, she supposed. It had been his money that had rebuilt the stables
and everything in them. She just wished he'd said something to her first.

Cash caught sight of her coming across the yard. At
first he thought he was seeing ghosts. More than once
today he'd felt as if the house's previous owners were
breathing down his back, but he hadn't seen a physical
emanation until now. The gray riding habit and the long
veil flowing from the hat startled him with their familiarity as the presence floated past wilted mock oranges and
darted through the shadows of the hedge. But when it
reappeared again on the other side, Cash recognized the

furious if dainty gait, and grimly he began to stride forward to meet her.

Catching Laura before she could say a word, Cash lifted her from the ground and all but shook her with the rage and fear whipping through him. "Where in hell is Jonathan? All I asked the damned man to do was keep an eye on you, and he can't even do that. For one tiny woman, you sure are a large baggage of trouble. Get out of here, Laura, and don't come back, whatever you do."

Shocked by his harsh words, Laura stared into Cash's dark eyes and tried to find some semblance of order in his actions. Surely he hadn't gone mad. There was enough inbreeding in these parts to produce the occasional witless aunt and eccentric uncle, but they were relatively harmless. Laura had never really known a truly mad person before. But Cash seemed to border on that description now.

"Just tell me what's happening, Cash," she whispered against the fierceness of his reaction. His hands crushing her arms hurt, but not so much as the violence in his voice.

"Nothing is happening, Laura. You haven't seen anything today. No one has seen anything. Do you understand me?"

Cash's hands gentled slightly as they lowered her to the ground again, but the grip was still tight while he awaited her reply. Laura clung briefly to his shirt, then let her hands fall when she saw he wasn't going to give her any explanation. 'No, I don't understand. I don't understand anything at all. Where is everyone?"

"They're eating supper. They'll be back at dark. Now, get yourself out of here before they return, and tell nobody what you saw."

"That's ridiculous." Laura turned her back on Cash's harsh expression, easily removing herself from his grip. She started back toward the house, knowing he would follow. "Every Negro in the county knows what you're doing out here. How do you think I found out?"

Cash swore slowly and viciously as he followed her up the hill. By the time they reached the kitchen yard, he had run out of curses. He caught her arm and swung her around, studying her face in the growing gloom. "You're the damnedest white woman I've ever known. Are you sure you don't have a touch of tar somewhere in your background? I don't know of one damned black who would volunteer that information to a white man or woman. You're the only one who has come riding out here to see what's going on."

Laura shrugged off his hold. She wanted tender words and phrases. She wanted to be in Cash's arms, feeling his kisses, hearing his reassurances. She wanted the feel of his warm body next to hers and the knowledge that he needed her as much as she needed him. Instead she got curses and insults. Once more she had fallen for a scoundrel and a rogue. She must be out of her mind, but she couldn't stop loving him for all that.

"My father was a Kincaid and my mother was from France. Believe what you would like to believe, it makes no difference. I really don't think being part black and part white makes it any easier to get along with both races, not any more than being wealthy makes it easier to get along with wealthy people. It might make it easier to get to know them, but knowing isn't liking. You, of all people, ought to know that."

Cash's mouth twisted bitterly as the barb hit home. "I appreciate your reminding me. Now, get out of here, Laura, or I'll throw you over my horse and carry you back."

"I guess you'd better do that, because it's almost dark now and I'm not leaving here until I know what's going on. You can do whatever you want with this place, it makes no difference to me, but I think I am entitled to some explanation."

She was right, but now wasn't the time to tell her. Cash had a brief wild vision of riding off into the sunset with her, finding a sheltered glen, and making passionate love to her in the scent of the grasses with the doves calling above them. He clenched his fists against the swell of heat in his loins as he glared down at her. She was so damned beautiful when she looked at him like that. He knew she wouldn't object if he took her right here on a crushed patch of herbs. That idea had its merits too, except he knew that the wagon drivers would be returning shortly.

From somewhere deep inside himself, Cash drew the only words he knew to explain and drive her away at the same time. "There's only one explanation I can give you right now. I love you. I daresay I've loved you since that day you saved my life, but a man doesn't admit these things, even to himself. So I'm a fool; go on and say it. But I love you too damned much to let you know what's going on here tonight. This is my decision, not yours. You have your own to make. Now, get the hell out of here and make up your mind, Laura. My patience is running out."

Struck dumb, Laura could only stare at the harsh angles of Cash's face as he spoke. There was no softness in the bend of his mouth when he said those words. He practically gritted them out between clenched teeth. His fingers were biting into her upper arm again, and he looked as if he would pull it off. Her heart began fluttering frantically against her rib cage, not knowing whether to light or flee, like some caged bird just discovering the open door.

But he didn't give her time to decide. Spying one of the returning men, Cash whistled piercingly, bringing him to a trot across the field.

"Jake, get this fool woman back to town. Take one of the cart horses and that Spencer rifle I left in your wagon. She's more valuable than the damned furniture, though at the moment I can't remember why."

He strode away without another word, leaving Laura to stare at his back as the servant raced to do as ordered. She wanted to scream and run after him, fling herself at his feet and plead with him to take her too. But she had too much pride to do any such thing. She had thrown her pride aside once before, with disastrous results. She wouldn't do it again. She had to have something left to hide behind.

When Cash disappeared in the direction of the stables, she slowly turned and returned to her horse. He loved her, and he was leaving her. To Cash, that would make sense. What she had to do was decide whether or not to follow. He had said he was giving her a choice. It was time that she made it.

They met Jonathan and Dr. Burke riding hell-bent down the road from town. The men reined in at sight of Laura and her bodyguard, their gazes switching nervously from Laura to Jake and back down the road to the farm. Laura knew then that they were in on Cash's plans, and her mouth straightened in a grim line.

"Jake, you can go on back to Cash now. These gentlemen will look after me. I suspect Cash needs you more than I do tonight."

She felt the men exchanging looks over her head, but she was in no humor to placate them. Kicking her horse into a canter, she started off without their accompaniment.

When they caught up with her, Jake wasn't with them. Satisfied, Laura rode silently, not giving them the satisfaction of her questions or her thoughts. Let Jonathan and Burke think what they would. She didn't care what they thought, what anyone thought. She had to decide for herself.

Cash would never have said words like that if he didn't mean them. But meaning them and doing what normal people did about them weren't the same things in Cash's mind. He hadn't loved Sallie, and he'd married her anyway, not caring what effect the marriage would have on Sallie, reasoning she had been a consenting adult and had made her own choice.

But loving someone, Cash would want to protect her. Laura knew that from her own experience. She wanted to protect Cash and Mark both. It was akin to forming a circle of wagons against the world. So if Cash loved her, he would want to protect her against the gossip, and the gossip would certainly fly if they did anything so rash as to marry within weeks of Sallie's death.

The conversation about the brush of tar came back with new meaning. Cash was still too aware of his own origins to want to compromise her with his reputation. She had never really been a part of the aristocratic society around her, but they had never snubbed her either. But unlike Sallie, if Laura married Cash, they would turn their backs without a qualm, muttering things like "blood will tell." So there was the decision he was telling her to make.

Laura looked to the man riding close to her, throwing her anxious looks. If she married Jonathan, she would be accepted everywhere. Cash knew that. He was practically throwing her into Jonathan's arms. Stupid, stupid man.

Laura threw her head back and set a careful pace back

to town. Perhaps blood did tell. She had grown up with
a gambler and a French singer for parents. She had spent
her early years on riverboats and trains. She had desperately looked for that same happiness in the home and
family at Stoner Creek. Maybe, just maybe, happiness
couldn't be found in a place.

She'd have to think about that a bit, but her heart
already knew the answer. Mark's heritage was here, in
the rolling acres of bluegrass that had fed and housed his
ancestors, but he was half Cash's too. And the Bluegrass
hadn't treated him very kindly.

And knowing that, Laura thought back on Cash's
words and the emptiness of the house, and a new desperation began to grow.

Death was much more final than California.

37

Laura heard no word from Cash that night or the next
day. Rumors abounded. She heard he'd been down at
the tavern drinking and carousing all night. She heard
he'd taken one of the prostitutes from the hotel to the
house. She heard he was broke and selling off the property. She heard many things, but she could believe only
what she saw for herself.

Since she had no mind to go down to the tavern on
her own, she would have to wait and see what happened.
Jonathan wanted her to go into Lexington and stay with
family. She probably ought to, just so she wouldn't be
putting him out of his house, but she dragged her feet
with one excuse or another. She had to see Cash, to
know that he was all right, and she couldn't do that from
Lexington.

Another night went by without word. Laura knew he
was still around. No one would let her forget. If she
walked down to the store to pick up thread, she was

stopped by half the town to ask after Cash's plans for
the farm and to advise her of where they had seen him
last. He was here, and he was alive, but he was avoiding
her.

She was being foolish to linger, hoping he would come
to her if she stayed. In all likelihood Cash was waiting for
her to leave to carry out whatever presumptuous plans he
had in mind. Jonathan obviously knew more than he was
letting on, and he wanted her out of town. Laura didn't
like the sound of that at all, but she couldn't be persuaded into leaving without knowing if Cash was going
to be all right.

And since they wouldn't tell her anything, she couldn't
leave. Steve Breckinridge stopped by with an invitation
from his mother to go shopping in Lexington for a few
days, and Laura knew then that he was in on this plan
too. It was hard to imagine Cash dealing with the Breckinridges, but they had never offered to take her under
their wing before. She stood her ground even more
firmly.

Steve looked impatient at her refusal. Jonathan looked
even more harried. Laura felt sorry for them, but she
was tired of taking care of everyone else. This time she
was taking care of herself. And taking care of herself
meant taking care of Cash. If he was bound and determined to do something foolish, she was going to be
around to pull him out. She couldn't bear to lose him
again.

The next day she heard that Cash had torn up the
tavern the night before, after the Raiders hanged another
poor soul just outside of town. Laura had an uneasy
twinge that the two incidents might be connected, but
she wasn't exactly certain how. No one else saw it that
way. They just clucked their tongues and expressed a
certain malicious sympathy that Cash was going to pieces
now that his wife had died.

By the end of that day Laura had almost made up her
mind to ride out to the farm to see if she could find him
on the morrow. She had made her decision; it was time
that Cash told her his.

She checked on Mark in his cradle, then sat down at
the vanity to brush out her hair. Since she had never
been blessed with Sallie's long luxurious curls, Laura

kept her hair trimmed to the middle of her back. It was easier to tend, and it looked thicker, fuller that way. Pulling a length over her shoulder to brush, she even imagined there might be a slight curl to the ends, and she tugged the brush through it at an angle to encourage it. The sudden choked gasp behind her made her swing around in fright.

Cash grabbed another candle and lit it, holding it high to fall on the shimmering halo falling about Laura's breasts and shoulders. The lacy yoke of her nightdress lay untied at her throat, revealing the shadowy hollow and swell beneath. He had thought he knew this woman intimately, but tonight showed he knew nothing at all. The warm and loving woman he had come to know could be a temptress as well, and his fingers ached to reach out and trace the rounded curves pressing against the nearly transparent cloth.

Once recovered from her fright, she knew her effect on him; Cash could tell that at once. Her eyes took on an emerald gleam as they moved over him, lingering at the open neck of his own shirt, halting mischievously just below the band of his trousers where the evidence of his desire was beginning to grow. Twisted around on the bench as she was, she leaned forward slightly, arching her breasts more clearly against her gown. It was the most provocative position he had ever seen, and Cash nearly dropped the candle in his hand as he fell victim to it.

"You're rapidly becoming a damned nuisance, you know that, don't you?" he asked harshly, setting the candle aside as he reached for her.

"You're such a romantic person, Cassius Wickliffe. Must you always swear at me?" Laura rose and stepped into his arms as if it were the most natural thing in the world to do. His hands clasped behind her waist, and she reached to wrap her arms around his neck. She was home now. She could smell it in the sweaty scent of lathered horse and leather and the fading odor of cedar shavings from his clothing. Cash had always smelled like that, from the earliest she could remember. She smiled at the wry twist of his lips.

The smile did it. Cash could no more resist that smile than a drowning man could resist a rope. He had expected harsh recriminations and arguments. He had expected objects flung at his head. He had expected the rejection that had so often come his way. But when he deserved it, when Laura had every reason to throw him out, she smiled at him with a come-hither look that tore him up by the roots and flung him against the wall.

"It's for your own good, Laura," Cash murmured, even as his mouth bent to take the kiss she offered. Her acceptance of the light brush of his lips ended the war raging within himself. Laura's lips never lied, even when they were silent. They met his firmly, responding to his every demand with an equal demand of her own. They parted without a fight, and Cash felt a shudder of deep, abiding desire as he drew her up against him and took her mouth with a hunger a mere kiss couldn't assuage.

Feeling her heart thudding against his chest, her arms clinging to his shoulders, Cash tried to move his mouth away, brushing his lips against her cheek and nibbling at her ear beneath the heavy cloud of hair. But the strain of keeping away would be too great shortly. He lowered her to the floor and allowed his hand to stray to the curve of her breast. "This isn't why I came here, love."

"Probably not," she agreed with a wry twist of her lips, her eyes never leaving his. "I'm certain it was some other noble reason that brought you here. You'll never make a gallant knight, Cash. But that doesn't matter. I always thought Scott's heroes were pusillanimous ninnies."

Cash nearly choked on the laugh threatening to swell his throat. "Remind me to have you repeat that again in the morning when I've had time to think about it. What am I going to do with you, Laura? You're like no other woman I know. You're supposed to be so mad at me that you'd take the first opportunity offered to get the hell out of here. I figured I was going to have to chase you down across half the country. Why can't you do what anyone else would have done?"

His hands were moving unconsciously up and down her sides, savoring the curve of her breasts and waist, and Laura had difficulty mustering a suitable reply. She tilted her head to look up at him with curiosity, reveling in the heated intensity that she found in his gaze. It wasn't difficult to answer the look in his eyes.

"Because I thought I heard you say you loved me.

Because I trust you. Because I don't want to ever be parted from you again. Is that too much to say all at one time? Should I scream the words at you and hit you so you'll understand?"

A chuckle lodged deep in his throat as Cash pulled her into his arms again. "Please, don't. I remember what happened the last time you screamed at me. The next time I make love to you, I want it to be with wine and roses all around. Lord, I've been such a fool, Laura. That first time, I just thought it was something that happened only once in a thunderstorm. I never imagined it could always be like that."

"Maybe it can't. Last time involved a thunderstorm too. Maybe all you require is thunder and lightning."

Laura gasped as she suddenly found herself flung back against the bed with Cash's arms propped on either side of her head. She discovered the erotic possibilities of this position quickly enough when she felt his lips brush near to hers where he leaned over her.

"You're all the thunder and lightning that I require, Laura. But now isn't the time to let you know that. You've got to get out of here."

Cash's mouth nibbled at the corner of hers, and Laura had to steady herself with his shoulders. Alarming sensations were beginning to sweep through her, but she had to retain her wits if she were going to get any sense out of him. Still, the press of his loins through her nightdress made her close her eyes and pull him closer.

"I love you, Cash," she whispered in his ear. She felt him stiffen, try to pull away, and she opened her eyes to meet his incredulous look. She ran her fingers into his hair and caught a hank, keeping him from going too far. "Don't look at me like that. If I'm going to be sinful, it might as well be for a reason. Maybe I didn't know what love was that first time, but I do now."

"No, you don't." Cash buried his face against the side of her neck and kissed her there. She squirmed deliciously beneath him, and he sought new zones to explore, producing a satisfying gasp as he nibbled her ear and rubbed an aroused nipple between his fingers. "You're just hungry for this, and I'm the only man who's given it to you."

Laura punched his shoulders and swung her feet in an

attempt to connect with his shins. "Cassius Wickliffe, you are a monstrous beast! Get off me before I pull every hair out of your head. I don't have to listen to your insults."

Her attempts to maim him lacked the fury of the last time they had fought. Cash brushed aside the open bodice of her gown and bent to touch his lips to her breast. She arched eagerly against him, all protest gone. She was the most responsive woman he'd ever had the pleasure of knowing, and he knew now that he wasn't going to leave until he'd had her once more. Just once more, that was all.

"Hold still, Laura, and let me love you as I ought to. And then you're going to leave Stoner Creek until I tell you it's safe to come back. Promise me you'll leave."

His tone was demanding, but Laura responded more to his actions. His lips had stopped their magic, and she understood the threat implied. If she didn't promise, he would go away, and she couldn't bear that, not now. She'd worry about his words later. For right now, she needed his love. "I'll go. Don't stop. Cash . . ."

Her words were cut off by the heated response of his lips. Laura gave a strangled cry at the sensuous tug and pull of mouth and fingers, and then Cash's hands were beneath her, pulling at her gown, lifting her against him, and her mind ceased to function beneath the barrage of sensations.

While his mouth lovingly attended to her breasts, his hand found the juncture of her thighs, and Laura was helpless to do more than tear at his shoulders and writhe beneath the wild waves of pleasure lifting her, washing over her, and throwing her into his embrace. When she finally felt his hand move to undress himself, she was frantic, and she cried in ecstasy when Cash returned with a swiftness that took her breath away.

Before Cash came along, she had always thought the marriage act to be something done furtively, under the covers, in darkness. This brazen act of pleasure that they performed now had never been within her ability to imagine. She did not even want to imagine it now. She only wanted the sensation of Cash inside her, his heavy body bent into hers. She wanted the scent and heat of him, the muscular strength rippling over her, as their bodies joined and thrust and fought for the order that would bring them together in the chaos of passion.

The hoarse sound of Cash's command, "Now, Laura!" was sufficient to release what little hold she had left. Her body exploded with his, the contractions ripping through them together while space and time ceased to exist for one brief moment. As the aftershocks rippled slowly through them, Cash lifted Laura more fully onto the bed and joined her there.

"Wine and roses next time," he whispered as she curved into him, reluctant to let him go.

"There will be a next time?" she asked sleepily, demanding reassurance.

"If that's what you want, there will be a next time," he promised, "but be certain that's what you want. Once I have you, I'll not let you go. I keep what's mine, Laura."

"I know." Eyes closed, drinking in the luxurious sensation of Cash's hard body holding hers, Laura knew she should be demanding explanations, asking questions, looking for some security for the future. But she couldn't shatter this peace with the world outside. She pressed her palm into the curve of his neck and shoulder and brought her lips to the base of his throat.

She couldn't have given him a more forceful reply. Gathering Laura into his arms and crushing her painfully, Cash covered her hair with kisses. He would succeed. He had to succeed. For everything he had ever wanted was right here, giving herself without question, without any strings attached. For the first time since he could remember, tears stung Cash's eyes. He'd thought it would be a cold day in hell before he ever cried. Instead, it was a brief glimpse of heaven.

"I've got to go, Laura. I can't stay here. Will you take the train in the morning? I've got to know you're safe."

She finally shoved away enough to see the shadows of Cash's face in the candlelight. His eyes were barely more than dark sockets, and she brushed her hand against the bristle of his cheek. "And how am I to know that you will be safe?"

A tender smile curved his lips as he touched a finger to the thick hair cascading over her shoulder. "It's never mattered to anyone before. I don't understand why it should matter now."

She regarded this nonsense patiently. "You know better than that. You've always mattered to me. Now, promise me you won't do anything foolish. I don't know what you're up to, but I'd rather have you alive than anything else that I can think of."

And strangely enough, Cash believed her. Laura had been the one to help him when no one else would, even when she was a little girl. She had been the one running at his heels when scarcely a soul would speak to him. Even now, she was the one who stood at his side when others turned their backs, who tended his needs when those who should have refused their duties. He found her devotion hard to believe, and he had denied it for years. But he would have to be the greatest fool alive to deny it now.

"I really think you mean that, *pequeña*." Cash caressed Laura's face with the back of his finger, enjoying the look of concern meant just for him. It was a rather heady sensation, he discovered, this caring and being cared for. It might take time to get used to. "And I'm not planning on getting myself killed. This time, I mean to be around to watch you grow round if I've planted something here." His hand moved to cover her abdomen.

Those were the words she evidently wanted to hear. Laura smiled and leaned back against the pillow, and Cash watched her until she slept, warming his hand against her belly.

He really did mean what he said, but he also knew life was full of uncertainties. What he was aiming to do was not conducive to a permanent existence in this world, despite his promise. He kissed Laura's nose and swung from the bed.

He'd just have to make certain he killed Marshall Brown before Brown could kill him.

38

Laura couldn't manage the morning train. She woke late, equally dismayed and delighted about the wanton abandonment she found herself in with her nightdress hiked up about her waist and her bodice undone and her nakedness arrayed across the rumpled sheets. She could still smell the scent of Cash against his pillow, and she buried her nose in it, holding it in her arms while she tried to adjust to her new role as wicked woman.

For what she had done was obviously wicked. Cash had never mentioned a word about marriage. He had simply walked in here as if it were the most natural thing in the world, took her to bed and had his way with her, and informed her he would do it again if that was what she wanted. She remembered his words very clearly this time. There hadn't been one word about marriage.

But he had mentioned what could have happened already. Laura touched a hand to her abdomen as if she could determine if Cash's seed had already taken root there. It would be a couple of weeks before she could know for certain, but she already knew they would have no trouble making babies. Some people did, she knew, but she and Cash had already proved their fertility once. She wasn't nursing anymore, and they hadn't done anything for protection. It was just a matter of time.

The thought really didn't frighten her as it should have. Laura stretched and flung her arms over her head and tried to picture Cash beside her in bed while her belly was swollen with his child. Just the thought aroused a longing for the act that would bring such a scene about. She was truly and without a doubt beyond the edges of wickedness. She wanted Cash's baby.

She didn't know what would happen to her if she didn't lose this craving for what wasn't good for her, but she wasn't going to sit here and find out. She had promised to leave today, and so she would. Cash had promised to come after her. That was all she wanted to hear.

Perhaps she was being deliberately blind. If so, she would suffer the results later. For right now she needed the heady happiness of Cash's lovemaking to remain untouched in her mind. She hated even to wash and scrub away the lingering scent of him. But she did so, content in the knowledge that he would come for her again.

Jonathan nearly collapsed with relief when Laura told him she and Mark would take the late train to Lexington. He offered to send for the Breckinridge ladies to accompany her, and when she refused, he offered to go with her himself. Laura smiled and touched his cheek and shook her head firmly.

"No, you've done enough, Jonathan. I feel like the most ungrateful person alive when I think of what I've put you through. I wish things could have worked out differently. You and I have so much in common, you'd think we would be perfect for each other. But I think we would only make each other miserable eventually."

He caught her hand and watched her face sadly. "You've seen Cash, haven't you? It's written all over your face. Even knowing what he is, you're going to throw everything away all over again and go with him. I'm not certain I know which one of us is the greater idiot. I should haul you to the preacher right now and save us both some heartbreak. I think we could be good together."

Laura shrugged lightly and turned her face away from Jonathan's all-seeing eyes. "Content, perhaps, but never really happy, and never really knowing why. It wouldn't work. I really do love you too much to make you unhappy. It's just not the kind of love that marriages are made of. I've seen those kinds of marriages, Jonathan, and that's not what I want for myself. It would be safe. I'd have the security every woman craves, but I'm old enough to know that isn't enough for me."

Jonathan released her hand and ran his fingers through his hair in perplexity. "Damned if I know what you want, Laura. I thought you wanted friends and family, the security of Stoner Creek, or I would have taken you to Arizona with me. I could still take you with me, if that's

what you want. Cash is a rover and a gambler and there's
no telling where he'll be next after he shakes this place
from his shoes. You've got a child to think of."

"I know." Laura smiled softly and turned her gaze
back to linger on his kind features. "A child who needs
to know his father. I know what I want, Jonathan. I
don't care if I have to live on riverboats to get it. There's
the difference between my love for you and my love for
Cash."

He managed a wry grin. "I know what you're telling
me, Laura, even if I don't like it. I left you behind, but
not my work. There are some things from which we're
just inseparable."

She smiled in relief. "Thank you for understanding.
I'll always want you for a friend. I don't know where I
would be now if it weren't for you, and if you should
ever ask anything of me, you know I'll move mountains
to comply. Please remember that, so someday I may be
able to repay this enormous debt that I owe you."

Jonathan lifted her chin and kissed her cheek. "You've
already named one son after me, what more can I ask?
Just let me bask in the rakish glory of being the father
of your child for a little while longer. It rather enhances
my reputation with the ladies."

Laura laughed, and they parted amicably. She could
tell by the look in his eyes that he would be returning to
Arizona soon, and she might never see him again. She
just hoped he would stay long enough to see that Cash
would come after her, and that she could be happy with
him. She wanted everyone to be as confident of Cash as
she was.

That was probably quite a ridiculous notion, Laura decided later as she settled the hat Cash had given her on
her head and gathered up her bag in one hand and Mark
in the other. She had quite lost any sense of perspective
where Cash was involved. He had left before and forgotten about her. He had made love to her and married
Sallie. Even now he was fighting her every step of the
way. Once she was out of sight, he would probably
breathe a sigh of relief and disappear into the sunset.
But she was going to trust him anyway.

Jettie Mae and the children came to the station to wave

good-bye, and Laura gave them brave smiles as she climbed on the train. She couldn't descend on her relatives with the entire crowd in tow, but she had promised to make arrangements for them as soon as possible. They could stay with Jettie's mother for a little while, but she had made a vow to see that Ward's son would be raised as a gentleman. If Cash fell through on his promises, she didn't know how she would keep hers, but she would find some way to do it.

The train pulled away from the station while Laura's mind was still on the farm and the little school she had started there. She'd had so much hope at the beginning of the summer. How silly she must have looked to everybody, with her plans to change the world. She couldn't even change her small part in it.

But she wouldn't give up trying. Perhaps when Cash came for her, he would take Jettie and the children with them. It wouldn't be the same as teaching a whole farm full of children, but it would be one small step in the right direction. And if they went to California, they would be free from the stigma of slavery. She'd heard all kinds of things about California. Cash would be considered a gentleman there. It would work. It had to work.

So immersed in her thoughts had she become that she failed to notice when the train started to lose speed. Only when Mark began squirming restlessly and Laura looked up to see the tense faces of the other passengers around her did she realize that something was wrong.

Glancing out the window, she could see nothing untoward, but she knew there was no stop along this part of the line. She bounced Mark up and down and tried to hear what the other passengers were whispering. Nervously she kept looking out the window, until she finally saw a man on horseback with a rifle in his hand.

Even then, the significance didn't occur to her. He was probably a farmer waiting for the train to pass. But the train didn't pass. It rumbled to a gradual halt with a belch of steam and a grinding squeal of brakes.

The panic around her began to have its effect. Train robberies had become quite frequent in these lawless days, but Laura had understood they came at night, when

Marshall and the Raiders and other lawless gangs were on the loose.

Just that thought caused Laura's eyes to widen, and fear snagged its steely barbs in her heart. Marshall! This was all about Marshall. Cash had known when those men would attack the farm. Cash had overturned the tavern when he had not learned of the hanging of that innocent man in time. Cash somehow knew what Marshall was planning, and he had tried to get her away. But not soon enough.

He couldn't have known that Marshall would hold up a train in broad daylight to get at her.

While other people were hiding their valuables, Laura hastily ripped a flyleaf from the book she had been reading and scribbled Mark's name and Jonathan's address on it. There was enough room to include her cousin's address too, since the train would get to Lexington first. That should be sufficient to identify him. Folding the precious note carefully, she tucked it into the pocket of Mark's little coat, the one she had made for him. Jettie had laughed at her when she made it, but he looked just as cute as could be sitting there in his long coat with a tiny hat perched on his head, his bright eyes watching her expectantly.

Taking a deep breath, Laura picked him up and stood in the aisle, leaving her bag on the floor and pulling her long gray traveling skirt around her. She ought to be wearing mourning, but somehow there had never seemed to be enough time to dye the proper clothes. It wouldn't matter now, if her guess were correct. Nothing would matter again.

Smiling at a nervous young couple she had noticed earlier, Laura stopped and lowered Mark to his wobbly little legs. "I'm afraid whenever I get nervous, I have to . . ." She paused delicately and nodded toward the partitions at the rear of the train hiding the crude facility for ladies. "Could you watch him just a moment? I hate to impose . . ."

The woman looked delighted at the sight of Mark's charming grin, and the man threw her a grateful look for distracting her at a time like this. Without trying to ascertain more of these people she had to judge by instinct, Laura lifted her skirt and hurried away.

If she were wrong, she could climb right back on the train before it pulled out. But if she were right, if that was Marshall and his gang out there, she wasn't going to wait here and let them find her.

The terrain she had seen when the train went by wasn't promising. But there was enough old blackberry bushes and locust saplings along the track to conceal her for a while if no one was looking. Without her holding Mark's hand, Marshall would never recognize the child, so he should be safe enough with the young couple. She had only to conceal herself long enough to escape.

As she climbed from the train, Laura prayed she was wrong. The sun was still too bright in the September sky for this to be real. She had to be imagining things. She would look back and laugh at this someday. There was probably a cow on the tracks. Or the engineer had had too much to drink and decided he just couldn't make it to the next stop. She was going to be embarrassed to death if . . .

A shot rang out farther down the line and a woman screamed. Without one more thought, Laura pitched herself into the bushes at the side of the track. Praying as fast as she could for Mark's safety, she began to push her way through the brambles, cursing her long skirts, protecting her face with her hands as she tried to find the densest thicket.

She used to make play houses in the bushes back home when she was a child, but she'd always had more sense than to choose blackberry thickets. Pain lanced through her as thorns tore at her hands, ripped through her jacket, and whipped at her face. But the force of panic pushed her on.

She could hear horses and men cursing. There was another shot, close by. Too close. Laura halted and held her breath. The blackberry leaves were fading with the cooler weather of September. She was small, but not so small that she would be entirely concealed if anyone looked close enough. She prayed they weren't looking out here. Surely, if they knew she had taken the train, they were searching inside.

Perhaps they weren't looking for her at all. Perhaps it was only her own enormous conceit that made her think anyone knew where she was or cared. But instinct was a tremendous urge, and Laura had to abide by it. She was willing to look foolish afterward.

A horse started this way. She could see its legs through the leaves. If she could see that much, anyone looking could see the gray of her suit. Please, don't look, she prayed as the horse slowly walked by. The rider shouted something to someone farther down the line. They must have worked their way through the train by now. She could hear loud protests trailing through the open windows of the car just above her. Men cursed, women wept. Please, Lord, let Mark be all right.

And then there were several men and horses almost within hand's reach, and it was all over. A rough fist grabbed the back of her jacket and jerked. Laura threw her arms over her face until she emerged from the bushes, then attempted to free herself from the trap of her suit. A man with a pillowcase pulled over his head jumped from one of the horses and stopped in front of her, blocking any hope of escape. Before Laura could fight free, he raised his fist, and the blow ended any notion of anything at all.

Within view of the other horrified passengers, Laura slumped forward, and while they watched, the thieves carried her off to a waiting horse.

39

Laura woke to throbbing jaw and aching head. Holding her eyes closed until she was certain her head wouldn't explode, she tried to determine where she was from the sounds around her. Male voices drifted from somewhere below, and she stirred uneasily, vaguely recalling the events of earlier. Alarm began to replace the demands of pain, and she held her eyes closed until she could determine if she were alone.

She heard no one else in the room. A branch scratched

at a window nearby, and cautiously Laura opened her
eyes to survey the room's growing darkness.

She must have been unconscious for quite a while. The
sun was close to setting, judging by the gloom around
her. She strained her eyes for some familiar sight, finding
it in the scorched posts of the bed where she lay. Sallie's
bed. Uneasily Laura let her eyes roam to the gaping hole
in the ceiling, then down to the broken and unboarded
window below. A tree limb still protruded through the
shards of glass. Cash had left this room untouched.

If Laura knew Marshall's mind at all, he had brought
her to the only bedchamber left with a decent bed. Cash
had been systematically stripping these rooms when last
she had been here. He would have taken the undamaged
furniture first. Not liking the direction of her thoughts,
Laura raised herself to a sitting position. Escape should
be the only thing on her mind.

Gingerly holding her jaw, she stood and crossed to
the window. The lightning had broken the burned elm
somewhere at the crook of one of its mighty limbs. All
the small branches had been burned off, so the limb coming through the window was fairly thick and heavy. But
Laura couldn't see where it connected to the tree, or if
it connected. It could be completely severed from the
trunk and just resting here at an awkward angle, waiting
for a strong wind to blow it away. In desperation she
might try climbing out on it, but she could be committing
suicide by doing so. Vowing that suicide would be better
than what Marshall had planned for her, Laura began to
survey the room for other escape routes.

The hole in the ceiling looked promising, but it was
easily five or six feet above her head. These rooms had
been built to let the summer heat rise to the top, keeping
the air at human level cool. It made cleaning the ceilings
nigh onto impossible, and put the escape hatch well out
of Laura's reach.

Laura glanced around for something to be used as a
ladder, but the small chest of drawers would not make
her tall enough to reach the uncovered lath, and the
wardrobe was too large for her to move. She wasn't at
all certain that the lath would hold her, but it looked so
much more promising than the room . . .

At the sound of approaching footsteps, Laura ran for

the door to Sallie's sitting room. Tugging at the knob, she cursed the water that had warped and swollen the old wood until it held tighter than a tick on a dog. Swinging around, her skirt swirling in a frantic circle about her ankles, she stared at the tree branch. Did she dare take it?

The point became moot as the door to the hall swung open. Framed in the light of a single candle, Marshall assumed an image of evil in her mind. A holster rode low on his hip, and he had disguised himself carefully for his role of respectable husband and responsible lawman. Wearing dark trousers and a long coat pulled back to reveal his gun, he stood in the doorway, savoring the sight of his captive as she backed toward the broken window.

"Well, wife, we're home at last. It's not the sight it once was, but I daresay once we find some lawyers to find out where your cousin's thieving husband hid the cash, we'll bring it back to normal. He can't have sold off all the furniture yet. I'm sure we'll be quite comfortable once we find it. Until then, this will have to be our marriage bed. I'll have some of the men move it across the hall in the morning. But it will suit for what I have in mind now."

"You're not my husband." They weren't the words she wanted to say, but they were the only words that came to Laura's tongue as Marshall stepped into the room, shutting the door behind him. She felt her throat closing and fear freezing her muscles as he advanced on her. She knew what he would do to her, and she knew she would die if she let him. The tree was beginning to look more promising.

"The town thinks I am. We can take care of the technicalities later. You should be happy about that, Laura. Wickliffe was going to rob you blind and leave you to starve. I'm a better man than that. I'm going to get your home back for you, Laura. This will be our home. We'll entertain like royalty once we get the place fixed up again. It's a pity you can't look a little more like your fancy cousin, but maybe in a new gown you'll shine enough to look the part of mistress of Stoner Creek."

She wasn't going to stand and talk with a madman. Swirling around, Laura raced for the window and the tree. She wished there were time to rip off her petticoat, but she would manage somehow. Tree-climbing had never been one of her talents, but she had sufficient inspiration to learn.

She screamed as Marshall caught her arm and jerked her back against him. She had forgotten how strong he was. His hand twisted cruelly at her arm, bringing her around until his foul breath was in her face. He had been a handsome man once, but meanness had marked his features until they were a caricature of themselves. Laura cringed backward as his thin lips twisted in an evil slant.

"The almighty Cash Wickliffe ain't gonna help you now. Even as we speak, my men have a gun to his head." He shifted her so his hand could come around to scrape her breast. "Perhaps you're not so plain as I remembered, wife. Now that you've got your figure back, you're not so hard to look upon. Maybe whelping brats is good for you. If so, I'll see that you always have one in your belly. There's plenty of other female flesh around here to ease my needs when you swell up."

His free hand caught in the ties of her traveling jacket, and Laura felt the hard brush of his hand through the bodice beneath. She jerked as if he had hit her, but Marshall's gaze was avidly fixed on her bosom and he gave no sign that he noticed her fear.

As his fingers began rapaciously tearing at the clothing protecting her, Laura reached for the tree limb, praying for a breakable branch. She would die before she let Marshall take what belonged to Cash alone, but she would damn well take Marshall with her before she did.

His informants had warned Cash that Marshall meant to act tonight, and he had been prepared for the brute who had attempted to stave his head in earlier at the tavern, but he hadn't been prepared for this. Cash blanched a shade of white hitherto unknown to his features as he watched Marshall's gang ride up to the house with a woman flung over the saddle of one of the horses. There was no mistaking that gray skirt and slender form. Even Breckinridge, beside him, recognized her, and he grabbed Cash's arm before he could break from their hiding place.

"You'll only get yourself killed going in there alone. If you know how, practice praying."

The wide sweeping lawns of Stoner Creek offered next to no protection should he be foolish enough to race after Laura, but that didn't stop Cash from contemplating it. The thought of Laura helpless in Marshall's filthy hands tore at Cash with a viciousness he had never known. He ripped his arm from Steve's restraining hand and turned a fierce look in the other man's direction.

"If praying would stop the devil, the world would be a better place by now. I'm going in after her." He stepped forward, and then another look passed over his face, a frozen look of fear and agony that penetrated every man within a distance to see it as he turned back to Steve. "Where's Mark?"

"Who?" Too startled by the sudden change in the man before him, Breckinridge replied without thought.

"My son. Where in hell is my son? She wouldn't have left town without him. My God, what has he done with my son?" And before another man could stop him, Cash started across the side lawn, loping over the shadowed grass, rifle in hand.

Ward's brother stood still a minute longer in the hidden depths of the row of trees lining the lane, watching the anguished man racing to certain death, letting pieces fall together in his mind with sharp little clicks. Never having fought in the war, Steve didn't know the military commands needed right now, but he had years of experience at wielding authority. Turning, he spoke curtly to the man behind him, and his orders began running up and down the line of hidden figures.

Unaware of the explosion of events behind him, Cash reached the safety of the old elm without being seen from the house. He could hear the crash of glass and male voices arguing within, but no feminine screams yet split the air. He almost wished he would hear her. At least then he would know she lived. He couldn't imagine Laura allowing anything short of death to part her from her son.

The shattered tree presented no problem in climbing. The angle was such at the top that he could practically run up the cracked limb. The only problem that presented itself was which limb to take. Choosing the one closest to the roof, Cash eased himself upward, testing the strength of the burned and broken wood beneath him.

It was a damned sturdy old tree. He would plant a dozen more like it one of these days. Swinging his foot out over the roof, Cash cautiously found the gaping hole and lowered himself through it.

What he was doing was pure madness. He'd been up in the attic only once to inspect the damage. He didn't know if the rotten boards could still withstand his weight. But he didn't have time to find out. Finding handholds where he could, he slowly made his way downward until his feet were touching solid wood; then, releasing his grip, he held his breath and took his weight on bent knees until he was certain the floor would hold him.

Lowering himself to his stomach, Cash crawled toward the flickering light coming through the washed-out ceiling. There hadn't been a light upstairs when he had run toward the house. He had hoped to lower himself unnoticed into the breach. Luck was running against him if the room below were occupied. Grasping his rifle calmly, Cash inched across the floor. He would shoot his way through if he had to. He couldn't leave Laura in Marshall's hands for the time it would take to plan this more carefully. He had promised to protect her. It would be with his life, if necessary.

Praying Breckinridge would have the sense to storm the house once the shooting began, Cash eased himself toward the fragile edge of the attic floor. Rotted lath and fallen plaster stretched out from this point toward the eaves. There would be just enough room to lower himself through, but he would like to have some idea of who was there before he entered.

Hearing voices, Cash halted. Panic forced his heart into double time as he recognized the calm sarcasm of the feminine voice almost below him. Never would it occur to Laura to placate the criminal with feminine wiles. Once cornered, she would fight like a wildcat, as he well had reason to know. But Marshall wouldn't be gentle with her.

Terrified he would be too late, Cash pulled himself out past the floor along a beam, searching the candlelit gloom for some sign of his target. The sight illuminated

below him brought a rush of rage and the taste of nausea
to his tongue, but he forced his fury into control as he
raised the rifle barrel. Whatever happened now, Marshall
would die first.

As Marshall tugged at the tiny jet buttons of her bodice, Laura fell back against the tree and grabbed for one
of the broken branches. She didn't fool herself into thinking she had the strength to kill him with a stick, but any
distraction would suffice.

The crack of the wood caused Marshall to look up
just as Laura's arm came swinging downward. The blow
glanced along the side of his head and he howled in pain,
grabbing at her shoulder to disarm her before she could
swing the weapon again.

Twisting Laura's arm behind her, he forced her head
back with his arm until she dropped the stick. Her sudden gasp of horror caused Marshall to follow her gaze,
and red rage consumed him at the sight of the rifle and
the man holding it.

"You're supposed to be dead, Wickliffe. You must
have the lives of a cat, but you've reached the last of
them. My men control this place now. If you try to use
that rifle, you'll only harm Laura and bring my men running up here. There isn't a thing you can do, so drop the
gun and come on down before I shoot you down."

This wasn't how he had planned any of this. Cash held
his tongue and cursed silently at the horror and fear in
Laura's pale face as their eyes met. He had meant for
her to be gone from here when Marshall took over the
place. He had meant to blow the whole damned house up
and Marshall and his gang with it. Laura was supposed to
be in Lexington by now.

But as usual, his plans had gone awry. Only instinct
worked at times like these, and instinct as well as experience told Cash he couldn't shoot Marshall while the
scoundrel was holding Laura. Nor would he be of any
use to Laura if he were taken captive too.

With a look he hoped would reassure, Cash and his
rifle disappeared into the blackness of the attic.

Marshall cursed vividly and shot at the hole where his
nemesis had been. The shot that followed came from
below, not above. Emptying a few more rounds into the

ceiling, Marshall twisted Laura against him and peered
through the window to the gathering darkness below.

Shooting erupted somewhere on the front lawn, but
from this position they could see only the occasional darting movement of men running through the bushes. The
hard arm around Laura tightened, and she held her
breath in fear as Marshall hesitated over some decision.
She strove to hear some sound of Cash in the attic, but
over the barrage of gunfire coming from the house, she
could hear nothing.

She knew the moment Marshall made up his mind,
and she steeled herself for the worst. She wanted to live.
She had a son who needed her, and a love she had yet
to share. But she would die if necessary to protect them
both. And she knew beyond a shadow of a doubt that
Cash would do the same. She had to protect him from
his madness in whatever way she could.

So when Marshall held his gun to her ribs and told her
to walk, Laura did as she was told. There wasn't anything
Cash could do for either of them while Marshall held
that gun. Obedience seemed the better part of valor in
this case.

Her courage almost gave way when she realized Marshall intended to take the back stairs to the kitchen rather
than face the battle out front. She closed her eyes in
brief prayer as Marshall half-dragged her down the narrow stairway. Cash had planned this confrontation with
Marshall; she had known it all along. Jonathan and Dr.
Burke and Steve Breckinridge were all in on it. If she
had only listened and left when they told her to, they
would have trapped Marshall and his men and put an
end to their marauding forever. It would be all her fault
if the plan fell through.

The least she could do was make it easy for them.
Marshall obviously thought he could sneak out and never
be seen. She didn't know what his plans were beyond
that, but she knew they wouldn't be pleasant. She would
rather die quickly now than suffer slow torture later.

Laura waited until they had slipped out the back door
into the relative silence of the kitchen yard. The slave
cabins along one side would be deserted now, she knew.
And Cash had taken all the horses from the barn, and
probably the grooms too. With all the firing from the

front, there would be no one here to see them leave. Unless she did something now.

Marshall had relaxed the gun pressing at her side as he made his way to the horses still saddled in the paddock where his men had left them. He thought she was harmless. Perhaps she was, but it was time they both learned if she could be something different.

It would be easier to act without thinking. Blindly Laura jabbed her elbow backward until it connected with Marshall's ribs. The blow wasn't strong enough to give him pain, but it was sufficient to startle him into loosening his grip. With another swift movement that she hadn't thought herself capable of, Laura slammed her arm into his gun hand.

The weapon exploded in the night air, sending the horses whinnying into circles in the paddock, focusing attention on this darkened corner of the yard. It wasn't enough to save her, Laura realized grimly as Marshall grabbed her waist and ran for the gate, but it had accomplished one small thing. Cash's wild cry from the roof behind them warned he had discovered their escape route.

There still wasn't anything he could do. Laura turned and caught sight of him as he came running over the roof, rifle raised, but he couldn't take aim while she was still here.

She struggled in Marshall's grasp, but her efforts were useless against his greater strength. He dragged her into the saddle with him, and even as men ran around the corner to stop them, he sent the horse racing into the darkness, away from what little protection the presence of others afforded.

Despair engulfed him as Cash watched the horse and rider escape. Leaping to the roof of the cabins below, he clambered to the ground. Some of the men he had gathered raced to join him, while others held the gang trapped inside.

Without a word, Cash slid under the porch, where he had planted some of the blasting powder with which he had meant to put an end to Marshall and his gang. It had seemed appropriate at the time, blowing up Stoner Creek and the man who coveted it, putting an end to past dreams and lost hopes. He could carve whole new worlds with Laura at his side. He didn't need old ones.

But he needed Laura, and he wasn't going to let her get away. Steve Breckinridge grabbed one of the canisters from his hand as Cash raced for the shrubbery hiding their horses, but it didn't matter. Cash could easily kill Marshall with his bare hands. First, though, he had to get Laura.

He was aware that some of the men followed, grabbing their horses as he plunged his stallion through the shrubbery and into the open field in the direction Marshall had taken. He didn't care. All he could think about was Laura in the wretch's hands, and his stomach churned and roiled as he kicked his mount to land-eating strides.

There wasn't a horse in the county that could match this one; Cash had made certain of that when he'd bought him. He could easily keep pace with Marshall, reduce the distance between them. The men behind weren't so lucky, but they followed at their own pace. Breckinridge would have the best mount. He would be nearest. These wandering thoughts kept Cash sane as he felt the muscles of the horse beneath him stretch and contract and carry him closer to Laura.

Laura. The images raced past him much as the familiar trees did. Laura in the too-big hat and solemn expression. Laura with his son at her breast and a look of love in her eyes. Laura reaching for him, holding him, welcoming him as no other woman had ever done. His hearth, his home, his wife.

The thoughts steadied Cash even as he watched disaster happening before his eyes. Marshall's mount was tired, lagging, even before he aimed at the stone fence marking the boundary. Cash wanted to scream in warning, but the man was beyond common sense.

But not Laura. As the horse gathered its waning strength to make the leap, she shoved free of Marshall's grasp and flung herself into the scrub brush of the fencerow. The horse sailed over the fence without her, its rider bent on escape from the hell-born stallion behind him.

Crying, calling her name, Cash hauled on his reins, but before he could come to a halt, Laura was scrambling to her feet and reaching for him. He jerked her up in front of him and turned the horse for the nearest gate. He was going to kill Marshall, but he'd be damned if he killed his horse in the process.

Laura clung to Cash's warm ribs as the wind whistled around them. Tears choked her throat and eyes and she could only take grateful breaths and hold on for dear life. She felt the rage in him, felt the hate and anguish boiling to get out, but at the same time, his hold on her was gentle, protective. She didn't know where he was going or what he meant to do, but she no longer cared to argue with him. There were some things she knew and could do that he couldn't, but there were others well beyond her reach or comprehension, and this was one of them. Laura buried her face in the security of Cash's hard chest and prayed.

When she looked up, she recognized the hill that they raced toward. Turning to look, she could see the scarecrow of the old Watterson place rise against the sky. She had known Cash owned it, had lived in it, had stayed here these past nights since Sallie's death, but she had never been inside. She wondered at their destination until she caught sight of the horse staggering to a stop near the front door and the man racing for the protection of its solid walls.

Cash reined the stallion to a halt and stared up at the two-story edifice Marshall had just claimed as his fortress. Cash kept no servants there any longer, but the rooms were packed with stored goods. Marshall could hold out there for months, if he liked. Cash didn't intend to wait months for freedom from the fear he had seen in Laura's eyes.

With grim determination he lowered Laura to the ground, out of range of Marshall's gun, then edged his horse into the yard.

"Come on out and give yourself up, Brown. You'll get a fair trial," he shouted at the house, well aware of the reception his offer would receive.

A shot exploded in the dust at Cash's feet as Breckinridge and the others raced up the hill to join him. They arrived in time to hear Brown's reply.

"You're the criminal here, Wickliffe. You killed your wife and now you're trying to steal mine. It won't work, you know. Call the sheriff, if you dare. He'll tell you who he's going to believe."

Steve Breckinridge sidled his horse next to Cash's. "The sheriff's busy rounding up the gang back at the house," he murmured. "Shall I send someone back for him?"

"Only if you need a witness for the execution," Cash replied grimly. Then, raising his voice, he called to the man who had done his best to destroy the life of the woman he loved, "The sheriff's back at the farm. Come on out and we'll take you to him. I'm warning you now, I'm not leaving here until you come out, dead or alive."

Marshall laughed triumphantly. "Then you'd better come in and get me, Wickliffe. I'm not stupid enough to put myself in your hands."

Without another word, Cash swung his mount back to where Laura waited. Handing his rifle to the man who rode beside him, Cash jumped down and pulled Laura into his arms, kissed her, then shoved her toward Steve. "Get her away from here."

Laura started to protest, but quieted at the look in Cash's eyes. It was his turn now; she no longer had to fight alone. The relief of that knowledge overwhelmed her, and she turned away from the set expression of his grim features, letting Steve guide her back down the hill to where the others waited. She could only pray that Cash would be careful and rely on the belief that he wanted to live as much as she did. Marshall wasn't worth wasting his life on.

Cash knew precisely where he had stored the gunpowder. Leaving his horse at the fence, he pulled the explosive from his coat pocket and his flint from his trousers as he climbed back toward the house. In the yard he bent down and gathered a pile of sticks from the old river birch hanging nearby. Carefully he set fire to the kindling, making certain Marshall watched his every move.

Then, standing, Cash held out the canister of explosive where it could be seen. "This is your last warning, Brown. Come out now, like a man, or I'll blow the house up around you."

"Smatter molasses from here to kingdom come; it's your loss," Marshall mocked. Then, shooting again in

Cash's direction, he retreated farther into the safety of the house. A single charge of powder would barely penetrate the old log walls.

Cash had known that would be his choice, but he felt only a fleeting regret as he set the fuse to the dying blaze and heaved the explosive toward the rear window and the storehouse of powder.

As he threw himself down the hill and rolled away, Cash felt only satisfaction at the blast of the old house shattering into oblivion, blowing the past to the hell from whence it had come.

Flames shot up behind him as Cash staggered to his feet and a small figure ran across the ragged lawn to greet him. He grabbed her in his arms and swung her up against him as fire erupted through the old cedar-shingle roof of the house on the hill. The touch of her lips, the soft warmth of her body against him, eased the hurts and the hatreds that had led to this moment, letting them leach out and dissipate into the air in the same way the fire became smoke. Cash clasped her tighter, burying his face in her hair.

"We'd better get Laura back to town now." Breckinridge came to stand beside them, imposing his propriety on the new scandal emerging from this night. "They've brought a wagon 'round by the road. Laura can ride in that."

Arms around Cash's waist, head against his chest, Laura felt him stiffen. Lifting her head to meet his dark gaze, she smiled softly at the concern she found there, then turned to Steve with a look not to be denied. "Only if Cash goes with me," she murmured in the polite tones that covered the steel of determination.

Steve and Cash exchanged looks over her head. Behind them the old Watterson place gave another small explosion as some combustible material caught fire, and the flames flared anew, carving a beacon against the blackness of the heavens, a memorial to the innocent who had worked and given their lives there.

As if taking warning from the flames, Steve nodded and walked away. Laura's fingers crept into Cash's hand as they followed him down the hill to the waiting wagon.

40

"I changed my mind. Take us back to the farm. It's closer, and I've got horses there."

"I'm going with you."

The small hand wrapped in Cash's remained firm as he glanced down at her. Laura's head barely met his shoulder, and she was staring stubbornly forward as the driver began to click his horses into motion.

Around them, the bushes were filled with the sound of rustling as men emerged on foot and horseback to examine the damage. The house was beyond saving, and no one seemed in any hurry to determine the fate of the occupant. But a singular number of horses began to form a protective circle around the wagon. One of the bigger horses rode close, and Laura could make out the outline of Steve Breckinridge's broad shoulders against the dying glow on the horizon.

"Let me take her home with me. She'll need the women around her."

Laura squeezed Cash's hand harder as she once again defied Steve's authority. "Mark is still on the train. I've got to go after him."

Both men answered at once, Cash's furious "The hell you will!" mixing with Steve's "Don't be foolish!" before the man on the horse submitted gracefully to the man who not only had more reason for concern but also seemed to have a better technique for handling the obstinate miss.

"We'll find him, Laura. You've had enough for one day. I'm taking you home."

Home. The only real home she had ever known was now an empty shell, but Laura relaxed slightly at Cash's words. She knew he meant their home, and she wouldn't argue with that, wherever their home might be. Steve interrupted before she could say anything at all.

"I'll ride into town and wake the telegraph operator. We'll have a wire at the station before the train arrives. I'll also have a wire sent to Uncle Taunton at the same time. He'll find him."

"I put Cousin Bessie's address in his coat. If there's some mix-up, they might take him there. You'd better warn her too."

The familiar cadence of family names and homely conversation created a circle of security that Cash could only marvel at. Sitting tensely on the hard bench of the wagon, his arm protecting Laura's back from the wagon's jostling motions, he felt suddenly uncertain of his position. He had the woman he loved in his arms, but the world she belonged to was pulling at her, trying to close her in, and he wasn't at all certain that he was being included. From prior experience, he was more than certain he was not.

"Cash?"

Steve's questioning tone caught him by surprise, but he understood what was being asked. It was hard, this asking something of others, accepting favors from people who had once turned their backs to him, and on his own, Cash would never have agreed. But feeling Laura's weight sagging slightly against him, he swallowed his pride and nodded agreement.

"I'd appreciate it, Breckinridge. I've got to see that Laura's safe first, then I'll ride into Lexington to bring him back. Just make certain someone wires back that they've found him and let me know."

"It's your decision," Steve replied gruffly, "but Laura knows her relations well. Her Aunt Bessie will spoil the kid and will jump at the chance to ride the train out here. But she'll have heart failure when she finds Laura isn't with us. You might do better to send her on until this is straightened out."

Steve discreetly omitted the reason he would defer the decision-making on Mark to Cash, but always alert to the slurs against him, Cash stiffened at the reference to Laura's relatives. Before he could say something cutting, Laura quietly intruded.

"I'm not a piece of luggage, Steve, I can speak for

myself. And if Aunt Bessie has any problem with my behavior, you can send her to me. It's not your concern."

The driver beside them chuckled softly as the mighty Steven Breckinridge seemed at a loss for words to reply to this defiance from a lady. Finally the man on the horse bowed his head briefly in acceptance.

"All right, Laura, if that's the way you want it. I just hope you know what you're doing."

She murmured a weary "I do" and rested her head against Cash's shoulder, letting him handle the rest of the situation.

"I won't see her hurt," Cash answered the other man's silence. "I'll do whatever is necessary to protect her."

Steve finally made an ungentlemanly noise of agreement. "You've made that point very clear. I'll not stand in your way, that's for certain. All right, I'm riding into town. I'll get you word as soon as I have it."

There wasn't time to do more than settle Laura more comfortably against his shoulder before another rider approached, this time on a long-eared mule. The man's face was unclear in the darkness, but Cash thought he recognized the voice of one of the county's smaller farmers.

"Me and some of the others been talkin', Mr. Cash. When you're ready to rebuild, we'll be there to help you. Can't rightly do more than that, things bein' as they are, but we owe you. What those . . ." He cut the expletive off with a glance to Laura, then continued, "What they did to my Edna Mae shouldn't have been done to a livin' soul." Anger tinted every word, although the speaker strove to control it. "She's gone now. She never did get well after that. Those bastards deserve to roast in hell just for that alone. What I mean to say is, we all got reason to be grateful for what you did. You just get the word out, we'll be there."

He rode off, but the message was the same from every man who walked or rode by as the wagon rolled slowly down the road. Cash remained largely silent at the unexpected accolades, but Laura could feel the tension building inside him. Unused to kind words, he was undoubtedly waiting for the next cannonball to explode. He would have to find out for himself that people weren't all what they seemed. She could do nothing more than stand by his side.

The wagon twined through the darkness of country lanes, turning up the rocky road to Stoner Creek despite Cash's protest that they could walk the drive. When the driver stopped before the now-empty house, he merely tipped his slouch hat at Cash's offer of gratitude.

"My boy fought for the Union and came home with only one leg. Those varmints shot it out from under him. There ain't a soul in the county won't be glad to see the end of this feudin'. You done us all a favor. We won't be forgettin' it. Take care of Miz Laura, now, and we'll see that the boy gets back home."

The wagon pulled away, leaving the two of them standing before the darkened house.

Without a word, Cash lifted Laura into his arms and carried her over the threshold, into the house where she had always lived and which would now be theirs together. There was too much to be said to say it now. Laura wrapped her arms around Cash's neck and held him close as they ascended the steps. She knew where he was taking her and why, and she offered no protest. The time for proprieties was gone.

When she woke, the sun was streaming in a newly cleaned window, and she luxuriated in the golden rays warming her nakedness. A hint of autumn coolness brushed her skin, but rather than reach for covers, she gravitated toward the source of heat next to her.

Cash reached for her and hugged her close, and Laura turned in his embrace, her breasts brushing against his muscled chest as she met his dark gaze. A day's growth of beard roughened his jaw, his hair made a disheveled mat across his forehead, but the look of wonder in his eyes was as gentle and loving as she could request. She pressed a kiss to his bristly cheek. "I love you," she whispered.

Cash studied on that a moment, his gaze drifting over the rosy hues of Laura's throat and shoulders and down to the gentle curve of her breasts where she snuggled against him. He had been aroused the moment she had touched him, and his hunger didn't diminish with his inspection. He could remember her response last night to his smallest caresses, and he knew he had found the treasure he had spent a lifetime in searching for. It had never occurred to him that riches could be found in small feminine packages, but he was learning a lot of things these days.

But one of those things Cash had learned was the rarity of love. He brushed his lips across her silken hair and pressed her closer, unwilling to let her go. "Laura, you don't have to say that just because of what we've done together. I know what I am and what you are. There's really no common ground for us. I've not brought you any happiness, just destruction. You'd do better to let me go."

Laura found the light mat of hair upon his chest and tweaked a curl. "Are you questioning my judgment?"

Cash caught her hand and held it still. "I'm questioning your sanity. I love you. I want to keep you. But there are walls of obstacles in the way. You need time to consider them before you make any final decisions."

Laura pressed a kiss to the flesh beneath his arm, then began to nibble between words. "I'm not leaving."

Cash groaned and caught her hair, dragging her head back so she could meet his eyes. "I'm not looking for a mistress. I want a wife, a mother for my children. Any woman who marries me will be tainted by what I am, what I was. It will never change."

"What are you trying to say?" Laura ignored the fear eating at her heart, opting for the courage to fight for what she wanted, remembering Sallie's words. This time, the only person likely to be harmed was herself.

Cash read the fear in her eyes, and he steeled himself for the inevitable. It had to be said, though. There was no other honorable course. What he would do when she turned him down, he could not imagine, and he hated to destroy what they had with haste, but there was literally no other choice. "Will you marry me?"

The fear disappeared, and Laura snuggled back down to his shoulder. "Of course." Her hand began an exploration of his bronzed chest gleaming in the September sun, locating old scars and smoothing them with her touch.

"Of course?" Stunned, Cash stared at the ceiling. "Of course? I've just asked you to condemn yourself to a lifetime as an outcast of society, and you just say 'of course'? Don't you even want to think about it awhile? Shouldn't we argue over where we're going to live, how we're going to live? Shouldn't there be some expression of concern over whether or not I still have the funds to support you? Laura, you can't just say 'of course' to a question like that. Maybe I better go ask your Aunt Bessie for your hand. You obviously need a keeper."

Laura slid her fingers to his side and tickled him under his arm until Cash squirmed and turned over to face her. His gaze was wary as he met her gentle smile. Unshaken by his suspicion, Laura merely took this opportunity to admire his manly shoulders, running her fingers over them as she spoke.

"I'm not Sallie, Cash. I should certainly think you would know that by now; I've told you often enough. I've loved you since I was a little girl. Why should I throw away now what I've spent a lifetime wanting? I'm sorry, Cash, you're trapped. I'll have all my relatives hold you at gunpoint until you say the words in front of a preacher. You're going to make an honest woman of me whether you like it or not."

A chuckle began to build and rumble upward from his chest as Cash caught her wandering hand and brought it to his lips. He pressed a kiss to the palm, then began nibbling on each finger, pulling them sensuously into his mouth while he watched the wonder grow in her eyes. When she moved instinctively to close the gap between them, he carried her hand downward, pulling her hips to meet his.

"I like it. I like it a lot. Honest women should be revered. If marriage is what it takes to make you honest, I'll be happy to oblige. Come here, *pequeña,* I want to give you a taste of what lies in store for an honest woman such as you."

Cash's nonsense filled Laura with joy, but the love in his touch raised her to new plateaus of ecstasy. Running her fingers through his hair, splaying her hands across his back, she took the love with which he showered her, and gave it back threefold, opening her body to accept his, taking him into her heart, and offering all she possessed into his care.

Cash took what she offered with gentleness at first, then with fierce desire as all that they could be became known to them. Love outpaced passion, and they were well and truly one before their bodies sealed the vows their hearts had already taken. The aftermath of pleasure was just one reward for their loving.

Tears streamed down Laura's cheeks as Cash lifted his greater weight from her. She arched upward to hold him a little longer, and he bent to press a kiss against her cheek, discovering the moisture there.

Touching a finger to the tears, he stroked her face wonderingly, gazing down into her eyes. "Tears, Laura?" He couldn't believe they were tears of regret, not after what they had just shared. But he was as yet uncertain to the sources of feminine emotion.

She shook her head defiantly. "I never cry."

Cash smiled at that. "I know. I can remember you sitting on that ridiculous little pony, your little lip quivering as you told me that your daddy got blown up on a boat. You didn't cry then. Or when your big dog died. Or when we laid Sallie to rest. Even last night, you didn't shed a tear. You're a hard woman, Laura Kincaid."

She burst into tears at that, and buried her face in Cash's comforting shoulder as he turned over, taking her with him. All the years of holding back broke through the dam of loneliness, flooding the present, clearing a path for the future. Cash held her tight and wished he had been a wiser man. So much could have been prevented if he had been.

But there was time yet to make up for it. Stroking her hair, he asked, "Where would you like to live, Laura? The wagons are loaded and ready to go anywhere you want."

Sobs lessening, she accepted the handkerchief he rummaged from the table. "Live? I thought you would be returning to California."

"That's still a long and dangerous trip, love. We could take the river halfway there, but the railroads don't go to California yet. We'd have to find a wagon train. Or go by ship around the Cape. I'm not about to put you through that. By the time we got to the desert, you could be with child, and the journey is just too dangerous. I'll sell the ranch, and we can settle anywhere else you like."

Laura had scarcely given it any thought. She had always assumed he would return to California, away from the slurs and insults he bore here. She studied the matter awhile. "I don't know anything about the North except that it must be cold a lot, and different from here. I don't know if I would like it. I suppose we could go south. They say so many were ruined that land is practically free for the taking, but I'd feel like a vulture preying on other people's grief. I just always thought you would go west. I don't know enough of what is out there to make that kind of decision."

Cash lay propped against the pillows, holding the woman he meant to marry against his chest. Their future rested on this decision, and he wanted it to be the right one. "I can't see you living in a sod hut on the plains. That's not what I want for you."

"It has to be somewhere where we can take Jettie and the children. I promised them a home. I'll not let Ward's child be raised in ignorance. Is there somewhere like that?"

"Not in this world," Cash admitted sadly, gathering her hair into his hand. "Not in the world we know now, leastways. We'd have to make a new one."

A new one. A new world where people were accepted for what they did and not what they were. A world where Cash could be seen as the man he was, and not the boy he had been. The thought appealed to Laura, and she played with it, letting the feeling spread deep down inside of her.

"We can build one," she offered recklessly. "The old one is gone. The war took everything, don't you see? It's gone. Watterson's place is gone. The slaves are gone. Society as we know it is gone. There aren't enough men left to quibble over which ones are blue-blooded gentlemen. There's no one left to work the farms. Clothes are being made by machines, not by hand. It's all changing, Cash. Can't we change with it?"

Cash ran his hand up her nape, gripped his fingers in a hank of hair, and lifted her up so he could see her face. Excitement danced in her eyes, and he regarded it with innate suspicion. "I'm not sure I'm hearing what you're saying. Do you want me to sell the farm and buy a machine? I meant for Mark to have this land. He has roots here, no matter where we go. I don't want to sell it."

Laura propped her hands on his shoulders and gave him a smile. "I don't want to sell it either. We both have roots here, Cash. This is our home. We know the problems we face. Why run from the problems we know to ones we don't know? If we stay here, maybe we can change the world just a little bit. You heard those men last night. They're willing to help us rebuild. You've got friends here, Cash, you really do. It can work. We can make it work."

Her excitement was contagious, but Cash felt the need to play devil's advocate just a little while longer. This was her future she was gambling away. He had to make certain she understood all the ramifications. "Sallie hasn't been buried a month, Laura. There will be hell to pay if we marry now, and I don't intend to wait a year for propriety's sake. If we go somewhere else, no one will know that Mark was born out of wedlock. I'll adopt him, make it legal, but the scandal will never be there as it will here. I can pass for anything I want anywhere in this country but here. You're asking to be cut off from all proper society, Laura. I can't do that to you."

Laura made an unladylike face. "What's one more scandal or two? I should think everyone would breathe a sigh of relief once Mark has a proper daddy and they don't have to worry about which man I'm seeing now. They can find some new amusement for a change. At least we'll know who our friends are. And anywhere we run, there's always the chance that rumor will follow. I'd rather have it right out in the open. The days of hiding family secrets in the attic are over too, Cash. The newspapers are making certain of that. Can we try it? Will it cost too much?"

Cash's gaze softened as he found the hope in Laura's face, and he lowered her gently to his chest, holding her there. "I'd like to add a new wing on where the tree fell in. It could have a sun porch just for you and chambers for us, and a nursery, and a new sewing room. It will be grander and more modern than anything Stoner Creek has ever seen, and it won't take a bevy of slaves to keep up. People will be so eager to see the insides, they'll ignore the scandal just to get invited. And horses don't require a lot of manpower. I know horses, and the demand for them is strong right now. We can build a stable that they'll come wide and far to find. Then we can start exploring your notions abut machinery. I've heard about some that can make a difference at harvesttime. They're a gamble, at best, but I'm willing to take a few risks."

"A master of understatement, you are, Cassius Wickliffe," Laura chuckled against his chest.

"And you, my wife-to-be, are too clever for your own good. You're going to hear about it if you go starting that school for ex-slaves. And I don't think I even want to know what you have planned for that sewing machine. Maybe I should arrange it so you have no time for anything but sewing baby clothes."

"Baby clothes are easy." Laura dismissed this threat with a scoff. "But there's always a need for new fashions. If I can teach Jettie Mae . . ."

Cash's kiss stopped her words from going any farther. "Later, Miss Machiavelli. Right now I'm going to make love to you. Then we're going to meet the train and pick up Mark. And then we're going to find a preacher. Practice agreeing with me. Say 'I will.' "

Laughing, Laura tangled her arms around him as he flipped her over. "I will." And then she pulled his head down for a kiss that straightened him out all the way to his toes.

Cash came up grinning. "You're damned right, you will. Want to try that again?"

And she did.

ONYX (0451)

SUPERB TALES OF ROMANCE
AND HISTORY

☐ **THE ROAD TO AVALON by Joan Wolf.** Shimmering with pageantry, intrigue and all the magic of Camelot, here is the epic story of Arthur—the conqueror, the once and future king who vanquished the Saxons and loved but one woman, the beautiful Morgan of Avalon.   (401387—$4.50)

☐ **BORN OF THE SUN by Joan Wolf.** This compelling saga about a beautiful Celtic princess who gives her heart to a Saxon prince explodes with the passions of love and war. "Triumphant ... majestic ... a grand adventure!"—Booklist   (402252—$5.50)

☐ **THE EDGE OF LIGHT by Joan Wolf.** Two headstrong lovers vow to fight to change the world rather than forfeit their passion—in the magnificent tale of Alfred the Great and the woman he could not help but love.
                                    (402863—$5.99)

☐ **WHEN MORNING COMES by Robin Wiete.** This is the story of a beautiful young widow, alone with her small child on the American frontier, seeking a white man who lived among the Shawnee to heal the child. They meet in a wilderness ravaged by violence, only to discover that they are not strangers but lovers ... "Tense and tender, sweeping and intimate ... a poignant love story."—Karen Harper   (403363—$4.99)

☐ **WILD RAPTURE by Cassie Edwards.** The untamed frontier, set aflame by a passionate and fiery forbidden love as a Chippewa man and woman from Minnesota stake their undying love against the forces of hate. "A shining talent!"—*Romantic Times*   (403304—$4.99)

Prices slightly higher in Canada

Buy them at your local bookstore or use this convenient coupon for ordering.

NEW AMERICAN LIBRARY
P.O. Box 999 – Dept. #17109
Bergenfield, New Jersey 07621

Please send me the books I have checked above.
I am enclosing $_____ (please add $2.00 to cover postage and handling). Send check or money order (no cash or C.O.D.'s) or charge by Mastercard or VISA (with a $15.00 minimum). Prices and numbers are subject to change without notice.

Card #_____ Exp. Date _____
Signature_____
Name_____
Address_____
City _____ State _____ Zip Code _____

For faster service when ordering by credit card call **1-800-253-6476**
Allow a minimum of 4-6 weeks for delivery. This offer is subject to change without notice.